Americans in Space

Also by Mary E. Mitchell

Starting Out Sideways

Americans in Space

Mary E. Mitchell

THOMAS DUNNE BOOKS
ST. MARTIN'S PRESS
NEW YORK

This is a work of fiction. All of the characters, organizations, and events portrayed in this novel are either products of the author's imagination or are used fictitiously.

THOMAS DUNNE BOOKS.
An imprint of St. Martin's Press.

AMERICANS IN SPACE. Copyright © 2009 by Mary E. Mitchell. All rights reserved. Printed in the United States of America. For information, address St. Martin's Press, 175 Fifth Avenue, New York, N.Y. 10010.

www.thomasdunnebooks.com
www.stmartins.com

Library of Congress Cataloging-in-Publication Data

Mitchell, Mary E., 1951–
    Americans in space / Mary E. Mitchell. —1st ed.
        p.   cm.
    ISBN 978-0-312-37245-3 (alk. paper)
    1. Single mothers—Fiction.   2. Family—Fiction.   3. Self-realization in women—Fiction.   I. Title.
    PS3613.I8596A84   2009
    813' .6—dc22

                                                            2009017064

First Edition: October 2009

10   9   8   7   6   5   4   3   2   1

In memory of my father, Bartholomeo (Bernie) Fussa,
who once shook hands with an astronaut

And for my mother, Dorothy Fussa,
who kept all of our feet on the ground

ACKNOWLEDGMENTS

I would like to thank my wonderful editor, Katie Gilligan, for her guidance, patience, and wisdom, all of which sustained me during the process of writing this book. My Tuesday Night Writing Group kept me going, greatly assisting in making this novel the best it could be. Bottomless thanks to Angela Gerst, Mike Scott, Betsy Fitzgerald, and Sherry Nadworny for their unwavering support. I was also supported by my fellow writers of the Two Bridges Writers Group, who read huge chunks of this novel at a time and helped me to understand the flow of it. I am grateful to you all and honored to be counted among your membership. Love and thanks to my first readers and dear friends, Elayne King, Judi DeCew, and Donna Moore-Ede, who read this manuscript in its draft form and provided encouragement on how to proceed. To Erin Brown, my gratitude always for your belief in me.

My greatest thanks goes to Melissa Mitchell, who, after she becomes a lawyer, should really become an editor. You will be the best editor in the world and will surely guide and encourage more writers than just your lucky mom. Thank you for the time and thought and dedication you have shown me and my work. I must have raised you really well.

Finally, I'd like to acknowledge the compassionate, loving, and skillful women I call my workmates in my "other job," at Bethany Hill School. Sr. Denise Kelly, Sr. Betsy Conway, Sr. Jane Schacht, Connie Pagan, Nikki Zani, Cherie Baden, Joyce McMahon, and

Denise Sheppard, thank you for the love and insight you bring me daily. You have no idea how much it enriches my writing.

To my beautiful family, Ross, Joe, Melissa, Sara, and Chris, thank you for the joy you bring me and the support you provide always.

Americans in Space

ONE

If You Love Something

He died the way lots of people do. He just went to bed and didn't rise the next morning. He had the thickest head of black hair I've ever seen on a forty-two-year-old male. Had he not died, I'd have had a husband in my old age whose hairline hadn't even receded. Do you know how rare this is? It is a terrible thing to bury a husband who has a full head of hair.

This, of course, is not what the children miss about him. Kyle was one of those perfect daddies, a man whose chest visibly swelled at the sight of his daughter on a soccer field or his infant son chewing on the bumper pad of his crib. My beautiful man, whom I have freely and openly idealized since the day I buried him, knew how to love his children without spoiling them. He did not believe, for example, that Charlotte needed the first-chair violinist from the Boston Symphony Orchestra to teach her violin. But he listened to Charlotte play every week, after every squeaky lesson with Mrs. Otten down the block.

He had had no history of heart trouble. Maybe he was too young for the doctors to go looking. I spent a few months being furious at his doctors, even the podiatrist he'd seen only once, who'd removed his plantar wart. But then I gave it up. There were just too many people to blame. I found it exhausting.

It's been two years since Kyle died, and I have heeded all the advice of the mothers, aunts, friends, and grief counselors not to make major life changes during those first two years, not to sell the house, for instance, or remarry on the rebound, or dye my wild red hair a surreal shade of silver-blond. There has been some progress. I have more energy and less depression. My children no longer eat microwavable instant dinners. I buy Christmas gifts for others again. That first year, when I'd suddenly discovered on Christmas Day that I hadn't bought my mother a gift, I'd hastily rewrapped an unopened set of honeysuckle soaps I'd found lying around the house. When my mother ripped off the reindeer wrapping, Charlotte was perched on the armrest of her love seat, ready to disclose my sin. I have a clear memory of the smirk on my twelve-year-old's face as she ratted me out.

"Nice one, Mom," she had said. "Regifting your own mother on Christmas."

It hasn't been easy raising the children without Kyle. He left me with a daughter poised on the slippery slope of adolescence, her anger erupting as violently as her complexion, her favorite word, on her best days, *no*. The eye-rolling. The fury. The agony of losing her handsome father, the soccer coach, and being stuck with lame old me. Hunter, Kyle's and my love child, recklessly conceived at a time when sensible parents knew better, was only two when his daddy died. He was born ten years after Charlotte, but I guess we thought we'd still have plenty of time to raise him. He was not a particularly verbal two-year-old, but he showed signs of his loss in other ways.

From the day the ambulance left with his daddy's body in it, Hunter developed a deep attachment to ketchup bottles. Empty or full, their undulating shape and smoothness, the colorful labels, their nice narrow necks, so perfect for the grasp of little hands, drew him to them. Our house empty of the sound of a man's voice, Hunter began toddling around with Heinz as his closest companion, the bottle braced against his heart, as though he were protecting it from something. I thought, perhaps, he'd lose interest in time, but when he'd acquired two or three more plastic squeeze bottles from the bowels of our unattended kitchen cupboard, he began stashing them in an empty Huggies carton, left beside his changing table in his sad yellow-walled nursery. One day Charlotte fixed him up with a handle for his box, cutting a slot in the side and sliding through one of Kyle's belts. After that Hunter pulled his cache of ketchup bottle behind him wherever he went. He'd stop and settle the carton beside me when I was doing the dishes or on the phone. He'd stand there until he had my attention. His eyes were tired for a two-year-old's.

Now here I am, waiting in the Guidance Office of the Alan B. Shepard High School, an embarrassing place to find myself, as I work here as a guidance counselor. It would be fine to be seeing Mr. Johnson if Charlotte and I were going over some PSAT scores. But it's only September, and we're seeing Tom Johnson because Charlotte, a mere ninth-grader, has been skipping school. Three times already. Plus, she's had her tongue pierced—not that this is against school policy. It's just further evidence that I'm a lousy mother of a fourteen-year-old girl. I don't even know how or where she accomplished her mutilation. Who would send their own child to me to devise a scheme for getting into Harvard?

The counseling offices at Alan Shepard High orbit a small waiting room designed by some genius architect who thought it would be fun to gather all the distraught and embarrassed parents in one space while they waited for appointments to discuss their incorrigible children. Although it's not necessary to wait on the slippery faux-leather chairs in the full glare of Gladys Panella, our ancient guidance secretary, I have chosen to sit here rather than spend another moment in my own office avoiding phone calls. Gladys nods curtly, looking puzzled. I nod back professionally, but offer nothing. I am restless with my work these days. I find it hard to execute my duties pleasantly.

I cannot stand my job, if the truth be told. I cannot, in good conscience, speak with one more overachieving parent who wants a letter from the Dalai Lama to put in his son's college admissions packet, one more clueless mother who has not caught on to the fact that the SAT sign-up ended last week. I am deeply resentful of these parents of malleable, compliant children, students who dutifully build latrines in Mexico during their summer vacations in order to boast about it on their college applications, although they do not like poor people and abhor outhouses, even on camping trips.

I hate the suburbs, too, although here I am, living a slow death in one of the fanciest ones outside of Boston. I remain here both for work and for personal reasons, such as access to the schools I want my own children to attend and the pension plan and benefits the Appleton Public Schools provide. I try to hide my loathing for my work by walking into school with a happy smile each morning. No one suspects a woman with wild red hair and a happy smile to be anything but a positive person. Only my children and my neighbor Marge know what a miserable human being I really am, and possibly Jack, the driver's ed teacher, who says I look demented.

Tom Johnson's office door opens and he walks toward me with his sheepish fifty-year-old's smile tucked somewhere between his mustache and goatee. It's embarrassing for him to be speaking to one of his colleagues about what a disaster her kid is. I feel for Tom, but have always thought he should be more embarrassed about his mustache and goatee.

"Kate," he says, squeezing my shoulder before I rise. "Come on in."

Gladys frowns at a stack of something on her desk as I head toward Tom's office. I pass by the poster on his open door, following his long lean back inside. He dresses like the guidance counselors in the *Mad* magazines I once read as a kid. He wears sweater vests and corduroy pants with shiny spots on the butt and the knees.

If you love something, set it free . . . , the poster on his door airily begins. *If it comes back, it's yours. If it doesn't, it never was.*

Half the poem is enclosed in the cheesy graphic of an open birdcage. I have always wanted to draw a mustache and goatee on the bird who sits smugly in the cage.

If you love something, lock it up, I invariably think. *If it gets away, yell at it when it comes back.*

Now, there's a poster I could warm up to. Tom is stirring a cup of instant coffee for us both, so sure he knows me after eleven years of working beside me.

"Where's Charlotte?" I ask him, plunking down on one of the two conference chairs opposite his desk. "Weren't you going to pull her out of class for this meeting?"

Tom sighs like a guidance counselor and gives me one of his significant looks. He has a long narrow face. My mother has a set of glass Christmas ornaments that are exactly this same shape. "I would've pulled her out of class," he says, speaking slowly, in case I am on anti-anxiety drugs, "if she were *in* class today." He rests my coffee gently on the front end of his desk, as if it might be a volatile liquid.

"Shit," I mutter, and there goes the last semblance of professional behavior.

"Kate," Tom begins gently. "This is not necessarily the end of the world. The kid's been through a lot and she's just acting out a little. It might be a good time to find her a really good therapist, though, and—"

"And have her skip those appointments too?" I feel anger at Charlotte surging up and down my arms, beneath the sleeves of my cardigan sweater. "And then come home with pierced nipples and an invoice for a hundred fifty bucks?"

Tom struggles between a smile and frown. Is he my friend or my child's counselor? He is trying to decide, tugging at his whiskers as he does so.

"Sorry," I say, rubbing the plastic arms of the conference chair.

"Kate . . . ," Tom repeats. Then his voice wanders off, as if there is so much more to say to me. *Stop being a poor widow. Give your kid a break. Smile, for God's sake.*

I can't do any of these things. Somewhere in the cocoon of sadness of the last two years, I misplaced all of my niceness. I used to be popular with the students and faculty. I used to be popular with my children. But all that is gone now, vanished as completely as Kyle.

"Look," I say, rising from the uncomfortable chair. "I know you're trying to help. And I know I'm being unreasonable, but let's just reschedule this thing for when we can actually get Charlotte in the same room with us."

I turn and leave his office. The nasty smell of the instant coffee follows me out. I feel terrible, of course, because Tom is one of the nicest, most caring human beings on the planet. I vow to tell him this the next time I see him. Gladys waves some form when she sees me coming, but I pretend not to see, ducking into my own office for my jacket and handbag.

"I've got an appointment," I tell her, a total lie, on my way out.

I can almost feel Gladys shaking her head in disapproval, her steel-gray permanent wave undulating the slightest bit in my wake.

A bell goes off in the corridor and kids pour out of classrooms, laughing and cuffing one another around the neck. A thousand iPods go by, hundreds of thousands of dollars spent by parents on kids who don't like their parents. You can almost smell the hormones. The kids act like I'm invisible, but this suits me fine. Coming toward me, a football-player-type guy guffaws good-naturedly. *You dick!* he cries out. A brace of chaste girls clutching books to their bosoms glance down at their feet. I think of my own daughter in her awful cutoff, navel-baring T-shirts, the one that says *These ain't silicone!* right across her perfect little round-as-chestnuts breasts. She used to love books. She used to love her violin. Once I watched her playing a simple Bach piece for her girlfriends on a perfect summer's night on our back deck.

I lock myself into my car, warding off principals, parents, possibly truant officers. An image comes back to me from the night Kyle died, of how, in the middle of the night, I awoke briefly to discover that he had hogged the top sheet, as usual. I remember with clarity the way I'd registered a twinge of irritation with him before yanking the sheet back. There'd been no resistance or response from Kyle. Was this because he was sleeping or because he was dead?

I suddenly have a deep desire to pick Hunter up early from the Bright Lights Early Learning Center. I long to hold my little Bright Light in my arms, which he still allows me to do at four, to smell his scalp, which still holds a faint trace of the baby scent, and to reassure myself that I know my child. By the time I reach the end of the school parking lot, my decision is made to head over there instead of home. Traffic flows by, impeding my escape. I idle beside the school's sign, a giant stone monument that looks like a gravestone. ALAN B. SHEPARD, the engraved lettering announces, FIRST AMERICAN TO JOURNEY INTO SPACE. I glide my car into an opening between two trucks, wondering where my other child is, my raven-haired firstborn, the spitting image of her father, the girl who doesn't seem to like me, or school, or her life anymore. My Charlotte, just another American journeying into space.

TWO

The Comfort of Ketchup

I spot Hunter immediately in the fenced-in playground of Bright Lights. He is standing by himself, holding an empty ketchup bottle, smiling peacefully at a tree. A group of four or five other boys are barking orders at each other, over by the Buckminster Fuller geodesic jungle gym.

"Hunter, honey!" I call from the other side of the fence. My little boy turns, and the September sun glints off his wispy blond hair. He looks nothing like his father or me. He looks like the child a woman has with the milkman. But I see a lot of myself inside of Hunter, even though he is only four. Something heavy weighs down his small soul already, something he came with that was not caused by the loss of his father.

"Mama!" Hunter cries in a soft voice that hardly carries over the bossy boys.

Courtney, his favorite teacher, waves at me from her post by the slide. "Hi, Kate!" she calls. "You taking him early?"

I nod as she catches the last small body hurtling to the foot of the slide. Then she scoops up my Hunter to deliver him to me. "He's had a wonderful day," she says. "Didn't you?" she adds, turning to my son.

Hunter wraps his free arm around Courtney's neck and hugs her. It's amazing the things he can do with a ketchup bottle in one hand. But he's had half a lifetime of practice.

"He played for twenty-six minutes without his ketchup bottle today, didn't you?" Courtney says, kissing my son on the cheek. Hunter nods gravely, as though he is accepting praise for an Academy Award.

"Good job!" I say, though the larger part of me registers the pathetic job I've done helping this child through his grief. Our mutual goal, Courtney's and mine, is to get Hunter to kindergarten next year empty-handed. If anyone can do it, Courtney can. I love this young teacher, with her brave twenty-two-year-old's energy and the quiet way she's registered Hunter's and my loss.

"We should celebrate your twenty-six minutes without a ketchup bottle," I tell Hunter in the minivan as we're driving home. "Should we have ice cream cones?"

I spot the grave little Hunter nodding in my rearview mirror. He is wild about ice cream cones with faces. Raisin eyes. Strawberry Twizzlers mouths. Beside him I swear I see Kyle, strapped in like Casper the Friendly Ghost, his big knees almost in his face. It is not the first time he's taken a car ride with us since he's died. The Kyle ghost nods. It's only early September, and the whole family is playing hooky.

"Want to have some lunch?" I ask my silent boy as I unstrap him from his big-boy car seat. He nods trustingly and the two of us go inside, Kyle vanished. This is when the quiet part of our day ends.

Charlotte is sitting on a stool at the kitchen counter eating a salad smothered in bean sprouts. A large coolata is half raised to her lips, frozen there at the sight of us. Positioned beside her lunch, her open laptop casts a pale blue glow on her Goth-white skin. She slams the laptop shut at the sight of me.

"What are *you* doing here?" she asks. Her indignation makes me feel like a home invader. I collect myself before answering, calmly helping Hunter out of his jacket.

"I should ask you the same question," I say, but this only heightens her defenses. I see it in the way her shoulders rise.

"What'd you do?" she asks. "Quit your day job? No more Mrs. Cavanaugh and her *Teen Beat* Touchy-Feely Group?"

She is making fun of the weekly group I run for emotionally disturbed and at-risk students, which is called, in actuality, New Frontiers, and isn't nearly as hokey as she makes it out to be. Charlotte, in fact, is a perfect candidate for the *Teen Beat* Touchy-

Feely Group. Oh, how I don't want this. I want my daughter back, the sweet one who used to braid my hair into tiny dreadlocks while we watched *Beauty and the Beast* together. I can almost feel her fingers on my scalp, see the teapot dancing with the candlestick.

"You're going to flunk out eventually," I tell her.

She shoves a huge forkful of salad in her mouth, in an effort, I suspect, to buy some time to think. I cannot help noticing how beautiful she is, despite the way she has piled her hair on top of her head in a sort of Pebbles hairdo. There are Kyle's eyes, though they're narrowed at me in disgust.

"Did you intentionally blow off our meeting today with Mr. Johnson?" I ask.

She gnashes violently and swallows. "No, Mom. Not everyone's universe is centered around the Guidance Department at Alan B. Shithead High."

"Watch your mouth!"

There is a skittering below me, somewhere around my knees. Hunter suddenly bolts from the room, silent as a country mouse, holding his ketchup bottle to his cheek. Charlotte looks stricken.

"Hey, buddy!" she calls after him. "Let's play ketchup train later!" Her face grows even paler. I see how she hates upsetting her brother.

"Nice way to talk around Hunter," I cannot help saying.

"You are so wicked *harsh!*" Charlotte shouts, slamming her coolata down on the counter. The plastic lid comes loose and mocha-colored sludge flies into the air, landing on her T-shirt and speckling her face. She wipes angrily at her cheek with the back of one hand. "Don't you see what a *loser* you are? Don't you see what you're doing to Hunter?"

In my work, we call what Charlotte has just said *projection*. She is really angry at her father, right? For what *he* has done to Hunter? Correct? There is no way to process this with her, though, as Charlotte is stomping out of the room now, her awful Doc Martens scuffing the floor in her exit. She swings open the back door with the fury of a rabid animal. "I can't stay here another second!" she shrieks.

"Good!" I shout. "Try school!" The pictures on the wall rattle when she slams the door. I watch her perfect little ass recede as she heads next door.

"You're grounded," I hear myself muttering, but she doesn't hear, of course. There are tears in my eyes and my hands are shaking.

I grab a dish towel and wipe coolata off her two-thousand-dollar computer. I know where she's going. She's going next door to Marge's house. Marge will let her in with welcome arms and an understanding ear and a plate of something freshly baked. I know I should appreciate Marge for her warm outreach toward my unstable daughter, but instead I hate her just a little. I hate how easy she makes it look, loving a girl like Charlotte.

I wash my face and go and find Hunter. He is curled up on the TV room couch watching *Dora the Explorer*, his ketchup bottle cradled to his heart. I scoop him into my arms and the two of us snuggle up to watch.

"You want some lunch?" I whisper into his ear.

He shakes his head no and, yes, I smell it then, the last vestiges of the baby scent, rising from his warm scalp. Kyle used to love that smell. He would bury his nose in both our babies' scalps, inhaling the scent like oxygen.

"Charlotte's just a little upset now," I breathe into Hunter's straw-colored hair. "She went to see Aunt Margie."

I feel the slightest release of tension in his small body. He loves Aunt Margie. Everyone does. Across the room the telephone stares at me and I know, as I feel Hunter's bulk grow heavy and soft with sleep, that I should gently lay him across the Juicy Juice–stained cushions and pick up the phone and call Marge. Find out if she knows why Charlotte is skipping school. Find out if she knows what is wrong with my daughter. We named her Charlotte after Kyle's grandmother. But now Kyle's grandmother is gone and he is gone and Charlotte is gone, too. Maybe we should have named her Marge. She never goes away, ever.

THREE

Real Simple

I had a cleaning lady for a while before Kyle died, but she was from Brazil and it broke my heart to watch her try to fit into our culture by naming her children for American products. There was her older son Polident, and then the twins, Wrigley and Campbell. This is no worse than our own native tendencies in America to name our children after cities and states. Daily a parade of Madisons, Dakotas, and Parises glide into my office. Then there are the cheeses: the Brees and Briannas and the Camerons, which sounds a lot like Camembert. My husband and I used to joke about the cheese names. We promised each other that if we had a third child, and she was a girl, we'd name her Velveeta. Then, of course, he died.

I haven't needed a cleaning lady since the first day Marge, my neighbor, peeked over my backyard picket fence and offered to weed my perennial patch, "just for the fun of it." This was years before I was a widow, back when Hunter was a just baby, and, slug that I was, I told her sure, she could come and weed my garden.

Which was like opening Pandora's box. The lid flew off and the female version of Mr. Clean emerged. By the time they'd wheeled Kyle out of the house, our home was shining like a moonlit planet. It began with her mowing our lawn each Tuesday, "just to get out of the house." From there it escalated into a handyman—or handywoman—service. Marge has an advanced degree from MIT and works from the comfort of her home as a software consultant, but this, clearly, isn't enough.

When Kyle started sneezing from the dandelion pollen, she moved her operations indoors. Carrying over her new vacuum with the HEPA filtration system was no problem! While I sat in my office at the Alan B. Shepard High School, dust bunnies disappeared from the corners of our house faster than the Jews from Egypt. Exotic cleaning products, found only in obscure hardware stores or online, began showing up beneath my kitchen sink. New bulbs went into the perennial patch. "Green" bulbs went into the light fixtures. I should have been embarrassed by all the manual labor Marge happily provided, but Kyle was delighted with the improvements and never criticized me for allowing Marge to make them. If cleaning were sex, Marge would be a sexaholic. But she is just a tall, unmarried, middle-aged woman who lives next door. I suppose I must admit she is also my friend. No one seems to care more about me and my family than Marge.

I've set up the old baby monitor beside Hunter, where I've left him sleeping in the TV room. With the listening device in my cardigan pocket, I walk the perfect bluestone path to Marge's front door, still amazed that her spiffy Dutch Colonial and my ratty Dutch Colonial were ever meant to be comparable housing. I lift the gleaming brass knocker on her front door and let it fall, staring at miniature potted roses on either side of her door as I wait. The roses seem to be blooming symmetrically, which somehow annoys me. The door swings open and there is Marge, smiling her same old warm and welcoming smile.

"Come in!" she says, practically dragging me inside in a hug. At six-foot-one, she looms over me, as Kyle once did. "Is that a new sweater?" she asks. "Do you want some tea and a brownie?"

"Am I disturbing your work?" I ask, my usual polite, if bogus, question.

"Of course not!" Marge assures me. "I was just enjoying a cup of tea myself with your lovely daughter."

"Who should be in school," I say.

"As should you," Marge points out. She leads me by the arm into her living room, where everything gleams—the waxed furniture, the lamps, the floors—and whispers conspiratorially, "I think she's calmed down now. What happened?"

It's the kind of question the parent of a difficult teenager simply can't answer. What happened? The sweet kid with the Beanie Baby collection morphed into a monster. That's what happened. The girl who used to tell me I was *pretty* and *nice* and *smart* now sees only Mrs. Touchy-Feely, the awful joke of her high school. My cheeks feel warm and my eyes feel wet and suddenly I'm weeping, right there on Marge's carefully Scotchgarded Cabot House sofa.

Marge flies into action, kneeling in front of me with open arms, patting my back as she tries to quiet me. "Oh, no, this is no good," she says. "We can't have Charlotte in there hearing her mother cry."

For some reason this makes sense to me, even though I am taking advice from an unmarried woman who has never raised children. Marge hands me a tissue from a pack she's extracted from her pocket. "Here," she says, and I wipe my face gratefully. I take a deep breath and try not to dwell on one distinct fact: my daughter prefers Marge to me. But there's something about this Big Bird of a woman squatting in front of me in her plain cotton blouse and her baggy khaki slacks that makes me feel warmed, too. I can't deny this, and somehow it makes me feel closer to Charlotte to acknowledge it.

"Thanks," I tell Marge, but she just shrugs.

"For what?" she asks. "Kate," she says, putting an arm around my shoulder, "I had this great idea for Hunter. I've been thinking about his nursery and wondering if it isn't time to make him a big-boy's room." She rises to her feet, her grayish ponytail swinging. "I've dog-eared some pages from *Real Simple*, showing how we could build him bunk beds with steering wheels on one end. You know, sort of race-car bunk beds. I can show them to you later." She is guiding me now gently off the couch, walking me slowly toward the kitchen as she continues talking in her lulling tones. "Charlotte is ready to go back to school now for her last two classes, and then for her soccer practice. I think it's the freshman soccer team that's keeping her in the school game," she half whispers. "I'd use that in my conversations with her, for leverage," she advises, just before she opens her kitchen door.

"Here we go." She swings the door open and there is Charlotte.

"Your mom's all set to bring you to school," Marge cheerfully tells my daughter, who is sitting at her table eating a brownie. The whole room smells like a mother-daughter bonding project. Nothing says lovin' like something from the oven. Charlotte won't look at me.

"I have an idea," Marge says. "I'll stay with Hunter while your mom drives you back."

Charlotte wrinkles her nose, hopefully at the school and not at me.

"I want to have a look at that nursery anyway," Marge continues. "Just to get an idea of its measurements for our project." She pulls a magazine out from under Charlotte's nose. "Here's the pictures of the bunk beds," she says, handing the magazine to me. "Charlotte thinks we should get real steering wheels from the junkyard. Isn't that a creative idea?"

Charlotte sneers at me, then looks down. There is only one zit on her face this week but it's a pretty big cyclops one, right between her eyes. I feel a little bad for her. I remember how I wanted to hide in my room when I had a cyclops zit, back when I was in high school. But somehow my mother figured out a way to get me to school, whether I liked it or not.

Five minutes later, Charlotte and I are driving to the high school in silence. Charlotte stares down at her Nike bag, stuffed to its splitting seams with shin guards and sweatshirts and expensive water bottles. I glance in the backseat for Kyle's ghost, but no dice this time. Charlotte will not speak to me and I do not try to speak to her. Instead, I entertain the uncharitable thought that we really didn't need to have this child. I was barely out of college, the only married twenty-two-year-old Kyle or I even knew. Most of our friends still acted like children themselves, but Kyle and I wanted a child right away, that's how in love we were, that's how unhip. Today, at thirty-six, I have friends my age who are just contemplating having their first child. They are shopping for changing tables for the first time while I'm hauling this unpleasant teenager back to school.

I pull into the half-circle driveway in front of the school, a drop-off lane only, and the Grand Central Station of people-watching for all students. A few deadbeat-type boys sit with their backs to the brick wall, checking us out. I happen to know that one of them, the boy with the dyed hair sitting in the middle, smokes pot, and possibly sells it, too. There is simply no way to keep your children safe. Charlotte is turned away from me before I've fully stopped, jiggling irritably at her door handle in an attempt to open her door.

"Fuckin' thing," she mutters, pulling and yanking and finally pounding on the door.

"Charlotte!" I scold. "I will not tolerate that language."

"This thing won't open! It's, like, totally stuck!"

"It's the child safety locks," I explain, shifting into park. "Here. Let me come around and open it from the outside."

"No!" Charlotte shrieks, as though I have suggested exiting the car nude to moon the druggie boys on the curb.

"I'll just open the—"

"No!" she shrieks again, then jabs violently at the button that rolls down her window. She tosses the soccer bag out first. Then, lithe as a skunk in a sewer grating, she crawls out after it.

Anything to spare the world the sight of her mother.

I remain in the car, numbed. "Do you need a ride home after practice?" I shout out her open window.

Charlotte doesn't turn, doesn't answer me. I shift into gear, avert my gaze from the staring druggies, and for the second time in one day, drive away from Alan B. Shithead High.

FOUR

Your Space Is My Space

I find Marge sitting at my kitchen counter with Hunter. Hunter looks dwarfed on her lap, like a football stashed in a linebacker's arm. They're playing some computer game on Charlotte's laptop.

"Press this one, peanut," Marge says, guiding his small finger to a key.

"It's a bunny!" Hunter peals.

"Yes, and how many carrots are in his basket? Let's count them."

Hunter looks anxiously at the countertop, where his ketchup bottle rests beside the dregs of his lunch. Marge has fixed him his favorite carrot dish, one where the baby carrots are inserted like rays of the sun into a blob of peanut butter. A raisin face has been pressed into the peanut butter. Hunter likes faces on most of his food, not just ice cream cones. Sometimes I fear he responds better to condiment bottles and peanut butter faces than to people.

"One, two, three carrots," Marge chants. Hunter wriggles out of her grasp and runs to greet me, throwing his arms around my leg. "Where's Sissy?" he asks. This is what he calls Charlotte. Hunter is great with the *s* sound but not too hot with the *sh* and *ch*.

"She's at school," I explain.

His brow furrows beneath his bangs. "Why *I'm* not at school?"

"Because . . . ," I begin, but then I forget why. Then Hunter doesn't seem to care. He bats his empty ketchup bottle deftly off the counter with one hand, catches it, and leaves.

"How'd it go with Charlotte?" Marge asks.

I pull up a stool on the opposite side of the counter and sit down. My purse goes *whump!* when it hits the floor. Marge puts a hand over mine. We sit quietly like that for a few seconds. This is the kind of friend Marge has become since she first weeded my perennials.

"Okay," I finally say. "You are free to return to your quiet and sane life now."

"It's boring over there," Marge says, popping a baby carrot into her mouth. "Besides, I love your kids. Hunter and I are so in love we've decided to get married."

I hear the strangest sound coming out of my mouth and discover, with surprise, that I'm laughing.

"I'm writing a purchasing and inventory system for a water district in central Ohio," Marge tells me. "How exciting does that sound?"

"It sounds perfectly exciting, at a hundred seventy-five dollars an hour. A nice quiet office. No one getting anything pierced or tattooed down the hall. The money flowing in."

"Money isn't everything, especially if you can't use it for the things you really want. I was in Target the other day, and I wanted to buy this little pair of size-zero pink sneakers so bad that my hands itched. They had these teeny-tiny lights in the heels that flash when you put weight on them! But who was I going to buy them for?"

We both fidget a bit on our stools. Marge's long face grows longer. Poor Marge, taller than anyone she has ever dated. She didn't ask for her brilliant systems analyst's brain, only for a husband and kids. But she got stuck with the systems analyst's brain instead.

"Now listen," she says, and her dreamy smile vanishes and her hazel eyes bore into mine. "Concerning Charlotte, we got bigger fish to fry than tattoos and piercings."

"What are you talking about?" I ask, but already my stomach begins to contract.

Marge turns Charlotte's laptop to face me, then walks around to my side of the counter. A screen-saver picture of floating skulls makes me dizzy. My stomach contracts some more. I am unwilling to digest another scary thing.

"I wouldn't ordinarily go snooping around in someone's private business," Marge says, the most ridiculous lie she could ever tell, "but when I was playing the number bunny game with Hunter, I couldn't help seeing that Charlotte had left a few windows open."

My mind flashes back to the quick bang of the laptop lid when Hunter and I entered the kitchen. I glance again at the screen. The floating skulls smile.

"You know a Web site called MySpace?"

"Of course," I respond, slightly insulted. What person working in a high school doesn't know MySpace? Every kid in my caseload has a profile, a blog, a favorite music listing, and a photo gallery on that Web site. They say terrible things about each other on their home pages. They show YouTube videos of teenage girls beating each other up. Of course I know MySpace.

"Okay," I proceed cautiously. "So Charlotte probably has a MySpace page. . . ."

Marge swallows once, squares her big shoulders, and looks at me. "And have you *seen* your daughter's home page?" she asks.

A memory comes floating back to me, apropos of nothing, of Marge and Kyle laughing together in this same kitchen, on these same stools, the week before he died. I'd been folding laundry on the dining room table, something that always calmed me on a Saturday morning and still does. I will never cease to love the way a tangled basket of many people's business can be smoothed and sorted out, all confusion reduced to right angles and sharp creases. Hunter must have been still asleep. Charlotte would have been watching television, the one morning of the week we'd allowed it. I remember glancing into the room and finding Marge and Kyle's even-in-height-and-breadth shoulders shaking with laughter. I have no idea what the joke was. Smoke curled from their coffee mugs and the sun struck the counter with such brightness that the world looked like a Tide commercial. They both appeared so strong and permanent. A feeling of safety washed over me, swirling upward from somewhere in my center.

I turn the screen away and hop off the stool. "I'm just going to check on Hunter," I tell her, and maybe it's true. Maybe I need to know he is safe before I venture into the brave new world of Charlotte in cyberspace.

FIVE

Cheerios and Bar Tricks

I love to sleep alone. People wouldn't believe me if I told them this, so I don't bother to tell anyone. But I love waking up with my own arms wrapped around me, comforting me as only my own arms can, my knees drawn to my chest like a child in utero. I have been held by men since Kyle died—not in a bed, but held— and the awkward squeezing, patting, circular rubbing of the back have felt to my body like alien gestures. *Here, here*, they say. *There, there*. These are the clumsy comfort hugs. Then there are the other hugs, the ones that implore you to give something up. Give it to me, these hugs say, or I will squeeze it out of you.

Kyle's embraces said different things, but with Kyle gone (and only occasionally showing up in the minivan) I am just as happy to hug myself. I can trust myself. I know myself. And so I awaken this morning at that hour when the sun is still a weak suggestion of light, finding myself in my own arms.

I stay like this for another few minutes. I glance at the fancy Bose stereo alarm and remember that it is Saturday, a soccer day. And then I remember that my daughter is sleeping in her bed in the room next door, that I watched her come in at eleven at night and go straight to her room. I did not question her as to her whereabouts; I hadn't the energy. Today is the day I will tell her she's grounded. Today's the day I begin to set rules.

I pull my warm bones into a sitting position. Her game is at nine at the high school. Will she want me there? I wish I could ask her.

She is safe in her room, but has left a thousand doors open in the ether of MySpace, inviting strangers in to see photos of her with her tongue sticking out, the silver stud winking. Marge made me look. There is one photo of Charlotte in jeans so low on her hips that the slightest bit of a tattoo peeks over the waistline, inked onto one side of her pelvis. I had no idea Charlotte had a tattoo. It made me realize that I haven't seen her fully naked since I stopped taking her out of the bathtub years ago. She wears a one-piece bathing suit when she comes swimming with Hunter and me at the YMCA pool. There is another photo of Charlotte in those same jeans, her body arched in a half-back bend, her exposed stomach shining like a polished stone surface, a shot glass in one hand and flames shooting from her mouth. Marge says this is a bar trick she has seen. You fill your mouth with cognac or something else one-hundred-fifty-proof, then carefully light it as you're blowing out. To me, it looked like self-immolation. The background in the photo doesn't seem to be a bar. It looks like some other mother's empty kitchen.

There are pamphlets all over the Guidance Office warning parents of the signs of a child gone awry. The moodiness, the truancy, the change in wardrobe. Have I ever smelled alcohol or pot on Charlotte's breath? Does she list when she walks, after a night out?

What would Kyle think I should do? The ghost in the minivan resolutely offers no advice. I doubt Charlotte would drink if she is on the soccer team. *Go to the game*, I decide Kyle would say. *Show support.*

I wrap a robe around myself and knock gently on Hunter's door. He's a hard sleeper and often needs extra time to get up. When I swing the door open I am surprised to find him on Charlotte's lap. They are looking at the *Real Simple* magazine that Marge brought over. His hair is mussed and his thumb is incongruously in his mouth. No ketchup bottle. I guess Charlotte is talking to Hunter about the race-car beds. Just for a second, in that tiny flash of time before she sees me, I glimpse the gentleness of her expression, feel the affection she has for her little brother, hear the soft cadence of her voice as she begins to say something to him. Then it is all sealed up again, as if a string has been pulled, a shade dropped. It happens so fast, I feel the catch in my own throat.

"Breakfast?" I ask.

I don't even wait for a response. Instead, I close the door and head downstairs for the kitchen. As I'm mixing pancake batter I hear the shower going upstairs. A few minutes later the smell of the griddle brings them down, Charlotte in her soccer uniform with the long socks and bright orange jersey and Hunter still in his pajamas.

Charlotte lifts Hunter onto his booster seat. "Doesn't that smell yummy?" she asks him.

I risk a glance at her and there is my warm sweet child again. The evil twin is gone. I don't even try to understand. I block from my mind the thought that there is a tattoo of . . . *something*, just inches above her pubis. What good does it do to dwell on this?

"Maybe after the game we can go over to Home Depot and check out some supplies for those bunk beds," I venture, sliding pancakes onto a plate in front of Charlotte.

"I think we should wait for Aunt Margie," she says, but not in a snotty way. No, not at all. She has rebuffed me, sure, but the rebuff warms me because it is so civil. For some reason, this makes me feel hope.

"Do you like the beds with the steering wheels?" I ask Hunter, ruffling his hair on my way back to the stove.

"Yeah," he says. "I like them. I like pancakes, too."

"Then maybe we should make you a pancake bed," I say, and yes, it is true, I hear Charlotte giggling. I put down the spatula and sit for a moment on a stool, almost as if the wind has been knocked out of me.

"Maybe we'll make you a Cheerios mattress," Charlotte tells Hunter, poking him lightly in the ribs.

"Hah!" says Hunter. "Cheerios mattress."

"And we'll pour Log Cabin syrup all over your blankets."

"Yucky! No!" her brother cries, gleefully banging down his fork, and for one full minute I just sit there, breathing in the sounds and sights of our family acting happy.

SIX

Don't Even Try

The sun is gold-leafing the world as only a September sun can. A crisp autumn chill cuts the morning pleasantly, causing me to zip up my fleece and chase Hunter around the perimeter of the soccer field with his sweatshirt. He has found another little boy to play with. The other boy, of course, is wilder. I have come to the conclusion that four-year-old boys are *supposed* to be wild, and that Hunter's wildness has been stunted by his father's death. It makes me happy to see him rolling in the grass, spinning in circles until he drops, screeching and running toward no evident goal.

I turn my eyes back to Charlotte, who stands in front of the net in her usual position as the freshman girls' goalie. The morning sun is so strong that even Charlotte's black hair has taken on a golden crown. She has pulled it back severely with an elastic band. Her face looks focused, even harsh. The muscles in her calves ripple behind the shin guards. *Don't even try*, her narrowed eyes, her hunched shoulders, tell the other team. She is a natural protector, my Charlotte. She would protect her brother barehanded from a pack of wolves. With the same fierceness, she protects her feelings, outside of the negative showy ones, from me.

"Let's get GOING, girls!" one of the parents is yelling, a blond woman in a fleece vest that looks a lot like mine. "Get that ball MOVING!"

"Is that your daughter?" a man's voice asks, and I turn to find a tall guy in jeans standing over my shoulder, arms crossed, eyes on the field.

"The goalie. Yes."

"Aren't you a teacher at the high school?"

I turn a second time and take in my interrogator. Early to mid-forties. Attractively graying blondish hair. Craggy but intelligent face. "A counselor," I tell him. "But yes, I'm at the high school."

"Must be tough to have your own daughter walking around the place you work."

Now I study him full-face. What a charming thing to say. After weeks of dirty looks from Charlotte, who is upset to find her mother walking around the place *she* works, this stranger has turned the problem on its head. Light glints off the lenses of his expensive shades. I can't see his eyes but his smile is nice. "And *you* are?" I ask.

"Foster." He extends a hand and I shake it.

"As in Foster Grant?" I ask, staring at his sunglasses.

"Sorry. Foster Willis." He laughs and removes them. "My father always told me it was impolite to speak to people while wearing shades."

Brown eyes. Very nice with the blondish hair.

"But look at that sun," he continues, waving a hand at the sky.

"Kate Cavanaugh," I tell him. "As you probably know. Which girl is yours?"

He points to a tall thin girl with hair his color. "Bree," he says. "Number twenty-seven."

Oh, no. A cheese name. I turn away from Foster Grant, ostensibly to check out his daughter, but actually to hide my smile.

"She certainly looks like you," I say, when I think it is safe. "Unless your wife has the same-colored hair."

"No," he says dismissively. I glance around at the clusters of coffee-sipping parents, trying to guess which is his wife.

"No wife, I mean," he says. "Divorced, actually. This is my weekend with the kid, but perhaps you know that routine."

"Every weekend is my weekend with the kids," I tell him.

He digs his hands into the back pockets of his jeans. I watch him trying to decide what kind of schmuck I'm divorced from, some man who doesn't come around on weekends to see his own kid play soccer.

"Actually, I'm widowed," I tell him.

It isn't so bad to say this, I notice. Even though Bree Willis's father stiffens a little in the usual awkwardness my announcement causes, I myself feel okay saying the words out loud. *Progress*, I think, and suddenly feel like celebrating. First Charlotte was nice to me at breakfast, and now this.

"Don't let it *in*!" some hysterical mother shouts, and I turn to the net again and there is Charlotte, staring down a pack of sweepers heading her way with the ball. One of them kicks it and I watch my daughter leap into the air, like a ballerina in cement shoes, and grab the ball to her stomach. She rolls into a ball herself then, a cloud of dirt rising, and a swell of cheering erupts from the sidelines.

"Yaaay! Charlotte!" I hear myself screaming. She looks out at me briefly and there it is, a smile. The freshman girls are huddled together around Charlotte, jumping up and down. High fives are distributed. Hunter appears out of nowhere, grabbing me around the leg of my jeans. "Sissy did it!" he says.

"Yaaay!" I cry again, and Hunter beams. I see his little row of baby corn teeth when he smiles.

"Quite a player, your girl," Foster Willis says.

I had forgotten he was still standing there.

"And who is this sport?" he asks, ruffling Hunter's hair.

The baby corn teeth disappear behind a frown. "Don't!" Hunter says, and then he does it, he lifts his tiny red Converse All Stars and stomps hard on Foster Willis's foot.

Later that night, after Hunter is bathed and tucked in, I go into my bedroom and lie down with the *Real Simple* magazine. The dog-eared bunk bed article bores me immediately. My mind flitters instead back to the morning, and how sweet Charlotte was with her brother and me. It's almost as if even *considering* parenting her better has had a positive effect on her.

It's possible, Kyle's voice whispers, and I turn, startled, to the almost-warm spot beside me on the bedspread. Apparently my husband's ghost has gravitated from the minivan to the bedroom. I can't see him this time, but I almost feel his breath on my face and my ear tingles from his voice. I drop the magazine into my lap.

You're still very hot, you know, Kyle whispers in my ear, confusing me further. The topic of Charlotte has seemingly been dropped.

Cautiously I rise from the bed. I have read in my counseling courses about people who carry a dead person's voice in their heads, but never dreamed I'd be one of them. None of us do, I suppose. At least this dead person told me I'm hot.

In case Kyle's still in the room, I move to the full-length mirror to study myself. Compliments from the dead are not a thing to take lightly. I start at the top of my head, examining the unruly red hair that has escaped my tortoiseshell barrette. The curls stand up all over the place, as if they are laughing at me, dancing around and having a party up there. The color is nice, if you like loud. The way the tendrils frame my face makes me look, even to my own eyes, youthful.

Green eyes stare back at me tiredly. Kyle used to call them cat's eyes. I, however, have always seen myself more like the freckle-faced girl you find on white-bread bags, whose coloring is meant to be cloying and heart-melting at the same time. I drop my gaze south. Something is stuck to the fleece on the front of my vest: a blade of grass? One of Hunter's noodles? The vest itself hugs the contours of my torso nicely. Widowhood does have its perks. I am ten pounds thinner than my husband ever saw me. Leave it to death to whip a body into shape.

"I'm definitely grounding Charlotte tonight," I say, but no one answers.

My eyes move to my painfully bright Nikes, still too new to dim down. What would make a living man want to buy dinner for the woman I am looking at? To me, the whole reflection says Van-Driving Soccer Mom. Nothing sexy there. Maybe Van-Driving Soccer *Widow* is a turn-on. I don't know. I don't know much of anything these days and this is perhaps why I told Foster Willis yes, I'd have dinner with him next week. Gave him my phone number. Smiled and waved and said, *See ya*, right in front of Charlotte. Or maybe it was because I was having such a good day. Or maybe I said yes as a way of apologizing for Hunter stepping on his foot.

"Mom?"

Her curt little voice spins me around from the mirror in a flash. "Charlotte," I say, trying to hide my embarrassment with a cool professional Mommy Tone. "I'm glad you came in. I want to talk to you."

She is still wearing her soccer jersey, the bright orange nylon reflecting against the pale skin of her neck. Her arms are crossed, like a rock star with an attitude. "What are you doing?"

She is frowning, studying me as though I am a sample in her science class petri dish.

"Nothing, just . . ."

"Just staring at yourself in the mirror?"

There is that beat of silence in which I understand that I can't satisfactorily answer her. It won't do to tell her that I've been chatting with her dead father. And I can't explain to a fourteen-year-old girl that her mother—her *mother*, for God's sake—occasionally still thinks of herself in terms of her sexual attractiveness.

"Do you miss Dad?" she asks, pointing at the closet, with its mirrored door. "Is that it?"

She silences me. Smart girl, our Charlotte. She has wrested the wheel from me in short order. I laugh to cover my surprise. "Dad's not in there," I tell her, gesturing at the door. "It's not like Narnia. I can't just walk through the wardrobe to find him."

Charlotte laughs, but it's mirthless. Her good humor seems to have vanished. I have intentionally referenced the C. S. Lewis books her father used to read to her every night. I have done this so she will think about annoying little fauns and sacrificial lions, rather than think of her mother pining for her dead father. But she's come in here with an agenda; a parent can always tell when a child has come to her with an agenda. Something is hard in the soft perfect oval of her face. I watch her plunk down on the edge of my bed. What has she come here to say? I decide to say something first.

"You're grounded," I say. "No going out after school, except to soccer practice."

"How long?" she asks, nonchalant.

"A week." I make this up on the spot.

Charlotte remains placid.

"Do you know what you're being grounded for?"

A disinterested shrug is her response.

"You know, you could get into a lot of trouble posting pictures like that on MySpace."

She whips her head around to face me. "You went on my MySpace page?"

"You left the window open when you—"

"That's your excuse?"

"I don't need an excuse—"

"You don't need an excuse?"

"It was right there in front of me—"

"That's not the point!" she interrupts, her voice rising high and agitated. "The point is, you just, like, invaded my privacy?"

"You left it open," I repeat, "on *my* counter. I am your mother. So I glanced at your profile page."

"You glanced at it? Is that what you call it when you, like, don't respect another person's—"

"Look," I cut her off. "I have a right to know what's going on in your life."

A dark cloud forms above my furious daughter's brow. She stays where she is, though. I stop, think, measure my next words. Visions of flames shooting from my daughter's mouth race before my eyes. I take a deep breath. "I just want to say," I begin calmly, "that your profile doesn't seem to reflect the real you."

"Maybe you don't know the real me," she sneers, swinging one foot lazily from the bed.

"How can you say that," I reason, "when I've been your mother for fourteen years?"

"Well, for twelve, anyway."

She might as well have slapped me. The guilt. The accusation. As if I'd stopped raising her when her father died. Will it ever end, her resentment for the empty shell of a mother she'd found after her father's death—the blank gaze, the limp arms, the one-word answers? It's painful now to remember Charlotte and Hunter staring at me, waiting. Had it been mere days, or was it weeks or months that I wasn't available to them? I pat my daughter's leg gently.

"You're still mad at me, Charlotte," I tell her. Cautiously I lower myself beside her on the edge of the bed. I feel her shoulders tense and am amazed at the power I have to change her whole metabolism just with my proximity. I stare down at the toes of her bulky soccer socks and wonder if Tom Johnson isn't right.

"Maybe it would help if you could talk to someone," I venture. "You know, a therapist. We could go—"

Outrage carries her to her feet, as if her body is propelled by a mixture of Coke and Mentos. Stupid Mr. Johnson and his stupid suggestions. Charlotte's arms cross in a defensive shield and I cringe while awaiting her response. "I don't need some retarded therapist," she spits. "I didn't come in here to talk about any stupid retarded therapists."

Why retarded? I am thinking. Why does she think a therapist would, necessarily, have to be retarded? The fact that I am asking myself this helps me to understand that I am not thinking at all. Just warding off the blows.

Charlotte lets out a steamy huff of breath before continuing. "FYI, Mom, Bree Willis is a weenie. Which makes her father a dick. Just for your information."

"What?" I ask.

"Don't act like you don't know. You're planning on having dinner with the father of a girl who can't understand the difference between a rock and a mineral. She's, like, the biggest moron in our science class."

"You're worried about this?" I ask, genuinely surprised.

"You know it's sick," she says. "You're, like, a *counselor* at the high school. The guy is a parent! How ridiculous is that? How pathological are you?"

Pathological? I turn around and look at her.

"We'd just be having *dinner*, Charlotte."

"Why? Don't we have any food here?"

"Stop it!" I command.

Smart-ass. Thinks she knows so much. My daughter with the smart mouth really doesn't have a clue about her mother's life. She doesn't see me mumbling into my cereal in the mornings, looking for adult company. But doesn't she think I could use a little?

"I'm not in *love* with the guy," I tell her, incredulous. "It's just dinner."

Miss Pathological sits up straighter on the bed and plants her hands on her hips. "Hunter was right to step on his foot, you know. Don't you think your own son was, like, *on* to something?"

Now I almost have to laugh. This child makes me bipolar. One moment I'm angry, the next sad, the next hysterical. I wave my hand dismissively. "I think Hunter is a little boy who wanted his mother's undivided attention."

"Good luck to him on that front," Charlotte says, but I let the jab go.

"Charlotte," I say. "This is no big deal. Really. Sometimes it's just nice to have a little adult company."

"So have dinner with Aunt Margie. She's excellent company. This guy's no Dad, you know."

"Yeah, well," I snap, "Aunt Margie is pretty strange herself, don't you think? Why is it okay to have dinner with *her*?"

I am stunned that I have said this. Marge, my friend who has stuck with me since Kyle's death. Marge, the closest thing to a re-tarded therapist my daughter allows, when she runs away from home because she hates the sight of me. Charlotte won't even look at me now. She flops down on the bed again on her back. The edge of her tattoo winks at me from the top of her belt.

"I can't believe you say you loved Dad," she mumbles, her part-ing shot. Then she raises herself from the bed like a gymnast, swivels around in a well-practiced maneuver of turning her back on me, and leaves.

It was a lot easier than loving you, I want to tell her. But, of course, as a good mother, I don't.

"Grounded," I say instead. "One week."

SEVEN

Ask the Retarded Therapist

I begin thinking about what it would mean to be a retarded therapist. In my years as a counselor, I've more than once worked directly with developmentally disabled students. I've always found them to be heart-wrenchingly honest. If they are happy at the sight of you, they will tell you so. If they want the piece of the half-eaten pie you raise to your lips, they'll ask you for it. If you have frightened them, or hurt their feelings, they will inform you immediately, rather than stuffing their reactions for another day. I'm having a hard time seeing why these wouldn't be good qualities in a therapist. If you told your retarded therapist—say her name is Harriet—about your problems, she would surely tell you if she thought they were good problems, and then she'd tell you how your problems made her feel. She would never charge you a hundred fifty dollars. Never. So what's wrong with that?

I'm sitting at my desk on Wednesday morning, flipping through Alan B. Shepard's official high school newspaper, the *Shepard's Staff*, while waiting for my Touchy-Feely Group to arrive. I amuse myself by imagining a monthly column in the paper, a sort of a Dear Abby–type thing, called Ask the Retarded Therapist. I honestly believe the column would be a great success. Every kid walking the halls of this school is wracked with problems of the heart, the hormones, grades, girlfriends, boyfriends, expectations, broken families, and more. And high school students, famous for their love of the politically incorrect, would surely gravitate toward anything in print with the word *retarded* in its title. I shift in my chair, remembering last weekend's dissatisfactory conversation with Charlotte. *Dear Retarded Therapist*, I begin in my mind. *My husband's dead and my daughter disapproves of me. I'd like to*— But then there's a knock on my open door that precedes Tom Johnson walking right in. This causes me to close the *Shepard's Staff* abruptly and sit up.

"You look flushed," Tom says.

"It's a little hot in here."

Tom laughs, though I don't think I've said anything funny, then he sits down in the chair across from me.

"I want to apologize," I tell him right away, "for the way I left your office when we met last week."

Tom waves away my apology with a swish of his hand. Then he stares at me with eyes I cannot read.

"What's up?" I ask, reorganizing the papers on my desk into piles. It feels as if Tom has overheard me composing my Ask the Retarded Therapist column. But then he does the strangest thing. He runs a hand through his thinning hair, just the way George Clooney does in *Ocean's Thirteen*. Tom is no George Clooney, not even from the back. Tom has the worn angular face you might expect one of the Joads to have had in *The Grapes of Wrath*. Any color or attractiveness it once possessed has been eroded away, as if by a dust storm in Oklahoma. He smiles now, and his face colors. I flip through the *Shepard's Staff*, alarmed.

"Nothing's up," Tom says finally, crossing his legs the wide way, so one ankle rests on his knee. My eyes are riveted by his argyle sock. I remember having a stuffed monkey once in this same argyle pattern. If I'm not mistaken, our dog ate it. "I just had a minute. Thought I'd drop in and ask you how Charlotte is doing."

I feel relieved. I remember my promise to myself to tell him what a caring, good man he is, the next time I saw him. Another guidance director might come by to see why you've missed a meeting or haven't responded to a memo, but Tom is here just because he cares about Charlotte and me.

"It's really nice of you to be so concerned about us," I say, and the smile he rewards me with is slightly startling. "I was just thinking of her now. Not that I wasn't working away, as well," I assure him, though I have never defended my work habits to him before. Something about this visit from Tom is making me speak like an ass. Fortunately, Tom doesn't seem to notice.

"I've grounded her," I tell him. "For a week."

Tom nods, to let me know he is listening.

"I also mentioned to her that she might like to speak to a therapist, as you had suggested."

Tom drops his crossed leg to the floor. "And?"

"And she basically told me to go screw myself."

"Hmmm," Tom says, as though he is processing how one might accomplish such an act.

"Hmmm," I repeat, feeling a little sheepish. I'm beginning to think that Charlotte has succeeded in knocking me off my rocker. Why else am I speaking this way to my boss?

For what it's worth, Tom seems not to have heard me. He remains in his own world. "I was wondering," he says after a minute. "Would you like to grab some dinner sometime, so we could talk more?"

Fortunately, I am sitting down. Or else maybe I would have fallen down. Would I like to talk more with Tom Johnson over dinner sometime? As in, say, a dinner date? I watch myself curl the *Shepard's Staff* into a tight tube, squeeze, then let go. I do this a second time.

"Tom! That is so nice of you!" I finally say, embarrassed by the sound of my own falseness. "You are such a nice person!" I continue. If I say *nice* again, I might have to shoot myself. Where are my guts? I try clearing my throat, digging deep inside myself for a teaspoon of guts. "Let me be honest," I manage, and already I can see his face falling the slightest bit. "Tom, I'm not ready for the real world yet."

There is a readjusting of knees, ankles, and argyle socks. "I understand," Tom says, but I can see that he doesn't. He is thinking: *She doesn't find me attractive.* He is thinking: *How long can it take a person to enter the real world again after a spouse's death?* He is thinking: *What a crappy-ass counselor this woman is.* Mercifully he rises, patting my hand where it rests on the desktop. "You just let me know how I can help you," he says, and immediately I feel like a pathetic charity case, a hopeless depressant, *pathological.* I deserve it all, and more. I watch Tom smile bravely, and walk with false jauntiness to the door. The shine on the seat of his corduroy pants is the last thing I see before the door closes.

I listen to the wall clock tick. I feel bad. Tremendously bad. After a few seconds, I get up and open the door again. Time marches on and I push a few chairs together, preparing for my New Frontiers Group, which will be walking through the door momentarily. Two men have asked me to dinner in the space of a few days. What does *dinner* mean in man-talk? I'm dragging my desk chair into the New Frontiers circle, trying to remember the last dinner I ate with Kyle. What had I cooked for us the night he died? Or had we brought in—maybe Chinese? Or maybe those Thai summer rolls that Kyle loved so much? The thought of Kyle raising a veggie-stuffed roll between strong fingers to his mouth, the memory of his square white teeth, that shadow of beard on his upper lip, the tiny S-shaped scar at the left edge of his lip, it all leaves me breathlessly sad.

I push the last chair into the circle, then fall into it. How many times did I tell Tom he was nice?

In Touchy-Feely Group, we discover that Alphonse has succeeded in planting his seeds. Alphonse, who studies horticulture arts in the voc-tech school, tells us he is going to become a father. His girlfriend, who goes to another high school, is pregnant.

"Holy crap, dude," Hector says, when Alphonse announces his news.

"Hector," I admonish. "Language."

He hangs his head like a little boy. My authority with children who are not biologically mine awes me. A delicate gasp emanates from the floral couch. I watch Phoenix rise from it and hug our young father-to-be. "That is totally amazing," she breaths into Alphonse's neck. "No matter what dies, something new is born."

I am hoping that this is something Phoenix has read in a bad poetry book and not her philosophy of life. But then she falls back onto the couch and begins delicately sobbing, quieter than a cat. We're all silent for a moment. Phoenix does this from time to time, no more often when she's sad than when she's happy. There's a lot I could say, but I wait to hear from the others.

"It's just the circle of life, dude," Alphonse says, scratching his arms until he has loosened a scab and begun to bleed. This reference to *The Lion King* seems to cheer Phoenix. She raises her red eyes to Alphonse and smiles.

Alphonse and the rest are assembled in the small circle in my office, not a seat empty. Attendance is always excellent in September, even in its last weeks. Hope radiates in my maladjusted rebels' hearts, bright as the white spots on their new sneakers. It's a brand-new school year. The slate can be cleaned. To the last they hold with the amazing belief that things can go differently than they have in the past. Success can be achieved. Even Phoenix believes.

A heavy silence falls on the room. Apparently Alphonse's news is tough for them; things like this are not supposed to happen in September. No one comments further on the pregnancy and I decide to leave it alone for the moment. My mind flips and flops, trying to configure how best to support Alphonse, while wondering to whom I must report these new developments. It is hard to maintain trust with a sixteen-year-old father-to-be when the county authorities must be alerted to his problems. And then there is Phoenix. Curled into the couch like a fallen leaf, you'd think it was this delicate girl herself who'd just discovered she was pregnant.

"Oh, my God," she moans, breaking the silence. "I'm so wicked tired." She's claimed the whole of my ratty couch, as she always does, forcing the others to sit on the uncomfortable school chairs. I pat her head, as I often do, and she flashes a microsecond of a contented smile. She distractedly strokes the buttermilk skin of her long neck, her iPod ear buds draped across one shoulder.

"Are you sad about something?" I ask her.

"No." She smiles. "I believe new life is a beautiful thing."

Her straight blond hair hangs down her back. She looks nothing like my Charlotte, yet I often imagine Phoenix to be my daughter's psychic twin. She is sensitive, intelligent, volatile. If my own daughter were blond instead of dark, and named for a city instead of Kyle's grandmother, Charlotte might *be* this lovely waif in my office. Except that Charlotte didn't swallow a whole bottle of ibuprofen last year. Phoenix did.

"Yo, Phoenix. Earth to Phoenix," pipes in Hector, my acting-out Latino junior stuck in a high school full of upper-middle-class

Jewish kids and *Mayflower* descendants. Hector has been in love with Phoenix since the day he first walked into New Frontiers. But he's also been in jail. His father is a Western religions professor at a renowned liberal arts college in Boston, but this is never evident to the cop shining a flashlight on Hector's brown face, or checking his pockets for pot. Hector's pockets get checked for pot a lot more than his friends' pockets do.

My entire group is an advertisement for drugs. They are on Ritalin and Prozac and Xanax and Ativan. These are the drugs their mothers and fathers give them. Then there are the drugs they choose for themselves. Those drugs *upset* their mothers and fathers. This is less confusing for my students than it is for me.

"So," I say, rolling my desk chair back a little, "would someone like to share how their week is going?"

I wait for the awkward wiggling and silence that always follows this invitation, the uninterested stares that mask an anxiety most people haven't felt since they were sixteen. I wonder, in this pause, why these kids trust me, and how it is they see me. They are ever respectful of my authority, even when they're swearing or swinging at each other. They're hardly ever absent; they cling to me emotionally like a toddler to a mother's leg. Sometimes I see only their hormones in action. The boys leer at me as if they see a sort of Mrs. Robinson potential in their Touchy-Feely counselor. Though certainly Adam, who is gay, is not lusting over me. If anything, he's probably dying to do a makeover.

I cross my legs in the other direction as a dollop of shame shoots through me. After unspeakable fantasies of a retarded therapist, I now have shown an unacceptable lack of Understanding Diversity. Truth is, I love Adam. He is smart, sensitive, and uncommonly handsome. As far as I'm concerned, it's the world he tries to exist in that needs a few sessions on my ratty couch.

"Adam?" I say, perhaps by way of a secret apology. "I heard from Mr. Weisman that you've asked him for a college reference. And he told you he'd be honored to write it. That must feel good." (It's more like I'm saying, *It* does *feel good. Feel good, Adam. Tell us you feel good.* But I've got to get this group going, and Adam is always our most generous participant.)

"It does feel good, I guess," he says, his handsome features brightening the slightest bit.

And we're off.

"Are you looking forward to going to college next year?" I ask Hector. A glance at Alphonse makes me sorry I've asked. Alphonse is a senior, too. The only place he'll be going next September is Babies "R" Us.

"It's sketchy," Hector says, wiggling his hand back and forth, making his silver bracelet jiggle. "Don't know if I can do four more years with the white man."

Adam shifts in his chair, uncomfortable now with being white, as well as being gay.

"People of color go to college, too," I suggest to Hector. "People of color even become president."

"Maybe I should skip the whole education thing for a while"— Hector shrugs—"and hang with my homeys."

This is just the kind of thing Hector's father wouldn't want to hear. Hector's whole life is about resisting what his father would like from him. My heart squeezes a little for Hector, a bit more for his father.

By the hour's end I've taken the emotional reading of my charges. I see some positive things in the works. Phoenix has tried out for, of all things, cheerleading. She seems excited about it. Hector has gotten his record expunged after being arrested last summer with marijuana found in his sock. Alphonse seems to genuinely care for the girl he's knocked up. Adam is proceeding on his college admissions packet. When the last student leaves my office, I put my feet on the couch and try to reflect on the small successes.

Then I think about Charlotte.

I have no idea what's going on in her cyber-life. Now she's blocked her MySpace profile with a "friends only" message, so probably Marge can get in, but I certainly can't. I am making a mental note to ask Marge to do so when there is a knock on the open door and I look up to see Phoenix again.

"Can I come in?" she asks. She is leaning against the doorframe as if depending on it for some kind of support. She smiles timidly while her wide eyes survey the room. She has never been to my office before when there was just me in it. She's a hard girl to figure out, sometimes righteous and outspoken, other times shy, like now.

"Of course," I tell her, and she wafts into the room, hair flowing behind her, like an angel. She is a golden child, not quite of this world. She heads for her floral couch like a homing pigeon.

"What's up?" I ask once she's settled in, feet tucked beneath her in their usual nesting position.

She shrugs one slender shoulder and a look of pain flitters across her features. It is almost not there, but I spot it. A mother can see it. "Do you think I'd make a good cheerleader?" she asks, a ridiculous question, which she well knows. She is the poster child for cheerleader. She is beyond too beautiful to be a mere cheerleader. Unlike Charlotte, who possesses a fierce athletic streak, a toughness that surfaces when confronted with a pack of spike-wearing others, Phoenix is all softness. She seems to float through space, only partially occupying it. Just like a cheerleader, I think.

"I think you'd be wonderful," I tell her. "But, you know," I warn, "sometimes these selection committees are unpredictable. Sometimes they choose the least likely candidates and not the most obvious ones. It's good to be prepared for that."

Phoenix shrugs again, like she couldn't care less about getting in or not. "You working late?" she asks. I know not to answer this honestly. I cannot say to Phoenix, this girl I care so deeply for, that I must get home soon to be sure that my daughter's grounding is properly supervised. Phoenix studies me with shrewd eyes. She is so much like my Charlotte, only gentle where Charlotte is angry.

"I wish you were my mother," Phoenix says, apropos of nothing, or maybe she has read my thoughts. "My mother follows me around the house, reminding me how much she doesn't trust me, ever since . . ." Her voice trails off. She looks down at her lap.

"Ever since you took the bottle of ibuprofen?" I ask.

When she doesn't look up, I wrap an arm around her, sitting beside her on the couch. She leans into my shoulder like a rag doll.

"You know," I tell her gently, "if I were your mother, I would act the same way. No one wants their beautiful daughter to not be safe."

Her tears wet my shoulder as she quietly sobs.

"Are you seeing your therapist each week?" I ask.

Phoenix nods into my shoulder.

"Do you know that everyone makes mistakes, not just you?"

She nods again.

"Do you know that everyone feels really sad sometimes?" I hug her a little closer. "You can always come and talk to me when you feel that way. Always."

We stay like this for a minute more, then Phoenix looks up with rabbit eyes and says, "Thank you, Mrs. Cavanaugh." When she leaves I wonder why it is so easy to comfort her, yet so difficult to comfort my own daughter. So easy to reason with her, but not with Charlotte.

It's after four, which means she is at her soccer practice. If I close my eyes, I can imagine her there. I can feel the sun on her head. I can see the other girls and the short hurricane fence and the yew bushes at the ends of the field. She is safe on a field where only cleats and wild balls can hurt her. No one wants her beautiful daughter to not be safe. I allow myself a few seconds of peace. And then the door swings open once more.

EIGHT

Bad Reception

Jack Hayes walks into my office holding two mugs of steaming coffee—the real kind, not the instant.

"It's a little late for coffee," I tell him.

"Hear about the two antennas that got married?" he asks. He's carelessly placing a mug inches away from a pile of permanent records. "The wedding was terrible but the reception was great."

"And your point is . . . ?" I ask, but he's already made me smile, as he always does.

Jack Hayes is my friend and also our driver's ed teacher. He's one of the most popular teachers at the high school—not because he has a car with two brakes, but because he is young and cool and apparently hot. He reaches a startlingly white hand across the desk and rests it on my shoulder.

"Your reception, baby," he says. "It's killing me."

I sip the coffee and recognize the taste of Nurse's Office brew. She has a Krups down there that whips the pants off the Mr. Coffee machine we all share in Guidance. I wonder silently if I need to tell the nurse about Alphonse's girlfriend. The girl doesn't go to this school anyway.

Jack lowers himself into one of my chairs, then pushes his straight blond hair out of his eyes. He is blonder than Hunter. He has the kind of looks that belong on a Dutch Boy paint can, but try telling that to the high school girls who follow him around like he's a rock star.

"How are things going with the Wild Thing?" he asks, a terrible way to inquire about someone's daughter. He always talks this way, intentionally provocative, putting into words my worst unspoken fears.

"I think you know how things are going," I tell him. "She's pissed at me, as always. And she doesn't listen. She skips school. Now I've found out that she's got a tattoo."

"Awesome! Does it say 'Mother' on it?"

"Not funny, Jack." I glance at him and he's grinning, his platinum hair rakishly covering one eye.

"I'm trying something new with her," I tell him. "She's been grounded for a week. I'm going to be more firm and consistent. And I'm going to set limits."

"Sounds hideous." Jack yawns. "And by the way, I don't believe she doesn't listen to you."

"Meaning what?"

Jack shifts a bit uncomfortably in the chair. "Well," he says, moving a bit away from me, as if for his own safety, "there was a time there when you weren't listening to *her*—"

"Jack"—I cut him off—"my husband had *died*. People get distracted when their husbands suddenly drop dead—"

"I understand, I understand. I'm just saying that kids have this way of getting back at you when they've been hurt."

Guilt. This is what Jack has brought with my coffee. I rest the mug on my desktop, my taste for it suddenly gone.

"I think it's great that you've grounded her," Jack tries. "Very good parental response."

I give him a look that could scald his coffee.

"Oh, come on, Kate. She's a *kid*."

Not helpful. Not helpful at all. I take a deep breath, exhale, and frown at my driver's ed friend.

"Imagine you, the driver's ed teacher, have this daughter at the high school," I say, "and she drives into the sides of buildings and up on the curbs. She takes out the neighbors' dogs, and maybe a few of the neighbors, too. Then everybody chats about it in the teachers' lunchroom."

"Oh, please," he says, rising from the chair again. "Everyone skips school! And half the student population is inked. I'd be a lot more upset if my kid brought ketchup bottles to class."

"Well, thanks, Jack. That cheers me up."

"You're missing the point! I'm not saying you shouldn't be firm and consistent." He makes a face, curving his fingers into quotation marks around my newest parenting strategy. "I'm just saying that maybe you should try enjoying her, too."

Jack crosses the New Frontiers circle and gives me a hug. "She's a cute kid," he says. "With a hot mama," he adds.

He smells like those little white mints in the tins that all the kids carry. He's just one more childless friend who loves me, who is full of useless advice.

"Gotta go," he says. "It's crash-dummy film day. Off to find the VCR cart. I just wanted to tell you, though, I think Charlotte has a boyfriend." He nails me with one of his looks. "More evidence that she is normal," he adds.

My feet flop off the couch and hit the floor. Damn Jack! He's always roaring into my office with surprising news. Always the one who knows first when Charlotte is up to something. I guess I'm supposed to appreciate him for this, but my instinct is to shoot the messenger.

"Who's the boy?" I ask, noticing my palms are suddenly moist.

"Don't know. Just some kid who keeps her in a half-nelson when they're not making out."

"Jack!"

"Just kidding," he says. "Well, not about the making out part. They pass by the driver's ed room right after first period. He looks nice."

"Jack, you have to find out who he is."

"Why don't you ask her?"

"You think she's going to tell me?"

"You'll have plenty of time to ask her, if she's grounded," he says, patting my shoulder.

"Well, fine," I tell him. "Now all the Cavanaugh women are dating."

Jack's head snaps around like an action figure. Two can play this game, I think.

"What does that mean?" he asks.

"Oh, nothing." I sigh, brushing down my sleeves casually. "I'm just going to dinner with some parent this weekend."

Jack's face registers nothing seismic, but I note a quick tensing of his smooth jaw. Maybe he's jealous, but probably not. We've been careful in this regard. We'd go tooth and claw for each other to defend our friendship. But the thought of waking in the same bed doesn't work for either of us.

"Who is it?" Jack demands, curious and proprietary and always someone who likes to cut to the chase.

I hesitate before telling him. "Bree Willis's father," I finally say.

"Bree Willis's *father*?"

Now I actually see color in his blank stationery of a face, a spill of red around the eyes and mouth.

"Do you even know who Bree Willis is?" I ask.

"Yes!" he says. "She's one of the crash dummies in this movie I have to show *right now*, and *you're holding me up!*"

Jack gives me a quick hug. "Don't eat too much bread at dinner," he counsels. "The carbs, you know." He inflates his cheeks like a blowfish to illustrate. "And make him buy the most expensive wine. *Milk* the guy." He waves from the door and then he is gone, my best friend at Alan B. Shepard High School, the twenty-eight-year-old man with whom half the faculty surely thinks I am sleeping, because no one can believe that the faculty stud and the young widow could ever just be friends. But all I see when I look at Jack is a sweet crazy pale guy who makes me laugh and endures my complaints with a surprisingly mature ear. My husband was dark, handsome, and olive-skinned. I used to sort his dirty socks and underwear imagining each piece of laundry against his skin, and this was enough to make me want him again.

I dissemble the New Frontiers circle, pushing the chairs back into their corners until next week. Who has my daughter found so irresistible? Is this really evidence that she's normal, or is she possibly dating some ax murderer she found in the voc-tech school?

.   .   .

When I get home I take a walk with Marge in my one free hour before pickup time at Bright Lights. The air is velvety cool and the colorful autumn trees cast long shadows that line and shade our neighborhood streets. We're each quiet enough to hear the slight panting of the other, my own thoughts consumed with Charlotte and some boy, Marge's thoughts unknown to me. We construe these brisk walks as something we do for our health, but I don't know if that's true. How is feeling stress while moving different than feeling it when standing still?

Grumble though I may about snooty old Appleton, its gracious homes look magisterial against a backdrop of golden-leafed trees and emerald-green lawns. We pass the Ferris house, the brown Tudor on the corner of Elm, with an outhouse perched on its lawn. A Pella sign is stuck in the grass, as though we all want to know what brand of windows the replacements are. Old Mrs. Ferris, who used to live there with her Scottie dogs, died last winter. No one peers out the window when you pass the house now, no one comes running out in a funny corduroy jumper and a big crooked-toothed smile to ask how you are and to tell you about her dogs' teeth-cleanings and who is getting divorced and whose son is going to Harvard. I frown disapprovingly at the Porta Potti. This is how we remember the dead in our affluent suburban neighborhood. We put their houses on the market so some soulless young couple—a capital investor who still can't grow a beard, and his shallow blond wife—can come in and knock the living daylights out of what was once Mrs. Ferris's life.

"Aren't the new windows nice?" Marge asks, pounding the sidewalk beside me in her Free Spirit farty old lady sneakers. Sometimes I wonder why she is my friend. But then I remember how much Marge loves this kind of craft work, how her hands must be itching right this moment to lay a level against the new sills and turn the screws in their casings and into the house's century-old wood. Kyle was like this, too.

I wonder if Mrs. Ferris thought of Kyle and me as some soulless young couple when we first moved in. I glance around the neighborhood and wonder which neighbors were as harsh in their assessment of us as I am being now. But we would never put an outhouse on our lawn for the "help." And Kyle was always smiling and waving to neighbors as he went about his yard work and home improvements.

"Remember when you and Kyle put that storm door up?" I ask Marge.

"Yeah," she says moodily. I glance at her face and watch something flitter across the features. Sadness? Nostalgia? What?

"So about this guy your daughter is starting in with," Marge says next. "I know a bit about him, if you're interested."

My head swings around again so quickly, I hurt my own neck. "How do *you* know about Charlotte's boyfriend?"

Marge studies me with concerned eyes. The sun, low in the sky now, glints off her sunglasses, giving her somehow a look of great wisdom. "He's not really a boyfriend." She frowns. "At least, I hope he isn't."

"That's where you're wrong," I tell her. "A teacher at school saw them making out in the hall today."

"Oh, this guy is long past high school," Marge says gravely. "He's looking at least thirty in the profile photo."

I hear myself gasping. My limbs lock and I am frozen on the sidewalk, grabbing Marge's arm, catching my breath before I speak.

"What are you *talking* about, Marge?"

"The MySpace guy."

"This is *another* boy?"

"He ain't no boy, my dear. Why don't we pick up Hunter and then we'll check out Charlotte's laptop?"

NINE

Click Here to Invite More Friends

Gimmee some some of that Sweet Sugah, honee B.

G So reads the illiterate heading of the MySpace message on Charlotte's computer. Marge shifts the screen so I can see my daughter's new friend's profile. He calls himself Big Butchie, a stocky man in a gold chain, jeans, and a white undershirt. He is smiling innocently, as a pit bull might, just before it rips off your arm.

"Not good," Marge says. "He's wearing a wife-beater."

"A *what?*"

"That's what they call the undershirt."

Huge muscles bulge from Big Butchie's sleeveless wife-beater undershirt. You can click around on his page by moving a little red devil cursor. There are photos and graphics surrounding his information: A stick-figure man with a swaying stick penis. A black-and-white photo of a woman lying spread-eagle atop a man on a beach.

What da buzz, babe? his message to my daughter begins. *Text me and we can get 2-getha.* I read further clever references to how he'd like to pollinate her in the hive. A regular biologist, Big Butchie is. *U R so hott n sexy*, he concludes. I hear myself gasping.

"Hot?" I croak, incredulous. "Sexy? She's a fourteen-year-old girl!"

"Not to Big Butchie she isn't," Marge tells me softly, squeezing my hand.

I gaze at the screen, stunned into silence. I force myself to read

Big Butchie's bio. Loves to watch his flat-screen TV, has a female Rottweiler, likes his Harley better than his mother. *One day at a time*, the last line says. Recovering alcoholic, or worse, I conclude. I know this, but does Charlotte? I stare out the window, watching the sky darken along with my mood.

"Has she written back to this guy?"

"Not yet."

"How did you get into Charlotte's account?" I ask.

Marge rises from her stool and opens the refrigerator. Even though we are at my house, she starts whipping up eggs. "We need to have a lesson," she says, reaching for a frying pan. "I'll make you and Hunter omelets. He can eat his while he watches the rest of his movie."

"Marge?"

She beats the eggs diligently. The whisk makes whistling sounds against the edge of the mixing bowl.

"*Tell* me, Marge. How did he get in?"

"Her password wasn't hard to guess."

"What is it?"

Marge doesn't look up. She's whipping the eggs into a froth.

"Marge? The password."

"It's Kyle," she says finally. "Kyle42."

I catch my breath, as though I've been punched in the stomach. *Kyle* . . . followed by the age of his death. I slam shut the lid of her laptop. *Dell*, it says on top, and I stare at this one simple word, so similar to *Dad*, really. A single word on the little box that channels my daughter into a big scary world. A world with Big Butchies in it, where all you have to do to reach them is type in the name and age of your dead father.

My stomach is in Boy Scout knots. The thought of eating something is absurd, but I don't have the energy to argue with Marge. She has barged into my daughter's computer and brought bad news. Marge the Barger. I know I should thank her. I should do a lot of things that I'm right now incapable of doing. Hunter sits in front of a TV burning up brain cells when I should be playing with him. Charlotte will come through the door in the next ten minutes, dragging her stinky soccer stuff behind her. She can eat Marge's omelet.

The sound of sizzling butter fills my ears.

"There are security settings Charlotte should have on her page," Marge says, staring into the frying pan. "I can help her with that."

I walk to the sink and turn the faucet on full force. "There won't be any page. Any MySpace, any Facebook. Any anything." I splash cold water on my face, wetting the front of my shirt. "There won't be any laptop. Period."

Marge is quiet. I wipe my face with a dish towel. The smell of sautéed onions fills the kitchen, slightly soothing me despite myself.

"She can always go to another computer," Marge finally says. "I think it's better if we try to reason with her. Explain to her how she's putting herself at risk. Help her set up a profile that keeps her safe."

"Yeah, right," I say. "Like she's really going to listen to me. Like she's going to let me into her life. She hasn't even shown me that tattoo she has. I don't even know what it is!"

"It's a turtle."

"What?"

"The tattoo. It's a turtle."

"Oh, fuck you, Marge!" I cry, and my friend drops the spatula and takes me into her arms.

"I know," she says. "I know." She pats my back as the aroma of the onions goes from succulent to burned. "This is serious, but it's probably fixable. Charlotte's a great kid, but she's suffering a bit right now." Pat, pat, pat goes the child expert. "And I know," she adds, "she's giving you a run for your money."

"Your onions are burning," I seethe into her armpit. The clock on the wall says 7:10 now, and still no Charlotte. She could be still at practice, or merely thumbing her nose at being grounded. What does Marge know, and what does Jack know, either? Marge releases me and attends to our ruined dinner. She turns off the stove just before smoke rises, just before the fire alarm starts screaming its warning, making me wonder if it's too late to catch this girl of mine in time, or if a fire is already blazing out of control.

TEN

Red Alert

I want red!" Hunter shouts, startling all of us in the garage as we're unloading supplies. Marge is leaning the custom-cut maple planks against the wall while I stash the stains and paints on a high shelf, far away from four-year-olds.

"It's a long time until we start painting the beds yet," Charlotte tells him. "We haven't even built them." She is sorting through her father's old Craftsman toolbox, even though Marge has brought over enough tools to build a second house.

"Where's the hammer?" Charlotte complains.

"I think it's on the wall by the rake," Marge replies, and I wonder, momentarily, why she knows this and I do not. I'm still in shock that we are proceeding with this Saturday afternoon project. Why would Charlotte want to build race-car bunk beds? She seems to almost enjoy being grounded.

"Red steering wheels!" Hunter insists. He clutches his ketchup bottle to his chest, covering up the *G* of his sweatshirt, so it only reads *AP*. It worries me that he wants the red because it's the color of his favorite condiment.

"We don't even *have* the steering wheels," Charlotte mutters, digging through Kyle's screwdrivers and wrenches. Apparently the hammer was not in its place. Nothing's been in its place since Kyle died. A late afternoon breeze wafts through the open garage entrance, lifting her arrow-straight hair slightly away from her face. She's hardly speaking to me after Wednesday's conference with

Marge and me. Three and a half days of the silent treatment. You'd think I was the only one who'd busted into her private business.

"All right," Marge says now, brushing her forehead with a work-gloved hand. "We've got the baby stuff out of your room, Hunter."

"Yeah, baby stuff," Hunter agrees. None of us comments on the tantrum he had when we dragged out his old changing table, and then the carton with the belt through it that holds his stash of ketchup bottles.

"Now we can begin building these beds," Marge continues. "Charlotte? Have you got the nails over there?"

"Nails, pails, whales!" Hunter sings, dancing his Heinz bottle around the garage in his arms. He slides on an empty plastic bag that sends him hurtling forward, heading toward the lumber leaned against the wall. "I'm Handy Manny!" he yells.

Marge gives me a look that says, *Get him out of here.* I read it in its exactitude.

"Come on," I tell Hunter, taking his hand. "We've got to go upstairs and get the room ready."

"Get the room ready," Hunter repeats, allowing me to lead him toward the door to the kitchen.

"Plus, Mom has a date tonight," Charlotte says, swinging savagely through the empty air with Kyle's hammer, which she has found. "Apparently Mom is the only one allowed to date around here."

I keep walking, not turning to respond to Charlotte. An unknown guy who makes out with her in the school corridors. A thirty-year-old man in a wife-beater undershirt. These are the people my daughter wants to date. "Nails, snails, pails . . . ," Hunter sings.

I make baked macaroni and cheese for dinner. Banging and drilling and sawing noises keep me company as I grate cheese and melt butter. Hunter lies on the floor at my feet, asleep on the hooked rug at the kitchen's center, exhausted by a day of early morning soccer, tantrums, and then the building project. I pop the casserole dish into the oven at five, then carry Hunter to the TV room, where I lay him down on the ratty couch there. He doesn't stir. He smells of little boy and old sunshine and sleep. There are food stains on the front of his gray sweatshirt. The love I feel for him almost hurts my teeth.

I head upstairs to shower and dress. Marge plans to stay and work on the beds while I am on my "date," as Charlotte calls it. But I don't think it's a date, despite what I've told Jack. Is it really a date if you eat dinner with one different person at one different table? This is what my daughter thinks. And what exactly is a date to Charlotte? Does she think I'm dying to jump Bree Willis's father's bones? That's more her style than mine, from what Jack has told me.

The table is set and I smell like jasmine and cedar, having sprayed myself with perfume from a crystal bottle that, to this day, had remained unopened. Kyle had brought it back for me from a business trip to Bermuda only weeks before he died. I remember the warm color that flushed his cheeks the evening he described for me the little wooden perfume factory in the field of flowers outside of St. George's. There was something wild in his eyes as he described the place, a place I've always wanted to know more about but we never got to return to together. He'd left the Hamilton offices where he had been working all week, had rented a scooter, and had ridden off in search of a gift for me. The way he'd told me about that journey—driving in the left lane down narrow roads that hugged cliffs and shorelines, roosters roaming through the whitewashed headstones in the cemeteries, the smell of rosemary and the sea—the ways his hands wrapped around the pretty pink box when he'd held it out to me, I remember it all so clearly as I dress for my date that it leaves me light-headed. If Kyle could see me tonight, standing at our bureau in a blue silk dress, he would tell me I was beautiful. He would approve of the way my hair falls softly to my shoulders, the way the overhead lighting makes my shoulder bones gleam like pearls. He'd love the scent of the perfume he'd chosen on my skin.

All I see is sadness on my made-up face as I apply a light coat of gloss to my lips. I hold the crystal bottle of perfume in front of me. "Hey, baby," I tell the bottle, or my dead husband, or no one. "I'm going on a date." Kyle doesn't answer. He is an inconsistent ghost. I wipe my eyes and head downstairs, grabbing the small purse that matches my shoes on the way out.

"Something smells like a soap store," I hear Charlotte comment, before I even turn the corner into the kitchen. They are all at the table, Marge serving the macaroni and cheese, Hunter on his booster seat, blinking back sleep, Charlotte sitting in Kyle's chair. The air smells moist with baking scents. They turn and examine me in my fancy dress-up clothes, and the reactions are mixed. Hunter looks miffed. He knows that when Mommy puts on her high heels she's going out. He crosses his arms and glares at me, and I see how he is too big for his booster seat, really. He's grown up a lot while I haven't been watching. Marge is right to start moving him out of his baby world. Her expression, as she studies my outfit, is kinder than my son's. She beams at me like I am a princess out of one of Hunter's storybooks. "Look at you," she says, piercing the judgmental silence of my children. "Lovely."

"If you're looking to get laid, I suppose," Charlotte adds beneath her breath, but not beneath it enough.

"Thanks, Charlotte," I respond coolly. "Maybe I could borrow one of your pornographic T-shirts to tone things down a bit."

"Mom!" Charlotte slams down her knife and fork. "Nice way to speak to your child."

"You started it," I point out, and Marge bolts from her chair and raises her hands like a referee.

"Okay, okay," she says. "Charlotte, your mother looks nice. Kate, Charlotte didn't mean it." Charlotte makes a snotty face, but Marge plows on. "She's sorry she was rude. She's worked hard today on her brother's beds. Your daughter's an excellent craftswoman. You ought to go out to the garage and take a look. They're beautiful already."

I rest my little ivory clutch bag beside a loaf of Italian bread on the counter. I have stooped to Charlotte's level of adolescent cat-fighting. Only Marge has stopped me from doing more damage. I pull out a chair and sit down at the table. A deep breath and I start again. "I can't wait to see Charlotte's work," I tell Marge, trying to sound like I mean it. "Perhaps if she works more and opens her mouth less, we would all get along better." I check out Charlotte's reaction from the corner of my eye, then soften. "Her dad would be so proud of her if he knew what she—"

Bing, bong! The unmistakable chimes of the front doorbell interrupt my attempt at making amends. The hair on my bare arms rises. Hunter, whose knees in his booster seat are almost at eye level, raises his fork like a weapon.

Bing, bong! I sigh and push my chair back. That would be my date.

ELEVEN

Ever Been to North Carolina?

Foster Willis looks handsome, if nervous, in his expensive golf shirt and linen pants, a sweater slung preppy-style around his shoulders. He allows me to lead him into the kitchen where my family awaits, wearing the cheerful expressions of unhooded executioners.

"This is my friend Marge," I say, moving toward the only friendly face.

"Foster Willis," he says, smiling and shaking Marge's hand, which is larger than his, I can't help but notice.

"Pleasure," says Marge.

"And this, of course, is my daughter, Charlotte."

Foster Willis is not foolish enough to offer his hand to Charlotte. He has a fourteen-year-old daughter of his own, after all. He tucks his hands back in his pockets. "Nice work on the soccer field this morning," he says in lieu of a greeting. "Bree says you're in her earth science class."

Charlotte grunts once in what I imagine to be confirmation. Hunter stares at his sister, attempting to mimic her expression. He juts forward his bottom lip convincingly, bracing himself to be spoken to next.

"Hi, Hunter," Foster says in a sweet daddy voice. "Great game today, huh?"

As Hunter reaches for his ketchup bottle, he never takes his eyes off the man standing beside me. He throttles the empty bottle around its smooth plastic neck, then lifts his foot and plants it squarely in his plate of macaroni and cheese.

"Hunter!"

Noodles cascade everywhere. Hunter's eyes bore into Foster's as Marge leaps from her chair, swiping the plate out from beneath his foot.

"Someone's outgrown his booster chair," she says evenly. "Looks like it's the same guy who's big enough for bunk beds."

"Bunk beds!" Hunter says, remembering.

"Come on." I watch Marge lift him down from the booster, the gesture smooth as silk, and take his hand. "Let's go take a look at them."

Charlotte is giggling behind her hand as Marge guides my silent, ill-behaved son from the kitchen. "Have a nice date," she says in her sweetest voice, flashing us her shit-eating grin.

"I know they were awful but, believe it or not, you're the first man I've dated since their father died," I say, not daring to look up from my brass plate of samosas. "They're just not used to seeing their mother with another man."

I am the best dressed diner in the small Indian restaurant Foster has taken us to, with the exception of our hostess, who wears a pretty pink sari.

"How long has he been, ah . . . deceased?" Foster asks. He's swirling his wineglass in circles, looking concerned, or maybe anxious.

I sip at my own wine, slightly stunned by his question. Up until this moment, I had always believed that only very old men and women were "deceased." The rest of the people we loved and lost were simply dead. But no, he's saying my husband is deceased. A giant sob escapes me. Foster looks up from his glass and pats my hand. "This must be hard for you," he tells me kindly.

Not as hard as it must be for you, I think, but I don't say it. "At least you understand," I only say. "I mean, I'm just glad you have a fourteen-year-old, too."

"Who is named for a cheese," he says, causing me to look up, then down again.

"What do you mean?" I ask, feigning confusion.

"Charlotte told Bree that her mother doesn't like it when people are named for cheeses or cities."

A swell of heat flushes up my neck, and it isn't the curry. "These samosas are so crisp," I say, my hundred and seventeenth stupid statement on this date.

"The thing is," Foster muses, staring at his wineglass again, "your own daughter is named for a city. Ever been to North Carolina?"

I take a huge gulp of my lukewarm white wine. "Actually," I say, and I notice my voice sounds a bit testy, "Charlotte is named for her father's grandmother."

"Who is also named for a city." Foster Willis flashes a shit-eating grin that outstrips even my daughter's.

"A city named for a queen, I believe," I tell him coolly.

Foster smirks, like all of this is just good fun. "Which perhaps explains why she acts like such a royal pain." He waits for me to laugh along at his little joke.

Now there is nothing between us but the piped-in sound of a yodeling Indian soloist. The woman's voice sounds half happy, half in agony, like a child whose finger is stuck in a vending machine door. Foster Willis is still smiling, but now the smile looks glued on, like a piece of a collage. "Sorry," he says. "I thought we were just having a good laugh about teenage girls and all."

The woman yodels on and on, a peppy sitar accompanying her.

"You know," he says carefully, "with all due respect, a lot of people, including myself, have lost their fathers."

I look up at him sharply. "Yes, but Charlotte is a *child* whose father is dead." Snip, snip, snippy, I sound. Like a bitch to my own ears.

My date sighs carefully, staring down at the wet spots on his paper place mat. "I see it's too early for this conversation," he concedes. "I apologize."

"Good," I say.

"But it doesn't mean you should necessarily endorse your daughter's unpleasantness."

Ice water replaces the blood in my veins. Our waiter plunks

down platters of tikka masala and matter paneer. "And here is your rice?" he says, as though he is not sure.

I am sure of one thing. I'm not staying in this restaurant another second. I grab my little purse. "You obviously understand nothing," I tell Foster Willis.

His hand shoots out and covers mine on the table. "I'm sorry," he says again. "You're right, of course."

I stare at his fingers, long and elegant, with tiny forests of hair at each knuckle.

"I just don't enjoy watching a beautiful woman like you being abused."

"I'm not abused," I snap.

"You forget I was there at your place tonight. I watched how—"

"Look, this is not your fault," I interrupt. "It's my fault for coming out tonight. I don't want to discuss any of this with you and I'm obviously not ready for the dating market." I pull my hand from beneath his and rise, pushing the chair back on the wooden floor a bit too noisily. "In addition to being a crappy dinner date, I admit it, okay? I'm having a tough time with my daughter right now."

"Let's not forget your son," he says. "He put his foot in his dinner. Remember?"

I can feel the waiter standing behind me, can almost feel him breathing and waiting to see how things settle. I look straight into Foster Willis's nice brown eyes. "I'd think you'd have a little empathy," I say, my voice coming out scratchy and raw, "at least because you have a teenage girl."

"Actually, my daughter's very sweet," he says.

"Perhaps it's because she doesn't know a rock from a mineral," I tell him.

"What?"

"Nothing."

From the corner of my eye I glimpse the waiter now, withholding our platter of garlic naan. "Look, I'm not ready for dating, okay? Let's just leave it at that."

"You're probably right," he muses. "But there comes a time to get back on the horse."

I rise swiftly to my feet, my chair almost falling. "Same to you and the high horse you came in on," I say, sounding, to my own ears, like a seventh-grader. There is nothing to do now but swivel around and stomp past the startled waiter.

"I like your perfume," Foster Willis calls as I'm exiting.

A brass bell peels spastically as I swing the restaurant door open and shut. The glass rattles in its frame. I don't turn back. I wrap my sweater around my shoulders and begin walking. Here's one Appleton restaurant I won't be returning to.

It's not that good anyway, Kyle's ghost suddenly offers. *Remember when we ordered takeout from there once and the vegetable pakoras were soggy?*

"Who asked for your opinion anyway?" I huff aloud, startling a mother and child walking past me. A stiff breeze stirs the air, ushering in the early darkness, but I just keep walking. Kyle keeps astride, emanating ghostly concern for the situation. "Did you bring a car?" I ask, angry at his uselessness and his unwillingness to defend me in the restaurant, to protect my honor and our daughter's. He told me to get back on the horse! He called our Charlotte a pain in the ass!

Hey, I'm dead. Remember? Kyle's ghost seems to laugh. I walk faster then, legs cold and heart aching for the real Kyle, the real husband I once had, who would have kicked Foster Willis's butt for saying the things he did. In my dreams he would have, anyway.

TWELVE

What Would Kyle Do?

"You walked all the way home from India Happiness?" Jack Hayes asks.

"My shoes are wrecked."

"*You're* wrecked," Jack says. We're trekking toward the high school from our lousy spots in the faculty parking lot. The distance between our cars and the school is not much less than the distance between India Happiness and home. At least I'm wearing work shoes. When I think of the price of the Jimmy Choos I ruined, I want to cry.

"Well, it's Monday morning," Jack says. "Time for new beginnings."

"Or New Frontiers," I tell him, thinking of today's Touchy-Feely Group, which at the moment feels like a mountain to climb, barefooted and without a rope. I button my blazer to the top as we walk. The sun is in hiding behind a clump of ripped clouds. A chill slips through the seams of my cashmere wool pants suit, my last Christmas gift from Kyle.

"Do you really think I'm wrecked?" I ask Jack.

He turns his handsome face to me and frowns. I am not used to Jack frowning. "Babe," he says, "you've been wrecked for a long time. People are worried about you! *I'm* worried about you. You think your dumb smiling act works, but a moron could see through it. You're telling me you walked out on a date with some guy just because he said Charlotte was a city?"

The occasional leaf crunches beneath our feet as I pound toward the school entrance in silence. "It wasn't just that."

"I'm sure it wasn't. . . ." Jack's voice trails off. He is squeezing the living daylights out of his lunch bag as we approach the high school. "Anyway," he comments vaguely, "I'm glad you're not going out with him."

"What's that's suppose to mean?" I ask.

"Let's just say . . ." He pauses, then is suddenly animated in that pigment-free-fooling-around-Jack way. "You're a wigwam! You're a teepee!" His eyes become wide and distorted. "You're two tents," he explains.

I rub my temples with my free hand. Isn't saying I'm too tense the same as saying I haven't gotten back on the horse? I stare at a convertible in the last row of cars before the interminable parking lot ends. WHAT WOULD JESUS DO? a bumper sticker asks. WHAT WOULD KYLE DO? I ask myself. What if he walked back into our living room today—not the useless ghost from last night but the flesh-and-blood husband and father—and was greeted by his sniveling, body-inked daughter, his son carrying a condiment, his wife who can't get along with others? Jack swings open the heavy entrance door. I walk through ahead of him, wondering if you've really lost your mind when you begin asking your dead husband for daily living tips.

"Stop by after first period if you want to catch Charlotte and her boyfriend making out." Jack gives me a quick hug and he's off. I watch a gaggle of girls close in on him as he attempts to make his way to the driver's ed office.

I'm walking to my office and worrying about Charlotte when I see Phoenix on the other side of the glass wall, alone in the empty student courtyard. She's sitting on the brick bench. Her legs spill like two creamy columns from the frayed hem of her short denim skirt. I stand a moment in the flow of students and study her, her glowing physical presence an advertisement for youth and good health. Beneath gold-spun hair, Phoenix's face is cast down in concentration on something. On what? I wonder. This beautiful child, the only girl conscripted to my bad boys' Touchy-Feely Group, may forever remain a mystery to me. I knock softly on the glass and she glances up and smiles. Her eyes look dull but her smile is radiant. I swing open the glass door and sit awhile beside her.

" 'S up," she says, stiffening the slightest bit at my presence. None of the openness she had showed me in my office is here now.

"Nothing much," I tell her carefully. "It just looked so sunny and nice out here that I thought I'd join you for a few minutes." I try not to shiver when I say this, so as not to look like a liar. It's freezing in the courtyard, even in my cashmere suit. Phoenix remains still as pillar. I pat her hand.

"How are you, sweetie?" I ask.

She moves her hand away, stares at her perfect knees. "Okay," she says without conviction. Then she looks at me and says, "You want to know what I was thinking about? I was thinking about how I might like to be an anthropologist when I get out of school. But then I was thinking there are probably enough anthropologists in the world already, so why bother?"

"Don't you think anthropologists are sort of like artists?" I ask.

"What do you mean?" A glimmer of hope lights her dull eyes.

"I mean that every artist or anthropologist interprets the world in their own unique way."

I watch her legs swing lazily as she thinks about this. "Maybe," she says.

"So if you decided to become an anthropologist, wouldn't the world get to see something new, something seen only through Phoenix's eyes?"

"Through Phoenix's eyes," she repeats. "That's a nice song title." Again she goes to that interior place, and I am left with only her downcast face and swinging legs.

"What makes you want to study cavemen?" I ask. "Is it the boys at this high school?"

The smile she rewards me with when she looks up is sad and beautiful. "I love you, Mrs. C.," she says, her hands not leaving the sides of the brick bench. I wrap my arms around this pixie of a sad girl. "You'll be all right," I tell her, although she hasn't said anything to indicate she's worried that she won't. Perhaps I am saying it not only for her, but for Charlotte.

"You think I can do it?" she asks.

"I believe in you," I tell her. We walk into the school together when the bell rings, Phoenix looking cheered, me believing I might have put one more anthropologist into the world. It's one of those moments that make the many rote hours at Alan B. Shepard seem worth it.

Gladys Panella is at her desk at Guidance Central, staring at my office door, which is open. "Good morning, Gladys," I say, marveling silently at the brightness and shininess of her red lipstick.

"You've already got someone waiting," she says. Her lips grow thin when she speaks, her rosebud mouth becoming two straight lines.

"Who's in there?" I whisper.

"A Mr. Willis."

I freeze in my spot in front of her desk. "Did he mention what his business was?"

"I wouldn't know, Mrs. Cavanaugh." Now the red lines are bent down at the corners, her mouth the direct opposite of a happy face. She is the only grown-up in the school who doesn't call me Kate. I draw my shoulder back. "Thank you, Mrs. Panella."

He is sitting on the couch that Phoenix likes to drape herself across during Touchy-Feely Group. He's wearing a suit and tie this morning, and it occurs to me that I don't know why. I never thought to ask Foster Willis what he does for a living. We never got that far on our date. He rises when I enter, smiling his good-looking-divorced-guy smile, and holds out a brown paper bag, neatly stapled at the top. "Your chicken tikka masala," he says, offering me the bag.

I rest my briefcase on a chair.

"Nice suit," he says, eyeing my cashmere.

"Thanks. So is yours."

Foster Willis laughs and reseats himself.

It's probably Brooks Brothers, his suit. He looks fidgety in his seat, like he's late to be somewhere. "What do you do, anyway?" I ask.

"I'm a lawyer."

I flop down onto my desk chair. "How can you tell when a lawyer is lying?"

"His lips are moving," he says, but his smile is mirthless.

I guess all lawyers know all these jokes. I am not happy that he's here. A wave of fatigue travels down my spine. "Have you come to see if I've gotten on the horse yet?" I ask, leaning back in my chair.

"Just to give you your food," he says. "And to apologize again. I think I could have been a more charming dinner date. And I should have given you a lift home."

"It's all right." *I wouldn't have accepted it anyway*, I don't say.

Foster Willis puts the bag down on my desk. I can smell the grease and curry through the brown paper.

"About the date," I say, "maybe you thought I was in the witness box instead of a restaurant."

Ouch, Foster's expression says, and I feel a little guilty. He is a lawyer, though. Aren't they supposed to fight back? He pushes the hair out of his face, much as I've watched Jack Hayes do, but to far better effect. "It was more like a deposition," he only says.

I study him, offering no response. He is definitely the attractive alpha type. I can imagine him on the port side of a yacht, a dry martini in his hand. Yet nothing much happens when I look at him, except for the tiniest bit of anxiety rumbling around in my stomach. My libido appears to be atrophied, but what if I'm happy enough to have it this way? I only know that I want him to leave now, to go to his big office downtown and bury himself behind a pile of briefs and leave me alone. Not that I don't find him attractive.

I open my mouth to attempt to dismiss him and am visited by an unwelcome thought. *What would Kyle do?* I lean back in my chair. It occurs to me that I don't give a damn what Kyle would do. If Kyle hadn't left me alone in the world with two unhappy kids, this guy and I wouldn't be having this awkward conversation now.

We listen to a bell ringing in the corridor. Foster clasps his hands together. "Let me just ask you something," he says, "before I leave. Hasn't it been two years since your husband died?"

A surge of adrenaline shoots through me, as though I have caught him rifling through my underwear drawer. "How do you know how long it's been?"

He shrugs. "The city told the cheese."

I glance down, chastened. Charlotte. Where is the girl's loyalty? "Look, I'm sorry about the name thing," I say. "And I'm sure your daughter is, as you say, a perfectly charming girl."

He laughs a little under his breath. "You know the truth of it. She's fourteen."

I glance at him. It's nice the way his hair falls over one eye. Very boyish.

"I shouldn't have offered you unsolicited parental advice," Foster goes on.

"It certainly wasn't solicited," I agree. But then I think about my son's foot flying into a bowl of pasta and feel chastened. I don't want to feel chastened.

I stare at the wall clock, ripple through the pages of a manila folder. This is supposed to mean *go*, but Foster Willis won't. A heaviness settles on my chest, as if someone has placed a steaming bowl of pasta right there.

"You know," Foster says, "whether or not you ever want to see me again, there is something I'd like to say to you."

I shift in my chair, as if a small fire has been set beneath it.

"Here's the thing," he says, leaning forward on Phoenix's couch to look at me. "There is a whole beautiful world out there that I get the feeling you're not even seeing." His eyes grow soft as he looks into mine. "If you saw it—"

"I should get to work," I interrupt. I smooth the edges of the folders, then move them to the other side of the desk, slapping them down so hard it creates a wind. Foster is not so blind this time as to understand that I am, indeed, dismissing him.

"Right," he says, rising from the couch.

"Thanks for the chicken."

He shrugs, smiling at me. "It's gorgeous, you know."

"What?"

"Your hair."

He leaves the door open when he exits. It's quiet in his wake.

Where are you now, Kyle? I quietly ask. He apparently hasn't seen fit to weigh in on this scene, leaving me suddenly irritated with a deceased person. When he wasn't deceased, when he was very much alive, Kyle hadn't seen fit to tell me he had any heart problems, either. Hadn't a doctor warned him at any point, during any physical? I find it hard to believe that some doctor had not. But Kyle, with all the authority of his eight-year seniority, had only told me the things he wanted me to know. And I had accepted this. And now he won't tell me if he thinks it's okay to get back on the horse. He won't tell me at all.

I walk past Tom Johnson's closed door, where his bird-in-a-cage poster shines beneath the fluorescent lights, my thoughts switching to Charlotte again, and the scene last weekend when she met Foster. *(If you love something, but can't make it behave even in its cage, what's the point?)* I walk past Gladys, who frowns at me in disapproval, or perhaps this is just the way she takes in all of life. I head for the faculty ladies' room and lock myself in. I pat down the lapels of my cashmere suit, calm myself. The soft green wool is the color of wasabi, but my face rising above it is flushed and tired. So tired, the woman in the mirror looks. I splash water on my face, pat down my unruly hair. *Gorgeous.*

When the bell rings at the end of first period, I am stationed by the trophy display case on the other side of the driver's ed office. Classroom doors fling open on both sides of the corridor and students spill out, anxious to make loud noises after being trapped behind desks for fifty minutes. Hooting and laughter erupt all around me, making my blood race and adrenaline flow. I spot Hector coming down the hall with a small group of his boys— possibly the only other boys of color in the entire high school. *"Papi,"* he says, his gold chains sparkling, *"leesen."* He borrows his phrases from Hispanic students whose lives are nothing like his. There are no *Papis* in the Sifuentes household, only his mother and father, both Ph.D.s, and a brother at Harvard. Hector's slow sexy stride goes a long way toward keeping his low-slung pants up. He is the king of bling, no doubt the purveyor of a MySpace page as racy as Big Butchie's and owner of his own wife-beater undershirts. He spots me and waves, even though he is with his homies. I smile back, trying not to capture the notice of his friends, especially the pretty girl with black eyes who walks beside him. It occurs to me, as he pats the girl's bootylicious behind, that I love Hector. Even though I may not be able to help my own daughter, I would love to help this boy. I'd like to bring him home, buy him a pizza, and explain to him that he is not a member of the underclass. I'm midway through this fantasy when I see her, my Charlotte. And there is the boy, his arm wrapped around her as though he is attempting to prevent her escape. Charlotte is smiling in a way I haven't seen for a very long time. She doesn't look like she wants to escape. Not at all. The boy isn't too tall but he's very handsome. He's got a square jaw that would melt a girl's heart. His auburn hair matches his eyebrows. He has the kind of eyebrows women love—the James Bond kind. I shudder for Charlotte. He could be a blithering idiot, with eyebrows like that, and women would think he was a sexy genius.

"Stop it!" my daughter says, laughing, when the boy begins kissing her neck. I approve of Charlotte's response, though I am not sure that she means for him to stop. He keeps kissing. I keep watching.

The boy is dressed a lot like Hector, I notice, with the low-slung jeans and the gold chain glinting on his neck. Is his hand really on my daughter's ass? *Yes, it is*, a prissy little voice inside my head tells me. My mouth falls open. This is when Charlotte sees me, of course. I clamp my mouth shut immediately but it's too late. Charlotte's smile vanishes. The hand slides off my daughter's royal ass. The boy's eyebrows remain sexy. I cross my arms like a schoolmarm.

"And who is your friend?" I ask, my voice rather pedantic to my own ears. We are making a scene. Passing students are staring at us. Charlotte surprises me by doing something very classy.

"Mom," she says pleasantly, "this is Ren. Ren, this is my mother."

The boy extends his hand, the one that was on Charlotte's ass, flashing a killer smile.

THIRTEEN

Monkey's Bed All Broken

Charlotte was a baby when I went back to graduate school to become a guidance counselor. I took evening classes so Kyle could be with her and when I'd returned at night, I'd find Charlotte comfortably settled in the crook of his arm, the two of them on the couch that's now in the TV room, covered with Juicy Juice stains. His little Charlie. She'd usually be wearing only a diaper or, sometimes, a diaper and her teeny little cowboy boots, which she adored. They were pink and leather, tooled with swirling designs that Charlotte loved to run her chubby fingers over, a gift from my parents when they first retired to Texas.

"Hello, gorgeous," Kyle would always greet me, looking up from whatever Richard Scarry book they were reading together, the story of Lowly Worm or a rabbit named Tanglefoot, making me forget in an instant the twenty-two-year-old boys who had smiled at me in my statistical analysis class. Even back then Charlotte hardly glanced up to greet me. She was too contented being Daddy's cowgirl.

This weekend, Daddy's cowgirl is raking leaves. She has accepted the chore without protest, which surprises but pleases me.

The awful drone of leaf blowers has been our autumnal weekend music. Neighboring houses all around us have been serviced by fleets of landscapers arriving in elaborate pickup trucks with rackety trailers on back. We won't need leaf blowers and landscapers at our house because we have Charlotte. And Ren, as it turns out. I have mixed feelings about allowing him to be here while Charlotte works, yet couldn't deny her new boyfriend's offer of assistance. Plus, for obvious parental reasons, I want a closer look at him.

"Hello, gorgeous," the suave Ren now greets my daughter at the front screen door. It squeezes my heart to hear these words coming from another male's mouth. Still, Ren is quite the smooth little man. I can't help noticing how likable he is, except for the fact of where his hands go. In my world, Ren's hands shouldn't be magnets for Charlotte's choicest bits.

"Excuse me," I say, swatting his hands from my daughter's butt. He drops them chastely to his sides. Even so, Charlotte wraps her arms around him dramatically two seconds later.

"Please don't feel shy around me," I say, and they ignore me.

"You two ready to rake?"

They smile, though not at me. He is handsome with those eye-brows. And he does make Charlotte smile.

"Let's go," Charlotte says, patting Ren once on the butt of his jeans, inches above an artfully torn hole that exposes his startlingly white underwear. Off they go to their leaf-raking boot camp for naughty teens. The trees have cooperated by dumping a golden abundance on our broad front lawn. Hunter follows them out, drunk with happiness at the sight of the rakes in his sister's and Ren's hands. He has carefully placed his ketchup bottle on the front steps and now wields his own kid-sized plastic rake so that Charlotte will notice it.

"Sissy! I'm ready!" he cries. Charlotte pats his head and Ren says, "Let's go, little dude." Hunter doesn't stomp on Ren's foot, the way he did on Foster Willis's. Hunter likes Ren. Charlotte's T-shirt, I notice, hangs loose and long. She looks like a wholesome kid today, all traces of the MySpace girl gone. Perhaps this boy-friend is good for her.

See? I tell myself, watching them from the kitchen. *I can be an effective parent.* I celebrate by eating a granola bar. Although I've bought the variety box, containing countless choices of mushed fruit, I look for the one with the chocolate chips in it.

A few minutes later I'm gagging myself on a cloud of Pledge, pretending to be dusting, but really continuing to spy through the dining room window. It's fun to watch Charlotte and Ren tumble and play like puppies. Hunter sits in a pile of leaves, his eyes as big as quarters. You can tell that he likes hearing his sister laugh. The two big kids are a huddle of blue jeans and white cotton. The midday sun is shining on them, making them look all scrubbed and new.

"Polishing your table?" Marge asks incredulously, causing me to jump a few inches off the floor. She seems shocked to see me so domestically compromised, or perhaps she's disappointed that I've taken such a choice job away from her.

"You scared me! When did you come in?"

Marge ignores my question. A steering wheel hangs from each of her arms. "I came through the garage," she finally says. "I brought these over, to paint. God, they look like they're having fun."

Now we're both staring out the window, mooning at the pastoral scene before us. Charlotte catches us spying and sticks her tongue out. Marge and I laugh. Parenting is such fun through a pane of glass.

"I could do those leaves for you," Marge says.

"Marge, *no!*" I tell her, as though she is a naughty golden retriever. "This is Charlotte's chore, and I'm happy that she's actually doing it."

"Yeah," Marge says, watching Ren haul my daughter in a fireman's carry to a pile of leaves. "You're really teaching her the merits of hard work."

Ren dumps Charlotte into the heap and the shouts of laughter pierce the window glass. Charlotte rises like a phoenix from the ashes and throws her arms around Ren. They kiss passionately, shockingly, in public, leaves clinging to their backs and hair. Hunter runs for his ketchup bottle.

"Wow," says Marge. "If you can get that boy to go to school every day, I don't think you'll have a problem with Charlotte skipping anymore."

Later, after our dinner of tacos and beans and rice, Charlotte clears the plates as I load the dishwasher. Hunter leaps neatly from the booster seat he has clearly overgrown, carrying a Beanie Baby monkey in a taco shell out of the kitchen. His silky hair rises like butterfly wings as he leaves the room. Outside, the leaves are raked into nice big piles, which we can see from the kitchen windows. The sun sets on the conical heaps like a giant Van Gogh painting. There is a whiff of family contentedness in the air, along with the scent of refried beans.

It makes me want to call Foster Willis, just to tell him I notice. The whole beautiful world, that is, which he claims I am missing. Charlotte's flip-flops slap rhythmically against the tile floor, pleasing dinner cleanup music. We chitchat like old buddies, wrapping the unused shells and loading dishes.

"So what does Ren's name mean?" I ask, slipping dirty forks into their little plastic compartments.

"Why do you want to know?" she snaps, and suddenly a cold front comes through the kitchen.

"I'm just interested," I respond carefully. "It's an unusual name."

Her face is grumpy when I turn to look at her. "It's not a city. It's not a cheese. So what's your problem?"

I rub my arms with my hands, as if I can stop things from escalating this way. "I don't have a *problem*, Charlie," I tell her carefully. "I was just curious."

"Don't call me Charlie," she says.

Another blast of cold air. I do a quick review of our afternoon's exchanges, looking for some offense for which I am now paying. Charlotte slaps down a pile of dishes too hard. There must be something.

"That was Daddy's name for me, not yours."

"I know," I say. "But sometimes I can feel him right here with us still."

Charlotte eyes me suspiciously, then lets this go.

"You're not the only one who misses your father, you know," I tell her.

"Well, he's not here, so don't call me Charlie."

I study my angry child. The grass stains and sauce stains on her shirt make her look touchingly young from the neck down. "*We're* here," I remind her gently. "We can try to love each other the way Daddy would have wanted us to."

She turns her back on me, and I watch our happy day evaporate. I know she misses her father, but I've just told Charlotte that I love her. Shouldn't this count for something?

"He's named for a bird," she mutters into the counter, "without the *w*. Does that make him, like, a freakin' asshole in your book?"

"Language," I say, then, "No." We are silent. Why, I wonder, is this all so hard?

"Maybe that makes him a pecker," I offer, using the last tool in my box, a pathetic stab at humor.

"Mom!"

"Or perhaps a cock?"

"Stop it!" Charlotte cries, flinging herself around to face me again.

"Oh, lighten up," I tell her. "You can't tell a joke coming if it's sitting on a parade float waving at you."

Charlotte doesn't respond to this.

"The truth is," I say, "I like your boyfriend. You can believe me or not."

Charlotte stares at me like I'm a tub of cottage cheese with green stuff growing on it. "Well, I don't like yours," she mutters.

"My what?"

"Your stupid boyfriend."

"What are you talking about?"

"Oh, just, like, the father of the most retarded girl in science class. Just Bree Willis's dorky dad."

"Charlotte, honey, you bandy around the word *retarded* in a way that isn't very sensitive. Haven't you ever known any people who have developmental disabilities? Maybe at the high school? These are wonderful boys and girls—"

"I'm not talking about retarded kids. I'm talking about your stupid boyfriend."

Now it's my turn to be offended. "He is *not* my boyfriend, Charlotte," I assure her.

She pushes a hank of jet-black hair behind one small pink ear. "He'll, like, morph into your boyfriend. You and I both know it."

"He will not morph into anything," I insist, slamming the dishwasher shut harder than intended. "And you didn't have to tell his daughter about the cheese thing, either." Charlotte jumps back a micro-inch but I see it.

"You'll be inviting him over here all the time," she persists, "and he'll be sitting on the furniture and stuff."

"He will *not*."

"He *will*."

Bang! goes my fist on the counter. *Bang!* goes Charlotte's fist next.

"You think you know so much," I tell her hotly. "Do you really think Foster Willis could hold a candle to your dad? You think you knew your father so well. You don't know anything."

Surprise flashes in Charlotte's eyes. But I am unstoppable.

"He wasn't just your father. He was my husband! Do you think, in your little addled brain, that you know who's a good replacement for him? *No* one is a replacement for him! That's who!"

"Then why didn't you take care of him?" Charlotte shrieks. "If you loved him so much, why did you let him *die?*" She turns from me again, grabbing the counter's edge. Her back shudders and her sobs come out in giant gulps. "You just closed your eyes and slept while his heart stopped," she cries. "Just slept," she sputters.

"Oh, honey, that's not how it happened."

We stand our distances, each tangled in our own misery. Eventually I walk over to her, pulling her fists loose and wrapping her close to me. Her hair smells like fresh air and refried beans. I rock my skin-and-bones daughter in my arms, feeling the tenseness in her every muscle, feeling her trying to ward me off, trying to ward off death and sadness and loss. I remember holding her father this tight in my arms the morning he died in bed, his skin already cold and slightly blue, the ambulance not yet arrived. I could taste the blue as I held him, and it had terrified me. She sobs in my arms until we hear the staccato pounding of little feet which grows louder and eventually produces Hunter standing before us with a ketchup bottle in one hand and the taco shell in the other.

"What?" he demands. "I hear yelling!"

I want to tell him that everything's okay, that we're just talking in the kitchen, but I'm still holding his sister, who is sobbing. He doesn't wait for me to tell him anything. Instead, he squeezes the taco shell in his left hand, cracking it in half and then throwing it at us.

"There," he says, administering his punishment. "Monkey's bed all broken." Then he turns his back on us and leaves.

FOURTEEN

Girls' Night Out

Hand me two screws," Marge says. I take a couple out of a little plastic box and reach them up to her. All I can see is Hunter throwing the taco shell. All I can think is that Charlotte is right. I just let him die while I slept. I allowed the love of my life, the father of my children, the foundation of our family, to slide down the toilet while I caught my beauty rest, worried over who got the top sheet. As of last night I can add lying in bed with my eyes wide open to my list of idiosyncrasies. I'm suddenly watchful for change but, of course, it's too late. The only one who can possibly change (and this according to Jack and Marge) is me.

Marge has been here all morning finishing up the *Real Simple* bunk beds. She's like a bloodhound who can sniff the air and smell change in it. "Where's Charlotte?" she asks now, hollering down at me from the top bunk. She looks like a mythical creature up there, a giant with a hammer on a beanstalk.

"She's at Ren's," I tell her. The fact that I don't expand on this tells Marge everything.

"Already?"

"She's an early riser."

"You two fighting again?" she asks.

"No. She just thinks I killed her father."

Marge fits the steering wheel in place and bangs at it with her open hand. "Kids say things," she tells the wheel. "It doesn't mean anything."

I grit my teeth and sink deeper into Hunter's beanbag chair. *You don't know anything*, I think.

"So are you still seeing that guy who came over?" Marge asks, screwing something into the center of the wheel. She's on her knees, turned away from me, her strong back and spreading middle-aged butt facing me.

"What guy?" I ask, as if I didn't know. I burrow even deeper into Hunter's beanbag chair.

Marge turns and looks at me. "I hate it when you act dumb. Stick to your poor-widow act. It suits you better."

I throw a stuffed Elmo at her. It bounces off her shoulder and she laughs.

"Come on," she says. "I'm talking about that Fester guy that Hunter didn't like."

"Foster," I correct her. "Not Fester."

She smirks down at me, the hair around her face escaping her ponytail. "Hand me that Phillips-head," she says. "Well? Are you?"

I struggle from the nest of beans to pass her the screwdriver. "I'm not really into dating," I respond evasively.

"Why not?" she asks, jiggling the steering wheel. She looks as if she's actually driving somewhere. "He was really handsome. Did you mess something up with him?"

"Did it ever occur to you that I might not *want* to date anyone?" I ask.

"Frankly, no," Marge says.

"And why is that?"

"Why do you think?" She flashes me a hard look. "From where I stand, which happens to be six feet and one inch off the ground, dating a nice man like Fester would be very appealing."

"Foster," I say again.

"Go out with him and I'll call him Foster."

"Well, I don't want to," I say, crossing my arms stubbornly. I almost tell her that the most desirable models in the world are her height. But then I don't. The truth is, Marge looks nothing like a model.

"You're a frustrating person," she says, climbing down from the top bunk. "Sometimes I think you'd rather spend your time complaining about your awful hard lonely life than you would spicing it up a little."

"Spice is the last thing I need right now. Charlotte thinks I killed her father."

"You mentioned that," my friend says. A frown elongates her long face. "That girl will say anything to get a rise out of you." She rubs her chin with a big hand. "I think you need to pay more attention to Charlotte in some ways, but less attention to her in others."

"What is that supposed to mean?" I ask.

"It means it wouldn't hurt for you to give her some responsibility. Other than passionate raking with her boyfriend. Like babysitting her brother once in a while so you can go out."

This sounds ridiculous to me, almost like Marge has suggested I let Hunter drive the minivan into town.

"Don't you like to babysit the kids?" I ask.

"I'd be willing to forgo that privilege if it teaches Charlotte some responsibility."

"Wouldn't I have to trust Charlotte first?"

"How do you think trust is built," Marge argues, "if not by giving your daughter the responsibility for something important?"

"I have nowhere to go," I tell her dismissively.

"Yes, you do," Marge says. "You and I are going out Tuesday night, to the Claddagh. Some of my old school friends are getting together for a little reunion. I want you to come."

I turn away from her so she won't see my face. A pity date with my six-foot-one neighbor. The thought of the Claddagh, I must confess, always cheers me, it being an Irish pub in our very own Appleton, with lovely live flowers growing in wire baskets of peat all along its timbered front. But what would I do with a bunch of Guinness-swilling MIT geeks?

"What would I do with a bunch of Guinness-swilling MIT geeks?" I ask, following Marge out of Hunter's room, secretly hoping she'll talk me into coming. I don't tell her that I imagine her friends to be just the same as she, brilliant nerds of disproportionate size with plain faces and hearts of gold. I imagine them at the bar, tapping code into their iPhones with square mannish fingertips, sipping drinks composed of perfectly separated layers of liquors, lights blinking in their shirt pockets as their BlackBerrys silently record incoming e-mails.

We stop in the family room to peek at Hunter, who is still sleeping, crushed leaves in his hair and scuffed sneakers on the couch cushions. I turn off the television and then we both stare at him for a while.

"He's upset with his sister and me," I tell Marge.

"They get over these things quickly," Marge assures me, not bothering to ask what he might be upset about. Again I think about how easily this woman with no children dispenses parenting advice.

"So I'll cook dinner for the kids on Tuesday," Marge says. "Just something easy I can bring over in a casserole dish. You come home from school and off we'll go. We'll be there in time for happy hour."

Instead of glowering at me in her usual way, Charlotte nods like a cop at the front desk as I enter the kitchen Tuesday afternoon. I throw my briefcase down on a chair, inhaling the mouthwatering lasagna Marge is heating up in my oven. Charlotte stands beside her at the stove, a stolen Starbucks apron wrapped around her slim body, her attention once more on the cooking. Marge is lifting foil from the top of the lasagna so they can both study it. "See how it's bubbling along the edges?" she says. "That means it's cooked through. You can take the foil off now and brown the cheese."

"Brown the cheese," Hunter says, giggling sinisterly from his booster seat. The room smells of goodness, despite Hunter's strangely parroted comment. It's an idyllic scene of mother-daughter cooking, only Marge isn't the mother. I ruffle Hunter's hair, kiss the top of his head.

"I can take it from here," Charlotte says. Her cheeks are pink, and I can't tell if it's the excitement of being in charge or simply the heat of the oven.

"Thanks, Charlie," I tell her, her father's nickname once more sliding loose from my lips. She doesn't cringe or yell this time.

"We'll be fine," she says.

"We'll be fine," her brother repeats, hugging an empty ketchup bottle to his chest.

"You see?" Marge says, when we're sitting later at the bar, waiting for the geeks to arrive. "Charlotte will do fine."

I run my hand over the smooth polished wood of the bar's surface. "Smooth," I say. "Everything goes smooth when you play the mother."

Marge shrugs dismissively. She sips beer from the mouth of the bottle, and then a really handsome Asian guy with a pocket protector is tapping her shoulder, grinning widely.

"Hey, Margie Gates," he says.

Marge's eyes light at the sound of his voice, even though her name is Marge Carlson. Then I realize the handsome guy is nicknaming her after Bill Gates. Geek humor. Marge puts the guy into a crusher hug. I stare at the edges of his pocket protector, wondering if it's a prop or if nerds really still use them.

"Kate, this is Thomas," Marge says, introducing us. He shakes my hand, his beautiful almond eyes the color of chocolate. Pretty soon others flow in, too, until we've moved to a table with one beautiful blond genius who talks like a robot, two more Asian guys, a mousy woman with glasses, and a very black Nigerian engineer. Marge's sandbox pals. They all look friendly, but slightly off in the social department. I settle in at the table, more or less one of them, even if I don't know what they're talking about. Yeasty brew smells fill the air and "Toora loora loora" flows like syrup from a hidden jukebox. How corny. I look around the table and see how un-Irish we all look, except for me. I sit among these cerebral powerhouses like a poster child for the Claddagh, Miss Katie Cavanaugh, shopworn vestige of the Boston Irish.

The song on the jukebox has ended now and musicians who've been setting up for a session have begun playing. The light is sinking in the dusty pub windows and a mournful lad is singing over sweet fiddle music, "Will ye go, lassie, will ye?" I close my eyes and let the music in, while bits of MIT conversation I cannot understand float all around me. Marge laughs loudly, delivering a punch line I don't get to a joke I cannot comprehend. It is a side of Marge I have only imagined in the past. She seems fulfilled and joyful in the midst of these friends. I am happy for her, but also happy for myself. Here I am, out of the house, for once not stewing about things, only slightly stewed myself. No one at this table tries extra hard to include me, but neither do they know that I am a widow. It's freeing in a big way, an encouragement to order another stout. I sip my fresh Guinness, wondering how Charlotte and Hunter are doing, understanding via the miracle of alcohol that my daughter *really* doesn't hold me responsible for her father's death. She just needs an answer, and someone to blame. We all do.

A tap on my shoulder brings me out of my reverie. A man with hair as red as mine and smiling blue eyes stands over me. "Will ye go, lassie?" he asks, extending a hand. I glance at the dance floor and find it suddenly swelling with couples, all of them swaying and embracing, the music too sad, too beautiful to resist. I rise in a coma, let this man lead me to the floor, inhale the workman scent of him as he holds me close, guiding me through the chords and the voices, the Guinness and the moves, the music that pulls at something in my heart. We dance like this through several long numbers, not bothering even to introduce ourselves, contented with the feel of our hands on the other, our breath in each other's hair.

Then a somewhat familiar male voice is calling my name. "Hells bells, would you look at who's here," the voice says, and I look up from the redheaded stranger's shoulder to find Foster Willis lifting his beer bottle in a salute not five feet away from the dance floor. "Mrs. Cavanaugh," he says, still in his expensive suit, having stopped, apparently, for a quick one on his way home from the office. His fine thick hair shines like Rapunzel's gold beneath the pub's warm lighting. His smile reveals perfect strong teeth, making him look more like a young English oppressor than an Irish lad from the sod. My dance partner nods and thanks me for the last four dances and, when he sees no encouragement in my eyes to take things further, removes himself to his table of friends like a perfect gentleman. Foster swoops right in, standing in front of me with his handsome divorced-guy smile, and suddenly I, too, am removed—far away from this nice warm pub and back to the realities of bad dating and the Alan B. Shepard High School and children who do not behave well for their parents. How can the presence of one man carry such import?

"Have I taken you from your identical twin?" he asks, grinning at my dance partner.

"It's Tuesday night," I tell him. "Genetic Doubles Dance Club."

Foster lifts his chin when he laughs, showcasing the knot of his silk tie. "What are you doing here?" he asks, and I feel immediately guilty, as though I am a schoolmarm who mustn't be seen in such rough places. I point at the geek table, where Thomas now has his arm around Marge and the two are laughing uproariously.

"I'm out with Marge and some of her friends," I tell him. "A sort of geek reunion, only I never went to their school."

"And they never went to the School for the Gorgeous Redheads," Foster comments.

"Would you please . . . ?" I plead. "You sound like a substandard Austin Powers movie. I don't see your note from the homeroom teacher for you to be here, either."

"Divorced guys can do whatever they want," he says. "Buy you a drink?"

Why not? I think, and Foster turns to the bar and gestures to the bald bartender. Seconds later I'm set up with my fourth Guinness, wondering if Marge knew that Foster was a Claddagh patron all along. Even if she did, she was right to drag me out tonight, right to bring me away from my claustrophobic little household full of worrisome ketchup bottles and Charlotte's three-course menu of volatile emotions. Somehow, in the press of the crowd, Foster has found us seating at a tall table for two, where we hunch over our barstools shouting at each other above the music. Foster tells me about his firm in the Financial District— Something, Something, and Something—in a very historical Boston building where he is a partner. He tells me about a pub on State Street called the Black Rose where real Irish immigrants still congregate. We keep the conversation far away from our daughters and Indian restaurants and the whole beautiful world he had told me I was missing when he spoke to me in my office. There is no need to raise these topics in the moist steamy air of an Irish pub. Instead, I update him on the progress of the steering-wheel beds. My head swims pleasantly with the Guinness and the hum of voices, the music and the sight of Foster's very pleasant face. Across the room a man stands with his back to us, the inverted triangle of his upper torso reminding me of Kyle. He turns, looking nothing like my dead husband at all. The fiddle starts up again. Foster makes a joke, squeezes my hand, then lets it go again. Everything is easy and happy. I'd forgotten how wonderful bars are for molting off real life.

"Are you and Fester all right, then?" I hear Marge's voice asking, and when I look up, there she is, pocket-protected Thomas in tow, the two of them red-eyed and of equal height, a tangle of drunken arms before us.

"Nice to see you again," Foster tells her, thrusting a hand toward their tangle of arms. Marge shakes his hand, red eyes shining with happiness and alcohol; I have never really seen her in the bag before. My friend's inebriation doesn't go along with her Martha Stewart propensities, all that cooking and cleaning and bunk-bed-making, yet I notice it suits her in other ways. She seems relaxed, happy, utterly open, openly horny. She and Tom glom on to one another again, this time making out like schoolkids. It is an awesome sight, two towering adults, teetering slightly, sucking face. Foster looks at me, eyebrows rising, an amused smile on his face. I find I can't take it.

"Marge," I call over the bleating of the band and the low roar of the crowd. "MARGE!" I call again, and she pulls herself reluctantly free of Tom the Geek and looks at me. She seems startled and slightly disoriented, but she does not look embarrassed.

"Tom and I are leaving," she says. Tom smiles moonily, then squeezes her hand for emphasis. "You and Fester'll be all right, huh?" She tries to focus her vision on Foster. "You can bring her home?" she asks.

"Certainly," Foster says.

"Marge, wait—" I begin, but she just reaches down and kisses my cheek, then gazes at me with affection.

"We needed this night out," she tells me. Thomas takes her hand. Then they weave their way through the crowd toward the door. I sit on my barstool, gaping at them as the door shuts behind them.

"Well," Foster says. "I guess you're stuck with your bad date again."

"Are you hungry?" Foster asks from behind the wheel of his Lexus SUV. "We could grab a bite before I drop you off." We're traveling down dimly lit residential streets, a road tour of Appleton, lights twinkling in the windows of Tudor and Queen Anne and Georgian homes, making our way from the Claddagh to the Cavanaughs'. We're far away from any eating establishments, but maybe Foster's getting desperate. The Guinness has left me rubbery and soft-willed, but I'm resolved not to invite him into the house.

"Not hungry at all," I lie, leaning back on the plush leather seat. The truth is, if I don't eat something soon, I'll probably be sick to my stomach. I belch softly, quietly enough so I hope I'm not heard.

"Good one," Foster comments. "You're quite the suave drinker, Mrs. Cavanaugh."

I don't grace his insult with a response. My stomach growls, in case the belch isn't enough. There is lasagna in my house. I can inhale a huge square of it once Foster has dropped me off. I decide on this plan. It is better this way. He and Charlotte will never have to look at each other. I notice Foster and I are both quiet. I shift again on the slippery seat, hoping to fill the silence with movement.

"You don't like me very well, do you?" he says. He is looking straight ahead.

"Don't be silly," I exclaim, with a bit too much indignation. "It's just that it's late and it's a school night and—"

"And your kids are waiting at home, sharpening their weapons in case you invite me in."

"No!" I protest disingenuously. "It has nothing to do with the children."

Foster Willis hoots derisively. It fills his Lexus with a mocking sound that is difficult to ignore. "*What* has nothing to do with your children?" he asks.

How rude, I think. But then again, how foolish of me to lie about my children. They hate him. They do. Despite his rudeness, Foster is an intelligent man. He knows how my children feel.

"Over here," I say, pointing to my house when it finally appears. I am alarmed to find that most of the windows are dark, making me wonder where Charlotte is. I lean forward nervously on the leather seat. Did she fall asleep in Hunter's room on the new bunk beds? That would be my *good* Charlotte. Did she leave Hunter sleeping so she could go somewhere to drink cognac and blow fire out of her mouth? That would be my *bad* Charlotte.

The minute Foster has shifted into park in the driveway, I fling the car door open, anxious to see that my children are all right, that they haven't been abducted by a child molester while I was swilling beers at a bar and dancing with Paul Bunyan. "This was fun," I say to Foster, turning briefly to smile at him before exiting his lawyer-mobile. "Thanks for the lift."

"Good thing I was there," he says. "You didn't think you'd get dumped by your neighbor, did you?"

I laugh, but a part of me is agog over this new Marge. I glance at her house, which is blazing with lights, and wonder if she and Thomas are up in her perfect bedroom, or maybe humping like bunnies on her perfectly waxed kitchen floor. "Go figure," I say, jumping to the ground from the Lexus. "You think you know a person."

"You don't even know yourself," Foster says, just like that, his eightieth annoying statement since the moment I met him. My head spins to look at him.

"You can be pretty arrogant," I say, or maybe it's the Guinness talking. He says nothing. I hug my arms, anxious to get inside. His face is a frowning pearl oval behind his steering wheel. "I had a good time, too," he finally says. Then he reaches over and pulls the car door shut.

I'm at my front door before he's even down the driveway. He revs the engine like a teenager and peels away. *Whatever*, I think. I'm sorry if I don't want to hook up, or whatever it is Charlotte calls it. As a father, Foster should understand this. I fumble for my keys in my purse and become alarmed when I discover the door is already unlocked. Why has Charlotte left the door unlocked? How careless can a babysitter be? I turn the doorknob and enter the foyer. It's so painfully clear to me in this moment that Charlotte isn't ready to be a babysitter. There must be some course at the Red Cross, or maybe at Alan B. Shepard that might prepare her for this, but she hasn't taken it. Why do I listen to Marge, who is now having sex with a geek next door? Why do I listen to anyone?

I trip over one of Hunter's sneakers, while dropping my purse and keys in the basket on the foyer's radiator. Beneath it, lined up like soldiers, are four sneakers. I peer down at the line of shoes. No, it's one pair of Doc Martens and a pair of sneakers. Big ones. Bigger than mine or Charlotte's.

Ren's sneakers.

"Damn it!" I cry, to no one.

I race into the kitchen but it is empty. To my daughter's credit, it is also clean. Gleaming counters. Not a noodle on Hunter's booster chair. Big pots washed and resting in the dish drainer. Charlotte's laptop rests on the table, closed. An unfamiliar sweatshirt is draped across the back of one chair. I swipe it up and hold it in front of me. There is a photo of two goofy-looking kids on the front of it, one with teeth too big for his mouth, the other a bald laughing baby. CHARLIE BIT ME, it says beneath the photo. I drop the sweatshirt onto the chair. Where are they? I do an about-face and head for the family room.

This, too, is empty, except for the sleeping Hunter. He is curled on the couch in the blue glow of the television screen, zipped into a blanket-sleeper, snoring baby snores. A ketchup bottle rests on the floor beneath him. David Letterman is smirking in Technicolor on the muted television screen. I turn it off, try to regulate my breathing. Big breath in, big one out. My hands shake as I try to calm myself. I have done it again, left the helm, left my family in harm's way. What good is lying awake all night if I leave my children alone the following night to get into who knows what kind of trouble? Hunter, thank God, looks safe and undamaged, but it seems likely I will find my daughter and her boyfriend in bed somewhere. They could be having unprotected sex right now. They are that young and foolish. But what do I do—just burst in on them, or do I knock? What do I say when I find them?

I flop down on the couch beside Hunter's sleeping form to collect my thoughts. Didn't they think I'd be coming home? A hoot of bitter, incredulous laughter escapes my throat, filling the quiet air and making Hunter jump in his sleep. Unbelievable. The situation seems a cruel practical joke, in which people are having sex all around me—Marge with her almond-eyed classmate, my daughter with the suave, sexy Ren. My job is to stop them, or some of them, anyway.

"Mama?"

Hunter's thin wail halts me momentarily.

"It's okay, honey," I whisper, running my fingers through his hair. "Shhh," I say as his eyes close. I sit a minute to make sure he's sleeping again. The glint of a silver picture frame, illuminated by moonlight, catches my eye. I know what it is. It is the last family photo taken before Kyle died, snapped with a digital camera by his mother when we'd visited them in New Haven. I don't need to see the photograph to know it by heart—the four of us in the leafy park, Kyle heaving Hunter over one shoulder like a sack of happy potatoes, Charlotte, loose-haired and grinning, with her arms around her father's waist. And me, with arms crossed, slightly askance from the rest of them, the smile on my face that says, *This is all mine.*

Silly me. Grinning like a fool. Too young to understand that nothing's all mine, nothing's all anyone's forever. But Charlotte is mine for the time being and I must go find her. I tiptoe from the room, ignoring my stomach and heading for the stairs. I take them two at a time, full steam ahead to Charlotte's room. *Will ye go, lassie, will ye?* Have I even thought to discuss with her birth control, STDs, date rape, *mother*hood? And I, a counselor, no less, proving to be just like all the rest of the mothers, like Alphonse's mother, for God's sake, professing to be open and frank with my child, while believing in my heart that these kinds of things only happen to other people's children.

I open the door of Charlotte's bedroom, almost afraid to flick on the light switch. Light floods an unmade, empty bed, piled with soccer cleats and a backpack. No fornicating teenagers.

I head for my bedroom next. Blood pulses in my temples just imagining my child having sex in her father's and my bed. Can life really move this fast? I choke back a sob that seems to have arrived out of nowhere. Again I find a closed door, push the door open, call out to them. I flick on the light, blinking.

The bed is empty. In the harsh light, our marital bed looks massive and unpopulated, like a broad flat pre-Columbus world. I'd never wanted a king-sized bed, but Kyle insisted. It's been like sleeping on a small desert island since he died. But the island is deserted. I allow myself a few seconds of relief. Then I realize that this means they're gone. Hunter has been here alone.

I collapse on the edge of the bed as if I've been sucker-punched. I let her father die. Now she's let her brother sleep in an empty house. I lie all the way down, holding my stomach, resting my face against a pillow. I am not good at this single parent thing. I have not helped my children at all these past two years.

And then a voice calls out.

"You fart monkey!" the girl's voice calls. Charlotte's voice. Charlotte. Inside the house. With a fart monkey, but still.

I fly to my feet and into the hallway. "Charlotte? Charlotte?" I call. Stillness falls once more. "Charlotte!" I cry again, this time too loud and too panicky. No answer, but she's in here somewhere. I fling open the bathroom door, half expecting to find her and Ren taking a champagne bubble bath. Empty.

I rush down the hall to Hunter's big-boy room, the last unexplored territory, flinging open the door there. I snap the light on, wait a second for my eyes to adjust. And this is where I find them, huddled together on the top bunk.

"Some people, like, knock before they enter a room," Charlotte says, in a high voice that wants to sound ironic but instead sounds scared. Two sets of eyes peer at me over the rim of a red steering wheel. Charlotte pulls Hunter's Speed Racer bedspread up to her chin, but I see she's dressed under there—the top of her, anyway. Ren has a T-shirt on. He looks, for once, not so suave, but pale and worried instead.

"Hello, Mrs. Cavanaugh," he says, attempting unsuccessfully his James Bond smile. "I, uh . . . came over."

"So you did," I say, crossing my arms.

"To help," he adds, "with the babysitting."

I cannot respond to the handsome boy beneath the Speed

Racer bedspread, cannot collect my thoughts to say the right thing, or even the wrong thing. Charlotte smiles sheepishly at him, and for the moment I simply feast my eyes on the sight of the two of them. They are safe. Their hair stands up at odd angles on their smooth, strong heads, each strand shining with health in the overhead lighting. Here they are, whole and lovely and out of harm's way. For the moment, it seems enough.

FIFTEEN

The Grope Zone

Y ou okay?" Jack whispers, sliding me the doughnut box at a Guidance meeting on standardized testing. We're having a Wednesday morning full-faculty "in-service half day" at the high school, which means the students don't come to school until eleven-fifteen and Charlotte, for all I know, is tucked in bed again with her Ren friend.

The full faculty has already endured a keynote presentation in the oxygen-free auditorium on "Recognizing Gender Learning Differences," this followed by a stifling teacher's union meeting, and then an even more deadly talk by the fund-raising chairwoman of the PTSA. *What do we need?* the chairwoman kept asking the captive teachers and staff. *Computers? Audiovisual equipment? Software?* A nap, was all I could think.

For some reason Jack is required to be at this Guidance meeting. This is because the thought of a single faculty member not suffering, no matter how innocent, is intolerable to the administration. Jack notices the way my eyes wander, the lids fluttering, my thoughts a million miles away. He's probably alert to this type of behavior in his student drivers. No fluttering eyelids at a four-way intersection.

"Kate," he whispers again. "You okay?"

I nod, extracting a goopy jelly doughnut from the greasy cardboard box. I never eat stuff like this in real life, but I am furious at my dead husband.

He left before all the hard stuff, before Charlotte even began menstruating. He was gone when her oar-flat body began to take on curves and her moods began to change. He was gone when she went to middle school and was exposed to without warning a colored film on childbirth. That was a year before Charlotte had even gotten her first period. A cheerful male teacher my father's age just popped the tape into the classroom VCR and, voilà: dilation, crowning, blood, and umbilical cords. She came home looking a little blanched, explaining to me how she'd learned the result of the sexual onion at school that day. Then she asked me what a sexual onion was. On the positive side, it was the first time she'd ever shown an interest in vegetables.

On and on the counselors drone. All the windows are open in the conference room, but still the room seems airless. "We need to have a conversation," Bunny Lawton chirps, holding forth with her favorite phrase. She's our newest hire, freshly minted from Boston College, sentenced to the windowless office at the end of the satellite. She looks more like a Playboy Bunny than a counselor Bunny, with an old-fashioned sexiness that clings to her like lint. I have tried being friendly with her, but she seems to prefer our male colleagues. On and on she blathers, pink lip gloss shining, blond bob tucked neatly behind one ear. Her Manolo Blahniks look a little slutty for a guidance counselor.

"We must be careful not to simply *teach to the test*," Tom Johnson passionately exclaims. Heads nod around the table as I desperately yearn to vaporize into the room's stuffy air. *Scotty! Beam me up!*

Jack slides me a scrap of paper beneath the table, like a kid passing notes in homeroom. *Did you hear they discovered that diarrhea is genetic? It runs in the jeans*, his missive concludes.

I snort a little coffee through my nose, and Tom Johnson glares at me, more hurt than annoyed. I try to behave, while simultaneously remaining awake. A little while later, Jack hands me a second scrap. *Check out the Bunny's shoes*, it says. *I'm reminded of the blind prostitute. You really had to hand it to her.*

When the meeting finally ends, Jack and I limp to the corridor to make our escape to lunch. My knees feel stiff from sitting too long. My butt is numb from the hard chair.

"That Bunny person really annoys me," Jack comments, but I'm too prepossessed with Charlotte to bother to respond.

"What's up with you?" he asks, and I stare down at the floor tiles, willing myself not to open up about my latest problems with Charlotte. Not here. Not now, with twenty minutes available to us in a crowded lunchroom.

"Nothing much," I try, but Jack puts an arm around me and squeezes. "Spill, baby," he says, and this is enough.

"I found Charlotte in a bunk bed with her boyfriend last night." The words just come tumbling out. Like diarrhea. It must run in my genes.

"And?" is all Jack says.

I turn and look at him, aghast. "And she's fourteen, Jack," I explain. "Don't be a dunce."

Jack frowns like a dunce, deep in thought. "Did they do the deed?"

"No. At least, that's what they tell me. But what about next time?"

"Get her some condoms from Nurse Ratched," he suggests, possibly the dumbest thing he could say. I stop walking and turn to fully face him.

"Do you really think I want to involve the school nurse in my fourteen-year-old daughter's sex life?" I ask. "You think I'd like to encourage my daughter to *have* a sex life?"

"What are you, like, the abstinence lady?" Jack shakes his head in disapproval. "You're a counselor, for God's sake. You know what kids do. Do you think your daughter is different?"

"She's a little young for a sex life, Jack. Even you must have to agree with that. She's a freshman, for Pete's sake. She's . . ."

Suddenly my mouth is dry. Images of Big Butchie, then snippets of his revolting correspondence with my little girl, float through my reluctant mind. My hands grow damp and my head begins to spin.

"What's the matter?" Jack asks. "Have you had your flu shot?"

I grab his arm for support, and now Jack looks alarmed. "Jack," I whisper, although we are alone in the deserted corridor. "When you see Charlotte in the corridor, you know, when she's passing your office, does she ever seem to list?"

"To list?" Jack looks confused.

"Yes. You know. Listing. Have you ever seen her listing?"

Jack stares at me like I'm crazy. "You need to get out more," he says. "We should go to dinner tonight. We can talk more about your daughter's listing."

I feel heat creeping up my face. "It's not funny, Jack," I insist. "It's a sign of a child drinking or doing drugs. Has Charlotte ever seemed drunk to you, or maybe stoned on something?"

"No," he answers shortly. "No, she has not. Have that big Amazon neighbor of yours watch the kids." He takes my hand and guides me down the corridor. "I'll take you to that tapas place in Cambridge," he says, in a soothing voice you might use to reason with a maniac. "We'll drink pitchers of sangria and get quietly wasted. Then maybe you'll begin to make sense. And maybe we can talk sensibly about your daughter, who is a good kid, as I might have mentioned previously."

"I know she's a good kid, but she's been acting—"

"And then," Jack interrupts, "after we've eaten some delicious scallops in saffron sauce, you can explain to me why Tom Johnson's acting weird around you."

This gets my attention. "I don't know what you're talking about," I lie immediately.

"Nonsense," Jack says. He fixes his pale blue eyes on mine and waits.

Mercifully, I am saved by a storm of doors bursting open in every corner. Kids pour in from the stairwells and around the bends of the corridors and, all of a sudden, noise and anarchy consume us and our in-service half day is over. Jack drops my hand as if a gun is being held to his head. We mustn't look as if we like each other. Half-naked students can swear and grope and thrust their tongues down each other's throats as they walk from algebra to English, but God forbid two teachers show any signs of even platonic friendship. A small fleet of long-haired girls is coming at Jack already and I feel him straighten up beside me, his body taking on a new formality that means he is a teacher, not a human.

"Get a babysitter," Jack commands, before they descend on him.

I turn and head back toward my office. I love Jack, but I don't want to get a babysitter. I simply want to go home and find Charlotte studying cheerfully in a straight-backed chair. I want her to look up from her textbook and exclaim, *You're absolutely right, Mom! Careless sexual activity leads to a myriad of unnecessary and dangerous consequences!*

My feet feel heavy as I walk back to my office. I've approached an undertaker's office with more relish than I now approach my own.

"We need more hotties in here, *mami*," Hector says later, arriving first to the New Frontiers group. His gold chains gleam in the fluorescent lighting.

"Hector," I ask, "does your father like those chains?"

Hector shrugs, scratching his smooth olive chin. "He has one himself. With the Blessed Virgin on it."

Yes, but that's different than a diamond-studded dollar sign, worn by the son of the Western Religions professor. I smile at Hector, pace a little, stare at the empty couch. It used to be our TV room couch, before we moved the old living room one in there. Kyle and I hauled it up the high school stairwell ourselves, though it was more my idea of a good thing to do than his. And of course I hadn't an inkling about his heart. "They'll love it," I'd only told him. "My kids need comfort at the end of the day."

A time bomb, his heart was. If I close my eyes I can see Kyle lying on this couch, his struggling heart resting somewhere beneath his shirt buttons, his long legs against the flowered cushions. We'd sometimes made love on this couch, when the kids were tucked in and HBO hadn't caught our interest enough. Now it belongs to Phoenix, but she is late for group.

"Where is Phoenix today?" I ask Hector. He only shrugs, which surprises me. When a boy likes a girl at the Alan B. Shepard High School, he knows exactly where she is at every moment of the day. This is because, along with groping and making out, stalking, too, is condoned at our high school.

"You know, *mami*," Hector says. "You should let your daughter be in our group." He gazes moonily at the ceiling. "She's so beautiful, your girl."

I sit down too quickly in the circle. It's more as if I've fallen into my chair. My misfits know their own kind and now one of them has identified Charlotte, my beautiful violin-playing, soccer goalie girl, as one of theirs. I gaze at Hector with his gleaming gold jewelry. He has only seen her tattoos and piercings, and I have not explained to him their cause, or who she really is. But I remind myself that every kid has an underlying cause for the chains, the ink, the grill, the slutty tank tops. Every kid is really someone else, beneath the disguise.

"What's the matter?" Hector asks.

"Nothing," I tell him, brushing down the front of my slacks. "Just waiting for Phoenix to arrive." The door opens, and it's Alphonse who drifts in, smelling slightly of fertilizer, flopping down into a chair, two over from Hector, one over from me.

"Hello," I say, searching his face for everything. Tension oozes from Alphonse. His eyes brush angrily past my face, a scouring pad going over a dirty frying pan. "Are all women bitches?" he asks. "Because my girlfriend is one."

"Alphonse," I admonish. "Language."

"Sorry, Mrs. C.," he says.

"Maybe it's hormonal, man," Hector offers helpfully. "You know, knocked up and all."

Alphonse looks as though he might cry. Then he scowls again, glaring down at his soiled Skechers. He's a great skateboarder, according to the word in the halls. Just what a baby needs: a skateboarding father with peat moss on his expensive sneakers. I see how today's session will be a difficult one and yet, for a second, a split second only, I'm grateful for the sight of these children who come to me willingly, unlike my Charlotte. They honor the tiny undamaged part of me still capable of comforting someone else. I glance at the clock, willing Adam and Phoenix to get here, so we can begin.

Adam complies a few seconds later, walking through the door with a furious swish. The others don't see it; he would never swish in front of Hector or Alphonse. It is meant for me, a defiant railing against who he is not supposed to be, not on the school bus, certainly not at home with his career Army parents, but nonetheless is.

"Yo, Adam, my man!" Hector says. He takes in Adam's belt, a handsomely tooled and studded creation that hugs his narrow hips like an expensive harness. "That is phat, dude," Hector comments, pointing at the silver spikes. Alphonse looks up from his soiled Skechers, smirking.

"Shut the fuck up," says Adam, and we all turn to look at him, this quiet scholar with the chiseled face of an angel.

"Adam?" I say, surprised. This is not our sweet Adam who glares up at me, eyes burning with pain and anger.

"Don't need this shit today," he says. His eyes are wet, and he takes a moment before whispering his rushed apology.

"No problem, man," Hector says, and this is how it is confirmed for me that there is no street in Hector. If Hector were living in the Dorchester section of Boston, he might have to shoot Adam now. Instead, our Appleton Hispanic sheepishly strokes his gold chains. The dollar sign swings left and right.

I watch Adam's face close up; his eyes grow expressionless.

"Tough day?" I ask, but he just turns from us in his chair, as if my question exhausts him. Maybe later we'll hear what happened to him on the bus, or in the boys' locker room, or maybe at the brick wall outside where everyone goes to smoke. Sometimes I want to take all of them home.

"Has anyone seen Phoenix?" I ask the small group.

"I saw her yesterday afternoon," Hector says, strengthening my theory that he stalks her, "by the gym. They posted the list of who got into cheerleading."

"Thank you," I tell him, but the news secretly worries me. Either Phoenix is missing because she has made the cheerleading squad or she's missing because she hasn't. A glance at the wall calendar tacked above my desk offers a third possible explanation. It is the final day of September, the day when most struggling students acknowledge that everything's exactly the same in their impossible lives as it was last June. I have seen this year after year, the hope for miracles drained from my students' hearts like helium from a party balloon. In the minds of my little posse of outsiders, the dappled autumn sunlight on the golden trees outside my window means nothing. These bright perfect crisp days are a ploy. None of it changes the fact that tomorrow will be difficult, and the day after that, and the day after that one, too.

We all look up when the cracked door swings fully open. But it is only Tom Johnson filling the space. The diamond-shaped pattern of his sweater vest lies flat against his fleshless ribs, looking more like a modern art canvas than men's apparel. There are worry lines creasing his forehead, running perfectly parallel to his side-parted sandy gray hairline. Unlike earlier in the day, he has no trouble looking me straight in the eye.

"Mrs. Cavanaugh?" he says. "May I see you privately for a moment?"

SIXTEEN

Slipping Through the Cracks

Rising from the circle and moving toward the door, I feel as if I'm floating through a mind-altering gas, something that deprives me of the gift of speech and tosses my emotions like a salad. I know this is bad; I know this will be about Phoenix. Either that or one of my children is dead. A hit-and-run. A tumble from the top monkey bar. Charlotte has set herself on fire with cognac. My father has clutched at his chest and fallen like a stone to the floor. Now my mother knows how I feel. Now she sees. Now—

"Mrs. Cavanagh? Can we close the door a second?"

Just like that, a plank of wood and a doorknob separate my New Frontiers Group from Tom Johnson and me. He looks at me with his angular face and small features, a frown causing his thin lips to linelessly stretch. "Kate," he says, in the tones of an undertaker—wasn't I just thinking about undertakers earlier today?—"Kate," he says again. "It's Phoenix."

Of course it's Phoenix, I feel like shouting at him, but discover that my voice is missing and my mouth doesn't work, it doesn't even open. Tom's mouth opens just fine, though, and now he is filling the air with words I don't want to hear.

"I'm afraid she's overdosed again. This time, though . . ." He rubs his temples with a thumb and forefinger and I watch, mesmerized. "This time, though, she has succeeded."

I stare at him, dumbfounded. A darkness crosses Tom's face, clouding his eyes with grief, bewilderment, and . . . what? Anger?

Is it anger at himself for having said such a foolish, obscene thing out loud? Is it anger at me for not having prevented it? If my voice worked, if my feelings were able to order themselves sufficiently for me to speak, perhaps I would ask him. Instead I seem unable to move. A paralysis of disbelief has robbed me of my hearing. A soft roar, like a vacuum cleaner running in another room, envelops me. Tom leads me by the arm to the circle of faux-leather chairs in the central waiting area, where I sit down hard. Gladys rises to shut the Guidance Department door. My beautiful Phoenix. She will be a cheerleader. She will be an anthropologist. Her mother will stop following her around and learn to trust her. Tom is studying me, worry lines appearing like magic on his forehead and around his grimacing mouth.

"She apparently did it sometime this morning," Tom is saying, standing over me, one hand on my shoulder, as if to steady me for the awful things he continues to say. "Her mother found her in her room when she came home from work. Sleeping pills and a quart of vodka. They tried pumping her stomach, but . . ."

We hear loud laughter coming through the wall of my office. It sounds like Hector, fooling around. "Let me just dismiss these kids," Tom says. "We don't have to tell them anything yet. We've called in some grief counselors for tomorrow morning, and the news will circulate soon enough."

I rise from the chair like a rocket, suddenly having found my voice. "These kids are *waiting* for Phoenix."

Tom is silent a moment. "Okay," he says. I hear him clear his throat. "We'll talk to them in a minute. But first, look at me."

Why does he keep talking to me? I remember the sun glowing on her legs out in the courtyard. Strong smooth legs. I remember stroking her hair in New Frontiers Group, when was it? Only days ago. She'd purred like a kitten, she'd let me comfort her. She'd promised she'd come to me if she felt sad again.

"Were you aware of any suicidal ideation Phoenix might have exhibited in your group?"

I finally look up at Tom. What can his question mean? Phoenix was sent to me with a record of her ibuprofen overdose right there in her files. That was why she was invited into New Frontiers, why the floral couch was reserved for her lovely young presence each Wednesday. We were a family to her—Hector, Alphonse, Adam, and me. We all knew what her demons were. This doesn't mean we could conquer them.

"Kate?" Tom says.

"No," I reply.

"Do you know if she was seeing her private therapist?"

"Do you know if she made cheerleading?" I ask.

Tom rubs his mouth with his hand. "Yeah," he says. "She made it."

I don't know why this is the thing that makes me start to cry. Tom rises and stands above my chair, patting my shoulder. "It's a tragedy, Kate," he says. "But it's no one person's fault. Somewhere, she slipped through a crack."

We can't hold them much longer in my office. We hear their wisecracking and laughter, the groan of chair legs against the floor. Their restlessness is palpable, even through the closed door. I wipe my eyes with a Kleenex Gladys offers me, rise from the faux-leather chair, and look at Tom.

"You know you can do this tomorrow," he says.

I shake my head.

"You want me to come in with you?"

"No. I can do this."

Tom nods and I see in his face that he believes I can. I am grateful for this, for I must go in there now, must sit among my small New Frontiers circle, must tell them that one of us is gone.

"I'm here if you need me," Tom tells me. He says it with kindness, but what can Tom do? He can't change the news I must carry to these children. Turning from Tom and Gladys, I place a hand on the doorknob, fighting a numbness that almost prevents me from turning it. I've done it again, let someone I love slip through the cracks, beneath the bedsheets, beyond retrieval or resuscitation. Charlotte's accusations come flooding back uninvited, traveling down my arms first, then up my spine, and then to the part of my brain that stores the hurting things. I didn't do anything to save her father, just lay there like a slug while his heart stopped. And what had I done to keep Phoenix safe? Stroke her hair? Sit with her for two minutes in the student courtyard? Listen to her, while not hearing a thing? *If you love something, keep it from dying*, I think, and then I turn the knob.

They are quiet before the door is completely open. Their horsing around stops midmuscle. They are frozen at the sight of my face. Adam is twisted forward in his chair, his graceful torso in a half arabesque. Hector stands at attention, hands stuffed in the pockets of his low-slung jeans, all the hip-hop bleached out of him by dread for what is to come. Alphonse slouches on a chair with his head down and his legs sprawled apart, staring at the space between his Skechers. The tension in the room is strong as an electrical current. Here is the hardest moment, then.

"It's Phoenix," I say, light-headed with the words leaving my mouth. "Our Phoenix."

I sit down, bracing myself for their outcries, but not one of them says a word. No one asks for clarification. Only their bodies respond. Alphonse never lifts his gaze from the floor, but his shoulders begin to shake softly. One expensive sneaker kicks futilely at air. I watch Adam's eyes glaze over with disbelief, watch the color drain from his chiseled, handsome face. I kneel in front of his chair and hold him in my arms. "I know," I tell Adam, rocking his sad bones in my arms. "I know."

But the truth is I don't know anything. I didn't know about the cracks and why she fell through them, and now their friend— the pretty, sad girl left in my care—is gone.

"Oh, *mami*," Hector sobs, somewhere behind, and I wonder why these children would trust me.

They wander out with their arms around one another. I hear their footsteps in the silent corridor, and then it is still. I stand by the satellite of faux-leather chairs in the empty Guidance Office, breathing in the heavy silence. Even Tom has gone home. He knocked once while we were still in my office and I told him to go. Mrs. Panella has left her desktop in pristine condition, her marble pen holder the sole object on its gleaming surface. Tom's door is locked; the bird in the open cage stares blankly at me. I pace the empty office. I wander over to my mailbox and pull violently at a pile of junk mail. Why do they keep killing trees? Why can't people understand that most communication happens now in space? Like e-mail, and Big Butchie's MySpace page, and the ghost of Kyle whispering to me from the minivan's backseat. I toss catalogs and credit card offers and vacation getaway opportunities into Gladys's trash, and this is when I see it, stuck between two other pieces of junk mail. It's a small piece of yellow lined paper. My name is scrawled on the folded surface. I snatch it from the basket and unfold it. Green ink from a felt-tip pen forms neatly printed letters on three lines.

> *I love you, Mrs. C.*
> *You know how to listen.*
> *I just want to go now, that's all.*

The lettering is open and bubbly, the kind of font used in cartoon captions over the heads of puppies and bunnies. There are tiny hearts and *x*'s and *o*'s all along the bottom of the sheet, marching from one margin to the next, like an exiting parade. I stare at the tiny sheet of paper until the letters blur into one another. I don't go home until I'm done crying.

SEVENTEEN

The Little Tree That Had to Die

In the United States alone, over thirty thousand people die by suicide each year, the equivalent of one major airliner, filled with passengers, crashing every two days. This is what I read online last night, after putting Hunter to bed. Thirty thousand people. That's a lot of slipping through the cracks. It's never one stressor, either. It's the intersection of several stressors. This I clearly remember learning in graduate school. Always several stressors. I'm thinking about this as I fold the wash on my kitchen table, this early sunless morning after Phoenix's death. What was bothering Phoenix, besides her mother following her and cheerleading? What had I missed? What could I have done?

My laundry basket is almost full. It's five A.M., too early to hear even the thunk of my newspaper being thrown against my front door. I have been up for hours. Charlotte is finally sleeping. Sleep was impossible for either of us last night. We sat up late, listening to Nightline's opening monologue, then Jimmy Kimmel's, then watching the Appleton Public TV station, where a student-made video on a polluted Appleton pond reeled itself over and over again. We dozed off on the couch like this. When I awoke in the half-dark circle of morning, Charlotte's head was leaned against my shoulder in slumber. Her proximity moved me to tears, even if it was accidental. Here she was, safe and sound, my daughter.

At six I awaken both children for a real breakfast. The three of us pad around the kitchen as if we're at a wake. We've told Hunter nothing about yesterday, yet somehow he knows something bad has happened. He wolfs down his French toast and scrambled eggs like it's his last meal, ending up covered with syrup. It's a good thing he's still in his pajamas. I'll have to rinse him off before he dresses. Charlotte just stares at her plate, though I make myself believe that the kitchen smells comfort her. There are dark circles beneath her eyes. A cruel god has made this day a gray one. Rain drizzles on the windowpanes. Only the sizzle of the frying pan punctuates our silence. Even with his big appetite, Hunter keeps his eye on his Sissy.

"Come on," I tell him, not bothering to sound cheerful. "Time to get dressed. We all have a big day ahead." I help him down from his booster, another transitional object he refuses to relinquish.

Charlotte insists on taking the bus to school. She follows us out to the car and allows me to give her a quick hug before I buckle Hunter into his car seat to take him to school.

"I'll be there all day," I remind her, but her blank gaze looks right through me. "Find me if you need me," I tell her, but she just pulls away from me. Here's the second person she's known who has died on my watch. Her hair is falling out of the elastic on one side of her face. I wonder if Charlotte thinks she is next. A chill travels up my arms for allowing myself this thought.

"There will be grief counselors at the school today," I remind her before climbing into the car. She's heaving her hundred-pound backpack onto her shoulders.

"I'll just look for strangers who are acting like they give a shit," she says, and then she is gone.

Hunter and I drive in silence down suburban streets where life looks mundane and safe and normal. There is a dead girl's family grieving behind one of these closed Appleton doors. It feels unreal watching two boys on a corner toss a lunch bag like a Frisbee between them, laughing like all the world is a flying bologna sandwich.

We find Bright Lights unexpectedly closed when we arrive, the doors locked and several teachers standing outside. It seems to be causing an uproar among the other working parents. We stand in a cluster of them in front of the building, rain drizzling on all of us. Parents complain and wail and squeeze their little ones' hands too tightly. "What are we supposed to do?" they ask each other and the locked door. Their tots huddle beside them like baggage, unused to feeling unwanted. The brave young Courtney is taking it on the chin. She stands with her arms wrapped, shivering in her too-light L. L. Bean jacket, rain darkening her naturally blond curtain of hair. We can all feel winter in the air.

"Why didn't you people have the decency to call us, so we could make other plans?" one extremely pissed-off father asks Hunter's young teacher. He is one of the older parents, with a very young wife and a new second family. You can see how he only sired this child to please his new wife. It makes me sad how so many kids arrive on Planet Earth without an adequate backup plan. So many Americans in space. Perhaps Phoenix was one of them.

"I'm sorry, Mr. Price," Courtney is explaining, speaking calmly to the parent like he's one of the four-year-olds. "We didn't know any sooner than you that the electricity was out."

Hunter holds Courtney's leg, glaring at Mr. Price. I am touched by his defense of her, if a little slighted by where his loyalties lie.

"Come on, sweetie," I say, extracting him gently from his teacher's leg. I give Courtney a quick hug. "Courage," I whisper, and she smiles and waves good-bye to us.

"Where we going?" Hunter asks, strapped back into the car seat.

"To Mama's work," I tell him, and I think I see his eyes brighten. Lord knows what I'll do with him when we arrive.

The grief counselors are due at seven forty-five, and when homeroom ends at eight we are supposed to have them briefed and oriented, a plan in place for how they'll meet with students. No plan has been put into place, of course, for a four-year-old boy. But there is nothing to do but swing open the Guidance Department door and walk my little boy in. Gladys Panella's eyes widen at the sight of him striding toward her desk, a half-full ketchup bottle in one hand.

"Careful that cap is closed," I whisper to Hunter, and Mrs. Panella frowns at me as though I am an enabler.

She'd be a lot more upset if Hunter spilled ketchup all over her office. I don't bother to explain to her that only one of Hunter's bottles is ever really full, but that it just happens to be the one he's traveling with today. The others, mostly all empties, rattle around in his Huggies carton, making their plastic hollow sounds when he drags them behind him. Gladys Panella continues to stare at Hunter, her giant wedding ring set drooping sideways on her wasted arthritic finger.

If only she and I could talk. If only she weren't this cement wall of disapproval who insists on calling me Mrs. Cavanaugh, then maybe I could acknowledge in this moment that yes, my son is a little different from other four-year-old boys. I am not blind to this. I have seen his friends running around their mothers' kitchens with dish-towel capes tucked into the neckline of their pajamas, terry-cloth superpowers flowing behind them. They are Spiderman, Superman, Batman. Which makes my son what? Mr. Heinz? I squeeze Hunter's free hand tighter. Then Gladys surprises me by rising from her desk with a smile on her face.

"No day care today?" she asks, squatting down beside my son.

"Today of all days," I tell her. "Not quite sure how I'm going to figure this one out."

"I can watch him," Gladys says. "We can keep busy, can't we, Hunter?"

Hunter stares at her, his lips sealed.

"You can help me make these paper clips into a necklace. Oh, I do want a paper-clip necklace."

It occurs to me that Gladys Panella sounds *nice*. Gladys Panella.

"Okay," I hear my son finally say. "Necklace."

They get to work, Hunter sitting Indian-style on Gladys's desktop, a pile of striped paper clips between them.

"What your favorite color?" Hunter asks her, clips spilling from his closed fists.

"Oh, I'm partial to red," she tells him, and I think I see a meaningful look pass between them.

. . .

The awful day goes by in a blur. Every classroom has an open door. In each room a stranger from the suspiciously named Student Support Counseling Center sits with a group of silent teenagers, making eye contact, nodding, listening. What kind of counseling service sets itself up in anticipation of impending tragedy? Sometimes I am troubled by my own profession.

We guidance counselors, who knew Phoenix the best, have been assigned traffic control. We pat stunned-looking students on their shoulders, directing them to this room or that. One grief counselor, a middle-aged woman wearing Birkenstocks and a flowing denim skirt, comes into the Guidance Department to grief-counsel us. I don't tell her about the note on the yellow paper. I will never tell anyone.

Sometime during the course of the morning, Courtney calls to tell me the electricity is back on. Marge shows up and drives Hunter back to school. Jack drops by, useless without his usual grin. He plops himself down in my office on one of the chairs still set up in the New Frontiers circle. "We never got to have our dinner out," he says. We stare at Phoenix's couch, empty.

"She loved that couch," I tell him, and then, neither of us can think of anything else to say.

The house is empty when I return home. I come in through the garage and drop my briefcase onto a kitchen chair. The refrigerator gurgles a greeting and then the late afternoon air is still again. I am in those strange hours, the time when most working people are still at work and only the teachers and guidance counselors are in their quiet houses, reflecting on the choices they have made in their lives.

I flop onto a chair, pulling *The Boston Globe* free from its home delivery bag. Hunter is still at Bright Lights. Charlotte is who knows where. I spread the paper on the cleanest part of the table, farthest from the sticky spot where Hunter sits, then check the index for the obituaries. *Deaths*, they're called now, not *Obituaries*. Kyle's *Death* had been in this paper, the entire backbone of my life reduced to a square inch of information. Just a tiny box with his last name highlighted and his family listed and the arrangements detailed. Phoenix gets her own story on the cover page of the Metro section. I can hardly read it.

I turn pages as though I know what I'd like to read next. But there is nothing in the world I'd like to read today, and each page holds only worse news than the page before. On the back of section C, a full-sized ad for the Blue Man Group stares up at me with its grainy photo of a grim man painted the shiny color of my mother's favorite Fiestaware. Kyle and I went to see these blue men the year before he died, lured by an extra set of tickets belonging to neighbors we didn't like very much who had bought four. I hated the show, a frightening spectacle of menace, noise, and wasted toilet paper. Afterward, as we sat sipping drinks in Boston, I'd declared to all assembled that I thought the blue men were psychotic. I railed over my apple martini that only a crazy person could like them. Kyle thought I was funny, but we were never asked to join these neighbors on a date again.

Folding the paper in half, it now dawns on me why I hated the blue men so. I must have had the prescience to know that startling surprises aren't generally entertaining, and that real blue men generally aren't breathing. Had I seen how an evening spent anticipating the unthinkable is no way to live your life?

I heave my tired bones from the chair, leaving the paper unread, and head upstairs. So much sadness at the high school. I seem to be carrying it all upstairs with me. I'll try to nap before dinner. I pass Hunter's open bedroom door, where the red steering wheels on his race-car bunk beds are as cheerful as apples. Approaching Charlotte's room, I'm surprised by the sight of Charlotte herself, asleep on her own rumpled bed. I step inside. Her clothes are still on and her arms are thrown wildly to her sides as she sleeps on one cheek, belly to the mattress. Her half face against the pillow suggests a serious girl dreaming serious dreams. I sit gently on the side of her bed and stroke her hair once, lightly. She doesn't even stir. It is impossible to imagine this same child in bed with a boy. Her backpack rests on the bed, zipper open and contents precariously threatening to spill out. Red ink scrawled across the top of one paper catches my eye. I tug a little at the document's corner until the words disclose themselves. *Unacceptable*, is what the red ink says. A small fist clutches inside my stomach. I pull out the stapled report and bring it with me to my own bedroom.

I kick off my shoes, remove my slacks, and lie on top of the bedspread. Bolstered by fat throw pillows, I begin to read Charlotte's environmental science paper, written for Clarissa McClure, a science teacher who went to Harvard and has had a mastectomy at age thirty-nine. All the counselors know that students either love or hate this teacher. A blend of brilliance and indignation, Clarissa usually takes out her rage on polluters or McDonald's, litter bugs or lobbyists. And then Charlotte handed her this paper. The title alone worries me: "The Little Tree That Had to Die." I read on with trepidation.

> There was once a little tree that had to die. This is because stupid women kept peeing on the toilet seats in public restrooms all over our gross disgusting nation. Oh, no, they couldn't sit down! They couldn't aim! Finally some selfish men who drove giant shiny Hummers met for an important meeting in a posh Manhattan office. They made bad decisions while Mexican valets parked their Hummers. "We'll find the cutest little defenseless trees that are left in our ugly deforested land," they said. "And we'll chop them down and make paper toilet seat covers for the sloppy selfish stupid women." These men were sloppy, selfish, and stupid themselves, but could, however, aim when they peed.
>
> A little tree named Leafy cried when they cut him. He became a thousand toilet seat covers. A thousand behinds pressed down on him, after which yet another ring of his heart was flushed down the New York City sewer system.

I take a deep breath, then let it out. I turn the paper over, to think about what my daughter has written. I don't know whether to laugh or cry. I could imagine Charlotte reading this story to her little brother and Hunter being riveted by it. She's a good little writer, really. Yet even Al Gore would be disturbed by the story of Leafy. I flip the report to the last page, wondering what Clarissa McClure has to say. There, I find her sole comment.

There is a waiting list of students who deserve to be in this class.

I shoot from the bed like a geyser. Is Clarissa McClure questioning my daughter's right to be here? How dare she even use those words? A part of me wants to rush back to Charlotte's room and gather her into my arms. Another part wants to storm the Alan B. Shithead High School and demand that McClure be fired. But my daughter has written a paper about women's behinds pressing toilet seats. And the school is preoccupied with the death of a girl like Charlotte. A disturbed girl, just like Charlotte.

Driving over to Bright Lights to pick up Hunter, I find Kyle sitting in the front seat this time in his blue long-sleeved shirt, my favorite, his cuffs rolled back the way he likes to wear them. I'm not too surprised to see him here. These past few weeks I've been seeing quite a bit of him. His broad back at the Claddagh. His hair on someone else's head. His eyes twinkling in another man's skull, as if he is borrowing the body like a rental car to come and see me. These flashes of him don't include his visitations in the car's backseat, buckled in beside his son. But now he sits in the passenger seat beside me, patting my hand and telling me that Charlotte's all right.

It's only his ghost, of course. The real Kyle would never tell me such nonsense.

"I'm worried about her," I confess, staring straight through the windshield with my eyes on the road. I don't want to look demented to the other drivers—a woman in an empty car whose lips are moving, no cell phone or Bluetooth in sight. "She's getting weirder and weirder," I say. "It's scaring me."

I glance at the passenger seat and he is gone. Once again, he's done me a lot of good.

"If you can't help Charlotte, maybe you can help Phoenix," I shout after his shadow, just in case he can hear me. He might as well take care of someone's daughter, if he has the time.

I realize, parking the car, that the person I should be most concerned about is me. I am, after all, chatting with my dead husband's ghost the way most women dish with their girlfriends at Starbucks. I had a girl once come to my office after the unexpected death of her mother, worried that she'd seen her mother's ghost at her chorus recital, sitting in the back row smiling at her. I knew what it meant. I knew the girl had unresolved issues with her mother, that some merciful part of her brain was seeking peace and resolution. But what was it left unresolved between Kyle and me—other than the rest of our lives? "You tell me," I say to Kyle's ghost, but he is long gone from the vehicle.

I walk briskly toward the Bright Lights play lot and find teachers and kids outside, idling away the final minutes of a long day beneath a late afternoon sun. There is Hunter, sitting by himself under his thinking tree, a small Japanese maple given to the school by one of the parents. Hunter loves its waterfall of red leaves, the way the willowy boughs dance in the wind. I often find him beneath it, looking very Zen, when I wish he was playing with the other kids instead. Courtney finds me as I'm relatching the gate, always a sign that she wants a small conference with me. "Can we talk?" she asks.

"Break it to me gently," I plead. "It's been one of those days."

"It's nothing, really," Courtney says. "Just a little altercation during the tug-of-peace."

"The tug-of-peace?"

Courtney looks embarrassed. "It's really tug-of-war," she says in a low voice, "but we're not supposed to use the *war* word."

I stifle a smile. I'm all for presenting life to our little ones as an endless opportunity for peace. But two groups of red-faced kids tugging at opposite ends of a rope has nothing to do with harmony. Sometimes Appleton is politically correct to a fault.

"I love Hunter, as you know," Courtney says, and I begin to see this might be bad. "But he bonked Brayton Weeks over the head with his ketchup bottle during the tug-of-peace."

"Full bottle or empty?'

"Empty. Thank goodness."

Visions of dilated pupils, lumps, and concussions thankfully vanish before my eyes. Then a new fear arises. "Is he a bully with other kids?" I ask.

"Not at all," Courtney says firmly. "He just got a little frustrated and lost a round with impulse control." She flashes her beautiful reassuring smile. "It happens all the time, with all the kids. I just wanted you to know."

"Why isn't he playing with the other kids?" I ask.

"He loves the tree," Courtney says gently.

"And how is Brayton?"

"Brayton is fine, and the three of us had a good talk. Hunter even let me take his ketchup bottle away. Can you imagine that?"

I can imagine Hunter letting Courtney do anything.

"Thanks," I say, wanting to hug her for making my child sound normal. Then Hunter spots us from beneath his tree and is running toward us. "Mama!" he cries, pounding toward me in dusty sneakers.

The sight of him tugs at my heart. Here comes my boy, smile on his face, lunch on his shirt. My own little tug-of-peace.

EIGHTEEN

Tie Food

They all arrive on time for the first New Frontiers Group since Phoenix's death. For once, they look serious, grounded, outwardly devastated instead of cocky. My beautiful, sad, Touchy-Feely misfits. I just want to hold them. I want arms long and elastic enough to encircle the entire paltry bunch of them—handsome Adam with the shadows beneath his eyes, clueless but fertile Alphonse (I never noticed before how young he looks, how his curly bangs rest against skin that looks smooth as a baby's), agitated Hector.

"Oh, Sister Kate," Hector says, addressing me as though I am the choir director at his church, "this is fucked. This is totally fucked." He wrings his hands together, and his silver bracelet moves up and down his wrist. I don't bother to correct him because I don't think he hears himself swearing. None of us can really listen. There is a low buzz in the room, like the piercing shriek of a silent fire alarm that can't be turned off. We stare at the couch where Phoenix used to lie, almost as if we can all still see the indentation there. No one dares sit on it. Can she really be gone?

"Can I ask you something?" Adam finally says, after we've sat in silence for over five minutes together. "What is the point of all of this?"

The grief counselors who ran the high school last week advised us not to answer questions like Adam's directly. Just listen, they said. But Adam's blue eyes look liquidy and he has asked his counselor a question, a very brave thing to do.

"The point of all what?" I ask him, as though I will have an answer.

"Of this stupid group," he says. "Of a bunch of jerk-offs sitting together week after week, watching each other be gay, or be Puerto Rican . . ."

Hector flinches, but it is more pain than indignation.

". . . or be suicidal." He glares at me angrily. "Or be a widow, even," he says boldly. "What exactly are we supposed to do for each other, huh?"

Adam's irises flare like hot blue flames. The grief counselors were right. It would have been better just to listen.

"It gets me out of a science class," Alphonse offers helpfully. "Not that I don't have to make up the work."

I can hear the phone ringing in the kitchen when I pull into the garage after school. Charlotte, glassy-eyed and exhausted, thrusts the receiver at me when I enter the house.

"It's Grandma Lynne," she says. This means my mother, not Kyle's. Kyle's mother is happy with just plain Grandma. Charlotte wanders away in her droopy jeans and decent T-shirt and I drop my briefcase to say hello.

"Charlie doesn't sound too good," my mother notes, though she doesn't seem too concerned about it. Nothing short of the threat of divorce—her own—has ever seemed to jar her into excess emotion. She and my father have weathered two close calls and still they labor on in their loveless marriage as a couple.

"We've all been through a little rough time, is all," I explain, falling into a kitchen chair. I glance at the wall clock, wondering already when I'll be able to get off the phone with her. There's dinner to think about, then Hunter's bath. My mother's monthly calls can come at any time. I wish I could say they were a comfort, but mostly they feel like a chore. She's not a bad person and, in all fairness, she was there for us in the weeks after Kyle died. But these days when my mother calls, I feel like a vendor talking to a sales rep, as if it's my job to present her with appealing merchandise. Smart happy grandchildren. A vibrant daughter. A fully recovered family with no stain of grief blighting their name.

"That li'l rough time was over two years ago," Grandma Lynne reminds me. Her voice sounds pleasant and cool, the way I remember it as a child. What's new is a slight southern twang she's developed since moving with my father to Texas. The move was supposed to firm up their marriage, but it didn't. I often think about how much more fortunate I've been in marriage when compared to my mother. Even though mine was cut short, there was so much more love there than I have ever witnessed between my parents.

I decide not to tell her about Phoenix, or the way the three of us have survived my endless faculty meetings this past week, eating Styrofoam-packaged take-out dinners too late at night. How, since Phoenix's death, we've been basically sleepwalking through family life. I don't tell her how we eat and live in our individual cocoons—Hunter hugging a ketchup bottle and staring at a TV screen, Charlotte with her earbuds in, or else text-messaging the family into bankruptcy. Me flopping into bed the moment I can. How Marge picks up Hunter at Bright Lights, then stays at the house until I come home. Ren is often here when I come home, too, no more substantial a presence than Kyle's ghost. I don't tell my mother any of this. I don't believe she calls to hear my news anyway. She's just looking for a sounding board—one more attentive than my father—while she talks about her life.

I sit back and listen. She and some of the other gals have started a book club. Why don't I join a book club, too? she inquires.

"Mom, I just don't have the time now," I explain, and then I see Marge, waving from the dining room, Hunter on her hip as she carries him to the bathroom.

"I found the cutest pair of pint-sized chaps at a leather shop last week, when me and the girls were on our shopping trip. I'd mail them to Hunter, but who knows what would happen if I left them in the care of the U.S. postal system?"

"Who knows?" I say, my fingers itching to hang up.

"Why don't y'all come to Texas and visit us instead?" she suggests. "You have that long Columbus Day weekend coming up, don't you? The kids have off and so do you."

The prospect of visiting my parents in Texas is right up there with a root canal. "Airfare's very expensive," I tell her. "Especially on holiday weekends."

"Well," she says, sighing, "you could plan ahead to drive down for Christmas. That wouldn't cost as much."

The thought of being trapped in the car with my children for all those miles makes the root canal sound appealing. I'm feeding her lame excuses for why I couldn't possibly drive to Texas when the kitchen door flies open. I turn to find Jack, of all people, holding a stack of pizza boxes.

"Gotta go, Mom," I tell my mother. "The pizza delivery boy just arrived."

Jack grins at this. "Domino's!" he shouts gleefully, making sure my mother can hear it. His announcement brings the children into the room quicker than ants at a picnic. I hang up the phone with such gratitude for this surprise, I almost kiss him.

"Thank you!" I say.

"For the pizza?"

"For that, too," I tell him, and he says, "Let me guess. You were on the phone with your mother."

"How'd you know?" I ask.

"You were talking in that classic whiny adult child voice. It's a dead giveaway."

The kids have already dug into the boxes, spreading them out across the countertop. Ren has materialized out of nowhere, gazing more amorously at the pepperoni pie than I've even seen him look at Charlotte. Hunter has sauce all over his face and is failing in his attempt to manage a droopy slice successfully in his small hands.

"Plates, everyone!" Marge orders, already in the cupboard pulling out dishes. "Let's make this a civilized meal." Marge slips a plate in front of each of the children, then says hi to Jack. The two shake hands like business associates, an amusing sight to observe.

"Nice to see you, Mr. Hayes," Charlotte says pleasantly, between stuffing her mouth with a vegetarian slice.

"Nice to see you, too, Miss Cavanaugh," Jack replies in his teacher voice. He nods at her boyfriend formally. "Ren," he says. "How are you?"

"I'm fine, Mr. Hayes," parrots Ren the charmer. My warm kitchen has become a contented place, the steamed windows holding us in place, the scent of oregano in the air. I'm taking it all in when Jack hands me a plate with two kinds of slices. It's silly how happy I suddenly feel. Charlotte pours everyone milk in paper cups and passes them politely around. Marge uncorks a bottle of Chianti, which she has found in the back of the high cupboard, stashed there since who knows when. She finds four stemmed wineglasses that haven't been used since Kyle died and she doesn't even rinse them. She pours the wine for the three adults and we clink glasses with the kids' paper cups. "A toast!" Jack says.

"With butter!" Hunter demands. It's the first time in weeks I've heard laughter in my house.

Hard as it is to believe, life goes on. Phoenix, with her buttermilk skin and fairy's hair, is gone, but Mrs. Cavanaugh is back in her office, same as before, her door open for the college-bound junior, the failing sophomore, the flailing freshman in need of an aptitude assessment. The grief counselors have packed up their wares and left us to fare for ourselves once more. A mere week later, it's back to business for the Guidance Department. Gladys Panella has resumed her unsmiling post at the central desk in headquarters. Tom Johnson has begun to act normal again when he's around me. No more offers of dinner or a sympathetic ear. Death knocks flirtation right out of the ballpark, if you're in a counseling department. I'm grateful for this, anyway.

After school I head over to a field behind Appleton Elementary School to catch the end of Charlotte's game. The games have helped us get through these long hot Indian summer days that have followed Phoenix's funeral. Even now, with emergency meetings no longer taking up half my afternoons and nights, the scent of tragedy remains in the air at school. Better to get outside, to watch strong determined girls kick the living daylights out of a little white ball and chase it down a field as if their lives depended on it.

A warm autumn sun illuminates the trees as I make my way to Charlotte's game. A fiery bower of red and gold leaves roofs the world. As I round the corner on Paradise Street, Charlotte's team comes into view, their orange jerseys dotting the green grass of the soccer field like a great ladybug convention. The other team is clad in muted grays and blues, no match for the Appleton girls' getups. I park the car in the school lot, but even as I'm slamming the door shut a shrill whistle blows. I turn to see the entire cast of them, bland blues and brassy oranges, moving to the edges of the field, as though a plug has been pulled and the game itself is being drained. Too late, then. I don't even get to see Charlotte play. She's coming toward me already with her usual grimace on her face, a sort of walking advertisement for teenage angst. She's dragging her shin guards by the straps, raising dust as she walks.

"You shouldn't have bothered to come," she says in greeting. The loose strands of her dark hair are plastered to her cheeks with sweat. She looks like a Gatorade commercial. I feel a swell of pleasure looking at her, regardless of the abuse that will likely ensue.

"I'm sorry I missed it," I say. "I came as soon as I could. Who won?"

"Is that all you care about? Who won?" She's yanking on the car door, no doubt trying to unload her filthy shin guards in there.

"Of course not," I tell her, not unlocking the door, even though it would be so easy to press the key fob I hold in my hand. "What do you want for dinner?"

A look of disappointment flashes in her eyes for only a second, until she has wrestled it again into submission. "Don't you *want* to know who won?"

"Nah," I lie.

"I saved four goals," she says.

"Do you want Thai again, or maybe Chinese?"

"Mom! You're unbelievable!"

I laugh, cuff her head like a mother bear. My hand comes back damp from the sweat. "You're awesome," I say. "I'm sorry I missed it."

"We won," she tells me, in case I don't ask her again. "We kicked their asses good."

"Very nice," I say. "If winning is all that matters."

This time Charlotte grins. I press the unlock button. "Want a lift home?"

"No, thanks," she says, throwing her filthy pads right onto the seat. "We're going to get pizza."

"Who?"

"Me and Ren. And some of the team."

I glance behind her at the field. There he is, the handsome cocky Ren. "Great," I say, suddenly feeling appreciative that my daughter has friends and teammates and even this boyfriend I found in her brother's bunk bed—all signs of a happy well-adjusted kid, no? Assuming they aren't having sex at Ren's house.

"Be home in time to do homework," I tell her. I dig into my purse and hand my daughter a twenty. She accepts it without comment. I hug her against her will and she walks off. She walks with the swagger of a girl who doesn't need hugs, but I know better. Everyone needs hugs.

"Did she hit you up for the pizza?" a male voice asks as I'm opening my car door. Foster Willis is smiling when I turn around. He's wearing another great suit, and his striped blue tie looks so soft and silky, I'm almost tempted to stroke it with my free hand.

"Is Bree joining them for the victory party?" I ask.

"Yep. She's getting pizza. With *cheese* on it. But not Brie."

I laugh, despite myself. "I heard it was a good game. Did you get to see any of it?"

"I saw all of it," he says, the setting sun behind him tinting his hair pink. "Your daughter was amazing. I would love to see her in a courtroom, but maybe without the shin guards. She'd kick some serious ass."

"Funny you should say that," I comment.

"What's really funny is that your daughter and mine seem to like each other all of a sudden."

I hadn't known this, though I try to show no reaction. Hadn't Charlotte called Bree something awful, like the most retarded girl in biology class? Now they're friends? Ask the Retarded Therapist, I think.

"What are you smiling about?" Foster asks.

"Nothing," I lie. I study the strong lines of his face, trying to decide whether I owe him an apology for the night he drove me home from the Claddagh, or whether maybe he owes me one.

"I'm just glad they won the game, and that the girls are getting along," I only say. "Every now and then, I need to feel my life is like a Disney movie."

"Especially after this tragedy at the school," Foster says. "You must have gone through hell with the death of that student."

"She was in my caseload, you know."

"I didn't. I'm sorry. She was a friend of Bree's. They were trying out together for cheerleading."

I lean back against the heated shell of my car, my face suddenly hot. "She was the most beautiful girl," I tell him, and tell also the world, and any spirits or gods who might be listening. I close my eyes and see Phoenix's note on the yellow piece of paper. What does it matter if I've destroyed it? It's seared into my heart anyway. My eyes are suddenly wet and a breeze touches tears that spill surprisingly easily down my face.

"Hey," Foster Willis says. He raises an index finger gently, stopping the tears in their tracks and wiping them away. A car door slams somewhere behind us. My shoulders tense. I stand straight again. Foster retracts his hand.

"Have you had any dinner yet?" he asks. "Think there's a chance we could introduce food into our conversation without one of us bolting?"

I find my own fingers, against my will, reaching for the blue silk of his tie and touching it. It is as soft as anything I have ever felt. A tremor of pleasure and of old memories travels through me like a hot toddy. I think of my babies' powdered skin soft against my cheek. I think of my own husband's ties, the serious maroons and the moony blues, the power stripes and the elegant chevrons, and how soft they felt to my touch as I unknotted the knots and removed them.

"Do you like Thai food?" I ask Foster Willis. "We have a square mile of it in our refrigerator if you're interested."

I have his tie off while the Styrofoam boxes still lie open on the kitchen counter. I press him into the counter with my kiss and his elbow dips into a puddle of peanut sauce on a dirty plate. His poor expensive suit. Brooks Brothers Pad-Ka-Pow. Tom Yam elbow. He wraps his free arm around my waist and lifts me from the stool as if I am nothing more than a bunch of straws. The tie dangles from one shoulder, his blue ribbon, and me his prize. Where is he carrying me off to? It is hard to see when I am kissing his neck, sucking on it like a vampire, tasting his exotic cologne, or perhaps this is the scent and flavor of Foster Willis himself. I am ravenous; he is my dessert. The part of my brain that might put the brakes on an activity such as this is locked down, after two and a half years of scrupulous overtime. Dining room chairs go by, their backs shining curves of polished wood. We are leaving this room, me flying through it in the arms of a man who tastes like cedar, a man whose shirt is being ripped off by a guidance counselor who needs guidance.

Oh, how I need guidance. But not as much as I need to feel this man's skin against my own, listen to his beating heart against my ear, stroke the hair on his arms and his chest and his legs. He throws me down on the couch on which Hunter watches TV. *SpongeBob Squarepants. Dora the Explorer.* I explore Foster Willis, climbing on top of him, stripping him of his remaining garments, neither of us speaking, both of us hungry. Starved. We're starved.

NINETEEN

Stayin' Alive

W ow," Foster Willis says, pulling a tiny baseball mitt from beneath his back. I'm already zipping up my skirt, a demure blue-flowered number from Banana Republic.

"Here," I say, throwing him his pants. "Maybe you should put these back on."

"Why, Kate," he says, frowning a little and sitting up. "I feel used."

I toss him his shirt. "Hurry. Please, Foster. Marge could walk in here any second with Hunter." I glance through the window to Marge's yard. A single bird perches at her birdbath.

"At which point I could give him his baseball mitt." Foster smiles, slipping his legs into his trousers. "And ask Marge how her evening went with that geek guy."

The bird seems to be staring at me. "I'm serious," I repeat, but he just rises and wraps his arms around me, pressing my face into the still-moist flesh of his chest.

"Don't you think Marge will be happy for us?"

I pull away from him. "Button your shirt. Please. And tuck it in."

"Are you this rough on your kids in the morning? Do you want me to brush my teeth, too? Shall I show you my homework?"

I'm puffing up couch pillows, arranging them carefully on the back of the couch. It's easier than looking at him as he ties his shoes. I'm a recognized Appleton school personnel member. And I've just left four hickeys on Bree Willis's father's neck.

"I don't know what happened to me," I tell the pillow, socking it once more in its heart, presumably to reshape it.

Foster shifts slightly on the couch to avoid the next punch. "What happened to you is you came alive again," he says. "What's so bad about that?"

"Is this the get-back-on-the-horse thing again?" I shout. "Because I really don't need to hear the get-back-on-the-horse thing, okay?"

Foster is staring at me, his brow creased with concern, or maybe it is hurt. His hands are still in the pockets of his expensive trousers. His sandy hair is mussed and some of the flush of sex still remains on his face. We say nothing for a minute, just enough time for me to see that this is a very handsome man, a decent man, a man who was invited—indeed, *dragged*—into a tryst by yours truly. It's not really right for me to abuse him. It is my mistake, not his, if our afternoon was ill-advised.

"Foster," I say, my voice regaining some measure of calmness, "I want to apologize."

My gesture does not seem to please him. Still his brow remains creased, his mouth turned down in a ceramic-smooth line. I spot his tie on the floor and reach down for it. I offer it to him like a gift of atonement. "Foster," I repeat.

"I guess I wasn't hoping for an apology," he finally says. "I myself would like to say that I enjoyed that very much."

Out of the corner of my eye, I watch the bird at Marge's birdbath fly away. It flies right over Foster Willis's head in the window behind him. "I'm not saying I didn't enjoy it also," I begin, not sure that *enjoy* is the right word to describe what I've just done to this man standing in my family room. *Devour* would be more like it. "But . . . ," I continue, glancing down.

"But what?" Foster asks.

Crash! goes the door in the kitchen, swinging open. "Mom?" calls my daughter's voice. *"Mo-o-o-om?"*

I grab the tie out of Foster's hand and fling it around his neck like I might strangle him. "Put this on!" I hiss at his surprised face. I can only imagine what my own face looks like. Is it pink with afterglow, like Foster's? "Oh, my God," I moan to no one. Then I shout, "Coming!" like some stock character in a sitcom, running out of the family room toward the kitchen.

"Coming, Charlotte!" I sing again until I'm standing in front of her shocked face, in the smiling presence of the suave Ren. His jeans hang so low on his hips that I can see the curve of his pelvic bone. Charlotte takes one look at me, then at the mess still left on the counter, and her eyes go from baffled to severely mistrusting.

"Mom. What's up with this?" she asks, waving at the mess as Ren tries to hide a grin.

"It's nice to see you, Mrs. Cavanaugh," he says, attempting to repair his girlfriend's gaffe. I notice that for once in his life, his hands are not all over Charlotte. His lack of impropriety at this crucial moment disturbs me.

"*You're* home early!" I exclaim, apparently unable to shake my new sitcom personality. "Did you get pizza?"

"Mom. Why is there all this crap—"

"Was it a nice celebration?"

"What is, like, wrong with you?"

"Wrong? Nothing is wrong—"

You'd have to be deaf to miss the sound of Foster Willis suddenly coughing.

Charlotte is pushing past me now, moving me with her hand as if I am a chair in her path. "Who's here?" she asks. "What's going on?"

"Nothing is going on," I tell her, following quickly in her path, until the two of us are staring into the family room at a man sitting on the couch with a tiny baseball mitt in his hands. His tie is knotted again, but it's inside out and loose. He's got a handkerchief raised to his nose. "Sorry," he says. "Hay fever."

Charlotte gasps beside me.

"Hi," he says lamely, not even attempting to get up. "How was your victory party?"

Her head spins from Foster Willis back to me again. Ren is suddenly standing beside us, too, exhaling loudly. "This is sick," he says beneath his breath, with clear admiration.

"Your mom and I just finished the Thai takeout," Foster tells

Charlotte, whose arms are crossed like Mr. Clean guarding the threshold of the family room.

"Your jacket's on the floor," Charlotte informs him coldly, the stud in her tongue winking when her mouth opens.

Foster regards the wrinkled heap at his feet. "So it is," he says.

"Take it off in a hurry?"

"Charlotte!" I scold. "Don't be rude."

"Rude? Is *rude* what we're worried about now?" Charlotte shakes her head sadly and grabs her boyfriend's hand. "Maybe I should give you two the lecture on the dangers of unprotected sex."

"Charlotte!"

"Come on, Ren," she says. "We're getting out of here."

"Oh, no, you're not," I tell her, my fingers curling into fists. "You're going to say good night to Ren and stay right here. And do your homework!"

Charlotte squeezes Ren's hand tighter and turns her full, furious gaze on me. "What is it you want from me?" she asks. "You want me to watch?"

My opened hand comes down hard across her face before I can even think about it.

"Ooh," Ren says apologetically, dropping his girlfriend's hand. The three of us stare at Charlotte, watching her cheek grow crimson. I have never raised a hand to this girl in my life. She will not look at me. She just turns her back on us and walks toward the kitchen.

Crash! goes the door again. The silence that follows is unnerving.

"Well, I guess I'd better be going," Ren says. "Good night, Mrs. Cavanaugh. Good night"—he glances over at Foster, who is fiddling with his backward tie—"sir," he adds politely.

And then he also turns, and he's out of here. Leaving me frozen on the threshold of the family room staring at the crumpled suit jacket. And then I suddenly know something with certainty. We're out of here, too. The Cavanaughs are leaving town.

TWENTY

Just Love Them

Next morning, we're up with the birds. I dress Hunter and try to feed him, but still it's too early to drop him at Bright Lights. No problem, then. I'll take him along with me. At six-thirty I have a cranky kid strapped into the child seat behind me. Even Kyle's ghost isn't up yet. I back out of the driveway, determined to get to the high school by seven, before the kids start pouring in, before Tom gets caught up in his day. Before I lose my nerve.

Hunter scowls at me in the rearview mirror, gripping a limp Pop-Tart in one hand. In the other he holds his one full ketchup bottle. This isn't an empty bottle morning. No indeed.

A soggy landscape goes by after last night's rain. Green Appleton recycling bins, empty and filthy, rest on their sides all along the curbs and sidewalks, making our perfect town look messy and disjointed.

"Whe-e-e-re's Sissy?" Hunter whines in his babyish voice, the voice most four-year-olds gave up half a lifetime ago. I don't answer him. Sissy never came home. Marge rang last night to tell me she was at her house and was okay. I didn't even ask to speak with her. Let her go to school today in her dirty underwear. Or maybe Marge has sewn her up a new pair by now.

"Where *is* she?" Hunter asks again, banging the Pop-Tart like a gavel on his knee. Crumbs fly everywhere. Goopy fake fruit filling lands on Hunter's jacket and the car upholstery. He pours his juice box over his spread-opened hand. I squeeze the steering wheel, negotiate carefully around an unleashed dog licking the insides of one of the green bins.

"Hunter, that's enough, honey," I say, trying to be patient. After all, his crappy morning isn't his fault. "Drink your juice, sweetie. Don't squirt it."

For once, when I pull into the high school parking lot, there are plenty of spots up front, close to the school's main entrance. I release my reluctant son from his car seat and guide him, holding one sticky hand, up the steps to the double glass doors. He leaves a fruity handprint on one of them, a tiny perfect starfish.

"I'm hungr-e-e-e!" he whines, when we've reached the second floor.

"You should've eaten your Pop-Tart instead of flogging it to death."

"What flogging?" he asks.

"What *is* flogging," I correct him. "You should say: 'What *is* flogging,' or you could say, 'What *does* flogging *mean*?'"

"I WANNA GO TO BRIGHT LIGHTS!" Hunter screams.

He is grammatically correct this time, anyway. The Guidance Office door flings open and Gladys Panella is suddenly frowning over him, casting a shadow like the Bunker Hill monument. I'm sure she's heard everything.

"Good morning," she says, arms crossed in front of her. She stares at Hunter, her white knit cardigan draped over her shoulders like Superman's cape.

Hunter looks up, up, up. Gladys's shadow is angled across the bottom half of his face and all of his goopy jacket front. His eyes sparkle in the overhead fluorescent lighting. "Are we gonna play?" he asks.

"I wasn't planning on it," she says.

"Spiderman?" Hunter's face remains hopeful. "Paper clips?"

Gladys sighs. "Why don't you come in so I can show you something?"

Hunter looks intrigued as Gladys precedes him inside.

"Good morning, Mrs. Panella," I say, but she doesn't respond, doesn't even ask me why I'm in so early, trailing a kid. "Is Tom in?" I ask, but again she ignores me.

"Come over here," Gladys says calmly to my son. "Stand right here beside me at my desk."

Hunter doesn't hesitate to obey the meanest woman in the school. Gladys Panella is sliding a well-lubricated desk drawer open beneath his wide eyes. "Now just wait a moment . . . ," she tells him, rifling around in its deep pocket, until finally she pulls out the most amazing thing I have ever seen. Ever.

Now my eyes are wide, too.

Gladys has extracted from her drawer an empty plastic ketchup bottle that seems to be wearing something. Something colorful and crocheted. There is a little woolly strap-handle growing out of the sides of what appear to be tiny crocheted lederhosen. Lacy crocheted suspenders rest on the bottle's shoulders, secured there by a cross-strap and fastened with bright shiny buttons to the lederhosen's waistband. Gladys holds up the strap handle and we all watch the bottle gently swing back and forth, back and forth, the lederhosen leg holes empty but also lacy. Unbelievable as it seems, Gladys appears to have begun a wardrobe collection for Hunter's ketchup bottles.

Hunter rubs his sticky hands together like a greedy banker. "What are it?" he asks breathlessly, his eyes glued to the red buttons at the bottle's belly.

"What *is* it," I say, partially to correct him, but mostly to hear the answer.

"Oh, it's just a little something I worked up this past weekend," Gladys says. "Thought you might like it."

"I *do* like it," Hunter assures her, grabbing the swinging bottle from the air and holding it out for further inspection. "It got clothes on!" he says.

Just when I think I might need to sit down, the office door swings open and a tired-looking Tom Johnson walks in. His face visibly brightens at the sight of us, and I wonder briefly who it is that delights him—Hunter or me. Tom has no children, and he's been divorced for as long as I have known him. But this doesn't mean that he didn't want children, only that he didn't get any. I watch as his eyes scan the two of us, then alight on Hunter and stay there. So maybe, I think . . . maybe this is the great emptiness in Tom's life, the reason the corduroy shines at the seat of his pants.

"Good morning, Tom," I greet him.

Tom looks up from my son and produces a half smile. "Morning, Kate. You're in early," he says. "And I see we have company. Good morning, Hunter."

"It got clothes on!" Hunter says again, shoving the bottle toward my boss.

"So indeedy it does," says Tom, glancing first at the bottle and then at Gladys, whose head is bowed with some emotion—either pride or embarrassment, it's hard to tell.

"It's got more clothes on than some of our students wear, wouldn't you say, Gladys?"

I feel a sting in his comment, almost as if he and Gladys are standing around the office gossiping about the way my daughter sometimes dresses.

"Do you have a few minutes?" I ask Tom, reminding myself why I have come. "May I see you in your office?"

"Just you?" Tom asks, glancing at Hunter again. "Or you and Hunter?"

I turn pleading eyes toward the impassive Gladys. Just a nod will do, but her white snowy permanent remains stationary. "We'll be fine here," she finally says. "Won't we, Hunter?"

"How are things going?" Tom asks, once the office door is closed. I sit in the student chair as he arranges himself on the other side of his desk. I remain silent as he performs his morning rituals: jacket-hanging on a corner coat rack, a quick finger-combing through scant sandy hair, a clearing of the throat as he seats himself on his desk chair. My courage is draining like rain in a gutter.

"How are the New Frontiers kids getting along?" Tom asks, trying again.

I run a hand through my own hair, which I have worn loose today, too busy getting out the door with Hunter to even have gathered it into an elastic band. "I'm not sure they're doing well at all," I finally say. "There's nothing I can do to help them, either."

Tom rolls his desk chair back a little. "Kate," he says, "you know that time will be the greatest healer for these kids. It's hard to remember, I'm sure, when you're sitting in a circle, looking at their glum faces, but—"

"Well, that's just it," I interrupt.

"What's just it?" Tom asks.

"Their glum faces," I say. "Their glum faces are killing me."

Tom smiles a weary smile. "That's only because you're an empathic person, Kate. It's a good quality in a counselor."

Pull, pull, my fingers through my hair while I consider his comment. "No," I decide. "The truth is I'm a burned-out counselor. And also a burned-out parent. And if I do feel everything deeply, it's because I'm trying to *ward it off*, Tom. My *armor* is sensitive, not me." I shift a little in the uncomfortable plastic chair. "Good counselors aren't trying to ward things off, Tom. They're trying to let things in."

Tom considers this in silence. "Kate," he finally says. "We just lost a student, a lovely girl. I think we're all feeling a little guilty— even if it makes no sense."

I can't look at him when he says this. *I just want to go now*, the note said.

"What I'm trying to say," he continues gently, "is that it's natural, if wrong, to be feeling somehow responsible after Phoenix's death."

Outside the door we can hear Hunter singing something to Gladys Panella.

"I know you're upset, but anyone would feel this way, even though it isn't true. You *know* it isn't true, Kate." His eyes bore deeply into mine, but not with sternness or unkindness. It's concern, maybe even worry. My desire to tell him he is wrong, off track, pissing in the wind with his theories, evaporates.

"She was a sweet girl," he says. "And she really trusted you, Kate. I saw that."

"She didn't trust me enough. She's *dead*." I rub my eyes with my cold knuckles. "I didn't know she would *do* that. I swear, Tom, I saw no suicidal ideation, none."

"I believe you," Tom says.

"She was like sunshine in my group. Always cheering up the others."

"Uh-huh."

"If you could see the others, Tom. If you could hear them. They are *slammed* by this!" I bang the arm of my student chair and it squeaks in protest.

"And how is Charlotte doing with all of this?"

I sit up straighter. "Why do you ask?"

A smooth recrossing of the legs precedes his answer. *Calm down*, the gesture says.

"Well, I know you've been concerned about her this school year. She's been having her issues, right?"

"Charlotte is nothing like Phoenix!" I protest too loudly. The singing outside the door abruptly stops.

"Bingo," he says. "She really isn't, is she?"

"That's not what I worry about," I tell him, but then I don't know if it's true. When Charlotte goes into her dark place, isn't that when she scares me most?

I study the chipped nail polish on my big toe. It's too late in the season to be wearing sandals, but I'd found them the quickest on my way out of the house. It's too late in the season for a lot of things. This is what I'm trying to explain to Tom. "It's not just Phoenix, or New Frontiers," I tell him. Then the room is quiet for a few seconds.

"What do you need, Kate?" Tom finally asks.

I clear my throat. "I was wondering if I could combine my unused vacation and personal days and turn them into a leave," I say. "A sabbatical of sorts, where I could keep my benefits and take a little time."

Finally, it's out. The few scant sentences that could change my family's lives. And mine, of course.

Tom strokes his goatee. So much communication is done with these little shifts and gestures. A crossed leg here, a small cough there.

"When would you want to go?"

"Now," I answer too quickly.

He studies me thoughtfully. "Well," he says finally, "I'm sure that you've thought about how this would affect your children, taking off in the middle of the school year."

"Charlotte has been skipping school anyway," I offer unhelpfully.

"Isn't she doing a little better with attendance now?"

"Yes, but only because she's in Necking 101 with Ren McKenna."

Tom's eyebrows rise. "Ren McKenna? Isn't he the young man whose father was arrested for tax fraud?"

"Oh, great," I say. "Look, we all just need a little time off."

"But your daughter seems to be doing fine now," Tom says. "No truancies these past three weeks. Excellent grades in everything except . . ." He pauses. "Environmental science, I think."

I wince at the mention of this. *The Little Tree That Had to Die.* Women's behinds on toilet seats. "She got her tongue pierced," I tell him.

Tom shrugs. He's seen everything in his years at the high school. A little mouth hardware doesn't impress him. "Does Charlotte want to leave?" he asks.

"It might do her good," I suggest. "She's never really gotten over Kyle's death. A change of scenery would be healthy for all of us."

Even to my own ears, this sounds stupid. I stare at my toes and wait for Tom to tell me the truth, that I'm the one who needs a break, not Charlotte. Instead, he leans forward on his elbows, lacing his fingers beneath his chin like a little bridge.

"Perhaps I should tell you that Charlotte came to see me yesterday."

"She came to *see* you?"

"Yes," Tom says calmly. "You might recall that students sometimes come to see their counselors."

I am silenced by this news, and by his gentle rebuke.

"What did she say?" I ask, my mind spinning with the possibilities.

"That would be confidential," Tom says. "You know that, Kate."

"Are you crazy?" I say, half rising from the chair. "Of course it's not confidential! She's a minor. She's my *daughter*, for God's sake."

"Kate," Tom says again, but this time it's a sort of command. It means stop. It means give someone else a chance to speak—sensibly, perhaps. I squeeze the chair arms until my knuckles hurt. "I want Charlotte out of here," I blurt. "I want all of us to leave. Maybe for a while. Possibly forever. It's the only way for us, Tom. Don't you see it?"

Tom doesn't see it. He sits quietly, his face retaining its Mount Rushmore impassivity. He's quite skilled at what he does. He waits until I have calmed down, allowing me to sit in my cloud of shame for a minute, and then says, "You know what, Kate? You're right. Charlotte is a minor, so I'm going to tell you some things that might benefit you, as her mother, to know."

I grip the arms of the chair even harder, as if I'm on a vomit-inducing amusement park ride. "Go ahead," I say, as my mind screams, *Stop!*

"Well, here's the thing," Tom says, sighing his counselor sigh. "No one wants to live with someone who thinks they're all wrong."

"All wrong?" I repeat, feeling highly offended.

He sits up taller, rubs his goatee. "It's just that as her parent, you might want to show her a little more acceptance."

I'm half out of the chair again. I catch myself and sit back down. "Tom," I say, taking a breath, "with the utmost respect, may I remind you that you've never tried to parent a teenage girl?"

Tom winces like he's been slapped, but recovers quickly. I review what I have said, remain baffled at how I've offended him. It's *my* train wreck of a life we're discussing, not his.

"Has it ever occurred to you," he says, not quite looking at me, "that Charlotte finds her tattoo attractive? That it makes her feel pretty, and good about herself?"

"Give me a frigging break," I say, maybe not the best way to talk to my supervisor when I'm asking him for something. Tom just gazes out his window, like he's yearning to leap through it. Then he turns back to me with a distant smile, as if he's decided something. "I'm going to tell you a little story," he says. "Perhaps you'll call on your anger management skills to bear with me."

Ouch, I think. Fair enough.

Tom's expression grows wistful, almost sad. "A million years ago," he says, "when I was married to a very nice woman, we had a baby and we named her Alicia, and she died."

His voice cracks the slightest little bit. I sit frozen in my chair, feeling my heart sink like a heavy bag.

"She was twelve weeks premature. She was two days old. She had yellow hair. Her lungs didn't work." I watch Tom take a long breath. "This was a long time ago," he says. "Before I even started graduate school. We were very young, my wife and I. Very young and hopeful parents." His eyes are moist when he locks them on mine. "Doctors can save a lot of babies like Alicia, but they couldn't save ours."

Tom rubs his eyes, then glances back at the window, as if he is looking for his baby in the staff parking lot.

"I am so sorry," I hear myself say, and resist an urge to come around the desk and hug him. "That is just awful," I add uselessly.

"Awful enough to end my marriage," Tom agrees. "My wife was a nice person, but we couldn't look at each other after that. Counseling didn't save us. We still came home to an empty crib. Finally, the crib and she left." His harsh laugh comes out more like a sob. "And neither of us has remarried. But every single day of my life, when I walk down the halls of this school, I see a girl who could be mine. *That's Alicia's hair!* I think, or *Those are Alicia's eyes!*" Tom becomes animated as I have never seen him before. His eyes glow, as if backlit. Pain brings color to his face and strength to his slight build.

"I know it's not fair to tell you this story," he says. "But I wanted you to understand that I *know* loss. I know what it is, and I know what it can do. When I suggested to you that you and I have dinner in September, and you looked at me as if a dinosaur were asking you on a date, it was because I wanted to tell you this. I've been scared, watching you sink deeper and deeper into your grief, Kate, and taking your family down with you. I wanted to warn you, to *help* you somehow."

Now tears are running down my face as I sit on the chair across from him.

"Please," Tom says. "Get some help. And leave Charlotte alone, with her tattoos and tongue studs. Just love her," Tom says, looking at me. "Just love her."

I come around the desk and hug him.

"I'll see what I can do about getting you your sabbatical," he breathes into my hair. And I feel guilty, in the midst of his loss, for being grateful for this.

TWENTY-ONE

Role Models

After I drop off Hunter at Bright Lights, I swing by a 7-Eleven for a coffee on my way back to school. I pay for it black, taking my time afterward at the fix-up station, adding milk and Splenda, stirring slowly, inhaling the aromas of caffeine and morning. Tom's story reels over and over in my mind, fueled by the caffeine. Why would he choose to be surrounded all day by creatures who could have been his own? My heart breaks for him, yet I remain convinced that I am doing the right thing. If Tom's daughter had grown up to be a troubled fourteen-year-old, wouldn't he want to do something, too? I gulp down some coffee, scalding my throat.

It's only eight in the morning and the hardest part of my day is over. In the days to come there'll be more meetings with Tom to plan for my replacement. A few parents will be up in arms, but it's only the New Frontiers kids I will really worry about. The others will adjust to their new counselor, and they probably won't be surprised to see me gone. *Mrs. Cavanaugh has finally lost it*, perhaps they'll say. Or, *Mrs. Cavanaugh never got over the death of her husband*. Or, *Mrs. Cavanaugh started sleeping with the parents. One of them, anyway.*

"Miss? Miss!" The clerk, a twentysomething dropout—I would put money on this, based alone on his expression of agitated blankness—is trying to get my attention.

"You forgot your change here," he says, proffering a fistful of singles.

"Thanks," I tell him, juggling the coffee in one hand and accepting my money in the other. I stuff it back into my purse and leave.

I back out of the parking lot remembering Tom's little Alicia once more, and then remembering Phoenix's mother, too. Shame floods me; I welcome each hot sharp prickle of it as though it is my due. Who am I to complain about my healthy, beautiful children? I slip the minivan into the flow of traffic and head back toward the high school. Poor Tom. Lucky Charlotte and Hunter and me. We'll learn how to love each other again, the way we did when Kyle was with us.

After first period I sneak out of my office and wait for Charlotte to pass by in the driver's ed hall. I semi–hide behind the glass trophy case, hoping Jack will not find me. *Bri-i-i-ng!* goes the classroom bell, and I am reminded of that ancient disco song Kyle used to love. *You can ring my be-e-ell! Ring my bell.* The insipid melody and synthesized beat runs rampant through my brain now as I watch students flow into the corridor. And then Kyle himself floats into my mind, the memory of him this time and not his ghost, and he is dancing naked in our bedroom, singing this song to me. His big feet are sinking into the mattress as he hovers over me like Michelangelo's *David*, just without the slingshot. And I am laughing beneath him, a tiny postage–stamp part of my brain wondering whether the kids are still awake and listening through their bedroom walls.

Ding-a-ling-a-ling-a-ling, he's singing.

How can any adult be an actual role model for a child? I suddenly wonder. We all walk around with our good behavior on the outside, while nursing and savoring our naughtiest inside thoughts. He was beautiful, my Kyle, with great body hair (all on display during his bedtime disco dance numbers) and what my mother would call "bedroom eyes." He would have made any woman happy, even if he did snore and all the vegetables in the food pyramid seemed to give him gas. It all makes it easier to believe in Darwin rather than God, for why would God bother to make a man like Kyle if He was going to take him away again so quickly? I suppose this is what Charlotte must wonder sometimes, except she thinks that I helped her father get taken away. I, who lay beside him the night he died and did nothing. If you're given the privilege of sleeping with someone you love, the least you can do is check to see if he's still breathing. It's suddenly easy to see Charlotte's point of view.

I spot her almost before she materializes; mothers can do this. Here comes my Charlotte, alone now, with no Ren, her books hugged to her chest like she's modeling the seat-back flotation device on a jumbo jet. She's wearing clean clothes—jeans and a GOT MILK? T-shirt, the suggestive words spread across her tiny breasts. This means Charlotte has gone home this morning to shower and change, finding Hunter and me gone. Which was probably a good thing. God, I love that Marge. One day I will figure out a way to pay her back.

Charlotte frowns as she walks. She is in her own world, a serious interior place where not even boyfriends are invited. She doesn't see me until I'm walking beside her, wrapping an arm around her shoulder.

"Honey, I'm so sorry about yesterday," I tell her, looking straight ahead, for fear of my eyes welling if I look into hers. Hopefully, no one is watching us. This could kill her social life.

" 'S okay," Charlotte says, also staring straight ahead.

I could cry with gratitude for her absolution. I squeeze her shoulder, feel the strong bones there that ward off soccer balls. "No, it's not, sweetie," I say. "No one should ever lift a hand to someone she loves."

Charlotte suddenly stops—perhaps it's this last thing I've said—and looks me full in the face. Her own face, I am happy to observe, appears unblemished. No marks or high coloring advertising her mother's child abuse, not on the outside, anyway.

"I thought you were talking about that other thing you did," she says in a low voice. We stand stock-still in the middle of students swarming around us like a stream over pebbles. My face grows hot. Foster Willis. His elbows in the peanut sauce. His inside-out tie.

"You're right," I tell Charlotte, humbled. "Your mother must seem unrecognizable to you sometimes. But, sweetie, I'm gonna fix that, for all of us."

Charlotte looks skeptical.

"Come home today after practice today and we'll talk."

"Can Ren come?"

"No."

A flinch. I have said this too quickly.

"Sure. Okay," I amend.

"Good. He's got a new dog. I'll tell him he can bring it over."

"A new . . . ?"

Charlotte is gone, vanished into the classroom beside us.

TWENTY-TWO

My Love/Hate Relationship with Angelina Jolie

The TV is on for support and company as I ready the house for Charlotte's and my big talk in only an hour. Angelina Jolie, without makeup, is answering a reporter's questions about her recent UN visit to Iraq. I gaze at her image with a jumpy stomach.

Angelina Jolie is my hero. I love her because I hate her. I hate her because she appears to be an excellent mother, a woman who doesn't need Brad Pitt for anything more than eye candy when it comes to raising her children, who keep coming. No lying in bed eating bonbons for Angelina. She's chosen diapers and runny noses and endless trips to FAO Schwarz. Now and then a photo shoot with the most handsome man in the world standing beside her, shouldering an adorable Asian child or two. Who cares if they've had children out of wedlock? *Everyone* does! Always Angelina has time to be on the set, where the makeup lady first applies pancake over her tattoos, so she can be a housewife, an assassin, a tattooless dominatrix for the day. She does have nannies, of course. But I have Marge.

I click off the television. I've asked Marge to pick up Hunter today (and of course she's said yes), so I can have a quiet house in which to discuss with Charlotte our trip. Perhaps she will take it as cheerfully and as well as Angelina Jolie's children, when they discover they're all going to Thailand so Mommy can make a movie.

We're all going to Texas, I could say to Charlotte, *so Mommy doesn't lose her mind*.

I'm straightening up the house, putting away clean dishes from the dishwasher and stacking magazines on the coffee table (the one with Angelina Jolie on the cover, smiling confidently, cleavage amazing, rests on top), so that when I tell Charlotte about our plans, she will hear it all in an orderly environment. What will she say? Do I dare hope she'll be excited, possibly see this as an excellent road trip? I've changed out of my work clothes and into my jeans. This, of course, made me think of Jack's diarrhea joke.

Sure enough, the door swings open in the kitchen, seconds after I've finally settled myself on the couch in my tidied-up living room. I hear laughing and two voices, and then someone says, "Stop! Cookie . . . no!"

There's a crash, and then some more laughter. It's Charlotte's sweet-little-girl laugh, which I haven't heard in a long time. I let it wash over me deliciously, ignoring the fact that I've also heard the crash. Next Ren's voice, also sounding young, is cooing at someone or something. "You da bad 'iddle girl, aren'cha, baby?"

Loud deep barking, like Darth Vader, is the only response.

Does Angelina Jolie have dogs? I know Paris Hilton has a purse-sized one, but these are not real dogs. These don't smell up your house or shed on your favorite black dress. They don't pull your arm out of its socket when you try to walk them. They don't chew your couches or roll in dead fish. No, that would be the type of dog charging into my living room now, pink leash flying behind. That would be Ren's 'iddle girl.

Cookie is the size of a small horse. She has a skull like an anvil and mottled brown and white fur that looks like a marble cake. She's pounding in, swinging her fuzzy head side to side, checking out the room and then the lady on the couch, her tail whipping dangerously close to my table lamps. Spittle flies from her goofy grin like a thick spiderweb being formed before my eyes. Ren pounds in shortly after her.

"Cookie, come!" he commands in an impressive, if worried, voice. Cookie ignores him, galumphing like a giant puppy toward me, moving with the earnestness of a lost lover. With a surprisingly light-footed leap, the dog is in my lap, knocking the wind out of me.

"Cookie Dough McKenna. You get down right now!"

The dog ignores him. His sexy eyebrows mean nothing to her. She's as soft and lumpy as cookie dough, which is perhaps where she gets her name. She takes up my entire couch, smothering my lap in fur and my face in kisses. She has apparently eaten something rank before making her house call. Her breath is killing me, but still I find I am laughing. It could be nerves, or it could just be that I've always liked killer dogs and have never let myself know it.

Ren drags the happy beast off my lap by her pink collar. "Sorry, Mrs. Cavanaugh," he says, looking very young and very nervous. His underwear today is green and his jeans look in danger of falling down completely. Still, a child with a face so sweet and concerned could never plunder my daughter.

"We'll just put Cookie Dough in the kitchen and shut the doors, if that's okay with you, Mrs. Cavanaugh," Ren says, as Charlotte comes laughing into the room, one hand patting her tiny perfect chest as though she might pass out from mirth.

"Isn't that the coolest name?" she asks, beaming first at Ren and then at the giant dog. "You know how he spells it? It's 'Cookie' with a dollar sign after it." Charlotte traces a dollar sign with her index finger through the air. She is showered after her soccer practice, fresh and lovely in wet hair, a nonpornographic T-shirt and jeans. "Get it?" she asks. "Cookie *Dough*?"

Ren beams at her like she's just won the Toastmasters' award, and Cookie $ is loose once more, making a beeline for my lap again. This time I'm ready for her when she leaps. I protect my face with my hands, but forget to tighten my stomach muscles for the landing. "Oof!" I hear myself grunting, then Cookie $ is dragged off me and into the kitchen.

"It's nice that she isn't a barker," Charlotte comments as Ren is slamming doors on the dog.

"Honey," I say quickly, before he returns, "I really want to talk to you. Is there a time when just the two of us could chat?"

Charlotte turns to me with a perplexed expression that melts, as I watch, into disappointment. "This visit is about the *dog*," she says. "I am trying to share my life with you. I'm making an effort here, after, like, you know, your . . . actions yesterday."

A slap in the face couldn't feel more awful. I stare down at my lap, flooded with embarrassment. The lap itself is flooded with dog hair.

"I had to face Bree Willis today in soccer practice," Charlotte continues relentlessly. "How do you think *that* felt?"

The hairs on my arms suddenly stand up. "Charlotte," I say carefully, "you didn't say anything to Bree about—"

"You want me to cover for you now?"

"No!" I shriek, though I wish I weren't shrieking. What will Ren think if he finds us shrieking again? "No, Charlotte," I repeat, in a calmer voice. "I don't want you to *cover* for me. It's just that . . ." I take a deep breath and think. "It's just that you are fourteen years old. You don't understand everything about what it is to be your mother's age."

Charlotte crosses her arms and glowers at me. I go on bravely, saying things I believe need to be said.

"I think you're milking this thing with Bree's father a little much. This is a matter between mature adults. I'm not a teenager who's been busted for bad behavior."

"You are *so* unbelievable," is Charlotte's response. "A hypocrite."

"I'm not a hypocrite! Look, I'm sorry you had to come home when you did yesterday, but my actions, as you call them"—I try to look dignified—"are really my own concern."

I touch her arm, hoping to soften things. It's cold as a flagpole. When Ren enters the room again he finds his girlfriend grimacing at me like I'm a war criminal.

"Is this a bad time?" he asks.

"No," I say.

"Yes," Charlotte says. "My mother doesn't want to hang out with us."

"That's not true!" I protest. "I'd love to hang out with you and the . . . dollar dog." I smile at Ren, then look at Charlotte imploringly. "All I want is to set a time with you for *later*, when you and I can talk."

"Let's go," Charlotte says to Ren. "We'll take Cookie Dough home."

"Wait!" I cry, jumping to my feet, blocking the two of them like a traffic cop. Charlotte stares at me with wide eyes.

"I need to tell you something," I say quickly. "We're leaving Appleton for a while. We're going to Texas to stay with Grandma Lynne."

I watch the color drain from my daughter's face. This is not how I wanted to tell her. We listen to Cookie $ thrashing around the kitchen in the stunned silence that follows my announcement. Charlotte falls onto the couch. Ren rushes over and sits beside her, the two of them looking like Romeo and Juliet just before they kill themselves.

"You don't mean next week, right?" Charlotte asks carefully. "You mean for Thanksgiving. We're visiting Grandma and Grandpa on Thanksgiving."

"It could be next week," I tell her, "we're leaving as soon as we can."

Ren wraps his arm protectively around her. "Holy crap, dude," he says.

"We'll be back again, maybe," I comfort him.

The stare at me openmouthed.

"It's just that we need some time as a family to sort things out. Since Daddy died," I add.

"What the hell . . . ?" Charlotte gasps.

I do my best to speak for all of us. "You know how hard it's been for you at school this year, honey," I say. "Don't you think it would be great for all of us to start over, to get away, to have an adventure—"

"MOM!" Charlotte rises from the couch, fists clenched. "You're fucking crazy! You know that?"

Now it's my turn to be speechless.

"This is ridiculous," Ren says, rising from the couch and rubbing his hands together.

"Just because you feel bad about getting laid by Bree Willis's father doesn't mean, like, the whole family needs to leave town!" Charlotte screams.

Ren throws his arms passionately around my daughter. They cling to each other like they've been thrown into a lion's den.

"Language," I say, but Charlotte won't even look at me. "Come, sit down," I instruct them. But Charlotte shakes her head violently, and the two of them stand there wrapped together, all arms and legs. All the joy is drained from their faces.

"Sweetheart—" I say, but then there's a crash in the kitchen, followed by another Darth Vader bark. Charlotte and Ren rush out of the room. A door slams and the house is quiet again.

TWENTY-THREE

Blow, Blow, Blow

M arge takes one look at me standing on her threshold and knows that something is very wrong.

"Is Charlotte here?" I ask her.

"You don't know where Charlotte is?"

"No."

"You checked at Ren's?"

I nod and Marge frowns. Her salt-and-pepper hair hangs loose, making her face look softer than usual.

"Come on in," she says quietly.

I follow her through her spanking-clean rooms to the kitchen, where Hunter sits happily behind a counter of healthy snacks and wooden puzzles, toys bought by Marge especially for my son. "Mama," he says blandly, then returns his attention to the puzzle piece in his hand, a wooden cow with very large black spots. He will miss this part of his life, his wonderful, secure hours with his Aunt Margie. He started coming over like this when Kyle died. He was here the day of his father's funeral.

I perch myself on the stool beside Hunter's, give him a quick hug, which he shirks off. "This cow don't fit," he says, frowning.

"This cow *doesn't* fit," I say, placing my hand over his and guiding the piece into its precut slot. "No!" Hunter says, shaking the puzzle frame upside down on the counter. Barnyard pieces bounce to the floor, clacking against the tiles.

"What's going on?" Marge asks, closing up manila folders on the counter beside the toys and her laptop.

"Most recently? Charlotte hates me again."

Marge closes yet another manila folder, almost like she doesn't want me to see what's in there, then flips shut her laptop, too. "Why now?" she says with a sigh.

Hunter has jumped down from his stool. He's grabbed my ankle for support while he retrieves his puzzle pieces, pinching my skin and making me feel weighted down. "She caught me," I say, "with Fester." I'm surprised I'm not feeling awkward confessing this. "It was just a little fling," I add.

"Fling, string, bing," Hunter sings at my feet, still tugging at my ankle.

"It's about time," Marge says.

"The wrong time," I tell her.

"What? Were you in the middle of things?"

"Busted by the two of them."

Marge plants her long chin in her hands, resting her elbows on the cleared counter. "Bummer," she says, grinning. "Makes it hard to lecture kids about abstinence. Were you dressed?"

"Of *course* we were dressed. Sort of."

"Tops? Bottoms? What was missing?"

"Marge! Stop being voyeuristic. It was just inside-out socks and ties, is all."

"Has he called you since?" Marge asks.

I occurs to me that he hasn't. "Has Thomas called you?" I ask.

Marge picks up a purple crayon lying beside the puzzle and begins doodling. "No," she says. She draws a figure eight and then goes over it again and again. "But then, we don't have that kind of a deal."

Hunter has climbed into his Aunt Margie's lap. She drops the crayon and absently kisses the top of his head. He hands her a puzzle piece in the shape of a pig. Marge puts it down, then closes a final manila folder, clearing it to one side.

"Since when do you clean up your kitchen workstation?" I inquire.

"You want some pound cake?" she asks. "I just made it."

"No," I say.

"Yes," Hunter says.

Marge rises to get the cake, placing Hunter back on his stool again. "You don't have to be embarrassed that you had a little fun," she says, her back to me over the cake plate. "Get it while you can, as Janice Joplin said."

"I saw you emulating her philosophy at the Claddagh," I comment, but the joke falls flat. It was just a one-night stand. Marge wants more. Something in my heart squeezes for my friend, just for a second, as I think of her life in her handsome Dutch Colonial. I come over here day after day, complaining about the very things she wishes she could have. Children. A lover who comes back. Someone to cook dinner for. I sit at her counter, envying her her clean, tasteful rooms, her effortless way of making a living, her freedom, the very manageability of her life. Wouldn't it be wonderful if we could trade our lives for the lives of others, just long enough to start wishing for our own lives back again?

"There's something else, too," I tell Marge. "Another reason Charlotte isn't speaking to me."

Marge looks up sharply, as if she knows the next thing I say is going to be hard.

"I've asked the school for a leave," I tell her.

The knife stays poised in Marge's hand, floating above the cake like a guillotine blade.

"You've what?" She turns and studies me. "What the heck are you talking about?"

"I'm taking the kids to Texas. To my mother's house."

Marge puts the knife down. "You're serious?"

I nod.

"When?"

"Next week, if I can. It all depends," I tell her.

"Cake," Hunter says.

"Holy God," Marge mutters.

She slips pieces of cake in front of Hunter and me. A pretty silver cake fork rests on the rim of my plate, a SpongeBob fork on Hunter's. She won't look at me now. "Do you know what you're doing, Kate? Charlotte's in school."

"We'll bring along her books."

Now Marge turns and faces me. "You're the only one who

needs the leave," she says. "Why don't you just go yourself and visit your mother for a while?"

"Yeah," Hunter says, his eyes on a wooden chicken he jams into the puzzle frame. "I don't want no leave."

These two are against me, but my mind is made up. I gather my courage. "We're all going," I say, right in front of Hunter, and this is how I know I'm really doing this.

"You enjoy your mother that much?" Marge asks.

I poke at the slice of cake with my fancy fork. We're quiet for a while, each of us attempting to quell a storm. The only sound is the clacking of wooden puzzle pieces. Finally Marge sits heavily in the chair beside me and takes my hands in hers. "Kate," she says. "Isn't there some way I can help you, something we could do, so you won't have to do this?"

I shake my head, and watch worry lines appear on Marge's forehead.

"I know it sounds nuts, but I've got to do this, Marge. I need to get some perspective on things," I add lamely.

More silence.

"Mmmm, good," Hunter murmurs, stuffing a piece of pound cake into his mouth.

"Why don't you let Charlotte stay here with me?" Marge proposes.

Her offer should surprise me more, but it doesn't. "The point is, I want *time* with Charlotte," I tell her. "I thought this could be some time for the two of us to . . . just be together."

"In the middle of her school year?"

She sounds like Tom Johnson.

"Would you like me to keep Hunter, and just the two of you can go off?" she asks.

"I don't wanna go off," Hunter says, spilling crumbs everywhere.

"I don't know," I confess.

Marge sighs loudly this time, like she's given up. "Will you be coming back?"

I look at my friend's worried face. "It's hard to know until I leave, I guess."

"That makes sense to me," Marge says, surprising me. She removes my empty cake plate gravely, as if it's a dead bird she's found on the sidewalk. "If you want me to talk to Charlotte, I'll be here all night."

"Night, flight, bite," Hunter says, fixing a puzzle piece perfectly into its frame.

"I'm not going!" Charlotte screams, waking me from a sound sleep on the couch. I jump a little on the cushions, pull myself into a sitting position. My clothes are wrinkled and twisted. I tug at the sweater, ruined now, straightening up the front of it. Charlotte looms dangerously over me, glowing like an angry archangel. A single lamp I've left switched on backlights her loose hair and darkens her face. "Are you crazy?" she asks. "Are you *crazy*?"

"Keep your voice down," I say. "Hunter's sleeping."

"What are you *thinking*?" she shouts, even louder.

"Charlotte—"

"You *quit*? You quit your job?"

"It's only a sabbatical I'm trying to get," I try to explain, but she shakes her head and turns from me.

The room is dark but for the light of the one table lamp. I imagine a starless night on the other side of the living room drapes. It feels as though there could be nothing out there, nothing hopeful on a night like this.

"Do you want to sit down so we can talk?" I ask, but she just shakes her head again, and I see the weariness in the set of her small shoulders.

"Charlotte, honey, sit down." I pat the empty sofa cushion beside me.

"No," she says, though she looks as though she might drop from exhaustion if she doesn't. I have seen her exact expression on Kyle's face before. It's a combination of worry and a suppressed hysteria that must never come to the surface. When had Kyle looked this way? I can't put my finger on it. The insistent twitter of a bird pierces the silence. What time is it? I wonder. Then I wonder if Charlotte has kept Marge up all night. Or maybe she was at Ren's, comforting herself in his bed.

"Honey, were you at Aunt Margie's?"

I can't believe it has come to this—a mother inquiring pleasantly in the birdcall hours of the morning as to where her daughter spent her school night. When had Kyle worn this same expression I see on Charlotte's face?

"Sit," I say again. "Please."

She slumps onto the couch, crumbling into an embryonic ball, her back to her mother. And then, finally, I remember when it was I'd seen that expression of suppressed hysteria on my husband's face. It was in the birthing room of Appleton Memorial Hospital, on the morning Charlotte was born. Her collarbone had twisted around on the way out; she'd been stuck in the birth canal for a few tense minutes. Kyle tried so hard to hide his panic. He'd held up two fingers before my face, as he'd been taught in birthing classes. "Blow the candles out, Kate," he'd said. "Blow, blow, blow." Beneath his smile, like the face of a bride behind a veil, I saw the terror. And now this expression is a gift he's left his daughter.

I wrap my arms around Charlotte's back and hug the tense shoulders. "Charlotte," I say, "sweetheart."

"Go away," she sniffs into a cushion, and I think, yes, that's the *idea*, the idea that will make us all happy again, that will reset the odometer for the Cavanaugh family. We'll go away.

"You can't just pull me out of school, rip me away from my life, because you feel like it," Charlotte cries into the cushion. I imagine all that Goth eye makeup wrecking the fabric.

"Do you think you're the only one who gets to play hooky?" I ask, smiling foolishly at the back of her head.

"You can have sex with whoever you want to. I won't ever say a thing again. Just don't make us move 'cause I caught you."

"Charlotte, it's not about that—"

"I'm not going," she says. "I'm staying with Aunt Marge. She says I can stay, and I am."

I stare at the picture window, where wan light now peeks from the cracks in the curtains. I wait, as a thousand feelings wash over me. Do I love Marge, or do I hate her? Didn't I explain to her that I wanted Charlotte along on this trip? I suppress a desire to shoot to my feet and cross the lawn and swing open Marge's front door. I want to wake her, bang up the stairs and frighten her, make her explain. I want to tell her that this is *my* daughter, whether I'm screwing up her childhood or not. It is easy to feel sympathy for Marge's barren life, but it's difficult to watch her claim my daughter as her own. She cannot have Charlotte, not without even asking first. And yet, how can I force Charlotte to come?

Charlotte whimpers and stirs in her half sleep. I touch her shoulder and she closes up tighter on herself. Can I really run to Texas and drag my daughter with me?

"Honey," I say. "How can I leave my girl behind?"

"Just stay," she breathes into the cushion.

"I can't," I tell her truthfully. "Any more than you, apparently, can leave."

She rolls away from me, deeper into the polyester. "Then go," she says, her voice gentling. "You've had this thing with Phoenix, and you probably still miss Dad." She takes a ragged breath. "And you probably need a vacation from me."

I wrap my arms around her. "No, baby, I want you to come *with* me," I tell her again.

"I'll be fine with Aunt Margie. And I won't miss any school. And then you'll come back and everything will be the same again."

Nothing will ever be the same, whether I leave this house or stay. I want to tell her this, but it seems too harsh to say, with the sun rising so hopefully in our window. "Okay," I hear myself tell her, and then realize that I mean it. "You stay with Aunt Marge." My hand is swirling in soft slow circles on her small back. "At least for a little while."

We fall asleep on the couch like this, to the sound of more birds outside that have joined the chorus.

TWENTY-FOUR

Running in Jeans

I suppose I should be happy that Tom has worked so quickly. Maybe he just told the central office I was going crazy. Whatever he did, nobody will be looking for guidance from Mrs. Cavanaugh for the rest of the school year. The poor widow will even be paid, for most of the year, anyway. I'm free as a bird, free to go to Texas and have a miserable life there without my daughter.

This last Monday in my office, I waste time staring at walls. My hair is pulled back in an elastic band and I'm sitting at my desk in jeans and a sweatshirt. A box of personal effects sits at my feet, my kids' school photographs, a sampling of Hunter's artwork, the ceramic ashtray Charlotte made for me in third grade. But the college posters and class schedules, do these come down or stay up? Am I advertising a permanent escape or only a short sabbatical? I wish I knew.

I keep my door shut so no one will walk in and discover me moving out. Only Guidance knows of my sabbatical. Tom will send out a letter to staff and parents next week, explaining the temporary assumption of my duties by others in the department, just for while I am gone. I'll tell Jack myself that I'm leaving today. This will be my last and hardest task.

The message light blinks wildly on my telephone. I press play and listen to a litany of parental complaints. Most are about college packets, but there is one from a mother who says her daughter has stopped eating since Phoenix's suicide. "She's unhappy," the mother laments. "It's scaring us." It makes me sad that I don't know who this freshman girl is. Why do they give us caseloads of 250 students when they know we can't help all of them? I make a note to pass the information along to Tom. Then I rub my eyes, thinking of my own unhappy girl. Maybe if she stays in Appleton she will eat healthily. If she stays at Marge's she won't be able to avoid it.

Across the room still tacked to the bulletin board is Phoenix's senior picture, taken when she was alive, developed in the days after she was buried. Her hair looks so golden and healthy I cannot imagine it resting beneath the ground. *I just want to go now, that's all*, her note to me had said. *Don't we all, sweetie*, I tell her silently.

The phone rings and I pick it up. "Mrs. Cavanaugh," I say.

"Foster here," comes the voice on the other end.

I rise quickly and close my door.

"I just wanted to see how you are," he says. Behind him I hear a man's raised voice, which means he's at work.

"You mean, after the disaster at my house?"

"I wouldn't necessarily call it a disaster." He pauses. "Except maybe for the hitting part."

I wince.

"Didn't you like the rest of it?" he asks.

I ignore his question, sitting down at my desk again. "Did Charlotte tell Bree about, you know, what happened . . . ?"

"What does it matter?"

"It matters," I say.

"Not really," Foster says in a low voice. *No! No!* the man in the background cries. *It's the other file, Grace!*

"Who's Grace?" I ask.

Foster laughs. "Someone in the office. It doesn't matter if our daughters know we like each other," he persists. "This isn't Victorian England."

I tap on my computer keypad nervously. "It's just that I'm leaving," I tell him.

There's a tiny but sharp intake of air. "You're leaving? Where are you going?"

"Texas. To my parents' for a while. I'm taking a sabbatical."

"A sabbatical?"

We listen to the still air.

"What about the kids?" he asks, just like they all do.

"Hunter is coming," I explain. "Charlotte is staying. That's why I don't want any gossip about us pulsing through the school like an out-of-control blood clot."

There is more silence on the other end. "Very pretty imagery," Foster finally says. He pauses again. "Bree doesn't know anything."

"That's not what Charlotte says."

"She doesn't know from me, anyway."

We burn through more cell phone minutes in silence.

"Well, so long, then," Foster finally says.

"I would think you'd want to wish me a good trip."

"I don't."

I stare at the photo of Phoenix. She smiles at me, perhaps encouraging me not to put an end to things, as she has done.

"I'm sure we'll see each other again," I tell Foster.

"I'm not," he replies.

"Okay, then."

"Is there anything I can do to help you?" he asks, softening.

Let me count the ways, I think. "No," I say.

"Charlotte can stay with us for a while," he suggests. "Now that she and Bree are friends."

"Not necessary," I tell him quickly, before I realize it sounds ungracious. "She'll be staying next door at Marge's."

"She might see some sex over there, too," Foster suggests.

"It's not about that," I protest.

"Listen, Kate," he says. "Despite your seeing our relationship as a blood clot, I want you to know I really enjoy your company. Very much." I hear him breathe in, then exhale. "I'll miss you," he says. "I like the way you fight with me."

"Typical lawyer line," I tell him.

He laughs, and I think we're finished, but something in my foolish heart softens.

I hang up, thinking how Foster and I seem incapable of speaking without cross words. So different from with Kyle, who never liked fighting with me. I always made an effort to be pleasant, even when he irritated or angered me. Was I keeping my inner bitch from Kyle, and this is why, perhaps, now my outer bitch seems so immense?

I find Jack sitting still in his office in a contemplative pose, like Rodin's *The Thinker*. He's half hidden behind his steel desk, staring at a piece of paper. Fluorescent lighting shines off the top of his head, making his yellow hair seem transparent. He looks ephemeral, almost holy. I warm at the very sight of him.

"Saint Jack," I say. "Patron saint of the three-point turn."

He looks up, smiling.

"I'm here to order my pizzas," I tell him. "The family would like you to deliver promptly," I add.

Jack laughs. "A motley crew, your family," he says, and I wonder if he's thinking about large Marge, my dear friend, or Ren of the droopy pants, or maybe Hunter's ketchup bottles. "But it was fun," Jack adds, and I believe him. "Besides, I never got to take you to that tapas place."

Sadness twists my gut unexpectedly, then gently lands on my heart. Can I really live with my mother, so far away from a crazy wonderful friend like Jack? My mother is another brand of crazy, but not the warm, fun, thoughtful brand. My father reads his newspapers. I hear myself sigh, and find Jack studying me. So far, the only plus side of going to Texas is that it's not Appleton.

"I heard," Jack says, pulling me back to the room. "You naughty, naughty girl."

My hand flies to my mouth. "You heard?" I ask. "Already?"

Jack just looks at me.

"Oh, my God! The gossip around here is on speed dial! You can't do a thing without it being dissected over lunch."

"What?" Pink flushes through Jack's white jawbones.

"I know you didn't want me to go out with him, and maybe I should have listened to you. But come on, Jack! I know you didn't say it because you yourself wanted to jump my bones. Hah! That's just ridiculous!'

Jack's mouth is hanging open now.

"I never meant for things to progress to the point where Charlotte and Ren found me buttoning up after bonking Bree Willis's father in the family playroom . . ." I wring my hands.

Jack's eyes seem to be boring holes into mine now. "I didn't know you were bonking Bree Willis's father," he says.

"Huh?"

"Only that you were taking a sabbatical."

"Only . . . that?" I stand there staring at my friend. Were I to take my temperature in this excruciating moment, the mercury would burst. I squeeze my hands together tightly, glance at the door. There is no dignified escape.

"Damn," Jack says, leaning back in his chair. "Well, you're right about one thing. I wasn't thinking of jumping your bones. That is just so-o-o-o ridiculous."

I try to read Jack's face, try to understand his placid expression. Is he playing with me, or confirming what I always thought was true? That we are friends, nothing more.

Suddenly Jack flashes his trademark grin. "Though if forced at gunpoint to jump your bones," he muses aloud, "I guess I could get through it."

I can only endure his taunting for another second. Then I will melt into his industrial carpeting. Not that I don't deserve this.

"Well, well, well," he goes on.

"You should talk," I mutter, attempting to defend myself. "You with your harem of hotties in the hallways. It's different when you're the poor widow."

"I don't bed the harem of hotties," he assures me. "Whereas you've gone to bed with Bree Willis's father."

"Not to bed," I correct him. "To the TV room."

Jack laughs. I must be such fun to tease.

"What did you watch?"

"Jack!"

"Kate," he says. He's done with the taunting. I watch him take a deep breath, modeling maturity and calmness now. "No one is judging you. No one *cares* who you sleep with." He smiles unconvincingly. "Except maybe if it's Bree Willis's father."

This time I laugh, too. Then Jack gets up from his chair and takes me into his arms. I inhale his minty countenance as he hugs me close. "Now, as for your leaving Appleton," he breathes into my ear. "That I'm not so crazy about."

I press close into Jack's nicely tailored cotton shirt and feel my eyes begin to leak. Jack! What would I have done at this high school without him? I'm about to tell him I'll miss him, and that maybe I'll come back, not just to get Charlotte, but to stay. But then someone begins banging on the door.

"Mr. Hayes? Mr. Hayes!"

Jack's arms drop like two sacks of grain. We turn and see the bright eyes of a future driver of America peering through the door glass. A ponytail swings in indignation. "Remember we, like, have a *class* and stuff now?"

I can't help but smile. "Good luck with, like, your class and stuff," I whisper to Jack, before heading for the door. I nod politely at the ponytailed lass on my way out, but she just glares at me, another kid Charlotte's age who doesn't like me. It must run in their jeans.

TWENTY-FIVE

On the Road with Mr. Heinz

The miscarriage resonates like another loss. Even though none of us has met Alphonse's girlfriend, we will now never meet his baby. There are only the four of us left in New Frontiers, yet in this moment the room feels too full. Our little crew sits quietly in a circle drawn tighter. Phoenix's couch has been strategically moved, pushed against a wall outside the circle, intentionally stacked with catalogs and manila folders, so as to suggest another use. It has become Mrs. Cavanaugh's filing space—a more neutral role for the highly charged piece of furniture. In my own mind I think of it as the dead people's couch—first Kyle's favorite place to lounge, then Phoenix's.

Alphonse looks uncomfortable, slumped in a school chair, trying to explain his feelings to us. "She didn't have no warning, man," he says. "And then she just began to start . . . bleeding."

They all shift uncomfortably. With Phoenix gone, I am the only female left in New Frontiers. Talking to your friends about women's bleeding is one thing, but talking about it in front of an adult woman must be truly hard. Miscarriages are an adult thing. So should be pregnancies. Alphonse has waded into a grown-up world that is over his head, and now I watch him struggle to swim. "She's fifteen, man," he says. "I had to go visit her in a ward full of old ladies who had just had their babies."

Old ladies, I think. If the women were twice his girlfriend's age, it would make them only thirty.

"That sucks," Hector whispers, looking down at his bazillion-dollar sneakers.

"It must have been very hard to do," I say, and they all look up at me, waiting for me to deliver them from their pain, Alphonse with his flushed, puffy face, Adam with his fierce, intelligent eyes, Hector with gold chains gleaming at his throat.

"What do you think about Alphonse going to the hospital?" I ask the others.

"It means he's a man," says Hector.

"As opposed to being a homo. Is that it?" Adam mutters, but we all hear him.

Hector's jaw muscles flex. This isn't what he'd meant. Adam's self-contempt seems to grow by the minute. Since Phoenix's death, he has been beating up boys who look at him wrong inside the boy's locker room. But Hector would not be one of those boys. Hector is many things, but not homophobic.

"I think Hector is saying that going to the hospital was the right thing," I tell Adam. "Am I correct, Hector, that this is what you want to say to Alphonse?"

"I heard you were leaving," Adam says, glaring at me. His square jaw is locked in fury. Before I can recover from my surprise, Adam adds, "That would be typical around this fucking place, wouldn't it?"

I am sorry I allow these students to curse. It seems to pull the plug on a colony of anger that lives just beneath their skin.

"Please watch your language," I tell Adam, and watch his head drop, the closest thing to an apology I receive today. All eyes are on me now. I can even feel the eyes of Phoenix gazing down at our proceedings.

I shift in my chair a bit. My kids' beautiful faces look alabaster beneath the fluorescent lighting, even Hector's.

"I love you all so much," I tell them honestly, a breach of counseling etiquette and failure of technique, but who cares about etiquette and technique when little parts of the world are crashing down?

"It's true," I tell them. "I need to take some time, but I feel awful about leaving our group."

My stricken group stares at me, their faces all confusion.

"Did someone die in your family, *mami*?" Hector asks.

How to answer this? They all look down at the school carpet, dissatisfied with my silence.

"I won't leave you in a lurch," I promise. "There'll be someone very, very good to continue meeting with you."

"Who?" asks Adam.

"Maybe Mr. Johnson?" I'm making this up, but I can ask him later. "He's wonderful, you know," I tell my group.

Adam sighs loudly and crosses his arms. Hector's knee bounces up and down like a Ping-Pong ball. I imagine Tom Johnson welcoming these sad vagabonds into his birdcage of love, then leaving the cage door open. How many of them will fly away?

"Why?" asks Alphonse.

I can't answer this question, either.

"Dude," Hector says. "Does that mean your beautiful girl is leaving, too?"

Two days later, Charlotte watches me wheel a suitcase through the kitchen on the night before I will lock up our house and send her over to Marge's. She's sitting at the counter, staring at something on her laptop while she's really watching me. She hasn't offered a hand on my last few trips to the garage as I've hauled bags and valises and toys to the car. She will not lift a finger to assist. She wants no part of this departure. The calls were made yesterday to the utility and phone companies. Charlotte acted like she didn't hear them.

Paper cartons and plastic soup containers litter the space around her. Chinese leftovers will be thrown out rather than stored, as the electricity will be shut off in the morning. Charlotte narrows her eyes at a canvas tote on the far end of the counter, burgeoning with empty ketchup bottles. "On the road with Mr. Heinz," she says. "You think Grandma Lynne will be happy to see those?" She sips hard on a straw until it makes rude noises.

I drop the handle of the huge suitcase and walk to her. "Honey," I say, hugging her rigid shoulders, "you can change your mind, you know. You can come with us."

She shrugs off my embrace. "Earth to Mom," she says coldly.

"It's, like, the middle of the school year. All people who are not ridiculous are going to school."

This from my formerly truant daughter. I remember what Tom had said about accepting her the way she is. I hug her again.

"It'll only be for a little while," I tell her.

"How long?" she demands, because she knows I can't answer this.

I take her by the hand and gently pull her from the kitchen stool. She lets me lead her into the TV room, the room where most of her happiest childhood moments are stored, somewhere in the studs and drywall. Her daddy reading to her as she sits on his lap. Plates of celery sticks and chocolate milk served to her by her happy mommy as she stares, glaze-eyed, at *Sesame Street*. I want to talk to her here, in a place where she feels safe, and loved, and secure.

"Sit," I say, pulling her onto my lap as we fall onto the couch. We haven't been in here much since Charlotte discovered Foster Willis on the couch. Only Hunter has used this room, his safe hideaway with Arthur and Dora and Handy Manny. Charlotte smells like egg rolls and baby shampoo as she leans her skittish body against my shoulder. All the softness of her baby body is long gone; it is like holding a colt in my arms. "Remember when Daddy and you made a book in here for my Mother's Day present?" I ask her. "You drew all those pretty pictures and Daddy sewed them together with needle and thread?"

"That was Aunt Margie's idea," Charlotte says. "I heard her talking to him about it."

"When?"

"When you were at work or at school or something. Aunt Margie used to come over all the time."

I try to understand her answer. When I was at school? As in graduate school, perhaps? Aunt Margie was over all the time? Maybe this is just Charlotte deliberately trying to goad me.

I shake off my ruminations, stroke my daughter's hair. "Your father was as proud of that book as you were," I say. I think I can see her smile, even though half her face is turned from me. "But the mess he left in this room! Do you remember, Charlie?"

I tense a little. I'm not supposed to call her Charlie. But Charlotte again doesn't protest. No fireworks. "There was glue on that old floral couch," I continue in a singsong voice. "And you'd gotten marker all over the walls. And tiny bits of paper and thread were all over the carpet."

"He always did whatever Aunt Margie asked him to," is all my daughter answers. "It was like they were married or something."

My vision blurs slightly, almost as if my eyes are attempting to adjust to something new. In eight hours I will be driving very far away from this child, with her brother in the backseat of the minivan. Charlotte will be crossing our front lawn to the house of our neighbor, Kyle's and my friend, a woman with the face of a horse and the body of a linebacker. A woman with a huge, generous, and loving heart. How loving?

I think of Thomas, of course. Her geek one-night stand.

Charlotte's stockinged feet curl up like a kitten's onto my lap, and suddenly she becomes very small again. I stroke my girl's hair, my fingers cascading through the long silky strands of her father's black hair. "Honey," I say again. "You can always change your mind and come with us. Grandma Lynn and Grandpa would love it."

"That's okay," she says, not looking at me. "I'm used to being on my own."

Marge is still in her robe, arms crossed across lace I wouldn't expect from her, as she stands in my driveway with Charlotte beside her. The sky is still smudged with remnants of night, although the sun peeks, wanly now, from the branches of Marge's dogwood tree. Hunter is slumped in sleep in his car seat. In my rearview mirror, he looks like a beanbag doll carelessly slapped into a bucket. He'd hardly awakened for the transfer from bed to car. He threw his arms around Charlotte in half sleep, though, and clung to his Sissy like a baby baboon during her long, teary good-bye. I put the car in reverse, but hesitate to begin my descent down the driveway. My daughter stands in her pajamas, waving and crying. How does a mother leave a scene like this?

She just does, I tell myself. I throw a kiss, then slowly inch backward down the drive. "Good-bye!" Marge calls. "Drive safe and call us tonight."

"Wait!" my daughter shouts, loud enough to awaken the whole neighborhood at five-fifteen in the morning. She is running now by the side of the minivan, her sweatpants flapping, looking every inch like the athlete I'll see no more this season on the soccer field.

"Wait!" she shouts again, but I've already stopped the car, pulled on the emergency brake, swung the door open, stepped onto the pavement in my floppy clogs. She flings herself at me, her T-shirt rising, her turtle tattoo visible, her arms catching around my neck. "I want to go with you," she says, her hot breath in my ear. "Mommy, I want to come."

TWENTY-SIX

Flying

K yle is riding shotgun again as the miles fly past us on the Mass Pike. We've left hours later than planned, but who could ask for a more beautiful autumn day? Kyle and I smile at each other, listening to our beautiful loving children behind us. We sneak peeks at them in the rearview mirror. There they are, rosy with excitement, big smiles on their faces. Do they feel their father's presence in the front seat? I make myself believe that they do. We're giddy with our escape, like four convicts in a prison break.

"Here's the church," Charlotte is telling her brother in a sing-song car voice. "Here's the steeple." In the mirror I see her hands laced, two index fingers pointing skyward, Hunter grinning madly.

"Open it u-u-u-u-p . . ."

Hunter's eyes twinkle with anticipation.

". . . and see the friggin' people!"

"Friggin' people!" Hunter repeats, waving his fingers like a mad scientist. Naughty word, I know, but how long has it been since I've heard him laugh like this? It's tickle-fit laughter, full of gulping and abandon. It's medicine for their dead father's and my soul.

"Sissy, more!" Hunter gasps.

Red-and-gold-dappled hills flash by our windows as we make our escape. My heart feels a hundred pounds lighter. All the nay-sayers were wrong. I should have put the kids in the car and left

Appleton two years ago. We've lifted ourselves out of the black hole we've inhabited since Kyle's death. He's even come along for the ride. Hunter swings his ketchup bottle around his head like he's flying a plane. A few minutes later, he and Charlotte are playing some kind of rock, paper, scissors game, with lots of palm-slapping and screeching. The sun warms our faces. Hunter looks dehydrated with glee.

"Anyone ready for lunch?" I ask.

"I am!" my happy son screeches. "Let's get friggin' lunch!"

The minute we park at the service area, Charlotte is on her cell phone trying to call Ren. A dark cloud forms above her when he doesn't pick up.

"He's probably at school," I tell her, and she gives me a withering look.

"Where, like, maybe I should be," she mutters. She walks ahead of Hunter and me, her pert little butt bobbing up and down righteously. The October sun still shines on us, but the climate is changing abruptly.

"I'll have a salad," Charlotte says, staring up at the giant McDonald's menu. Then she disappears into the ladies' room with her backpack. When she comes out again, she's wearing full Goth makeup. She looks like an angry little mime. Hunter and I are already wary, hiding behind our lunch trays at the table.

"Did you reach Ren?" I ask.

"That would be my business," she says. There are tears in her eyes. She grabs her salad, still in the bag. "I'll eat this in the car," she says.

"I know you miss him, but he'll call you soon." I tentatively pat her hand. "I'm sure of it."

"Mom! Just, like, stay out of it, okay?" She is almost screaming. Surrounding diners stare. Hunter is quiet again. He's pulled a shade down on his face. He puts his Happy Meal toy on the table in front of his ketchup bottle. He and I proceed to the car like we are walking through a mine field.

Charlotte crams Kyle's ghost out of the shotgun seat. She no longer wishes to sit with her stupid brother. She wants me to have a full view of her misery. She wants me to understand what I have done to her by separating her from her boyfriend. I turn over the engine.

"I wanna get OUT OF THIS SEAT!" Hunter yells from the backseat.

"Jesus Christ! Would you, like, put a sock in that damn kid's mouth?"

Charlotte glares down at her lap, her mascara-gunked lashes casting angry shadows on her cheekbones. I glance at the dashboard clock. We're fifty-five minutes into our thirty-hour road trip.

"No car seat!" Hunter screams, oblivious to his sister's comments. We pull out of the Sturbridge service area on the Massachusetts Turnpike, the bright plastic action figure in my son's hand doing nothing to appease him.

"Don't *wanna* go driving!" Hunter hollers. I see it's not just Charlotte's mood that's upsetting him. It's dragging this kid from the magic of McDonald's, back to the purgatory of a car seat. I should have thought of this when planning this adventure. It occurs to me suddenly that I've never taken Hunter on a long car trip before. We stopped doing things like that when Kyle died. Now I understand that he sucks at it, unlike his sister, who used to drop off as if injected by a narcotic the minute the engine turned over. Cars whiz by us as we travel in the slow lane. It seems the safest lane to travel in while your family is disintegrating.

"Why don't you go back there and try to entertain him?" I ask Charlotte. She sits, flushed, trying to eat the McDonald's salad on her lap. The opened foil packet of her Caesar's dressing has dribbled onto her sweatpants. Why she is eating salad is beyond me. If anything, Charlotte looks alarmingly thin. I have only now noticed it, probably because she is sitting beside me. No one's knees should be that bony, even if you are a fourteen-year-old Goth goalie girl. I shudder as a thought wanders, uninvited, through my head. What if my daughter is anorexic or bulimic? Fear that she is makes me want to throw up myself. What will my mother think?

"I wanna get OUT of here!" Hunter screams—a complete sentence, I note. Perhaps this trip is having an unintentionally positive effect on him. I gun the car around an old lady going forty-five, her snowy head just cresting the steering wheel, the bumper sticker on her ancient yellow Neon reading EAT MY DUST.

"Hunter, please stop shouting," I tell him calmly. "We all want to get out of here, but we have to drive some more to do it." *Like nineteen hundred miles*, I think.

"No!" he says.

"Why don't you shut the fuck up!" his sister barks.

That does it for me.

I flick on my directional and yank the car roughly toward the shoulder. We bump and jerk to a rough stop in the breakdown lane and I'm ready, then, to break down. The car stinks of fried food and adrenaline. My hands are shaking in their gripped position on the wheel. How are we supposed to get to Texas like this?

I shift roughly into park. Thanks to my driving, Charlotte's lap is a bed of romaine lettuce. Her skin is pale and her mouth is open. Her tongue stud winks, and I wonder what my parents will think of this, too. Before I speak, I breathe in deeply, then exhale slowly. *Think*, I tell myself. *Think before you speak.* It is not hard to figure this situation out. Sitting very still, staring at my own hands, I suddenly reflect on the power that parents are given. They can refuse to have their children vaccinated, make them eat whole-wheat products, drive them without explanation to the other side of the country. No one will stop them, as no one has stopped me. I have not forced Charlotte to come on this trip, yet she glares at me with her usual adolescent loathing, and I am at a loss to understand who should be angry with whom. We listen in silence to the traffic *shoosh*ing by, each of us afraid to initiate the conversation to come. Yet here we are, on the shoulder of the Mass Pike. Someone must say something.

"Charlotte," I finally manage, when I think I've sufficiently collected myself. "First of all, you are never to use that language in this car, and certainly not when addressing your brother."

The storm cloud centers itself over Charlotte's head again, yet I continue.

"I want you to think about how much effort I have expended since five-thirty this morning," I say, "when you suddenly decided to come with us. Think about how I packed with you, then repacked the car, then dealt with Hunter, who had to wait for us, then called your school. I was set to leave at five-thirty. Because of you, we left at eleven."

Charlotte looks down at the salad in her lap and begins picking at vegetation. I can smell her resentment over the aromas of spilled dressing and hard-boiled eggs.

"Why have you decided to come," I ask, "if all you can do is complain?"

Charlotte flings a large romaine leaf into the Styrofoam plate, the way she'd like to fling her mother out the car door. At least Hunter's quiet. He is always quiet when we fight. He's become a keen observer of mother-daughter angst.

"Maybe I came because it's weird to be left behind while your mother's having her little breakdown," Charlotte says after a minute.

"Charlotte!" We glare at each other from our car seats. My ability to communicate evaporates like dew from a blade of grass. I want to smack her, pour her salad over her head. "That is unfair and you know it," I manage to say.

"No, I don't know it," she says, eyes flashing, tears suddenly puddling on her bottom lids. "Are you saying it's, like, *not* unfair that my mother wants to run away in the middle my school year? And why?" She looks me full in the face now. "Why are we making this trip? What do Grandma Lynne and Grandpa have that's gonna . . . *fix* you?"

"How . . . dare . . . you," I seethe. And then, instead of counting to ten, or counting the whizzing cars racing past our unhappy family, I let her have it. "*You're* the one who needs fixing!" I shout.

"Mama!" Hunter cries, but I am unstoppable, Tom Johnson be damned.

"What do you think Grandma Lynn will think of your tongue?" I ask her. "Think she'll like that stud in there? Do you think anyone does?"

"Mama," Hunter calls again, even more pitifully.

"And how about the goddamn turtle tattoo? Huh?"

"How about your stupid boyfriend?" she shrieks. "Are you gonna have sex at Grandma Lynn's house, too?"

"Don't talk to me about sex, young lady!" I yell. "Not when I find you in Hunter's bunk bed with Ren. And not when you're cock-teasing guys twenty years older than you on MySpace, okay? You're lucky you haven't heard back from any chain saw murderers—"

"Stay out of my business!" Charlotte shouts. "If you could possibly even *imagine* respecting my privacy, we wouldn't be, like, having this conversation, would we?"

"Respect your *privacy*?"

I am incredulous. My head is spinning faster than the traffic. "If I stayed out of your business," I say, though I know it's a mistake, just as this conversation is a mistake, just as this entire road trip is a mistake, "you'd probably be on the street by now! You dress and act like a middle school hooker! You're out of *control*, Charlotte. You're . . ."

I watch how her eyes are widening.

"You're a total pain in the ass!" I conclude.

She has her hand on the door handle, same way she does when I drop her off in front of the high school. She's squeezing it so hard her knuckles are white. "Why don't you hit me again!" she finally screams. Then she pulls on the handle, opens the car door, and runs.

To where? I'm wondering. I stare through the window as her retreating back grows smaller and smaller, until I see her entering the tall brush that begins where the mowed grass ends. Where is she going? Where does a person go when the edge of the road ends?

Down. She's gone down. Charlotte has disappeared into a sea of autumn foliage where the landscape drops off sharply, seeming to swallow her, seeming to swallow my only daughter whole.

"Where's Sissy?" Hunter cries, struggling against his seat belt, rocking his car seat back and forth like a bumper car. The heater fan is blowing hot air in my face, while the cold air from Charlotte's open door stabs at my arms and legs. I leap outside, slide open the minivan's long passenger door, and hurry to get to Hunter. He's already gotten himself half unbuckled. I unbuckle the rest of him at a furious speed, his hot breath on my face while I work. Lifting him into my arms, I begin to run. His long legs flap against my thigh and his weight pulls me down, but I run anyway, over the uneven dead grass, my clogs crunching its thin layer of leaves, my eyes fixed on the dip in the landscape and the tree line after, the place where my daughter has disappeared.

"Where we going?" Hunter cries. But then he abruptly stops as we make our descent down the gully, too stunned to continue, or maybe too winded by the roughness of his transport. We enter the wooded area and it is like plunging into a dark fairy tale. A light switch for the sunny autumn afternoon has been shut off. Gray shadows lay upon even the most colorful foliage. Nothing but foil candy wrappers and broken glass bottles glitters in this new world, litter hurled there by careless travelers or teenage lovers. Charlotte is not even a murky form in the maze of trees. I hike Hunter farther up my hip and run faster. My ribs hurt when I exhale, and sharp pain jabs at my shoulders like a sudden bolt of lightning. "Charlotte!" I hear my winded voice calling. "Charlotte, where are you?"

"Where *are* you?" Hunter mimics loudly. I turn to look at him and this is when it happens. First I notice how my charging foot refuses to move, locked behind a tree root or something else I cannot see in the fallen leaves. Then I'm pitching forward on my knees as Hunter sails from my arms like a football. I see the small bulk of him flying ahead of me, then landing in the leaves with a sickening thud.

"Ooof," Hunter says softly, then nothing else. Then he just lies on his face in his red jacket, one more colorful leaf on the forest floor.

TWENTY-SEVEN

We Are Family

It's almost as if she could smell the blood. Charlotte is standing over me as I turn Hunter over, blood covering my fingers, spilling in the spaces between them, warm and viscous and copious. "Hunter!" she screams. It's almost as if she's magically reappeared. "Oh, my God! Hunter!" she says.

She is clasping her hands in front of her, crying.

"Are you happy now?" I seethe at her. Hunter stares up at us with frightened eyes. The blood seems to be coming from his mouth, or is it a nosebleed? I quickly sit him up.

"You're not supposed to do that!" Charlotte sobs. "What if his back is hurt?"

Leaves are falling around us, whisked through the air by a cutting wind. Hunter is silent, eyes wide, blood dripping down his chin. I tear off my sweatshirt and hold the hem of it to his mouth. I gently press, holding him in his sitting position with my other hand on his back.

"Are you all right, honey?" I ask. "Tell Mommy if you're all right."

The wind rips the air again, traveling low across the forest floor. Goose bumps rise on my bare arms. Hunter shivers in his light jacket. There is blood in his hair, fringing his bangs like Halloween makeup. I am dizzy with fear as the sweatshirt grows dark and soggy with it. "Mommy's going to pick you up now and take you back to the car," I tell him. I press him into my shoulder as I carry him carefully toward the light. He is stiff in my arms, like a doll. "Everything's fine now," I tell him, but he doesn't answer. I remember how they say that head wounds always bleed more. It doesn't necessarily mean anything serious, not always.

"Mommy," Charlotte whimpers, clambering behind me like a lamb. I don't even turn to look. I am that furious with her.

"Oh, Jesus Christ, hurry," I hear her say.

We crest the hill and there is the van, its doors ajar, keys still in the ignition. I place Hunter on Charlotte's lap in the back seat and slide the door closed. Now we are all covered in blood, the entire family. It feels as though it were meant to come to this, from the day that Kyle died. He never should have left me with his family. Not everyone is meant to raise and protect a family. Should I dial 911 on my cell phone, or would that be overreacting?

"Keep the sweatshirt pressed to his mouth," I instruct Charlotte, and then decide to just start driving, fast. The last thing I want to introduce into this day is a bout of police reports, police escorts, police anything. "We'll take you to see a nice doctor," I tell Hunter, bumping our car back into the closest lane, then the middle lane, then the fast one. "He'll make you all better in a jiffy." I am going eighty but it feels like we're standing still. In calm white letters, an approaching sign announces NEXT EXIT SEVENTEEN MILES.

I have a bleeding child in the backseat! I want to shout back at the sign. But the sign doesn't care.

"Are you all right, honey?" I call back to Hunter, and when he doesn't answer, I yell to Charlotte, "Is he all right?"

Charlotte doesn't say. Her T-shirt is saturated with blood. Hunter has pressed his cheek against his sister's small chest, where he appears to be resting peacefully, waiting for the rest of his life to unfold.

Following the blue square signs with the big white H has led me to Mercy Hospital, a rather haunted-looking brick edifice with a giant statue of the Blessed Virgin Mary out front, holding her hands aloft in welcome. I don't know what town we're in, or even what state; we could be in Connecticut by now or maybe we're still in Massachusetts. I can see the ambulances lined up by a glass door that says EMERGENCY. Good enough for me. I swoop the van into an empty spot that says NO PARKING, lift Hunter from his sister's arms while the engine's still running, and rush him through the glass doors, which automatically slide open for us. "Miss!" I hear a man's voice yelling behind me. "Miss! You can't leave your car here."

Bite me, I think. *My son is bleeding.* If they tow the car off, perhaps they'll tow Charlotte along with it. She can think about her behavior in some tow lot until I find out where she is. Hunter feels calm and peaceful in my arms as I run with him, but this could just be the loss of blood. A balding man in a green coat is rushing toward us. He takes my son from my arms and I follow, the two of us now running through sterile white corridors, through swinging doors, until we are in an area of many beds, each of them cloaked by cotton curtains, some drawn, others opened. The man in the green coat lays Hunter down on a stretcher with wheels in one of the empty cubicles, then immediately begins examining his mouth.

"Let's just get you cleaned up here a little bit," he murmurs to my son. "Nurse! Some gauze?"

Hunter looks up at me with fearful eyes as two giant strangers now mess with his mouth, washing and prodding and pressing. I squeeze his hand, which seems so small. This helps me to keep standing. Someone else, a third person, has attached what looks like a plastic clothespin to Hunter's finger, getting ready to measure something.

"It's all right, Hunter," a soft voice calls from behind me. I turn, surprised, and find Charlotte with her arms crossed over her bloody T-shirt. Her mascara has run like watery poster paint all down her cheeks. "It's gonna be fine, buddy," she tells her brother.

"Did you leave the car running?" I ask her.

She nods, but then I realize that I really don't care if the car is still running. It's almost as if we've been anxious all day for someone else to drive it away with our lives inside.

"He's going to need stitches," the man in the green coat informs us. I see now, by the shiny little name plaque on his lapel, that he is a doctor. "Is he allergic to any medications?" He looks at us with placid green eyes, waiting for me to respond. Hunter looks a little green himself.

"No," I hear myself utter.

"He's also lost his two front teeth, but they're baby teeth anyway, so that's not a problem."

"How many stitches?" I ask, though the voice seems to come from far away, from the place where I am floating above the tiny cubicle. The doctor runs a hand through his sparse hair, pushing back a sandy fringe on his forehead and revealing deep worry creases. He's no beginner, this doctor. At least we haven't gotten some intern who's afraid of blood.

As I am, I suddenly remember.

"Hard to say," the doctor says, his bloody thumb still on my son's chin. "The thing is, we'll have to restrain him for the procedure, so he doesn't move while we're stitching."

"Restrain him? As in strap him down?" Charlotte asks, her voice high and offended. "I highly doubt that, dude."

The nurse, a big woman with a careworn face, rests her hand on my daughter's shoulder and holds her in her gaze. "Looks like you and your mom have been through a really rough day, dear."

If she only knew the half of it, I think.

"Why don't I bring you to the waiting room now," she continues, "and you can rest."

"Don't think so," Charlotte says rudely but bravely.

"We'll take very good care of your brother. Promise."

No dice for my tough little toothpick with the crossed arms. Funny how the nurse knows Hunter is her brother. After all, there are ten years between them, and Charlotte looks even older than her age in her happy hooker makeup.

Now the nurse swings her head around to look at me. Apparently I am sitting down, though there is no chair beneath me. She grabs my arm, catches me, seats me on the end of the stretcher.

"You need to take some deep breaths," she says.

"Thithy," her brother calls from beneath the doctor's thumb.

"I'm right here, buddy," she tells him.

"How about you, dear?" the nurse asks me. "Could I walk you to the waiting room?"

. . .

It's not that I'm a bad mother, it really isn't. It's not that I don't want to be there to comfort my boy as they strap him down like Frankenstein and stick needles through his skin. It's just that I don't think I'll do much good in there, and he's asked for Sissy anyway. It's not my fault that I'm no good with blood; it's the way I was made, with a trip switch that drains my own blood from my brain the minute I see it flowing out of someone else. Charlotte is in there with him, and the truth is, this comforts me. She is a brave, good girl. A pierced, tattooed, venomous, but good girl. Just what my Hunter needs right now. His Sissy. I feel my anger at her draining, like blood from Hunter's mouth.

I move the minivan, then do the admittance paperwork in the waiting room, while sitting beneath a massive wooden crucifix. The clock on the wall makes grinding noises instead of ticking. There is a Latino family wringing their hands in the plastic chairs beside me. I sip terrible vending machine coffee with chemicals in it to make it white. It is what I deserve. I dropped my baby like a bag of groceries on the forest floor, and now he must go through this.

Charlotte comes through the swinging door with the air of a young intern. Her face looks sensitive and intelligent and the veneer of hardness just disguises her pain beneath. Her sweatpants are flapping against her thighs, and the perfectly round salad dressing stain on her knee looks like a target. The Latino family stares at her. My daughter flops into an orange plastic chair beside me and sighs.

"They gave him something to make him sleep," she says. "But he'll be waking up soon."

"Is he all right?"

"Yeah."

"How many stitches?"

"Three."

"Will there be scarring?"

She gazes at me, as if to ask, *What kind?*

I shoot from my chair like a bullet. "I want to see him. Let's go."

"Wait," Charlotte says, pulling me back into my seat by my sleeve. She leans over her own chair to speak softly into my ear. "I just want you to know they were, like, asking me questions," she says. "They were trying to see if . . . you know, if you, like . . . did this to Hunter."

"If I *what*?" I cry, too loudly.

"Don't *worry*," she says quickly, sounding worried herself. "I was, like, *Are you fucking crazy?*"

I cringe at my daughter's language.

"They checked him all over," she continues. "They even found dirt in his mouth. They totally know it was an accident. He was calling for you the whole time, until he got whacked by the drugs."

Tears are coursing down my face now, and the family beside us bow their heads in sympathy.

"A kid doesn't call for his mother if he thinks she's gonna beat him up," Charlotte says.

Now Charlotte is giving her mother lessons on traits of the abused child. I think about how I slapped her, only days ago. That slap set the scene for us, the one where we were running through a forest by the side of the highway. I cannot seem to stop crying. "Come on, Mom," Charlotte is saying, sounding scared. "I only wanted to tell you so you'd, like, know. Everything is okay now. Hunter is fine. When he wakes up we can go."

The family beside us has turned away. The boy stares at a TV mounted on the wall, where a metal plaque screwed at its base says MERCY HOSPITAL. *Have mercy on us*, I think, looking at the giant crucific. *We're only Cavanaughs.*

When Hunter is ready to leave, they have fed him Jell-O and applesauce and given him a soft blue pillowy ice pack to hold to his mouth. He seems cheerful in his bloody striped T-shirt and light red jacket. Little drops of blood on his sneakers have turned brown. The winking lights in their heels flash merrily as he walks toward me, holding the big nurse's hand.

"Mama," he says, in an ice-pack-muffled voice. His face is puffy beneath one eye, though the other side appears normal. I can't see the stitchwork with him holding up that thing to his mouth, but I'm not sure I want to anyway.

"Baby," I say, scooping him into my arms and hugging him close. "You're all better now! I'm so proud of my big boy."

"They gave me Jell-O," he says into my shoulder. "Red."

The nurse goes over a maintenance care sheet while I hold my son tightly. "Come over here to the desk and we'll check you out," she says. I carry Hunter with me.

"You're limping," she says.

This is news to me. I look down at my ankle, which now feels too swollen for the shoe, and remember the root that trapped my foot into place, and then the twist of the ankle, but not the pain. I must have forgotten to feel it when I saw my son bleeding.

The nurse is on her haunches, squatting over my foot, poking at it gently. "We could X-ray that ankle," she says, "so long as you're here anyway."

"No," I tell her. "No more today. I'm fine."

"Well," she says dubiously, "at least let me give you another ice pack. But when you get home, if it's still hurting or the swelling won't go down, you should call us, or come back in and see us."

I accept the second ice pack from the nurse, thank her again, then hobble quickly toward the hospital exit, Charlotte trailing behind us. When I get home, if it still hurts, I can call her. She should only know that home, in the Cavanaughs' case, is a place with the heat on low, so the pipes won't burst during the long months of winter. Home is an empty refrigerator and a heart loaded for bear, every time my daughter or I open our mouths. We're certainly not going home, not even after this. But am I really going to strap my son into his bloody car seat and head on out to Texas?

I think about this, limping through the parking lot. The sun has all but exited the late afternoon sky and the crisp breeze we felt in the breakdown lane has turned nasty. My stomach rumbles with hunger and my ankle, for the first time I have noticed, hurts like a son of a bitch. None of us wanted to go to Texas anyway.

Hunter's face looks trusting and loopy, like the druggie he is, as I strap him into his car seat. He smiles at me benevolently, lowering the ice pack and exposing his stitched puffy lip, the gap in his mouth where the teeth used to be. "Where we going, Mama?" he asks.

"That's, like, a good question," his sister says with a sigh from the front seat. The ironic tone and breathy sigh make her sound just like Kyle when she says it.

And suddenly I know where we are going.

TWENTY-EIGHT

Skull and Bones Club

Kyle's parents have always lived in New Haven, and it seems they will stay there, despite the lure of warm-weather retirement communities that would offer them an easier life in their twilight years. They raised Kyle and his brother in the Gothic shadows of the Yale campus, surrounded by rich students' expensive sports cars with out-of-state plates that often were parked in his parents' residential spaces. There is a certain kind of toughness necessary for living in a town like New Haven, two or three blocks from the Skull and Bones Club. You have to be scrappy and fight for your parking. You have to teach your children to work hard in school and not expect that, just because a world-class Ivy League institution borders your backyard, you will be transferred from a New Haven high school to Yale University by mere proximity. Kyle's parents taught him well. He left his New Haven high school for Boston College instead of Yale, and as a result of this met me.

I'd taken a summer job at the Appleton Memorial Hospital just after graduating high school. My duties were mercifully removed from blood and open wounds, just part-time work doing preliminary intake at the Orthopedic Imaging Center. The patients would enter my little antechamber—a corridor, really, between the waiting room and the stacks of hospital johnnies waiting in the changing rooms—where I would check their computer records and double-check their health insurance carriers. It didn't take a Ph.D. to do the job, only good hearing, a clean white blouse, and fast fingers.

Once, a tired-looking old man with his arm in a sling was sitting on the other side of my glass cage, wringing out the brim of his woolen hat while I asked him, "Who should the hospital call in the event of an emergency?" I'd asked this question of hundreds before him, never even looking up from my computer screen.

"No one," the little man answered, and this time I looked up.

"Is there a next of kin?" I asked.

"No."

"A friend?"

"No."

The old man was still worrying the brim of his hat, and realized I had no more questions to ask him. I think that might have been the day I decided to become a counselor. While in my yearbook I'd professed to a future career in advertising and copywriting, the little man with the sad eyes and stooped shoulders and ruined hat taught me something I hadn't learned in all my years of living, having even been raised by my wandering father and distant mother. That some people in this world had no one. That loneliness, despite the existence of sophisticated medical technology, was incurable.

"Mom, are we almost there?" Charlotte asks, interrupting my reverie as the minivan hurls itself down 95 South.

"Almost," I tell her, patting her bony knee. Then I ask, the way you only can in a moving car, "Did you know that I met your father at a hospital?"

Charlotte, who has been sweet and cooperative since the accident, rolls her eyes.

"I know, I know," she says. "He, like, broke his arm or something."

"Right," I say. "He, like, broke his arm or something."

Behind us we hear the soft wheezing of Hunter, sleeping off his codeine.

"You were wonderful with your brother at the hospital today," I tell her.

She stares straight ahead through the window into night. Highway lights flash by, outlining her profile in silver filigree. "Whatever," she says, but she squeezes her hands in her lap, and the trace of a smile tightens her lips.

By the time we exit 95, both my children are sleeping. Their heads loll sideways in their dreamland states, and I am filled with an irrational hope that I can protect them forever. I circle the streets of the Cavanaughs' neighborhood, half looking for the impossible parking spot, half not wanting to park at all. So many memories on these streets. The lit windows seem to be hiding him somewhere behind the thick brownstone walls. The sidewalks themselves seem haunted with the presence of my Kyle. Not his ghost but my real Kyle. I pass a corner convenience store, a ripped canvas canopy and Greek letters painted on the glass, and almost expect the door to fly open and for him to walk out. We'd found chicken broth in there one Thanksgiving Day, when Kyle's mother was getting ready to make the gravy and discovered she'd had none. I can still feel the sting the air held, see the afternoon's blue sky as Kyle and I walked to that store. I can feel the weight of his arm on my shoulder, the healthy huff of his breath beside me. Only it wasn't healthy enough, and maybe too huffy already. How old had Kyle been that day we bought the broth? Thirty-five? Thirty-six? We wouldn't have believed God Himself if He'd told us that day that Kyle was in the final years of his life.

I circle past the convenience store one more time, its maroon canvas flapping where the canopy is torn, and decide to give up. I call Kyle's parents on my cell, tell them we'll be double-parking in front of their apartment, ask them to be there to bring in Hunter. Minutes later, the van door is sliding open and exclamations of tenderness are competing with the chill night air.

"My beautiful Charlotte," Emily Cavanaugh exclaims, pulling my crumpled daughter with her studded tongue and her turtle tramp stamp into her arms. Hunter is being unbuckled by the strong and sturdy hands of his grandfather, and then he is lifted with his fat lip into the world and against Kyle Sr.'s flannel chest.

"Thithy. My iceth pack," he calls, sounding startled. Charlotte reaches into the backseat and retrieves it for him. Bags are removed and placed on the sidewalk.

"I'll be back in a jiffy," I tell them, feeling rescued and suddenly teary-eyed. I cry so hard I can hardly see, as I circle the blocks again, looking for parking.

Maybe the neighborhood where I finally find parking is a bad one. It is hard to tell at night, even harder to tell if you don't care. I walk in a numbed state past boarded-up windows and storefronts locked behind metal grating. I pass an old woman wrapped in scarves, pushing a wire shopping cart. The world appears to belong to only her and me. I listen to the sound of my dumb L. L. Bean clogs, the very ones that tripped me in the woods, clip-clopping against the empty sidewalks. My ankle sends sharp stabbing pains up my leg with each step. I'd forgotten about that ankle until now. I'm grateful for its discomfort. It is an odd assurance that I am not entirely numb. Clip-clop-ouch. Clip-clop-ouch. I breathe in a mouthful of the evening's frigid air. Unwise though it may be, I let my mind travel to my nice warm Dutch Colonial in Appleton, the swing set in the back, the fireplace in the living room. I can see Charlotte's soccer equipment all over the kitchen. Hunter's toys in the big green toy box. The race-car beds, Kyle's and my king-sized bed in our toasty yellow bedroom with the bamboo shades. It's all there waiting for us. Yet here I am, limping through a bad neighborhood in New Haven.

On a whim I pull my cell phone from my pocket and dial Marge. I let the phone ring until it goes to her voice mail, astonished that she is not picking up. Isn't it Marge's role in life to *always* be there? I leave her a short message, meant to be funny. "Are you busy putting out the blaze at our house?" I ask. "Is that why you're not answering?"

What a dumb thing to say on someone's voice mail. If our house in Appleton were ever to really burn down, I'd be devastated. Possibly more than the kids, even. A tickle travels up my neck as I realize this is true. I hang up and punch in another number. I'm standing on a dark corner, staring at a red traffic light as the phone begins ringing.

"Foster Willis," a voice says. The light turns green, but I just stand there. It feels nice to lean on the good foot and take pressure off my ankle. It feels nice to hear his voice.

"I need a lawyer to help me with an insanity defense," I say.

"Kate? Is that you?"

"Yup," I say, noticing that I'm really cold now.

"Where are you?"

"That's where the insane part comes in," I say, and then I find myself telling him about my long, demented day, shivering now, with a pawnshop behind me and a traffic light in front of me.

"Does this mean that you like me?" he asks when I am finished describing breakdown lanes, hospitals, stitches.

"Did Bree have a soccer game today?" I ask, imagining my own daughter in her bright orange shirt, the bushes turned scarlet on the edges of the field, the patent leather sheen of Charlotte's black hair beneath the afternoon sun.

"Objection," he says. "Nonresponsive answer."

Fair enough, I think. The light turns red again and I gather my jacket closer around me, reflecting on Foster Willis's question. Do I like this man, or is he only attractive because he is there on the other end of the phone? My phone clicks in the way that means someone else is trying to reach me. "I have to go," I tell Foster Willis. "I'll call you back."

"When?"

"Soon."

"Kate?" he asks before we disconnect. "Are you all right?"

"That's a hard question to answer," I say. "It is possible I haven't been all right in a very long time."

"I hate to say I told you so."

Then don't, I think, smiling as I press the flash button.

It's my father-in-law. He sounds frantic for such an ordinarily calm man. "Where are you?" he asks, just like Foster Willis did.

"I'm almost there," I tell him, glancing around for landmarks, hoping I am right.

"Didn't you hear me, dear, when I said to just park in the church lot? The one right across the street?"

"I didn't," I confess.

"We've been worried sick," he says. "I could have moved the car for you in the morning."

"Don't worry about me," I tell him in a chipper voice, clip-clop-ouching hurriedly now through a red light and across a deserted street. "I'm just fine!"

"I'm coming to get you," my father-in-law says, just before the phone goes dead.

He finds me by the store with the tattered valance. "You're limping," he says, frowning. "And for God's sakes, you could have been killed." He steers me by the elbow slowly toward their grand, spacious first floor apartment. He is so much like Kyle, in his size and his seriousness. I glance sideways at his square jaw, set now in frustration and concern for his ditsy, confused daughter-in-law. Would Kyle's hairline have eventually receded like his father's, if he'd lived long enough? Tears fill my eyes again and Kyle Sr. stops walking. "You're crying," he says, frowning.

"No," I lie. "It's just a little cold out here."

He nods, though he does not buy it. We walk in silence the rest of the way, just me, Kyle Sr., and his son's ghost.

They offer me tea to warm me up, but I ask them for a scotch on the rocks. Emily goes into the kitchen to get it while my daughter sits across from me on an ottoman, glaring at me. "What the hell, Mom?" she says after her grandfather leaves the room, too. "Were you, like, trying to run away from Grandma's?"

"Of course not," I tell her. "It was just hard to find parking."

Charlotte hugs her knees and stares, looking a little frightened. We are jockeying for space on the ottoman, where my ankle rests elevated beside Charlotte's small butt. Emily has wrapped the ankle in an ice-filled dish towel, safety-pinning it snugly against the blue swelling. She'd tried to borrow Hunter's ice pack, but he wouldn't give it up. "Thith ith mine!" he'd told her, pressing it to his cheek possessively. It was defrosted anyway. They tucked him in with it, in the room that used to be Kyle's.

"How long are we staying here?" Charlotte asks, glancing into the kitchen to make sure her grandparents aren't listening. My ankle throbs but my brain is empty. Cotton has replaced the spaces that once held neurons. My only thoughts are: Why do people keep asking me things I cannot answer? Do I like Foster Willis? How long am I staying in New Haven? Why did Kyle die? Why did Phoenix kill herself?

"We just got here," I say to Charlotte. "Aren't you having a good time?"

"Yeah, sure," she says with a smirk. "Maybe tomorrow you can get me an ice pack, too, 'cause it's, like, totally fascinating to be with all you swollen, banged-up people." She wrinkles her nose. "Plus it smells like sauerkraut in here."

Oh, my poor Charlotte. I reach over my fat ankle and pull her into my arms. When Emily returns with the scotch she smiles benevolently as us, as if this is what she's expected all along. Her happy family has come to visit.

Emily and Kyle, despite my daughter's comment about the sauerkraut, have always been cool, hip grandparents, in my estimation. First of all, they seem to really love each other. There is still a lot of touching that goes on between them—a hand on a shoulder, fingers brushing a stubbled cheek, a pat on the backside in lieu of saying so long. They've always been this way, for as long as I have known them, and I used to think, right at the beginning of my marriage, that their comfortable love for one another was ultimately a burden. Kyle would visit my parents and see nothing of the sort, and this, of course, would make me defensive, even though I wasn't being attacked. I'd become agitated when Kyle was around my parents, wincing at their every sharp word as if stung by a bee.

"Leave it alone," Kyle used to say, trying to calm me down. "Let them be who they are."

But I couldn't leave it alone because I couldn't accept that Kyle didn't see my parents' terse interactions as a reflection of the woman he'd married. I guess I believed he deserved a whole package when he married me: one loving bride with two loving parents. The fact that my parents had almost divorced more than once, each time because of an affair my father initiated with someone at his office, weighed upon my shoulders like a heavy mantle of personal shame. In retrospect I see that Kyle couldn't have cared less. He was in love with me, not with my family. As for me, I *wanted* a new family, where the mother and father touched, cracked jokes, smiled at each other right in front of their two sons. I wanted that family desperately but had nothing with which to swap for them. My father seemed uninterested in the fact that I was marrying someone at all. My mother is a nice enough person, but she never acted over the moon about gaining a son-in-law, either. Growing up as an only child with her was something like growing up with a pleasant postal clerk in the house. *Will that be all?* her distracted smile at the dinner table seemed to ask. *Or do you need some stamps, too?*

Even now, in her late sixties, Kyle's mother is a pretty woman, with short-cut silver hair, but her smile is webbed with deep lines that she has come by honestly. Emily is not a woman who attempts to look younger than her years. Just a little eyeliner at parties to bring out her blue eyes, and maybe some lip gloss applied before a walk. Kyle Sr., well . . . he looks a lot like Kyle Jr. Or maybe it's the other way around. Anyway, it is easy to see why Emily loves him. There are these men in the world who aren't diminished, but seem burnished by age instead. Paul Newman was a good example. Kyle Sr. is one as well, and it breaks my heart to think how well his son would have aged, too.

Emily is teaching Charlotte to knit this morning. Her laptop sits unattended on the coffee table while she and her grandmother frown over something purple, knitting and purling away. I wrap myself in a quilt on the Cavanaughs' old couch, a soft brown leather one with built-in end tables. I call my mother, explaining to her the changed itinerary. Hunter is leaning against me like a stuffed doll, his thawed ice pack pressed to his face, staring at the television, which is turned off. "Say hi to your other grandma," I say, putting the phone to his ear, but he only shakes his head and stares. I'm not sure my mother is listening too attentively to my tale of woe, based on the number of times she's said, "Fine, honey," and "Okay, honey." Is it really fine that her grandson flew like a football through a breakdown-lane forest, losing his front teeth in the process?

"I'll get back to you and Dad when we know what we're doing," I lie to her.

"Okay, honey," she says. I almost expect her to ask if I need any stamps.

I put the phone down and give Hunter's shoulders a squeeze.

"Ready to go out and have some fun today?" I ask. Hunter just shrugs. I gently pull the hand that holds the ice pack away from his face and he opens his mouth in silent protest. The gap where his front teeth were freshly startles me. But the swelling has gone down, and the doctor said the stitches inside his mouth will simply melt away.

"You're gonna have a great time, buddy," I tell my son cheerfully. He presses the ice pack to his cheek again and frowns at his lap. His hair smells dirty, but I forgot to ask at the hospital if I can get his head wet. Bright morning sunlight spills through the Cavanaughs' large living room windows, the same sunlight that spilled on my husband all the days of his childhood. Hunter and I sit quiet a minute. We are still recovering from breakfast, which was strained. We've never sat together at the Cavanaughs' mahogany table without Kyle being there too.

His parents have been warm and welcoming since our surprise arrival last night, patient even with my stupid parking adventure. They haven't hounded us with awkward questions, such as why the kids aren't in school, or why I'm driving them away from their home, or why I'm not at work myself. Still, I see it in their eyes, the grief that will never go away. The celebratory meal they prepared for us this morning would add five pounds to anyone's butt, but there was nothing to celebrate. Two years after the death of their firstborn, I see how they struggle to smile while passing his survivors the syrup.

"Are you all right?" I ask Hunter, who is squeezed up against me like a Siamese twin. The smell of bacon is still in the air, as is the sweet scent of blueberry pancakes, Charlotte's favorite. Kyle Sr. buttered toast while he and Emily carried on a friendly conversation with the children at the table. Charlotte regaled them with tales from the soccer fields, just as if she were an ordinary girl and not some child who curses at her mother in the car. Not a word was uttered about her tongue stud. Now and then Kyle's parents gazed at Hunter, surely imagining their own son. Hunter spoke only once, staring longingly at a ketchup bottle his grandfather shook over his scrambled eggs. "I want that," he said.

Kyle Sr. has been gone for almost an hour, out looking for our car in whatever awful neighborhood I've parked it. Emily's back in the kitchen and Charlotte has put down her knitting and returned to her laptop. I get up from the couch and casually hover over her.

"Checking your e-mail?" I ask, lamely attempting innocent curiosity. I'm silently relieved to see that she's doing just that. She casts me a dark look and tells me to leave her alone. When I sit down again, she rises from the couch and leaves the room.

Kyle Sr. comes sailing through the front door, cheeks pink from the cold, Charlotte's soccer ball under his arm. On his face is the same grin Kyle used to wear, standing on Charlotte's soccer field, instructing the girls on teamwork. It is not a *similar* grin, but my own Kyle's soccer grin, exactly. I squeeze Hunter's shoulder too hard. "Mama?" he says, but my eyes are frozen on the sight of Kyle Sr. grinning his son's soccer smile. Except then he sees my face, and then the grin disappears.

"I found this in the van," he says, almost apologetically. "I brought it home to lure Charlotte into the park with us."

"That's great," I say, sounding anything but enthusiastic. Kyle Sr. looks uncomfortable. "I'll go find Charlotte," he says, bustling past us, clearly anxious to leave the room with the stricken woman in it.

I somehow nod, then rise again from the comfy leather couch. "Excuse me," I say, leaving Hunter sitting there like a potato. I limp down the hall to Kyle's boyhood bedroom. I close the door behind me and fall upon the unmade bed. Hunter's pajamas are strewn across one pillow. I bury my face in them, remembering the times Kyle and I made furtive love in this very bed. Such exciting sex in the early days, with his parents in the next room and the two of us not yet married. All the muffled laughter, our hands reaching, our arms embracing, our efforts to be silent in vain. No matter how happy a marriage is, how satisfying the sex life, I see in retrospect how nothing compares with the delirious, gluttonous sex before the wedding vows, the insatiable lovemaking that helps you understand that this is serious, that you get to have this for a lifetime, that you are starting now. I hug the pillow tight in my arms, close my eyes, and try to remember everything.

"Kate? Would you like some tea?"

A voice wakes me from my light sleep. I release a pillow in a yellow pillowcase and sit up, trying to orient myself to my surroundings. It is Emily calling. It's daytime. The children are out with their grandfather. The sun shines low through Kyle's slatted shades.

I find a comb in my purse, run it through my hair. I smooth down my clothes, then hobble down the hall to the dining room. On the way I pass Kyle's high school senior portrait, mounted to the left of his brother's. I study his shining black hair, his strong square jaw and startling white teeth. I lower my eyes when I can't take any more of it.

Emily has set up bright blue mugs and a plate of cookies on the dining room table. Beside these, a ball of yarn and six inches of what perhaps will be a purple scarf are displayed.

"She's doing okay with the knitting, don't you think?" Emily says with a smile, entering the room carrying a steaming kettle. "Irish Breakfast? Earl Grey? Peppermint?" She waves at a selection of boxes. "I also have plain old Tetley, if you're old-fashioned and boring like your mother-in-law."

I sit, taking the weight off the bad ankle. The setting sun bathes the air around us in a soft orange glow, and an aura of love and tranquillity rises like the steam from every corner of the room. Everyone should be old-fashioned and boring like Emily is. And then I wonder if it's really as simple as she makes it look, creating this feeling in one's home. I imagine myself pouring Tetley tea for Charlotte at our kitchen counter, while Big Butchie leers at us in his wife-beater from Charlotte's open MySpace page.

"She's been a handful, Charlotte," I surprise myself by confessing. I expect to see Emily's eyebrows rise in surprise, or perhaps in disagreement, especially after their *Little Women* morning together, all that knitting and flipping of pancakes and sweetly recounted anecdotes from the soccer field. But instead I see her eyes grow red as a rabbit's. She lowers the kettle onto a trivet someone made for her in second-grade art class, not even pouring water into our cups. Blue mosaic tiles, crookedly set, disappear beneath the hot metal.

"She's like her father was," Emily says. "Full of piss and vinegar."

I lean forward, elbows on the table, curious.

"Thickheaded and stubborn as hell, he was," she continues, smiling and shaking her head. "I was thinking of him this morning, when I saw Hunter's mouth full of missing teeth. Did I ever tell you the story of Kyle and the tooth fairy?"

"I don't think so," I say.

"Hmmph," she grunts, pouring the water now. "Every other child in the world looks forward to the day when he can tuck his tooth under the pillow and wait for the tooth fairy to come flying through his bedroom while he's sleeping." She runs her fingers through her own silver fairy hair. "All those shiny coins waiting there in the morning! It's something that usually delights normal children."

A little sting of shame shoots through my gut. Had I even remembered to suggest the tooth fairy coming to Hunter last night, before his grandparents tucked him in? Of course, his teeth are rolling around somewhere on a forest floor in Sturbridge, but still.

"I even sewed each of my boys a pillow with a pocket on it," Emily goes on, "just big enough to hold one little tooth. But would Kylie put his tooth in the pocket? No, ma'am."

"Why not?" I ask.

She looks up from her cup at me, and I see a mix of amusement and anger flashing in her blue eyes. "Why not? I'll tell you why not. Because *my* little boy wanted to *keep* his tooth. He refused to leave it around for any fairy! 'I don't want any strangers sneaking into my bedroom at night,' he said. Can you imagine a child saying this?"

The tea, unfortunately, comes up my nose. I should have thought to swallow it before listening to the punch line of my mother-in-law's story.

"Yes," I tell her. "I can imagine a certain girl child saying a thing like this. Only with lots of F-words thrown in."

Now Emily is laughing, too. It's wonderful to hear her great, extravagant guffaws. Tears are rolling down both our faces. Emily reaches over and grabs my hand. It's the closest I've felt to Kyle since he left me. "I saw her tattoo," Emily tells me, gasping for breath. "A turtle!" She cannot stop laughing and neither can I. "Can you imagine what Kyle would have said if he discovered a turtle on his daughter's belly?"

"Well, maybe Hunter should get an ice pack tattooed on his face," I say, and Emily howls even harder. Now we're beside ourselves, wracked with laughter, unable to breathe or speak or sit up normally.

"You should have heard Kyle Sr. in bed last night," Emily says, "trying first to work the tattoo out, and then the ketchup bottles!"

"How does he like Charlotte's tongue stud?" I manage to sputter. This doubles us over, too. We laugh and laugh until we are too tired to do it anymore. Then I lay my head down in my arms on the table. It's dark and safe in my little cave, and I close my eyes for a second to rest.

"So are you seeing anyone yet?" Emily suddenly asks.

TWENTY-NINE

Crusty and Brittle in the End

The mugs are washed and the tea put away. It has been one of those days that escapes entirely; a meal here, a nap there, a sip of tea with your mother-in-law, and the next thing you know, the sun is setting. I watch the sky grow burnt orange from Emily's kitchen window, the two of us in that state of limbo that too much family visiting induces. We love each other, but being together is an effort. Between us, we shoulder a million memories while attempting to pass time in the present. The memories of Kyle are a beach ball that must continuously be hit into the air at a ball game. Nap or no nap, I am exhausted.

Emily leans into the sink and stares at a wall clock shaped like a rooster. "They're really making a day of it," she says. I hear concern beneath the false brightness of her voice. I look up at the rooster and discover it's almost five o'clock. Slides and swing sets could hold very little appeal at this hour. Perhaps Kyle Sr. has taken the kids to the funky pizzeria, across from the convenience store with the torn red valance, to warm them up and to eat a few slices.

"Kyle Sr. is going to sleep like a baby tonight," Emily says, and I see we are sharing the same thoughts. "All that fresh air . . . ," she muses.

"And fresh kids," I add.

Emily laughs. "We'll bring in a few pizzas when they get back," she says.

"If they're not already eating some now."

"Oh, I don't think Kyle would do that," Emily responds quickly. "He always lets me know if the plan is going to change."

Not like his son, I think. He changed my plans without any notice at all.

I look at the clock again. Wouldn't Kyle Sr. call to tell us he was pushing my son on a swing in the dark? Perhaps he and Charlotte are finishing up a little soccer match, or maybe they're sitting on a pitted park bench, ignoring the cold bite of metal against their pant legs, quietly talking about Charlotte's dead father.

"You know," Emily says, settling on a chair beside me at her clean kitchen table, "it's been more than two years since our Kyle died."

Whose Kyle? I'm thinking, but of course I don't say this. My mother-in-law is a big-hearted woman, a generous person. She never tried to hoard her son's affections, once he'd brought me home.

"I wasn't joking, exactly, when I asked you before if you were seeing anyone."

I turn to look at her and what I see in her face is love for me, all along the small lines that frame her smile, and pain for herself, all around the eyes. She is talking to me about the advisability of replacing her son with another. Her blue eyes—Kyle's blue exactly—blaze with determination and something else, too. Is it courage to say the things she will say next?

"It can't be easy raising two kids alone," Emily continues. I know she has steeled herself for this little lecture and now must deliver, like a gymnast at the beginning of her floor routine. One more backflip, then a round-off, then the arabesque, and she is done.

"I certainly haven't *chosen* to raise them alone," I say, rubbing my eyes with my hands. "Neither did Kyle, for that matter."

"I know. But since you're doing it," Emily says, and then she takes my hand between her own small hands. "Since you're doing it anyway, and doing such a fine job—"

"Please," I interrupt.

"Yes, you are. You're doing a fine job. You're not the one who has made them unhappy. Kyle is."

Why she has said this I don't understand. But a stab of anger pokes at my ribs like a stick, and suddenly I am standing, rising like a volcano from my chair, until my voice explodes in the quiet kitchen. "Why the fuck did he die?" I cry out, first asking the stupid wall-clock rooster, with his cocky expression and arrogant tail. "He was only forty-two!" I scream, my hands shaking and my shoulders shaking and my vision blurred. "What kind of shit heart did they give him?" I'm still asking the rooster, who continues to sneer at me from behind the safety of glass. "Who dies at forty-two?"

"Exactly," Emily agrees, sitting still as a statue on her kitchen chair, hands clasped on her lap like a demure Catholic school student. "Who?"

Seconds later I am flying into her arms, kneeling beside her chair, my arms wrapped around her waist. We cry as only Kyle's women can cry for him. We are wracked with sobs, wracked with grief and memories.

"Here, wash your face," Emily says, handing me a clean wet dish towel with tiny poinsettias on it. I press the cold water against my eyes and feel suddenly soothed, oddly peaceful. Nothing to see but blackness. Nothing to feel but the cold soft cotton against my swollen eyelids. A scrap of a dish towel restoring my sense of calm in the world. That, and Emily's voice lilting somewhere above my head.

"Why shouldn't you have a companion to help you through this?" she asks, as if we are midconversation about my love life. "If just someone to have dinner with, go to a movie with, laugh with a little over a drink, what would be so bad, Kate?"

It's nice and dark and cool in my terry-cloth hideout. I press the towel a bit more into my closed eyes, say nothing. It is easy to think in this new place. I feel no pressure to answer Emily's questions.

"Do you ever do that, Kate? Just take time for yourself? Go out with someone? Let a man take you to dinner?"

Foster Willis has somehow made his way into my terry-cloth cave. He is offering me unsolicited child-rearing advice at an Indian restaurant with that little smile on his face. He's passing me a Guinness in an Irish pub.

"You're still young, Kate. Still a lovely young woman."

Press, press, press. How did Emily get into my hideout? Why won't Foster Willis leave?

"Sometimes I think you idealize Kyle, which is not surprising," Emily says. "We all do that with our dead, I suppose."

Now I pull the towel away from my eyes. "What do you mean by that?" I ask. The cold kitchen air stings my eye sockets as I study Emily's face, looking for clues.

"How old were you when Kyle dragged you off to the altar? Were you even twenty-two yet?"

What?

She crosses her arms, thin as sticks, just like Charlotte's. "He hoarded you like he hoarded his baby teeth. Kyle Sr. and I sometimes wondered why he couldn't have waited. Given you a chance to become the woman you were becoming. He'd certainly given *himself* plenty of time to grow up. Why couldn't he have given that to you?"

I stare at Emily, stunned. What is she talking about? "What are you talking about?" I hear myself ask, my voice high and incredulous.

"Kate," Emily says, taking my hand in hers.

I pull it free and ask her another question. "Did you disapprove of Kyle marrying me? Is that what you're saying?"

"Of course not," Emily says. "We loved you the minute we met you." She pauses, which causes my blood to freeze. "But Kyle brought home a girl, Kate," she says softly. "And he was a man already. And he wanted you right away. So he did the selfish thing and married you, before your girlhood was even over, before you even had a chance to grow into yourself. And then . . ." Emily sighs and recrosses her arms, leaving me breathless. "And then he left you, just like that. And it must be hard as hell for you to know who it even *is* that he's left."

I stand so quickly my chair tips. "Is that how you see it?" I ask Emily. "Is that how? I loved Kyle. I wanted to marry him. We wanted to get married." Even as I say this, I remember how it was Kyle who wanted the wedding to be as soon as possible after I graduated. And then I remember something else, how there was no breathing space between the graduation and the wedding. I remember hiding my disappointment at the diminished pleasure the actual graduation delivered, after four long years of studying. There was a wedding to plan. There were caterers to hire and then a band. There were dresses to buy and bridesmaids to fit. How puzzled my bridesmaids seemed at the timeline I'd given myself to get married. They wanted to go out and celebrate one last time our four years spent laughing and crying and drinking and studying together. They wanted to drink too many apple martinis at a campus bar, and tell silly stories about bad professors and worse boyfriends and near misses with undeserving men we'd saved each other from. But I was already ordering wedding invitations and drawing up guest lists. I was planning my move to the Dutch Colonial in Appleton that Kyle had bought for us. He'd gotten a mortgage easily; he was twenty-nine, after all.

Was I still a girl then, as Emily says?

"He was a hell of a good father," I say, as if I am defending Kyle as he stands beside me in the room. Oddly, though, even his ghost isn't making a cameo.

Emily smiles, eyeing me with the patience of a woman who has seen everything. The sun is completely gone now. A suspended light fixture the shape of a wagon wheel casts triangular shadows on the tabletop. I trace one triangle with a finger, wondering about the things she has said to me. I was twenty-one when Kyle became my life. How old did that make me now?

"Of course your instinct would be to go home to your mother," Emily says quietly, as though she is reading my mind. "You were a child when you left there. But what can they do for you, and Charlotte, and Hunter now?"

Tears are coursing down my cheeks as I ineffectively swipe at them with my dish towel. "She'll go crazy when she sees the ketchup bottles."

Emily shrugs. "He won't be taking them to college."

"I saw how he was using them, right at the beginning. I should have taken them away from him, distracted him with something else, two years ago."

Emily squeezes my hand. "We're human," she says. "We make mistakes. We're kind of like bacon, pink and hopeful in the beginning, crusty and brittle in the end. Life'll do that to you." She squeezes my hand again. Then we hear the door swing open and the two of us rise and head for it, floating on a cloud of relief that they are home.

Only it's not all of them.

It is just Kyle Sr. standing at the threshold with Hunter in his arms, my son's eyes puffier than my own as he chews his thawed ice pack.

"We've been looking for Charlotte for hours," Kyle Sr. says.

THIRTY

Into the Woods from Grandmother's House

Someone has seated me back on a kitchen chair where Hunter also sits, clinging to my lap with his arms wrapped tightly around my neck. My sweater is wet through from his runny nose.

"Thithy," he sniffles. "I want Thithy."

The rooster clock groans in the otherwise silent air.

"Want to sit on Grandma's lap?" Emily asks, placing a cup of hot tea before me.

"No," Hunter huffs into the wool.

A policeman is on the way over. Kyle Sr. is telling us the story again, of how he lost my daughter at a New Haven park.

"We'd left the playground area and were kicking around the soccer ball on the field there," he explains once more. "You know the park I mean, right, Emily?"

Emily nods slowly.

"There's nothing around it but houses and that one little coffee shop. And then there's just the highway behind it on the other side. You could see a person a mile off if they left that field."

I squeeze my eyes shut. He has told us all of this already. How long have I been sitting here while my child is gone? The highway runs behind the park. What part of it is Charlotte traveling now? What car is she in? Who is driving it?

"She told me she'd be right back. She was just going to get a can of soda from the coffee shop. We weren't two hundred feet from the store. Hunter and I kept kicking the ball and waiting."

I close my eyes again and see Charlotte slipping away, waiting for the moment when her grandfather's and brother's attention is diverted. Perhaps they were chasing the soccer ball. Maybe Kyle Sr. bent down to tie Hunter's shoelace.

"I thought maybe she'd had to use the bathroom, and that was what was holding her up," Kyle Sr. continues. "But after about ten minutes, we went looking for her. The sun was setting and it was getting cold anyway." He rubs his arms, as if he's still feeling the sting of dusk in the park. "When we got to the coffee shop, the guy behind the counter had just arrived for his shift. He didn't even know who I was talking about."

"Did you call the police then?" Emily asks, even though she knows he didn't.

Kyle Sr.'s brow crinkles with annoyance. "After ten minutes? Who calls the police after ten minutes?"

"It's a strange city to her. Charlotte doesn't know her way around New Haven—"

"She's not in New Haven," I tell them both. I shift the weight of my son on my lap. "Believe me," I say, "she's a long way from New Haven by now." I rise quickly, lifting Hunter and placing him down on his grandmother's lap. "Can you keep him?" I ask. "I'll come back as soon as I can."

"No!" Hunter screams, scrambling off Emily's lap like it's on fire. "*You* keep me," he implores, eyes wide with fright. His open mouth looks foreign again, until I remember the missing teeth.

"Kate, the police are on their way over," Emily says. "Why don't we wait a few minutes, to see if they can help us—"

"I know where she is!" I tell her, too loudly and too urgently, while attempting to peel my terrified son from my leg. "Or, at least, I know where she is headed."

"Yes, but perhaps—" Emily says, and then we hear the doorbell ring. We remain frozen in our tableau: two women facing each other, a child wrapped around a leg, a tall man with his arms crossed. Finally Kyle Sr. unfolds his arms from his chest and leaves the kitchen. We hear him open the door.

A woman police officer follows Kyle Sr. into the kitchen. She looks fiftyish, her iron-gray hair and tough-looking face competing with kind, intelligent eyes. She is big-boned and curvy, like

Sophia Loren stuffed into a man's uniform. I can see from her eyes that she hasn't found Charlotte.

"Are you the girl's mother?" she asks. "Why don't we sit down so we can talk?"

We all sit down, except for Emily. She somehow manages to situate Hunter in front of the television in the next room. Strains from "The Circle of Life" waft into the kitchen, Kyle's favorite song from his favorite Disney movie. Since his death, his daughter listens more to "The Circle of Poo," some disgusting song from the *South Park* Christmas DVD, featuring a talking turd named Mr. Hanky. The rooster clock groans.

"We've got several squad cars surveying the area," Officer Eileen Lynch says.

"I'm sure she went home," I tell her.

Officer Lynch nods once, then goes on with her careful litany of questions. What was Charlotte wearing? Was she carrying money? Does she have a Social Security card? No. Cell phone? Yes.

Good. Very helpful. The cop starts calling Charlotte's cell from another phone. No answer. Duh. Why have we come to New Haven? she asks next.

I explain it all to her again and again. After I offer the last bit of useless information that won't help us, Kyle Sr. is asked to tell his whole story once more.

This is when I rise a second time from the table. "She's going *home!*" I explain again, exasperated. "She's got a boyfriend there. The only question is whether she'll make it safely."

"Do you think she's hitchhiked?" Officer Lynch asks.

"I don't know. Probably," I say.

"Has she been talking to anyone online?"

This is the question that paralyzes me.

Big Butchie with his swinging-penised stick man, and who knows who else.

"Oh, my God," I wail, and then someone is sitting me down again. I see Charlotte's gazelle legs folded beneath her on the couch this morning, her face lit by the bright screen. She was only on her e-mail when I checked, but what about before that? Could she have been chatting with some pervert on MySpace, making plans to meet him at a diner or a Starbucks or a highway stop? I hear myself gulping like a drowning woman.

"Mrs. Cavanaugh, what is it?" Officer Lynch asks.

I can't speak as my brain dredges forward the worst images it can find. Child sex rings. Abductions. Girls found in shallow graves on the side of the road. It seems like every day I pick up the paper and read about these things. They go off willingly, maybe to catch a ride to their boyfriend's house, or to escape the smell of sauerkraut in their grandmother's house, or because they're sick of their bleeding baby brothers, or sick of their mothers.

"Mrs. Cavanaugh?" Officer Lynch says again.

"Kate?" Emily tries, gently pressing my hand. I gaze at her soft face, then through it.

Charlotte wouldn't do these rash things, would she? Charlotte is a smart girl. She has friends and a boyfriend, and a family who loves her. Tom's words flutter into my mind uninvited: *Well, here's the thing. No one wants to live with someone who thinks they're all wrong.*

I shake my head to dislodge the voice. Nonsense, I think. I tell her I love her all the time, if I'm not fighting with her. Or slapping her hard across the face.

"Mrs. Cavanaugh?"

My teeth are chattering. Apparently the others can see this. "A girl in her high school killed herself," I say, apropos of nothing.

Officer Lynch gazes at me.

"My daughter puts cognac in her mouth and lights it," I tell her, burbling on. "Not that she drinks it," I add helpfully. "But this older guy in a very bad undershirt did see the picture of her blowing flames."

Now the cop eyes me sharply.

"On her MySpace page," I explain. "But we made her get rid of him," I continue. "She changed her password. He couldn't find her now, could he? I don't really know where he lives. . . ."

Tears are streaming down my face. Kyle Sr. rises and puts an arm around my shoulder. I find it hard to breathe. Who is this person whose body isn't behaving at such a critical moment? I need to get going. I need to find my daughter and protect her from the wolves out there, waiting for broken little girls to come skipping by.

"Listen," Officer Lynch is saying in a soothing tone. "We'll check out her computer, but I don't want you to worry too much."

This sounds like the stupidest advice I have ever heard. Officer Lynch lets out a long steadying breath and continues. "Kids this age usually show up. Really. We'll contact the Appleton police so they can be looking for her, too." She pats my arm and rises from her chair, trying her best not to look anxious. "Meanwhile, can you show me your daughter's computer?"

Somehow I stand up. I lead them into the living room, where we stare at the laptop on the coffee table as though it might be alive. Emily and Kyle Sr. follow, making their way immediately to Hunter, who looks up from the television screen, alarmed at the sight of us.

"Let's eat cookies," Emily says, quickly leading my half-drugged boy, my only remaining child in attendance, to the kitchen. Hunter is too tired, too bewildered, and too outnumbered to protest. He allows Emily to lead him out, turning his head only once to whimper a disconsolate, "Mama?"

"We'll take this with us, just in case," Officer Lynch says, lifting the computer into her big, capable hands. Then she is gone. I stare at the empty coffee table, listen to the front door open and close.

She's fine, I think, wringing my hands. *Most kids her age show up.*

Kyle Sr. arranges a happy face made of raisins on the top of Hunter's Cream of Wheat so he will eat his dinner. Emily sits beside me, forcing me to sip the scotch she's prepared for me.

"Here," she says, pressing the sweating tumbler into my hands. "Drink this. I insist." It's the second scotch she's given me since I arrived last night. Purple half-moons shadow Emily's eyes; she looks as if she's aged ten years in the one day we've been here.

I call Marge and get no answer. I call Ren's number and get his voice mail. "Have her call me, please," I say, "the minute you hear from her."

Emily makes me get into bed. I lie there, listening to the sounds of my son in the next room. "I want Mama!" he wails, this followed by the soothing cajoling of his grandparents. Suddenly the door bursts open and there he is, arms outstretched, toothless mouth open, running for me. I gather him into my arms, curl him between my chin and my knees. Emily stands helpless at the open door, but I tell her it's okay, we'll be fine, I'll get him to sleep. The door shuts and we lie there quietly. I inhale Hunter's scalp, smelling shampoo and playground and sweat. My baby. When his breathing gentles and I know he's asleep, I think again about the note Phoenix left me, the day before she died. *I just want to go now*, she'd written, *that's all*.

But why did Charlotte want to go? Only yesterday she hovered so close to her brother's stretcher that it looked as if it would take the National Guard to persuade her to leave his side. She and I had been getting along. Was it the rest of the trip she couldn't bear? I roll on my back and stare at the ceiling. What was I thinking when I loaded my children into the minivan with their father's ghost? Of course Charlotte wouldn't want to go to my parents' house. Neither did I, though I wouldn't let myself see it. When I was Charlotte's age, I couldn't wait to get out of my parents' house. Maybe this was why I married Kyle in the first place.

I am up all night. I call the New Haven police too many times and get no new information. I pace Kyle's childhood bedroom. I listen to Hunter sleep. I dial Marge in the middle of the night and listen as her voice mail tells me to have a nice day, just before the beep. I go to the bathroom and stare at my face in the medicine chest mirror and ask myself for help, for anything. "Please," I tell my tired reflection. "Find her." Nothing. I order Kyle's ghost to visit me, demand he make an appearance, but he doesn't come. Maybe he is with Charlotte, protecting her. Maybe he's a colossal disappointment, an impotent nothing, a useless asshole who is never where you need him to be, not even in death. My anger fuels me, keeps me awake. I welcome it as a relief from the anxiety. I watch the sun rise this way, Hunter still sleeping in the crumpled bed. I pace Kyle's old bedroom. Endless, the hell is.

And then the kitchen phone rings.

I hear it through the closed bedroom door. I spring from the edge of the bed and race through the hallway in bare feet. I wince at the sunlight pouring through the kitchen windows. Emily is picking up the receiver. She holds the shiny white earpiece to her ear and says hello with a shaky voice. I cannot see her face, but I listen to Emily's silence as she clasps the white plastic to her ear. The wait feels interminable. "Sure," Emily finally says. "Let me get her."

She turns to me and our eyes lock. I try to read everything, but see nothing, just the cool blue irises of her son, and of my daughter. "It's your next-door neighbor Marge," she says. "For you."

I am a shard of ice melting into a puddle. I grab the phone from Emily, gasping with relief I pray is not premature. "Marge?" I say, or maybe I am shouting. "Marge? Is she there?"

"Calm down," Marge says in her sensible tone. "She just arrived. She's fine. Everything is fine. I found her here when I got up this morning."

Kyle Sr. calls the police for us. He puts me on the phone with Officer Lynch. "You see?" she says. "I told you they show up. I'm happy this worked out well."

We send Kyle Sr. to the station to pick up Charlotte's laptop. Emily makes a fresh pot of coffee and we sit for a moment, not speaking, just allowing our bodies to adjust to this new fact: Charlotte is safe.

Hunter soon awakens and runs into the kitchen holding the blue ice pack, his anxious face focused on me. "Where's Thithy?" he cries, eyes crusted with sleep, sensing a crack in the case. He pushes past his grandmother and climbs onto my lap. He strokes my hair with his free hand. I am giddy with love for him.

"Sissy's fine," I tell him. "She went home."

"*I* want to go home," he says, snuggling into my chest. I wrap him in my arms, kiss the top of his head. Not a trace of the baby smell left. It's time, I think. A year from now he'll be registering for kindergarten. I squeeze him again, then pull him from my chest to look at him.

"Sissy's waiting for us," I say. "We're gonna go home."

"Yaay!"

"You are my big boy now," I tell him, while he studies my blotchy face, looking worried.

"Yeth," he agrees tentatively, and this is when I do it. I gently remove the ice pack from his hand.

"And big boys don't need ketchup bottles, right?"

Gravely, he shakes his head.

"Or ice packs."

I watch a frown furrowing his forehead. He stares sullenly at the ice pack, then yanks it out of my hand again. "Thath's mine," he says. "The doctor gave it to me."

He quickly evacuates my lap. He brushed off the seat of his pants with his free hand. Emily and I watch him lift his chin in a dignified manner before leaving the room.

"Oh, well," I say when he's gone. "At least we're down to the ice pack."

THIRTY-ONE

I Just Want to Go Now

As I'm fitting things into our bags again, laying the suitcases across Kyle's unmade childhood bed, tucking in the neatly folded clothing Emily has laundered for us, I think about the special kinds of hell there should be for specific kinds of people. I do this sometimes to amuse myself, as when imagining a hell for male shoplifters where the man must wait outside a woman's dressing room forever, holding his wife's shopping bags. Or the hell I imagine for the tattoo artist who inked a turtle onto my fourteen-year-old daughter's left loin. His is a hell where he hangs from a tree, transformed into an unbreakable piñata. Overstimulated fourteen-year-olds swing a bat at him for eternity, waiting for something sweet to spill out that isn't there. I'm in the process of sentencing Big Butchie and his ilk to the piñata hell when Emily enters the room with a second load of washed clothes.

"Most of the blood came right out of your shirts," she says cheerfully.

I thank her, staring down at the open suitcase, feeling responsible for more than her tough laundry problems this week.

"It's just less you'll have to do when you get home," she says. "What with opening the house again and getting yourselves situated. You can't even run your own washes until the plumber comes to turn the water back on, right?"

"Right. Thank you," I say. I fold the blood-free tops into the suitcase, Hunter's little striped one on top of Charlotte's sweatshirt.

If I needed to do washes at home I could take a dirty basket over to Marge's. Doing my wash would be like porn for her. But I don't tell Emily this. She's just making chitchat anyway. We both know what I'll be doing when I get home, and it isn't laundry.

"Are you nervous about speaking to Charlotte after this?" Emily asks.

I look up from the suitcase and see her frowning at me.

"Seems to me," Emily says, "a child ought to know when her mother's angry with her."

"She's angry with *me*."

"Yes, but you're not the one in the acting-out stage."

"That's what *you* think," I say, pressing down the top of one suitcase. We both laugh, for each other's sake. It saddens me to think of all the things Emily doesn't know about her grandchildren's life with me. The slapping. The yelling. Her grandson flying like a football through a highway forest.

"You know what I mean about Charlotte," Emily persists. "It's different with a teenager than an adult. Next time you're feeling upset, you're not going to drink too many beers with a bunch of boys, or, God forbid, get yourself pregnant, or run away from home again because you figure you've got no limits."

"I'll speak to her," I promise Emily. "I'll call her from the car when Hunter nods off."

"Does he do that, too?" Emily asks. "Kyle was like that in the car when he was a baby. The moment we turned over the engine, it was like driving around a dead body in the backseat."

There's an awkward few seconds of silence while we watch Emily's joke go south. Then, strange as it may seem, we both laugh. It is our first Kyle-is-dead joke. It's not that we're glad he's gone, but we're glad to be able to acknowledge it, for the first time in two years, without the weeping and gnashing of teeth. When we're done laughing, we look away from each other in astonishment. I hug Emily very close, feel her small sharp bones against my chest.

"Thank you so much for everything," I tell her.

"You're the one doing the heavy lifting," she says. "Just don't forget what I said about finding some nice company."

.   .   .

Hunter's grandpa lifts him back into the van, just as he'd lifted him out a couple days earlier. Everything is repacked, except for the canvas bag stuffed with empty ketchup bottles. Hunter allows these to be left behind, even the one with the lederhosen.

THIRTY-TWO

Can You Hear Me Now?

D id you get a good night's sleep last night?" I ask my daughter.

"Yes, thank you," she says, polite as a catalog sales associate.

Here is our first attempt at communication since I wept into the phone, earlier this morning, telling her I was glad she was safe, telling her I loved her. She was at Marge's house then. Now she's on her cell phone, somewhere at school. There's lots of dead air in our conversation. We understand we're walking a tightrope with each other. Neither of us airs our grievances or defenses, each of us too happy with the outcome of Charlotte's adventure. It leaves little to say. The tires hum beneath the car.

"What did Aunt Margie make you for breakfast?" I ask, trying to fill the void.

"She made me turkey sausage and—" Gales of laughter suddenly blast into my earpiece.

"What's that, honey?"

"I just walked into the cafeteria," she tells me. "Someone here wants to say hello."

"*Hola*, Mrs. C.!" I hear Hector yelling in the background.

I squeeze the wheel and blink hard. "I didn't know Hector was a friend of yours."

There is a big intake of air on the other end, then the exhalation. Over the clatter of trays and chatter of students, she says,

"Mom, I going to tell you something, and I don't want you to get mad at me. Or at Hector."

"Go ahead," I reply pleasantly, throttling the steering wheel now.

"You know that picture on my MySpace page that you didn't like? The one where, you know, I'm, like, blowing flames? From my mouth?"

A hundred miles from her, I sense she can see my face. Blood-drained complexion. Disapproving frown. Forehead crinkled with fear. "Yes?" I say carefully.

"Well, we took that in Hector's kitchen. He's a friend of mine. We were just fooling around."

"Oh," I respond.

"We don't, like, actually drink or anything. Seriously."

"Great!" I exclaim, as a huge tractor-trailer truck passes. Hector, our briefly jailed marijuana salesman. He doesn't drink.

"He's been, like, a good friend to me," Charlotte says. "He was freakin' when I told him about all the blood with Hunter."

"Right."

"But seriously," Charlotte continues, "it's been bothering him since you found the picture and got mad, that he, like, had anything to do with it." She pauses so that only the cacophony of lunch hour fills the air. "Hector loves you," she says. "He's sorry we posted it 'cause he thinks you're way cool."

Flip-flop go my emotions, like a pancake carelessly thrown in the air. I take a breath, decrease my speed in the right lane. "I love Hector, too," I tell my daughter honestly. "Why didn't you ever tell me you were friends?"

There's more dead air for a moment, then Charlotte says, "I didn't think you'd approve."

As my stomach twists with guilt, I remind myself that everything will be different now. I'm coming home to be a better parent.

"I'm only telling you this 'cause, you know, if I'm going to bother to run away and all, I might as well start telling you the truth and stuff."

"Good plan," I say. "Thank you, Charlotte. We'll talk more when I get home."

"How's Hunter?" she asks then.

"He's fine," I say. I glance into the rearview mirror and find him slumped in sleep. "He's happy we're coming home."

"Are you?"

"Am I what?"

"Happy you're coming home?" she asks.

I stare at the trees at the sides of the highway. They're all a little barer than even a few days ago, when we'd traveled in the opposite direction. "Yes," I finally tell her, "I'm happy to be coming home."

At the Massachusetts Welcome Center, I park, push the seat back, and close my eyes.

"Mama?" Hunter says. He's as reliable as an alarm system, returning from the dead once the engine is cut. His dazed voice pipes forward from the backseat.

"Mama, are we at home?" I watch him in the rearview mirror, rubbing his eyes with small fists. He's strapped down in that slightly uncomfortable car seat position that is just another measure of my son's patience with life.

"Not yet, honey."

"Watha matter?" he asks, ever alert to the slightest shift in my mood.

"Nothing's the matter," I tell him. "Mama's just tired. I just want to get a nice cup of coffee. Do you want to come with me and get something from the vending machines?"

Hunter is quiet a moment, studying me. "Yeth," he finally says, as if he is doing me a small favor. He unstraps himself from his own seat and grabs his ice pack. We hold hands on the way into the visitors' center.

"Is Thithy at home?" Hunter asks a hundredth time, once we're on the road again.

"Of course she is," I assure him.

"I love Thithy," he says, and I think perhaps we're having a conversation.

"I love Sissy, too," I tell him.

"Sometime you hate her," Hunter says matter-of-factly. I

glance at him in the rearview mirror, shocked and hurt by his tinny proclamation.

"No, honey," I assure him, "I don't hate your sister, ever."

"Hmmph." Hunter sighs, raising his ice pack to his mouth.

"Hunter, honey," I say, "sometimes grown-ups who really love each other have arguments in really loud voices."

"Thithy's not a grown-up," Hunter says. "She's my thither."

My hands squeeze the steering wheel. I have been shut down by a four-year-old. "Everything will be fine when we get home," I say to Hunter. But the moving car has already taken its toll. I see in the mirror that the ice pack has fallen to his lap. Hunter is sawing logs.

I'm getting onto the Mass Pike, not far from the place where I dropped my son, when the cell phone begins chortling again. I check the number and then, a bit reluctantly, press send.

"How are things going?" Foster Willis asks.

"I'm almost embarrassed to tell you," I admit. "Aren't you in the middle of a workday?"

"You know lawyers don't really work," he says. "I sort of heard your embarrassing story already. About Charlotte."

My face grows hotter by the second, as an expensive minute ticks by.

"What'd you hear?" I ask.

"That she ran away to home. Bree told me this morning."

"How did she know already?"

"They're friends, remember?"

Something about this makes me sad instead of happy. "Are you sure you want Bree being friends with one of the wild girls?"

"I leave those decisions to the city and the cheese," he says. "And anyway, if I get to see the mother, I'm willing to risk the friendship."

"What do you mean by *see*?" I ask.

"I mean I enjoy your company."

I say nothing. A thought announces itself, unbidden. I *liked* having sex with Foster Willis. I pull the visor down, try to block the thought, but the stubborn fact remains. I enjoyed his company over spring rolls in my kitchen. He made me laugh. I liked looking at the nice cleft in his chin.

"I'm on my way home," I tell him.

"For good?" he asks.

"It's where I live, isn't it?"

"I thought you were moving to Texas."

"Without my daughter?"

"Run while you can."

"Very funny," I say, but I find myself smiling.

"Listen," he says. "I imagine your house is closed up still. So why don't you and the kids come over for dinner tonight?"

"That's sweet of you," I tell him.

"I'm a very good cook."

"Yes, but, let's say . . . it might muddy the already muddy waters."

"How so?"

"Well . . ." I pause. "As you might recall, Charlotte last found us dressing, in the room where she and Hunter watch PG-rated movies."

"Kate," he says, sighing loudly into the phone. "Let's get real about fourteen-year-old girls. I've got one, too, you know. They aren't that easily offended by the sight of a guy putting his tie on."

"The tie went on last," I remind him.

"Oh, please," Foster says. "Stop talking like a church lady when really you're this hot, sexy, beautiful—"

"Enough," I say, cutting him off.

"And your red hair is gorgeous. I'm really glad you're coming home." He sighs into the phone. "I could eat you up."

The highway stripes blink in their broken lines, some kind of Morse code I try futilely to read. I'm speeding toward Appleton to make things right with my runaway daughter. Snoozing behind me is a little boy who thinks I hate his sister. But there is a man across town who could eat me up.

"Kate?" he says after a while into the phone. "Kate?" he says again. "Can you hear me now?"

Rolling into our driveway, I'm engulfed in the sensation of having been away a very long time. It's only been two and a half days in reality, but the leafy copper beech that umbrellas our front lawn is now almost bare-limbed, as if it's given up like the rest of us and shed everything. Its leaves rest in neat piles on the lawn. Marge must have been raking. I put the van into park, engage the emergency brake, and sit a moment, studying this house that has held my family and my marriage and the whole of my grown-up life. The paint is still white, the shutters still black. Everything looks exactly as it did the day I first walked in the door. Shouldn't there be some sign of the crisis that ruined us, of a man being taken out dead and his family left inside?

Next door, I see Marge's front door swinging open and there she is, my friend, my rescuer, smiling broadly, ponytail bouncing as she walks toward the van with her big manly strides. Her hands are tucked into the pockets of her brown fleece vest, a walking advertisement for L. L. Bean. The afternoon sun shines on her forehead and picks up glints of gray in her hair. I roll down my window and immediately feel Hunter stirring behind me.

"You're home," Marge says, hugging me through my open window.

"Aunt Margie!" Hunter cries from the backseat, amid the clicking and clacking of belts being unbuckled, clasps being undone. When did he learn this self-release strategy from his car seat? Perhaps when his sister was running down a highway embankment?

We cross the lawn, where Marge's giant boastful mums seem to leer at us in greeting. Soon I'm nibbling on the delicious crumb cake she's baked this morning. I sip organic tea, imagining somewhere in Marge's organized cupboards a tightly sealed Tupperware container labeled CAKE CRUMBS. I imagine Charlotte sitting in this same chair this morning, eating her turkey sausage. We haven't spoken about anything yet, like how my daughter looked when she walked into this house. And who drove her here and what happened on the drive. Was she threatened, hurt, propositioned by a pervert, molested? Just because I haven't asked Charlotte about any of these things doesn't mean Marge hasn't. I also want to know if Charlotte felt the slightest bit sorry for what she put me through. But this last question I probably won't ask.

"I called *NSTAR* for you this morning. I saw someone over

there fiddling with your meter, so you probably have lights again," Marge says. Somewhere from the next room, the sound of Eddie Murphy screaming like a stuck pig travels to the kitchen.

"What's Hunter watching?" I ask.

"Shrek," she says. This explains everything.

"I can call Verizon for you, if you want your phone back."

I glance at Marge's kitchen clock, a rectangular space-age gadget that you wouldn't expect to see in her kitchen. Two-thirty, it says, though it feels like it's midnight after my long drive on no sleep.

"I asked Charlotte to be here by three," I tell Marge.

She nods, and I begin to become irritated.

"So," I say.

"So," she repeats.

"Aren't you going to tell me anything? What was she like when she got here?"

"She showed up at the door with Ren," Marge says quietly, as though she's afraid something might detonate if she says the wrong thing. "I think she hitchhiked as far as his house. They walked over together from there. He lives all the way on the south side of Appleton, as you probably know."

I nod as if I do.

"They both looked tired and cold when they arrived."

"Who did she catch a ride with?" I ask, feeling cold myself.

Marge sighs. "I asked her that, but she wouldn't elaborate. It was a guy, though. Ren told me."

A chill creeps up my arms. "What did Ren say?"

"Only that some *dude* picked her up in New Haven." Marge's imitation of Ren is pretty good, but not comforting. "He was heading for Boston anyway," Marge continues. "Or so the guy told her."

The inevitable thoughts overtake me a second time. She could have been traveling with a rapist, or a murderer. She could have been sitting across from a normally decent man in a business suit who took one look at her slutty attire—her midriff-baring skimpy T-shirt and her spiked tongue—and thought about his passenger in a new way. We all have our dark sides. Charlotte is excellent at conjuring them up in others.

"The main thing is she got home safe and sound," Marge says, reading my thoughts. She pats my hand. "And she knew to come here."

The first resentful thought threads its way through my neurons. Charlotte knew who to come to, but she also knew who to leave.

"And she knew to call you, too," Marge goes on. "That was her idea, you know, though of course I would have called you anyway. After we drove Ren home, she talked to me a little. She really feels bad about having worried you."

"Bullshit," I hear myself say, suddenly angry at my daughter, and maybe at Marge, too.

"No," she insists, "it's really true. She's a confused kid, Kate. But she loves her family."

"Nice way of showing it," I mutter into my cold tea.

"She tried going with you first, Kate."

"After you told her she could stay with you," I say.

Marge looks down. "I'm sorry about that," she says. "But the point is she tried going with you. That should tell you something."

A look passes between us, riding on cold air.

"It's hard for a kid to lose everything," Marge says. "She wanted to come home again."

"To who?" I ask. The look I give her is less than appreciative.

"Kate," she says. "I was home minding my own business when the doorbell rang. I—"

The door behind us swings open, cutting Marge off. I turn in my chair, and there she is. Holding hands with Ren.

She's wearing her wholesome-child clothes. A baggy sweatshirt hangs almost to her knees. Her jeans are loose and frayed at the hem. Her face is pale, but the cold has left pretty pink blotches on her cheeks. She looks like a porcelain doll, dressed in clothes-hamper cast-offs. She glances away from me as I study her. Ren smiles and nods cordially, hands buried in his saggy jeans pockets. Fair enough, I think. We each brought along our support system. Mine is a friend wiping down crumbs with a wet sponge. Hers is a guy whose pants might fall down. Charlotte looks at me once, then glances away again.

"Charlotte," I say. But then I don't know what to say next.

Hunter bounds into the room and wraps himself around Charlotte's waist.

"Thithy!" he cries joyously. Charlotte's face breaks into a grin. Yet another moment in which a hidden camera would reveal a happy family.

"Hey, little dude," Ren says, patting Hunter's head. "Where's your ketchup bottle?"

Hunter's face falls in an instant.

"Have you ever seen *Shrek*?" I ask Ren.

He frowns handsomely. "One, Two, or Three?"

"Why don't you and Hunter go in the other room and find out?"

Ren winks conspiratorially and his sexy eyebrow dips. "Gotcha, Mrs. C.," he says, suavely glancing at Charlotte and then back at me. Hunter drags him off by the hand and we stare at the back of his low-slung jeans, his omnipresent strip of exposed underwear. The kitchen gets quiet.

"Well," Marge says after a minute. "I've got some work to do in my office." She picks up an unmarked manila folder that rests beside the toaster oven and hugs it protectively to her chest. "Be good to each other," she says, as the kitchen door closes on her large khakied form.

THIRTY-THREE

Who's a Johnny Rain Cloud?

Y ou know she's adopting a baby from China," Charlotte says, scooting onto one of Marge's kitchen stools.

"What?"

"That's what she's doing with all those folders. Did you know that?"

I sit heavily on a kitchen chair, watching Charlotte roll the hem of her sweatshirt with her fingers. She and Marge have their secrets, just like her father and Marge had secrets.

"How do you know?"

Charlotte wiggles a little on the stool. "I saw all the papers on the kitchen table when I . . . uh, when I . . . got in."

"I see. And did you talk to her about it?"

Our tones are mild and friendly, like two strangers chatting on a train.

"A little," Charlotte says. "She told me it's kind of sketchy if you're not married. She's been trying for, like, forever. I think it's been two years."

Charlotte's forever is the exact measure of my widowhood. Something quick and hot twists in my gut. Poor Marge. She's been childless forever. Cagey Marge. She doesn't tell me everything.

I study my daughter, the shadow of her hood cutting her face in half like a broken piece of china. Did Marge talk to Kyle about adoption and Chinese babies, those mornings they were building the swing set for my son? Did they exclude me from these conversations because I was too young, too unworldly—a child, as my mother-in-law puts it?

"Well, anyway . . ." Charlotte clears her throat. She glances up at me, then away, her anxious face attempting to contain everything. I rise from the chair and walk over to her, wrapping my arms around her. She smells of Marge's laundry detergent and my little girl.

"Here's the thing," I tell her. "You scared me half to death." I take a breath to steady myself, until I feel I can proceed calmly. "I thought, after the hospital, we'd been getting along. You could have been hurt. I thought I'd lost you."

Just like that, Charlotte is crying. I hold her closer.

"*Any*one could have picked you up."

"I know," she whimpers.

"So who did?" I ask, pushing back the hood, kissing the top of her head.

"It was all right," she tells me, but then she's crying harder, which makes me believe it wasn't.

"Charlotte, honey, tell me what happened." I hug her close, sensing something agitating beneath her skin, something ready to explode.

"He kept *yelling* at me!" she says, when the explosion finally comes. I press her closer, feel the poky bones of her chest against my own. "He kept telling me that, like, if he were a different kind of person, he could do all these things to hurt me. If he weren't so nice, I'd be totally fucked. I'd be totally . . ."

Fucked. She'd be totally fucked.

She is gulping huge mouthfuls of air as she cries. As a baby, she used to give herself gas bubbles, crying this way. My baby would be totally fucked, was what the man told her.

I breathe in, breathe out. Nice cleansing breaths before I speak.

"Did he hurt you?" I ask, feeling the hairs on my neck rising as I brace myself for her answer. She shifts in my arms and I ask her again. "Did he, Charlotte?"

Nothing.

"Charlotte, please tell me."

"We stopped at a gas station and I locked myself inside the restroom. He banged on the door for me to come out, but I didn't."

I stare at Marge's space-age wall clock, imagining my daughter in some gas station ladies' room, her fist around a big wooden dowel upon which the key hangs. I can hear the pounding, see the sink with rust in it, the pee on a broken seat, a wad of toilet paper stuffed into a peephole in the door. *I've failed you, Kyle*, I tell his ghost, wherever he is hiding.

"How did you get home?" I ask, and suddenly Kyle is sitting beside me, waiting for her answer.

"Ren," she says. "He took his father's car."

Relief floods me momentarily. The remainder of Charlotte's trip involved no more than a stolen car. Thank God for that.

"It's gonna totally suck when his father finds out."

I don't even ask her why. Ren is, after all, fifteen.

"Where did he get you?" I ask instead.

"It was, like, right where Connecticut ends. He kind of dented the side of the car when he was pulling out of this rest stop—"

She is gulping air again. A loud wail escapes her. I pat her back, and then we hear a rumbling at the closed kitchen door. Hunter swings it open, frowning at us. Ren stands behind him with his worried face, wringing his hands.

We try to convince Hunter that his sister is all right. She's just tired, Ren and I tell him. Then Ren swoops him up, Three-Stooges-style, and carries him back out of the room laughing. I hear Hunter's shrieks of laughter.

Charlotte and I sit holding hands for a while. Then I smooth back her hair from her wet face. "We can talk more about this later," I tell her. "Should we think about dinner first?"

"Bree invited us to dinner," Charlotte says, brightening. "You want to go?"

I don't answer immediately, in case this is a trick question. Then I say, "I think we're all a little wiped tonight, don't you?"

"*I'm* not tired."

I pause again, before saying the next thing. "Don't you not like Bree's father?"

Charlotte shrugs her shoulders. "He's all right."

I rest my elbows on the kitchen table, rest my face in my hands. A ragged cloud of fatigue travels quickly and settles upon my shoulders.

"Can we go?" she asks.

"Honey, I'm really not feeling like—"

"Why can't we ever do anything *I* want?" she snaps. "Don't you want me to have friends? What's the point of living here?"

I look up at her pretty flushed face and surprise myself by very calmly answering her question. "The reason we live here is not so we can do everything you want," I tell her, "exactly when you want to do it. The reason we live here is, hopefully, to be happy together, and to love each other, and to help each other out. We can do that, can't we, even without Daddy?" I take her cold hands into mine and smile at her. She looks slightly stunned, but by no means down for the count.

"I *want* you to be happy, Mama," she says in her little-girl's voice, "and I'm trying to help you out. Daddy's not here, but some guy who's nice and has the hots for you wants to cook us dinner. Doesn't that interest you?"

"Doesn't it bother you?"

Charlotte shakes her head.

I close my eyes and try to imagine all of us sitting in a strange Appleton kitchen a few miles away, the perky blond Bree at one end of a table, my two misbehaved children at the other. And there is Foster Willis holding a steaming casserole dish, a smile on his face. An apron covers his family jewels, the only garment he wears. *I could eat you up*, he says. I smile inside my little hand cave, even though I'm exhausted. He does have nice family jewels, I think. Maybe he's a good cook, just as he claims.

I stand and stretch. "I'll tell you what," I say. "Why don't you tell me first why you ran away from Grandma's, and then we'll decide."

I watch her softness vanish as she becomes all sharp angles again. "Charlotte," I say.

"I didn't like being there," she answers. "I know they're nice to me, Grandma and Grandpa, but I feel like I'm *weird* when I'm there. And you seem to agree with them, too."

"What are you talking about?"

"You know what I'm talking about," she says. "The way they stare at me, just because I'm, like, an *individual*, who's decided to create my own look."

An individual, I think, staring at her indignant face. Look alike to feel different: it is the mantra of every high school student alive. Of course, I say none of this to Charlotte. But I do think again about Tom Johnson's words in his office. *Just love her*, he said.

"And you!" Charlotte is on a roll now. The color has returned to her cheeks. "You're *used* to my chosen sense of style, and yet you act all shocked and disapproving, as if you, like, *agree* with Grandma and Grandpa that I'm a total freak."

I'm speechless. What can I say when the truth is, I *did* agreed with them that she was dressed like a total freak? *Just love her*, Tom reminds me in my head again. It's fine for Tom to be so understanding because, let's face it, he's bargaining with God. And it's all right for Marge to smile and bake her things because Charlotte's not her daughter.

Or maybe these are excuses I've been giving myself for not *seeing* Charlotte, not seeing who she actually *is*.

Charlotte is rolling the hem of her sweatshirt again, her downcast face still burning with indignation. I think of my mother-in-law's face, the pity on it for me, when she described the way her son had robbed me of the formative years of my young adulthood. Married at twenty-one. Mother at twenty-two. Grad student at twenty-three. Was I really so happy as I tell myself I was?

I rub my eyes, then study the strong stubborn face of Kyle's and my child. Maybe I've been robbing Charlotte of her own chance to try things on and try things out in her formative years. Growing up is a messy business, beyond the tattoos and wardrobe choices. Maybe I could be there for her, just because I love her, even when I don't agree with her path.

THIRTY-FOUR

Of Snowflakes and Suicides

Charlotte occupies herself for a long time dressing for our dinner at the Willises'. She emerges from Marge's guest room in a pretty pink top with a lacy neckline that ends way too soon above her waist. She's standing at the coat closet in her skin-tight jeans with the holes that cost extra. "You look pretty," I say, and think I might mean it. I'm surprised, when I look up from my own coat, to find her frowning at me. Her eyes traveling from my scuffed clogs to my frumpy jeans, and then my sweater. The blue one. That I wear everywhere.

"What?" I ask, quickly zipping my jacket.

She's leaning against Marge's polished banister, brow furrowed. "It's just that we're, like, going to dinner at someone's *house*," she says.

"Yes? And?"

"And you're sort of not dressed appropriately."

I sit down hard on Marge's bottom step. "You're kidding me, right?"

Charlotte crosses her slender arms in front of her. "Well, seriously," she says. "Did you not, like, wear those clothes all day in the car with Hunter? I'd be surprised if a french fry didn't fall out of your sweater when we got there."

I am aghast at her assessment of my appearance. I remain where I am on a carpeted stair, trying to think. "And your outfit," I say, when I've finally found my voice, "that is, like, dressed up. Yes?"

"Well, duh," she says, preening a bit, if I'm reading this right.

"And if you could dress me yourself, you would want me to dress like . . . you?" I try to keep the judgment out of my tone, but it's hard.

"Of course not!" Charlotte laughs at the notion, her pretty, over-made-up face becoming soft and beautiful once more.

"Then exactly," I continue, unsure now, "how is it you would want me to dress?'

"Like a mother," she says, in a tone implying tremendous patience, "only a hot one."

"A hot mother," I repeat.

"Yes."

"And if I dress like a hot mother," I ask, "that means I'd be able to drop you at school without you climbing out the car window?"

She rolls her eyes. "You *are* going to see a guy you hooked up with," she offers helpfully. "Don't you want to look good?"

I rise from the step, heat flooding my face. "Okay, let's go," I say. "Get in the car."

Charlotte shakes her head. "It's too early," she insists, and then does the strangest thing. She smiles at me, just the way she used to in the days she thought I was *pretty*, and *nice* and *funny*. Just the way she used to when she was too young to loathe me. "Come on, Mom," she says, taking my hand, coaxing me up the steps. "Let's do a little makeover on you. If not for your sake, then for, like, mine."

Marge looks amused as we go by, hand in hand, passing by her office and heading for her guest room. Charlotte sits me on the edge of the bed, then opens my suitcase on the bedspread beside me. She digs through the laundered clothes there, tossing rejects over her shoulder like so many thrown-away wishes.

"Bad," she mutters to herself, hurling a pair of my jeans that have seen better days.

"Worse," she says, chucking a baggy fleece vest.

"Sick," she finally swoons, holding up an item of apparel she evidently approves of. She turns to show me and is holding her own top, a stretchy, form-fitting black sweater, admittedly modest for my daughter's taste, but definitely racy for mine. It's feminine in shape and soft in fabric and there's even a little lace around the V-neck and mid-length sleeves. It's just the Hell's Angels skulls, entwined in red roses, dancing across the front that make it the last item in the world I'd ever wear.

"So fine," my daughter coos, eyeing me like a steak in the meat case and then holding the sweater up in from of me. "And with that ridiculous red hair it's, like, a stellar choice!"

Charlotte's eyes glitter the way they once did at Christmas. Just the same, there is no way I'll be wearing the sweater.

"Charlotte," I begin, "I don't think this sweater's quite—"

"Mom, please!" she interrupts. "I'm, like, trying to work here."

"But Charlotte—"

"I'm trying to help you." She says this last thing softly, imploringly, taking my hand and squeezing it between her own.

"Those skulls'll be sitting right on my boobs," I plead.

Charlotte laughs naughtily. "Hot Mama!" she squeals. "At least you got some."

"It's still early in the game for you," I tell her, smiling at her tiny chest.

"Mom, I wasn't talking about me."

"Oh." My face heats again. "Sorry," I apologize. But Charlotte is busy finding me better jeans, better socks, better shoes. She only succeeds on the sock front, coming up with a pair of solid black ones, to replace the white tube socks I'm presently wearing, which Charlotte describes as butt-ugly. I am quietly offended. Defeated, I let her dress me in the sweater.

Once she has wrangled me into it, she studies my jeans more closely and pronounces them wearable. "They're decent, but not hot," she decides. "At least you're not some tub of lard, like some of the other mothers, and your butt still looks good."

"Charlotte!" I scold.

"I'm not being rude," she explains. "I'm saying you look ridiculously good for, like, somebody's mother."

She waits for me to thank her for this, a self-satisfied smile on her face.

I escape the makeover with only a few hairstyle alterations. Charlotte sweeps a clump of the front of it into a lopsided ponytail at the top of my head. The rest of it she leaves hanging in its natural, ridiculous state.

"Now you look, like, casually sexy," Charlotte explains as she weaves her magic. "Like someone who *is* hot, but pretends she doesn't notice it." I don't dare glance at the mirror when Charlotte is done with me.

"Very nice," Marge says with a smirk as we pass her office door again. "Fester will be thrilled to see you."

Charlotte is gregarious when we're finally in the car. "Let me just add, while we're on the subject of makeovers," she says, "that this minivan's a totally unhot vehicle." She shakes her head sadly. "Even a frikkin' Volvo station wagon would be better."

"Charlotte," I say. "Language."

"Sorry," she says. She smiles at me from the passenger seat. "You know, I'm seriously only trying to help you here. Bree says her father has the major hots for you."

"Charlotte, please."

"What?" she asks. "I'm adjusting, okay?" She throws her hair, which she is wearing loose, back. "Honestly, it's better to have a mother who, like, sleeps around than, say, one of those ridiculous *Birkenstock* mothers, who are such losers with their big frizzy 'dos, and, like, make their poor kids eat organic spaghetti squash and other crap, such as Ashley Minton's mo—"

"Charlotte! Enough!"

We're on the south side of Appleton now in my totally unhot vehicle, and I've begun to feel sorry we haven't taken Hunter along. He was sleeping when we left, knocked out cold on Marge's couch, possibly due to a concussion caused by playing with Ren. It made no sense to wake him. Also, he doesn't like Foster. But still, Hunter would be such an easy ticket home, should things become uncomfortable at the Willises'.

And why shouldn't things become uncomfortable? I think, as we wend our way through a ticky-tacky neighborhood of identical ranch houses. I'm arriving for dinner dressed like a biker babe with my runaway daughter. I could always explain to Foster that I've finally gotten back on the horse. Trouble is, I look like I fell off it again, on my head.

"You know Ren is coming tonight, too," Charlotte says.

"That's nice," I tell her, turning the wheel onto a clone of the street we've just left. "Is he a friend of Bree's, too?"

Charlotte gives me a dark look, trying to decide if I'm teasing her. When she's satisfied I'm not, she says, "We've been talking about forming a band together."

"A band? What a great idea."

"Yeah," she says, a little shyly. "It's like a major part of the reason I wanted to come home." She brushes something imaginary from her lap. "I might play violin in it. Sort of bluegrass," she explains.

"You might play violin again?" I ask, a swell of pleasure flooding my tired body. My head fills immediately with visions of a younger, sweeter Charlotte on the back porch, her small violin beneath her chin, delicious strains of Bach in the air.

"Well"—she hesitates—"it would really be like a hard rock band, but violin sounds good behind some of the bluesy stuff. Right here," she says, "turn left."

I jerk the wheel sharply and find myself turning into a fancy circular drive. Really fancy. I shift into park before crashing into anything. I'm finding it difficult to stay focused. Hard rock and circular drives.

"So why didn't you bring your violin over?"

"It's already here." Another surprise. I imagine the black violin case we all used to trip over in the dining room resting now against some wall in Foster Willis's house.

"Have you thought of any names for your band?" I ask, shutting off the engine.

She nods proudly. "It's the one thing we've decided. Weak Stream," she announces. "We named it after this thing we heard on a Flomax commercial."

I'm about to attempt responding to this, but find myself staring straight ahead instead. We seem to have turned, when I wasn't looking, onto Vulgar New Money Lane, where we've now landed in front of a serious McMansion. I sit in the minivan a moment, gazing in wonder at the stucco façade, the twin turrets, the Tudor touches, and the heavy oak door. I look outside for a moat.

To judge from Foster's home, divorce would appear to be a lucrative situation for the ex-husband. If Foster and Bree got this house, what did his ex end up with? I'm imagining the former Mrs. Willis in a small efficiency unit, a space heater going to keep her warm, when Charlotte taps my arm and says, "What're we waiting for?" Reluctantly I open my door and we head out.

Hearty mums that make even Marge's look lame line Foster's curvy bluestone path, tucked inside a riot of other fall flowers. As Charlotte and I crunch up the path, I begin to wonder how well I know the man inside. Well enough to call him when lost in New Haven. The thick front door opens and there is Foster, his hand resting on the gleaming brass doorknob.

"Ah," he says, smiling. "The lovely Cavanaugh girls."

Bree is poking her head out from behind her father. Charlotte bolts up the stone steps, nipping around Foster as if he is a Doric column. "Sweet!" I hear her cry, referring to something Bree must be showing her in the foyer, maybe Flomax, or her violin, or maybe it's the foyer itself that is sweet.

"Footman's day off?" I ask, an awful greeting, I realize, once it leaves my mouth. But Foster just laughs, holding the door for me as I pass through. I feel more like his cleaning lady than his dinner guest in my makeover outfit. Foster, on the other hand, is showing off his linens and wools to great advantage. My eye is drawn to the sleek black belt that lies at the flat of his waist. He's a good-looking man, but his black loafers have tassels. Kyle would never wear tassels. I am sure of this.

"You look a little dazed," Foster says, releasing me from a very nice hug. He gazes politely at my lopsided ponytail.

"Long day," I tell him. And then I just stare at the Sistine-high ceilings of his foyer.

"Ah, yes." He smiles, looking a little embarrassed. "These digs won't last long. I'm thinking of putting the house on the market and getting something smaller. In Appleton."

"But what about your wife?"

"She won't want it. It reminds her of me, even though she's the one who had it built. And may I remind you, it's *ex*-wife."

I see the foyer is really more of a rotunda, once I look around. A round marble table sits in the center of a gleaming hardwood floor. The silk rose arrangement on top looks very expensive.

"My ex is a decorator," Foster says, reading my thoughts. "Overbearing interiors are her specialty."

"I see." I clear my throat. "Quite a carbon footprint she's leaving."

"This is all her taste, by the way," Foster says with a laugh. "I'm more of a houseboat kind of guy myself. One table, four chairs, four plates and cups will do it for me. And a bed, of course."

He smiles suggestively. I turn away.

"But Bree, as you see, is with me, and not her mother, on a school night. Her mother, it appears, saw fit to accept a big job in the Midwest, even though her daughter lives in the Northeast."

Foster throws up his hands in a sweeping gesture. "Voilà!" he says. "Calling Daddy to live in the mansion. What's a good divorced parent to do?"

I throw up my own hands. "Live in splendor," I say. "What else?"

Foster laughs. "Here, let me take your coat."

I don't want to give him my coat, which is really just a ski jacket with a ketchup stain on the pocket, a souvenir from Hunter. I don't want him to see my makeover at all, but Foster is already removing my jacket from behind me, exposing my no-name jeans and the row of grinning skulls on my breasts.

"Whoa," Foster says, eyes twinkling with what only can be described as lust. "You're so hot, Mrs. Cavanaugh." His eyes travel up from my breasts to my ridiculous hairdo again. "And I can see so much more of your beautiful face with the thingamajig holding up your hair."

"I can explain," I say, feeling foolish. "You see, Charlotte wanted to dress me—"

"Good for Charlotte," Foster interrupts. He leans in to whisper in my ear. "And now I want to *un*dress you." I feel his hands on my back, pulling me in.

"Okay, okay." I push away from his nice embrace, confused as to whether I'm flattered or flustered. "I understand Weak Stream will be with us," I say, attempting to change the subject.

Foster looks at me blankly, then shrieks of laughter emanate from another room.

"Bree?" Foster calls. "Come back out and introduce yourself to Mrs. Cavanaugh."

"I already know her," Bree shouts back. "From school."

Another burst of hilarity erupts. Probably some joke about the Touchy-Feely counselor being in the house. Or maybe Charlotte's telling them about my makeover. Or maybe they're talking about how their parents bonked each other.

"Don't be rude," Foster calls, walking toward a room at the end of a long hallway. "Come and greet our guest properly."

They don't come, which makes me happy. Foster insists we go to them. We find the two girls curled up on a red couch the size of a yacht, hugging giant shiny throw pillows on their laps. They're painfully trying not to laugh, and the strain shows on their lineless faces. Bree manages to rise and offer a hand. "Nice to meet you," she says, golden hair falling over one eye. She is a pretty girl with a sweet face, smooth as a dinner plate.

"Nice to meet you, too."

When Bree Willis smiles, I can see the dear little girl she once must have been. Now she dresses much like my daughter, in low-slung sweatpants tonight and a very tight tank top. "We're gonna rehearse later," she tells her father. "Ren and Hector are coming over."

Charlotte looks at me, then away again. Is there no end to tonight's surprises?

"Is your homework done?" Foster asks his daughter. "We won't be done eating until at least eight o'clock." She tells him it is, as Foster guides me by my elbow from the room.

"Can the guys eat with us?" she calls after us.

"Sure," her father tells her.

"So let me understand this," I say, as we pass by the marble table and the silk roses and enter a stainless steel and granite-topped state-of-the-art kitchen. "The fourth member of Weak Stream is a boy named Hector Sifuentes."

Foster boosts himself onto the granite top of his kitchen island. "I don't know his last name," he says, seating himself beside an uncorked bottle of red wine. "But he calls my daughter *mami*. His father is some kind of professor, I think. Wine?"

I nod, no longer able to be stunned by anything. *Gourmet* magazine smells emanate from a wall oven behind him. For all I know, the entire New Frontiers Group might be coming to dinner tonight, with the exception of Phoenix, of course. Foster's legs swing from the countertop, as if he is poised to make scintillating dinner talk.

"Would you mind getting down from there?" I ask. "You look like an Internet dating ad."

Foster grins, jumping down and wrapping his arms around me. "I love how uppity you get," he says. "I might like that the best about you."

"Better than my hairdo?"

"Even better." He kisses my mouth nicely and I let him, tasting ginger and warmth and something with alcohol in it. "So tell me everything," he breathes, when he can speak again. "Tell me about your road trip."

"Wine," I respond. "I'd like lots of wine, please."

Foster pours generously into two red wineglasses with stems thin as threads. I take a sip and let it travel slowly down my throat. "Can we talk about the trip later?" I ask, feeling almost tipsy already.

"Sure," he says. "I'm no stranger to the long, crappy day. And Charlotte is home safely. So let's have a nice, quiet cocktail hour."

I clink my glass against his. "To a quiet cocktail hour."

"Oh! I've got munchies, too," Foster says, and something mischievous crosses his face. "I can't wait to show you," he says, opening a wall panel of stainless steel and revealing a refrigerator large enough to stock a hotel. He fumbles behind a white wine rack, pushing past a series of sliding crispers, until he extracts a brick of cheese that he giddily spins around to show me. "I've been saving this for a week," he says, "since before you ran away from home. Read the package." He thrusts it toward me.

It's only supermarket cheese, from the looks of it. Nothing to get excited about. But then I read the wrapper. *Hunter's Cheese*, it says. *Seriously sharp cheddar.*

"Gotcha!" Foster cries, his sandy hair glowing victoriously in the recessed lighting. "Seems your boy is named for a cheese. How do you like dem apples?" He reaches over and pokes me in the ribs triumphantly. "Now you've got the entire complement! A girl named for a city and a boy named for a cheese." He grins like a fool, poking gently again, and this time the wine shoots from my mouth in a fine spray that hits his linen shirt like tear gas. Foster looks stunned at first. But then we're both laughing as he pats at the stain with his bare hand.

"That looks like sign language for *I'm a jerk*," I tease, and then Foster tosses the brick of cheese at me, grazing my shoulder and making me spit some more. Then we're both laughing like crazy for who knows how long.

Twenty minutes later I'm tossing homemade dressing into the salad with sleek stainless steel utensils I've found in a drawer. "Did NASA design the cutlery?" I ask.

"Whatever gets the job done," Foster says, still happy. He pulls his pork roast from the oven and garnishes it with the cherries and ginger he has sautéed. The kitchen aromas are delicious. They bring in the others, a single file parade of Bree, Charlotte, and now Hector and Ren, too. Hector's handsome face lights up when he sees me. He charges around the granite isle to greet me, causing me to almost drop the metal salad bowl, a serious object that looks like it came out of an automotive supplies shop.

"Mrs. C.!" he cries, stopping just short of a hug. "Oh, Miss, I'm so glad you came back." He halts abruptly, catching himself. He crosses his arms on his chest, gold gleaming everywhere. There is a small new tattoo of a cloud on his wrist. How does this happen in one week?

"I've missed you, too," I tell Hector, and then I do hug him.

"Sweet," Ren comments, looking down.

"Sick," my daughter says.

"What happened to your shirt?" Bree asks her father.

"Nice sweater, Mrs. C.," Hector says.

We head into the massive dining room, where Bree quickly ensconces herself at the head of the table, probably in the chair where her mother used to sit. Hector sticks to me like glue. I can't tell if he's really missed me or if it's the Hell's Angels sweater. He plants himself between Bree and me on one side of the table. Charlotte beams at me from the other side, Ren beside her. The boy's smile, if hereditary, makes it easy to imagine his father committing tax fraud.

"You were great with Hunter today," I compliment the handsome boyfriend with the sexy eyebrows.

"No biggie," he says. "He's an excellent little dude."

"Salad, *mami*?" Hector asks, interrupting almost jealously. He passes me the heavy bowl and the space-age utensils. "So when are you coming back to our group?" he asks, surprising me by so openly speaking of the Touchy-Feely Group at the dinner table. But a quick glance around the table shows me how comfortable these children are with each other.

"Well?" Hector persists. "I hope you are coming back soon, 'cause it truly sucks now with Mr. Johnson in there and, you know, like . . . no Phoenix."

Hector winces, then gathers his feelings back in again. A silence settles on our ragtag dinner gathering. Hector's gregariousness dries up. Bree looks like she might cry. Charlotte's downcast face throws a sad shadow across her dinner plate.

"Mr. Johnson is a really great guy, you know," I tell Hector.

"We want you back, Mrs. C."

"It's just that we're all missing Phoenix," I add lamely.

"Duh," my daughter says. Then we seem to run out of conversation.

We stare at our plates, all of us quiet. Phoenix seems to sit among us, blond hair flowing down her back, that faraway smile on her lips. It's almost as if she is waiting for Foster to cut her a piece of meat. Finally Bree says, "Did you hear about that girl who was saved from lightning by her nose ring?"

"No!" Hector exclaims.

"It was on the news," Bree continues. "It came in through her feet and was grounded by her nose ring."

"Sick," Ren says.

"She could have died," Bree concludes.

Charlotte gives me a significant look.

Foster clears his throat, gently placing the carving knife back on the platter.

After dinner we set the kids free, preferring to clean the kitchen ourselves. We tell them they're excused to do their homework and rehearse, but the truth is, the grown-ups want to be alone. Foster and I clear and rinse, scour and wrap, wrapped ourselves in our own thoughts, and maybe each wondering quietly what the rest of the evening will bring.

"It's been tough on them, that student's death," Foster says, running water over his roast pan.

"She was a beautiful girl," I tell him, hearing weariness in my voice.

"I remember you told me she was in your caseload."

"She was," I say, my throat suddenly closing. "I thought she was doing okay."

"You can never really know how another person is doing. Or even *what* they're doing." He shuts the water off and turns to me. "My ex-wife taught me that."

"Still," I say, wiping down a granite countertop, "it's a terrible shock when someone is just gone like that."

"You would know," Foster says.

"How is Bree handling it?" I ask.

"Okay, I guess. They'd met at the cheerleader tryouts, right before the girl . . . did it. She says they weren't close friends or anything, but still . . ."

"Did Bree get into cheerleading?" I ask.

"No."

So neither of them would be cheerleaders, then.

"Does she miss her mother and you being together?"

"Not that she'd ever say," he says.

A dull quiet hangs over us as we finish our chores.

"The worst part is how the kids suffer," I say, and Foster turns and puts a zip-locked bag of meat down on the counter. Then he wraps his arms around me.

"What can we do about it?" he says. "Marriages end. People die." I smell the wine on his breath as he speaks, but now it smells sad instead of exciting. "It happens." He shrugs. "Even when you love your kid more than your own life."

"Yes," I say, believing we understand each other perfectly.

"The thing about you and your kids," Foster continues, "is that you didn't do this to them."

"No."

"But yet you walk through life apologizing for it."

I pull free of his arms with the little bit of strength I have left. "You know," I tell Foster, "I'm widowed and you're not. It's not always good to speculate on situations you don't know the first thing about."

Foster takes a minute to tuck the roast into his refrigerator. Then he asks gently, "Do I need to be widowed first before I can tell you what I observe?"

"It's late," I say. "I should go and check on Hunter. Thank you very much for a lovely dinner."

"Oh, would you please stop the little walking-out scenes?" Foster says, attempting to embrace me again. "Come on, Kate. Can't I say anything honest to you?"

"You want to tell me about the whole beautiful world I'm missing?" I ask, shrugging off his hug this time.

"Why?" he asks. "Is it too soon after your husband's death?"

"Stop it."

"Stop what? What exactly is it you would like stopped? Other than your actual life?" Foster frowns at me. "How old are you, Kate? Thirty-five? Thirty-six?"

"Look—" I tell him carefully.

"*Ninety*-six? Is that why you're finished with this annoying little activity the rest of us call living?"

"Stop it!" I shout. We both stare gloomily at our shoes. So much for quiet fantasies of a romantic evening. I just want to go home. "This has been very nice dinner," I say, when it's safe to speak. "But I've had a long and difficult day. I just—"

Foster slaps down his dish towel onto the granite counter, stopping me cold. "I like you, Kate. I really do," he says, his face flushing with wine or feeling, or both. "I think you're gorgeous. I think you're funny. I *think* about you all the time, as a matter of fact. . . ."

He pauses. I watch him rub his hands together, and realize I can do it if I want, just leave his house this very minute. I can turn on my heel with a thank-you, collect Charlotte, and go. But something holds me, freezing my fists to the countertop, tensing my shoulders to ward off his next words, while at the same time waiting to hear them. And then he says them.

"I could grab a fistful of your red hair and *live* in it," he says, his face contorted with frustration. "I don't know why I'm so attracted to you, but there it is. There's just one little problem, Kate, one little question that goes on and on, unanswered."

I watch, horrified, as his lips move to pose his little question.

"How long?" he asks, running a hand absently through his hair. "How long are you going to wait until you start living your life again?"

His gaze almost burns me. He's no longer handsome, just frightening.

"He's dead, Kate," Foster continues. "Your husband's gone. I'm sure he was a wonderful guy and a great father, but he's dead. And you have to let him go, just like I had to let my wife go, even though she's still alive."

"I didn't come here to be lectured by you—"

"This isn't *about* me," he says. "It's about you. And your kids. Your poor goddamn kids, they're *waiting* for you, Kate. They're waiting for some *sign* that their sad, old, behind-dragging mother is back." He grips my shoulders hard and looks into my eyes. "The best sign I've seen since I met you is the way you let your kid dress you tonight. When's the last time she had fun with you like that, huh, Kate?"

He shakes me, shakes the tears out of me, holds me by my shoulders until I pull away from him.

"Don't you see that your kids haven't just lost a father?" he says, as I'm leaving the kitchen. "They've lost both of you, Kate."

"Stop lecturing me!" I shout. I am weeping now, wiping my eyes angrily with the back of my hand. "What do you want me to do?" I ask. "Pretend I'm happy? I'm not, okay? You want me to lie about it?"

"Maybe you should just stop lying *in* it," Foster suggests.

I squeeze my eyes shut and when I open them again, he is still staring at me.

"Do you want to sleep over?" he asks.

"You're kidding, right?"

"No," he says. "I promise you, I'm not."

"Thank you for dinner," I manage to mutter, turning a second time to leave.

"Don't forget to smile," I hear Foster say. "You never know who's falling in love with you."

I walk blindly through the house, looking for my daughter, searching for a door that might lead to a basement. That's where they said they'd rehearse, in the basement, though I hear no music emanating beneath me, see no door that would lead to such a lowly place. His wife built this giant house and then left him. Why do people do the things they do?

"Charlotte!" I call out. "Charlotte, where are you?"

I follow a sound somewhere ahead of me, threading my way past modern art and family portraits. Finally, there is Charlotte, standing at a set of opened French doors, scissors in her hand. She looks worried. About what? I wonder. Her sad, old, behind-dragging mother?

"Mom, are you all right?" she asks.

The room behind her is strewn with paper. Streamers of white office paper rest in soft piles on the Oriental carpet. It looks like the aftermath of a confetti parade.

"Mom?" my daughter asks. Behind her, from the couch, three pairs of wide eyes stare at me, like baby raccoons on a tree branch. There is no way to hide distress from children.

"What are you doing?" I ask Charlotte.

She points to a place over her shoulder. I lift my gaze to the sliding glass doors where a dozen or so giant origami snowflakes seem to float in the black night. They are beautiful ghostly things. They dance against the darkness like a small miracle. I stare at them, feeling a thousand things, unable to articulate the simplest direction, such as *Get your shoes on, we're going home.*

"We're making these for Thursday," Charlotte says. "We're going to sell them at our Halloween UNICEF sale."

"We decided to do art," Bree adds.

"Because our band truly sucks," Charlotte says.

The peanut gallery behind her dissolves into laughter.

"We're weak," Charlotte adds, and they all laugh again.

"It's not that we suck, *mami*," Hector explains. "It's just that we don't feel like practicing. We feel like making snowflakes."

"I taught them how," Charlotte explains with pride in her voice. "Remember Daddy and I used to make them?"

I do. It almost doubles me over, remembering the two of them hurrying into the kitchen to present me with a droopy lopsided snowflake, fashioned out of junk mail from our recycling bin. It had taken them all morning to make it. This was long before Hunter. It must have been a cold winter Saturday or Sunday. They'd created a mess, similar to this one, in the family room. The whole morning was stapling and taping, folding and cutting. If I close my eyes I can see Kyle's big hand over Charlotte's small one, her fingers laced through her pink plastic safety scissors, the lines they cut jagged and ill-spaced.

"They're beautiful," I whisper, not able to look at her as I speak. Then I tell her we have to go home.

"Can't we just finish them first?" she asks, her voice a bit whiny, like a younger Charlotte. Her posse of friends implores me with their eyes. These are silent, obedient, good children, different creatures from the ones who walk the halls of the Alan B. Shepard High School. *Your children are waiting for you to live your life . . .*

"I'm showing them how to do it," Charlotte says, breaking the silence. "Just like Daddy showed me."

. . . waiting for their sad, old, behind-dragging mother to come back.

"All right," I hear myself say. Then I sit down in a leather chair across from them and watch. I watch them play like seven-year-olds, cutting and pasting and folding. I listen to them giggle about how hard it is to tape the little parts, listen as they burst into television commercials in harmony. They don't mind my being here. They've created this safe regressed place to replenish themselves, a world far away from MySpace and cheerleading tryouts and science tests and suicidal classmates. A mother in the background belongs in this world, in case they need a juice box or carrot sticks or peanut butter with faces in it. Last night Charlotte was locked in a gas station restroom with a possibly dangerous man on the other side of the door. Now she's at Bree's house, cutting snowflakes. I lean back into the chair, thinking how mothers need a safe, regressed place, too.

After a while I let myself out, finding the wide oak door in the foyer and opening it quietly. Charlotte has asked to sleep over, and I have said yes. In essence, I have dumped my daughter on

Foster Willis for the night, without the courtesy of asking him. But the funny thing is, I don't feel bad about it.

I'm not the slightest bit worried about his parenting. I'm confident that Ren and Hector will be asked to leave soon. There'll be a reasonable bedtime, and no tattoo parties or truancy on Foster's watch.

Teeth will be brushed. A house the size of Foster's must contain a spare toothbrush for Charlotte. Maybe there are fresh ones in the master suite bathroom, for when Foster Willis invites women over.

I crunch across the circular drive toward my minivan, aware of my stomach squeezing unpleasantly. I don't want him to invite women over.

Maybe the truth is I'm not really angry at him—only at the things he says that are true. I unlock the cold car and get in. And then I'm on my way home, alone. A light snow, the first of the season, sparkles on my windshield as I head for Marge's house to check on Hunter. Rubbing my eyes with my free hand, I drive through a quiet moonless night, out of autumn and into the next season. Perhaps it's the wine, or maybe it's the beauty of the snowfall, but everything feels brand-new again. Anything could happen.

THIRTY-FIVE

Open House

Instead of pulling up at Marge's, I swing the car into my own driveway. A sugary veil of white covers the blacktop already, sparkling ahead of me in my headlights. The house is dark. The world seems quiet.

Welcome home, Kate, Kyle's ghost says. He is standing in front of his garage. *How are the roads?* he asks.

I press the garage door opener and wait as my strong invisible man with his perfectly healthy ghost heart slowly lifts the heavy panel. The first lights at 32 Pleasant Street automatically flash on, warming the garage's interior like a cave. I sit, not moving the car inside, considering this workplace my husband once loved so well. There are his cans and boxes, stacked neatly on the high shelves. Hoses and tire pumps hang in tidy straight lines along the sides.

But wait, did Kyle hang things in straight lines?

I study the space hard, watching Kyle's ghost vanish. And then I realize I am looking at Marge's work, not my husband's.

Signs of her obsessive organization are everywhere. She must have done this after the bunk beds were finished, cleaned and reorganized Kyle's garage like a madwoman. Perfectly centered on the back shelf, I can see the shiny red enamel of Kyle's toolbox, which Charlotte had searched for when she helped build the beds. Smaller items flank the box on both sides like candles on an altar.

Shouldn't Kyle's wife be the one to build his altar?

Suddenly it feels as if I'm finding a bra beneath Kyle's pillow. It is a foolish feeling, certainly, and I can't even imagine what one of Marge's bras might look like. But nor can I shake this feeling, any more than I can move my car into the garage and close the door behind me. I am bolted to the seat of my idling minivan, having the irrational thought that this house was never all mine, that instead I've shared it with the six-foot-something woman next door who made my husband smile.

I shift into park, turn off the engine, glance at the clock on the dashboard. It's a little after ten. I decide that it's not too late to begin a conversation with Marge. If the clock had said three A.M., I would be on my way over to begin a conversation with Marge.

I am panting as I cross her lawn. I crush a mum in Marge's border garden, leaving a big gap in the line. I proceed up her front steps and ring the doorbell. I ring again and again, as if there is an emergency out here on Pleasant Street, but it is only me, an emergency in my own right, waiting to be admitted, waiting for explanations, assurances, answers, apologies.

There is the suck of air as the door is opened, then the crack of light, and then Marge's horsey face, smiling warmly, though her eyes look puzzled. "Come in," she says, holding open the storm door for me with one strong arm. "Is everything all right?"

I step inside, as I have done a thousand times, squinting against the welcoming warmth and light, the pleasing honeyed wood of the banister and moldings, the traces of dinner smells still in the air. It is such a nice house. What man wouldn't enjoy entering it? I think of Thomas again, the man she brought home from the Claddagh. Was he the only one?

Marge is still frowning at me, wondering what is wrong. "What is it?" she asks. "Is Charlotte all right?"

"She's fine," I tell her, removing my jacket and throwing it on her banister. I rub my arms beneath my Hell's Angels sweater sleeves to warm myself, and to calm myself, too. "Were you and Kyle in love?" I blurt out, just like that, swinging around and facing Marge. I have shocked us both, and sound to my own ears like some kind of madwoman. And I *am* mad. I'm mad and scared and fed up with being the person missing in action in my own life. And it's not just because of the ride home from Connecticut, or what Foster has said, or the rearranged garage, or the fact that Charlotte ran home to this woman, to this house, to this place where my son sleeps peacefully now, feeling he's arrived home again, too. It's more than all of these things, and it's less, also.

"Kate," Marge gasps after a minute. "Are you okay?"

"No," I assure her. I walk into her living room with all that Cabot House furniture and sit on a love seat. I bury my face in my hands and try to think.

"You need sleep. You've been under terrible stress these past weeks," Marge says.

"That's not it!" I tell her, dropping my hands to my lap and staring up at her khaki-clad knees. "I just need to know," I say. "I damn well need to know." And then I can't say any more.

I feel Marge kneeling before me, as if I am a child who has lost a Rollerblade, or is disappointed that she can't go out to play. But I'm not here to inquire about any lost Rollerblade. Is it possible I really didn't know him at all? Did I lose him, in the days before his heart stopped beating, to this big-hearted, super-nerd, Julia Child of a woman?

It's possible that I never had him, if you listen to my mother-in-law, that he just had me, his child bride, just some doll in a fancy dress that you put on a shelf and forget about. No. I shake my head no. I shake it and shake it. No.

"We had great sex, you know," I announce to Marge, or maybe I'm just bragging. "Right until the end."

Marge takes my hands into hers. They are warm and mine are cold and shaking. I look at her face and feel almost disappointed by what I see there. No guilt lines Marge's forehead, no shame pales her lips. There is only concern, the same concern Marge has always felt for me and my family, and there is a pinkness rimming her eyes that speaks of some kind of sadness.

"My mother-in-law thinks her selfish son married a child," I tell her, my face growing hot with indignation. "She thinks Kyle robbed the cradle, that I never had a chance to grow up, or grow *into* myself." I feel as if I have swallowed a lemon when I finish this confession. I wrap my arms around my belly and rock.

"Your mother-in-law sounds like a bitch," Marge says.

"She's not," I say, wiping my wet snotty face with the back of a hand. "That's the surprising part." Marge is becoming fidgety. I can feel how she wants to rise and find a box of Kleenex for me. But she stays, good friend that she is.

"Do you agree with her, Marge? Truthfully?" I ask. "Tell me. Was I an unfinished person when you met me? Like some immature kid with a husband, like some child bride handed over to a Latter-Day Saint polygamist?"

Marge rises from the love seat and wordlessly paces her living room carpet.

"You sound nuts," she muses, half to herself. "Latter-Day Saint polygamist?"

"I saw a special on it, on the Women's Entertainment channel."

"And who would the other wives be?"

Marge looks sorry she's asked me this. She's pacing in a slow bemused fashion, as if attempting to handle my feelings and her own at the same time. The artificial light is harsh on her long, lined face. Hair has escaped the elastic band of her ponytail. She looks tired, more ready for bed than I am. But I can't wait for Marge to be rested, even if the feeding and care of my son is the reason she's tired. I need to hear her answers to my questions. I need to hear them now.

"Marge, please tell me," I persist. "Were you and Kyle in love? Was I just his little *starter* wife? Did he enjoy your grown-up company more than he enjoyed mine? Did he ever even *want* to build a swing set with me?" I am crying in earnest now, sloppy and pathetic, and I don't care.

"Did he sleep with you? Did you sleep with *him*?"

I crumble against the love seat in an embryonic position. "Who the hell *were* we, Marge? Kyle and me?"

For the first time in our long friendship, Marge seems content to just let me cry. She settles on the couch across from me, watching and waiting for me to stop.

"Look," she finally says, her voice crushed as the mum I took care of in her border garden. "You know I can't have this conversation without tea and cake. Come into the kitchen." She rises and leaves then, not looking back at me.

I follow her in. I sit at her table, which is strewn with papers and manila folders and Marge's laptop. She sweeps everything into one quadrant and plops down a fresh cake in the cleared space.

"I know about the adoption," I tell her, staring at her mess of papers. "Charlotte told me."

Marge's face seems to age ten years before my eyes. "We can talk about that later," she says, turning her back to me and running water into the teakettle. "I'll just say it's another area of my life where being unmarried has felt difficult."

I stare at her slumped shoulders as water splashes into the kettle. It is such an odd thing, to see Marge look vulnerable, to see her look at odds with a solution to anything. Once the kettle's on, she lowers herself into a chair across from me, elbows on the table, rubbing at the dark circles beneath her eyes. I stretch a hand across the table and squeeze hers.

"I'm not much of a grateful friend, am I? All you've ever done is love and support me. And here I am asking you if you were in love with my husband."

"That's not all you're asking," Marge says, looking up sharply. "You're also asking if he was in love with *me*." She pushes her chair back and leaves the table, heading for the cups and tea bags, heading away from me. "What do you want to know first?" she asks. "Did I love him? The answer is yes." She reaches for two mugs on a high shelf and places them on the counter before continuing. "But does that mean that I don't love you? And your children? Did my loving your husband preclude that?"

"*How* did you love him?" I ask, my fingers tightly knotted on the tabletop.

"Do you mean did we sleep together? No."

A strange heat flushes through my arms and legs.

"But that doesn't mean that I mightn't have, if he'd been interested. I'd like to think I'd have restrained myself, acted decently, honored our friendship. But you saw the way I acted at the Claddagh."

"Marge!" Now I've pushed my own chair back and am on my feet.

"What?" she asks, turning around to face me. "Sit down. Please."

She reminds me of Foster, bossing me around. I sit down again. Marge sighs deeply, then smiles the saddest smile I've ever seen.

"Does that surprise you?" Marge asks. "That I fell in love with him? That the unmarried woman next door who's admired and envied your life from the day she met you would want some happiness, too?" Now it's big, strong, competent Marge who wipes tears from her face with the back of her hand. I almost hand her my napkin, but then I don't.

"All I've ever wanted in life, Kate, is a family," Marge says. "Some children in the yard, a man who looks at me the way your husband looked at you. Someone I could make laugh, and could cook for and sleep beside each night." Marge places the empty mugs on the table with a distracted air. "Why wouldn't I love Kyle? He was funny and smart and he liked to do things. He loved his children and he loved you, just the way I would want a husband to love me. And you want to know something, Kate?" Marge asks, her face suddenly radiant. "Yes, he did love me. He loved me, too. Just not the way he loved you, is all. So I guess you could say you were right. Kyle and I were in love."

The teakettle is whistling and Marge turns to pick it up. He loved her, too. When she gazes at my son's face over his plate of carrot sticks, I wonder if she is looking for Kyle in there.

"Did he think I was a baby?" I ask, and Marge just sighs again.

"Stop *being* a baby," she says, turning off the stove. "And stop being angry all the time. Consider for a moment how meaningless all of this is. Kyle is dead. I've never betrayed you, even if I imagined it. All I ever did was continue to be your friend."

"Well, you're certainly an honest one," I concede.

"To a fault, some might say."

Pouring the tea seems to take Marge's last ounce of stamina. I watch it stream from her mother's china teapot into our mugs, feel the heat of the liquid on my face.

"And what about the rest of it?" I ask. "Tell me if you think Kyle and I had a real marriage. Please be honest. Was I grown up enough?"

Marge shakes her head as if she is tiring of me. "Who cares what I think?" she asks. "The real issue is that you lost him, Kate.

And whatever growing up there ever could be was aborted." She throws up her hand in frustration. "Who knows? If you'd had enough time together, you might have become bored with Kyle yourself. He might've left you or divorced you, though I doubt it." Marge rubs her eyes again before looking at me.

"The thing is, Kate, he died. You didn't get the time to find out."

I watch Marge climb the stairs to her bed. For a little while, I lie beside Hunter on the pull-out couch in her den, tucking his warm sleeping body into mine, listening to the sound of his breathing. I kiss his head many times. Then I pull the covers to his chin and tiptoe out of the room. Through the living room window I see the van in my driveway and the light spilling from the open garage door. I decide to go home.

My shoes grow soggy as I cross the lawn. I enter the house through the garage, turning my key in the lock for the first time in days, though it feels like years. The door creaks, perhaps with the cold, and I fumble for the switch on the kitchen wall. Light floods the room, making its familiar landscape visible: the counter stools bunched together roughly like boys on a school line, the boxy toaster oven with its permanently smudged glass window, Charlotte's laptop glowing once more on the kitchen table.

I drop my jacket on the back of a chair and head for Charlotte's screen. I awaken her computer from hibernate by tapping on a few keys. Her e-mail is open, which is not surprising. I scan the inbox but see nothing alarming. *WASSUP?* Is the subject line of an e-mail from Ren. *I'm PIMP!* reads the subject line of another, this one from Bree. I open it up, unabashedly eavesdropping. Turns out PIMP means "peeing in my pants," which means laughing hysterically. *Okay*, I think. *That's okay.* There is one piece of spam in the inbox, titled *WELCOME TO WIENER WONDERLAND*, this one suggesting that extra inches make all the difference when seeking happiness. I am too tired to be upset by this. I hit delete, then delete it again from Charlotte's deleted items box. And then I think about Kyle and wonder if his wiener was the primary source of happiness in our lives. We certainly enjoyed it, but even after bragging about my sex life to Marge to-night, I think our marriage was a whole lot more than Kyle's wiener. Isn't every marriage?

I turn up the thermostat before climbing the stairs to the bed-room. I haven't even my suitcase with me to unpack; all of it has been left at Marge's. But it's not the lack of my suitcase that fills me with a feeling that everything I need isn't in this house. It's something else, perhaps something Foster has said.

Foster. I wonder what it would be like to make love to him in the room I once shared with my husband, in the dead-husband bed. I stand at the doorway of our room, gazing at the quilted comforter pulled hastily over the sheets. I hadn't made the bed very carefully before we left. When was the last time I'd changed the sheets? I sit on the edge of the bed and kick my shoes off. Fresh sheets haven't mattered to me much these past two years. When I pick up the phone on the nightstand, I'm relieved to hear a dial tone. They've turned the phones back on already! The phone, the heat, the water, the electricity—everything is back to normal so swiftly and smoothly. Not like when you lose your husband. Not like when you find a dead body on the mattress beside you, when you roll over and find your whole world has changed in the missed beats of a foolish heart.

I climb on top of our sloppily made bed and wrap the com-forter tightly around and around me. I am a hot dog in a bun, a pig in a blanket, a wiener in wonderland. I lie like this for a long time, the overhead light shining in my eyes, until I feel warm again. And then I say good-bye to Kyle. "Good-bye, sweetheart," I say aloud, in the same bed where we lay when he died. I didn't get to say this to him at the time. He was already dead, and I was saying things to him like, *Oh, my God* and *Wake up, no, this can't be. Stop it, Kyle, stop it.*

But the only thing that stopped was his heart. And so I hadn't said good-bye to him.

A few minutes later, after I'd dialed 911, the kids had come rushing in, Charlotte with wide eyes full of alarm, carrying her baby brother in her arms. The two of them were still wearing their pajamas. I remember the pink puppy dogs on Charlotte's pajama pants. *Puppy Love!* it said in the flannel hearts. She was still young enough to think her pajamas were *neat*. They were *cool* and they did not *suck*. Nothing sucked yet, not until that moment when my children looked into their parents' bed and found their father was not moving. I was trying to use my camp counselor mouth-to-mouth resuscitation on him. I had never used it at camp. Now it did not work, and I punched him and punched him in his chest, to start it up again. It was almost like a violent sex act. First the kissing, then the punching. Hunter began to cry. Charlotte began to hate me. The EMTs came and carted a quarter of our family away.

Now here I am, still wondering what Kyle would do if his daughter came home with a pierced tongue, if his son stopped talking, if his wife cut off a huge piece of her own heart and stopped feeling the things around her. I wonder if his ghost is still in the garage, waiting to lift the door for me again when I go outside to our minivan.

I pick up the phone a second time and punch in a number I've surprised myself by learning by heart. Even on the cell phone, I never speed-dial Foster Willis's phone number. I press each number individually to allow myself to understand my intention. I give myself a chance to stop, mid-dialing, if I want to. Sometimes I think when I'm calling him that he is an unpleasant man, slightly pushy and a bit forward. And yet I notice I'm not dialing Jack, looking for a laugh or to hear his next joke. I'm not dialing Marge, looking for an understanding ear. I'm dialing a guy who intrigues me, or who *might* intrigue me, once I've learned how to engage with the world again. I don't pretend to know what any of it means. Am I falling in love with him? Do I just need someone to argue with, the equivalent of asking someone to pinch me so I know I'm alive? I know that his arms felt wonderful around me in his stainless steel kitchen tonight. His neck was delicious when I ravished it in my own kitchen. His smell is nice. And to make love with him, oh, that was an angry and lovely and delicious thing. Perhaps it was an act meant to melt my anger, or perhaps my anger fed it. But delicious it was. Delicious.

"Hello?" he says now, into my bedroom phone receiver.

"I'm in my bed," I tell him. "Would you like to join me?"

THIRTY-SIX

Americans in Space

It doesn't feel like Kyle's bed at all. It feels as if the man who holds me takes up more space in the room than the bed we lie in. The shadow of his face across the pillow is foreign. He has kept his promise. He is living in my hair. My big tangle of unruly red hair, plaits of it stuck beneath him. I gently pull it free, stare at his sleeping face. The angles are sharp but the expression is soft. He breathes in and out. Soon his eyes open and I smile at him. Dusk has slipped beneath the shades and into the air around us. He sits up. His chest is practically hairless. Kyle's ghost cracks the door a fraction.

Yes, I tell him, *your chest had far more hair. But he's the sandy-haired type.*

Kyle's ghost nods thoughtfully, though not disagreeably. *Yes*, he says. *I see.*

Well, don't see, I tell him. *Don't see, my darling dead husband.*

He wafts away amiably, and I am distracted by live arms encircling me.

"I have to get back," he says. "I have to drive the girls to school."

"Yes," I say. "Get back before they know you're gone."

"I don't care if they know I'm gone," he says, hugging me again. "We're entitled to our lives, Kate. We didn't give them up just because we became parents."

I nibble his warm neck. This seems funny to me, what he has

said. Of *course* we gave up our lives when we became parents. But then, I think, lawyers will argue about anything.

"And what about you?" he asks, when he's risen from the bed and is slipping into his clothes again, shivering a little as he swoops his shirt above his shoulders. "Are you returning to work today?" he asks.

It is a new season, I want to tell him. Instead, I don't answer him. I have no idea whether there is a work for me to return to. I guess I'll eventually drive over to the Alan B. Shepard, knock on my office door, and see who answers. I'll endure another frosty smile from Gladys and proceed to Tom's office, tail between my legs. Tom will see where Charlotte got her talent for truancy.

"I guess I'll go into school," I finally say.

Foster is pulling on a sock with a lot of effort.

"Was it another guy who broke up your marriage?" I ask, and he grimaces like his tooth hurts.

"My wife and I are the ones who broke up the marriage," he says.

I stroke the back of his soft cotton shirt, feel the tension in his spine. "I'm sorry."

Foster pats my leg beneath the blanket. "I'm not," he says.

"And what about you?" I ask. "Did you cheat on her?"

"No."

"No nooky on the side with some young associate at the firm?"

"*God*, no. I would *never* date a lawyer. Who would?"

I reach across the bed and hug him. "It does seem foolish," I say. "But some of us are risk-takers, once we've come back from the dead."

"Have you come back from the dead?" he asks, breathing into my hair.

"I think so. I may still have a little frostbite, but the joints are all moving."

"They certainly are," Foster agrees.

"Hey," I say, before letting him kiss me again, "are you the type of guy who likes building swing sets?"

"No," he replies curtly. "I hire out for that sort of stuff."

"You hire out for a swing set builder?"

"Isn't that what the town playgrounds are for?"

I watch him tie a shoe. *Yes*, I think. *That's exactly what the town playgrounds are for.*

After he is gone, I take a long shower and lay out my outfit for the day. All of my school clothes hang neatly in my closet, just where I've left them. It is only my deodorant and face cream that are inconveniently locked up at Marge's house, inside my suitcase. I search the bathroom medicine chest for replacements but only come up with Kyle's old Speed Stick. I flip the blue cap and begin running the solid beneath my arms. I smell like a football fan, high on testosterone. But it's a clean smell and it will do. I slip into my charcoal pin-striped pants suit, coral silk shell beneath. I smear on my face the last globules of some ancient Noxzema cream I've found in the medicine chest. Now I smell like testosterone and a baby's behind. I practice in the bathroom mirror: "Hello, Tom. May I have my office back?" The thought of his response tingles as much as the Noxzema.

I click on the hair dryer and allow the blare of it to settle me down. So much has happened since my arrival home. I've held my daughter safely in my arms, watched her friends cut snowflakes, blasphemed my best friend as I ate her cake, said my goodbyes to my beautiful husband, and slept with another man. A lovely man who would never build a swing set. Marge would probably not like Foster, if I told her this. My hair falls into nice shining sheets of copper. I force each strand into submission with heat and brushes, perhaps because it's been complimented so nicely by Foster. It's been slept upon by him, by this man whose wife has left him and gone to the Midwest.

Closing the front door softly behind me, I tiptoe through Marge's front foyer to the room where Hunter sleeps. There he is, a tiny bump at the top of the pull-out bed, interrupting the smooth field of blankets there. He sleeps with his hands crossed in front of him like a mummy's, my little pharaoh, my little man. His ice pack rests on the pillow beside him, soft and cushy. It occurs to me, looking at it, that he'd never bonded with a teddy bear, the way Charlotte had at his age. No stuffed monkeys or bunnies, no stuffed anything has made its way into Hunter's heart. Just ketchup bottles, and now this. I glare at the blue blob, as though I believe I can hurt its feelings. It just lies there. Had Hunter liked stuffed toys before the morning he'd found his father dead? I squeeze my eyes shut and try to remember. There was his little plastic carpenter's bench that he'd liked. And Charlotte's soccer shin guards, grass-stained and sweaty, which he'd absolutely loved. So maybe he was strange even before Kyle's death. "Hey," I whisper, gently shaking him now, "who wants to go to Bright Lights and see Courtney?"

"Bright Lights . . . ?" He is up in a shot. He sits with his straight back and sleepy eyes and yesterday's T-shirt, trying to orient himself. "Mama," he says. "Where Thithy?" He sounds just like a baby.

"You're my big boy now, you know," I tell him again, just like I did yesterday, resisting an urge to gather him into my lap like my little boy. "You go to school each day, just like Sissy."

"Thithy in school?" He is rubbing his eyes with small fists, allowing me a chance to bat the ice pack off the pillow and onto the floor.

Take that, you nasty glob.

"Let's get you in the shower real quick, and then we can stop for an Egg McMuffin before we see Courtney."

"Thithy in school?" he repeats.

"Sissy *is* in school," I tell him, checking out his mouth, which is totally normal-looking, except for the missing teeth.

"Where my icth pack?" he asks, glancing around frantically.

"You don't need to bring your ice pack to school. Your lip is all better! Let's go into the bathroom and take a look in the mirror."

"Where *ith* it?"

"None of the other boys and girls bring ice packs to school, do they? Come on, let's get—"

"WHERE MY ICTH PACK?" He is standing on the mattress now, his face very pale, eyes very red. His fingers are twitching, as if they are groping for a missing digit. His T-shirt is twisted above his belly, making him look a bit mad. I see I have a choice here.

"Hunter," I say in my firmest voice.

"MY ICTH PACK!"

A chill travels up my spine. That was loud enough to wake the dead.

"Your ice pack is under the bed."

I watch him dive to the carpet, amazed at his devotion to plastic. He surfaces with the face of an angel, smiling serenely, ice pack in hand. "Thank you," he says, most politely. Then he struts happily out of the room.

Off we go to Bright Lights, just as if we'd never left. It feels almost like we belong in the sticky blue minivan as I strap Hunter in it for the zillionth time. Hunter seems to like it. He doesn't mind the restricting belts and buckles, the slight tilt of the world from his car seat.

Somewhere in the garage, I feel Kyle's ghost once more hovering. Perhaps he has always been in our garage, for wouldn't this be the best place to regularly see his children? Hunter is ushered into the world daily through it. And no matter how much Charlotte hates me, she'll usually accept a ride to school, passing through the kitchen door and into this garage. Kyle can stand by the paint cans and see how much she has grown, how beautiful she has become.

"All set, buddy?" I ask our freshly showered son.

"McMuffin," he orders, "then Courtney," he commands, as if I am his Bus Driver Bob.

Nothing has changed on the outside. I crest the hill, past the giant Alan B. Shepard monument that looks like a gravestone. FIRST AMERICAN TO JOURNEY INTO SPACE, it stubbornly insists. My head is spinning. Perhaps I am the second American to journey into space. I park, brush the crumbs of Hunter's Egg McMuffin from my collar, and head for the front door. The halls are empty when I open the door to Gladys's control center. There she is, her grim line of red lipstick, her scent of stale lilies, her droopy rings on her wasted fingers. Gladys, the woman who crochets lederhosen for my son's ketchup bottles, there she is.

"You're back," she says, stating the obvious. And then the

strangest thing happens. Gladys Panella's face lights up with a smile. It is so strange I almost shield my eyes.

"Hi, Gladys," I say.

"Mrs. Cavanaugh," she greets me. "And how are you?"

"Much better," I tell her.

We're quiet for a minute, just looking at each other. "May I ask you something?" I say. "Do you think you could call me just Kate?"

"I can't call *any* counselor just Kate."

"I might not be a counselor anymore. Would that help?"

She colors a little and glances at her computer screen. "Mr. Johnson's in," she says, "if you'd like to see him."

THIRTY-SEVEN

If It Comes Back

I do want to see Tom, but not right away. Curiosity points my feet toward my own office first. The door is open; I can hear someone talking on the phone in there. I circle the satellite of offices with something like dread, then steel myself and walk right in. Bunny Lawton beams up at me like Miss Congeniality. She's sitting behind my desk, her twentysomething shapely buns on my chair. An open file—probably belonging to a student in my caseload—is poised in her manicured fingers. A week ago she was in her own office, that dismal little cubbyhole on the other side of the satellite that the newest counselors must endure, almost like a hazing ritual, before we let them in. But apparently Bunny has been more than let in. She's been promoted.

"Golly," she says, smiling at me like an opportunistic virus, "what the heck are *you* doing here?" Her smile remains fixed. Her blond bob glows beneath the recessed lighting.

No one says *golly* in the twenty-first century. I open my mouth to tell her this, then close it again. I shake my head violently, as if trying to dislodge a bee from my bonnet. "I'm not really back," I tell her. "Just stopping by."

It kills me to say this. It requires pushing back a powerful urge to throw a Hunter-like tantrum on my office floor. This might be my most professional moment. I wave at Bunny and float out of the room again, as if I'm in a great hurry to get on to the next thing. But there is no next thing. I've been replaced. Suddenly

I understand my son a little better. I see how hard it is to give up things you believe are yours. *Mine!* he always says. And now I see it.

I pause in the satellite corridor and take a deep breath. I wipe my eyes and gather myself together. Then I throw my shoulders back and calmly walk to Tom's office.

The first thing I notice is that his door is naked, the birdcage poster gone, the sight of the bare wood almost as alarming as the sight of Bunny at my desk. Everything has changed, in just a few days. I hate change, I realize, knocking perfunctorily at his open door before striding in uninvited. "Where's your poster?" I ask, the moment I see his surprised face. He's leaning back in his chair with his fingers linked behind his head, as if he is on a beach in Aruba. His goatee is gone. More change!

"You're very observant," he says, sitting up. He looks thin and wan, even in his argyle-patterned sweater vest. "You always hated that poster, didn't you?"

"I *loved* that poster," I tell him, realizing that it's true. It was like a friend to me. I'm happy to see Tom's dear long face.

"Loved to make *fun* of it," he says. "And of me."

"Okay," I admit, flopping down in his student chair. "I thought it was a little cheesy, all that flowery *If you love something* language. But I always had fun talking back to it, and secretly rewriting the ending."

"With your own cynical thoughts?"

My head snaps up to look at him. "That's way harsh, Tom," I say, hoping to make him smile with a Charlotte joke. When he doesn't respond, I ask, "Have you heard about Charlotte?"

"I have," he says. "She came to see me yesterday."

"So she told you she ran . . . home?"

Tom nods.

I shift uncomfortably on the plastic chair. "I guess I totally screwed up, taking her out of school."

"You certainly got her attention," Tom suggests.

I don't know if this means he approves or disapproves of me. We sit in silence a minute. Then I say, "It must be annoying to see me so soon, after all you did to help me with my sabbatical."

"I'm never sorry to see you, Kate. Neither are your students."

"I don't think that's true," I blurt out. "I've already been re-placed."

"Someone had to take care of your caseload."

I squeeze the arms of the chair. "Can sabbaticals last only a week?"

Tom is still another moment. Then he swivels around to his computer screen. "Let's see what the dictionary says." Tap tap go his fingers on the keyboard as he frowns at the screen. "Okay. Says here that a sabbatical is *any extended period of leave from one's custom-ary work, especially for rest, to acquire a new skill or training,* et cetera." He looks up at me. "Did you rest?"

"Not really."

"Did you acquire a new skill?"

I think about last night in bed with Foster. I hope I'm not blushing when I nod.

"Good," Tom says. "And did you get a chance to think about Phoenix and your group, and find some resolution in all of that?"

"Yes," I tell Tom. "I've even seen some of my . . . the group members since I've been back."

He studies me long and hard, the way I sometimes find myself studying my children when they aren't looking. "How do you feel about returning to work?" he asks. "Honestly."

"I feel great about it," I tell him. "Is this a possibility?"

"It won't be easy."

"I understand," I say, lowering my head and seeing Bunny again at my desk.

"Chances are they'll put you somewhere else for the rest of the year. Maybe another school. And then, possibly, next year you might have your caseload back. How do you feel about that?"

"Whatever it takes," I say. I think about Hunter, leaving all those ketchup bottles behind at his grandmother's.

"Then there's the New Frontiers Group," Tom says. "As you might know, I've been leading it."

I nod, remembering Hector's dismal critique of the session. "Thank you," I tell him humbly. "Does Bunny sit in too?"

"No."

Good, I think.

Tom shifts in his chair. "Okay, then. I'll see what I can do."

I nod, holding back tears. "Tell the New Frontiers kids I miss them," I say.

"Why don't you do that yourself?" he suggests. "Come in this afternoon and tell them good-bye."

If he'd handed me a dozen roses I couldn't feel a fuller heart for him. "I'd love to do that, Tom. Thank you."

"You'd only stay for the first few minutes," he warns. "Then we'd have other business to attend to."

"Fine. Yes. Just so I can say good-bye."

"There's a new member now, too," he says.

I look up at him, feeling blood rushing to my feet.

"You've put Charlotte in the group."

"Do you object?"

This might be the hardest question he has ever asked me. I squeeze shut my eyes and imagine Charlotte sitting on the flowered couch, the same couch where she and her father read storybooks together. Will she remember this? Will she grow stronger and happier, plunked down in Phoenix's spot, surrounded by Hector and Alphonse and the angry Adam? I look at Tom, who seems to read these questions in my eyes.

"I'll take good care of her," he says. "I promise you, Kate."

I want to thank him. I want to tell him that I know he'll take good care of my daughter, just as he would have taken good care of his own. But my voice doesn't work. It is blocked by a lump in my throat the size of a soccer cleat. All I manage is a nod. Then I come around the desk and hug him. He feels frail and strong at the same time. He feels like my friend.

"You see?" he says when we disentangle. "The poster was right."

"What do you mean?"

He smiles as he explains. "If you love something," he says, "set it free. If it comes back, it was always yours."

"Put the damn poster back up," I say.

He squeezes my hand. "Be here at three. And by the way, Kate," he says, "you look great."

I think I see something wistful cross his face as I close his door.

THIRTY-EIGHT

Love in Complete Sentences

A lphonse, the shy one, arrives first. He pats me on the shoulder, looking down at his Skechers. "You're back," he says. *Pat pat pat.*

"How's your girlfriend doing?" I ask.

"Good."

Adam walks in next. He nods curtly at me, then smiles at something over his shoulder. "Dude," he says, flopping onto the couch, into the spot where Phoenix used to sit. "Thought you'd gone AWOL. Sorry if we scared you off."

"You did no such thing," I assure Adam, though I'm not sure this is entirely true. "I needed to take some time for myself, but I hated leaving you." Adam sprawls on the couch, an almost visible cloud of emotions swirling above his handsome head.

Hector comes through the door next. "Hello, Mrs. C.," he says. He looks surprised to see me. He stares at my chest, looks disappointed to find only a pin-striped blazer there. Then he glances a little anxiously behind him. Charlotte walks into the room in her expensive jeans and pink top, a pile of books pressed to her heart. Her eyes are wide with apprehension. I catch her eye and smile at her. She almost looks happy to see me.

"Over here, Cha Cha," Hector tells her, taking her by the hand and wedging her in on the couch, between himself and Alphonse. I take the chair beside Adam's.

Our little group sits in its tight circle, an unspoken ripple of

love and trust and disappointment traveling between us. I redis-
cover viscerally how much I love these children. I open my mouth
to tell them why I'm here today.

"Mr. Johnson invited me to visit with you for a few minutes."

"Visit with us?" Alphonse is incensed. "You're *ours*," he says,
scratching his arm.

"And you will always be mine," I assure them. "You'll always
be in my heart."

Adam rolls his eyes, but he looks as though he might start crying.

"You have a new member in your group, I see."

Everyone looks at Charlotte. She squeezes her hands together
and her face colors in that pretty way.

"Mr. Johnson said it was okeydokey," Hector assures me.

"Why haven't you invited Ren to the group, too?" I ask, smiling at my daughter.

"He's not fucked up enough, *mami*," Hector says, and they all
laugh, including Charlotte.

"Language," Tom says, walking in, as if appearing on cue.
"You know we have another guest coming today. We want to
show our respect by the way we speak."

My chastened group sits like good schoolchildren, looking
down at their laps. I scan the circle, studying them. I note how
Alphonse's acne is clearing. The hard set of Adam's jaw hasn't
changed. Tom will be good for him. Hector holds my daughter's
hand in his, as if they are waiting in line for a visa. Okay, I think.
Tom will become her retarded therapist.

"You know I can't be your group leader anymore," I tell them.

Adam sniffles a little, then wipes his nose with his arm. I accept
this as his parting gift. No one says anything for a little while.

Alphonse glances anxiously at the wall clock. "I don't know if
it's such a good idea that we invited Phoenix's mother in," he says.

I look at Tom and he nods. So this is the other guest coming
today. In the hands of someone less skilled, I'd worry about inviting a dead girl's mother to the group. But Tom will handle it
well. It could start the healing for this little band of shell-shocked
adolescents. I pray that it will.

"Why isn't it a good idea to invite Phoenix's mother?" Tom asks Alphonse, who still won't look at him.

"Her daughter's, like, *dead*," he tells the floor. "What are we supposed to say about that?"

No one speaks. Hector begins tapping his foot on the linoleum. We listen to the heat click on, then off, in the quiet room.

"Do you miss her?" I ask Alphonse.

He shrugs. "I don't know," he says. "I guess so." A tear spills down his cheek, but my sweet group of misfits, bless them, do not say a word to embarrass him.

"I absolutely miss her," Adam finally offers.

Heads nod gravely, including my daughter's.

"If I was straight I would've married her," Adam says.

"Could you tell Phoenix's mother that we miss her?" I suggest. "And that we loved her and that we were her friends?"

"I definitely will," Charlotte whispers, her first utterance in her new group. "People, like, *appreciate* it when you tell them you miss someone." She locks eyes with me so I will understand what my sins have been. "Then they don't feel all alone," she adds.

"We can't bring our friend back," Tom says softly, "and we don't even know why she's left." His eyes move slowly to each member of the New Frontiers Group. "But we can love her and honor her memory."

"I think Phoenix's mommy would like that," Hector says, reaching across the circle and patting my hand. "Right, *mami*?"

"Phoenix's mother hugged all of us," Charlotte says, riding shotgun beside me in the minivan later. We're on our way to Bright Lights to pick up Hunter. "She misses Phoenix even more than we do," she says. "She made us promise to talk to someone if we ever felt sad."

The car is quiet, the radio off. The tires hum beneath us. Outside our windows, lights flicker on in some of the houses. It is not quite dusk in this season of premature darkness. But spring will come, I remind myself, if only we learn how to endure things.

"If you ever feel sad," I tell Charlotte, "you can talk to Mr. Johnson, or to your friends in New Frontiers."

"Or to you," she says.

I pat her bony leg as tears fill my eyes. She presses her hand over mine. It is enough.

The children are on the Bright Lights play lot, running around in the afternoon's last light. Courtney brings them out at the end of each day, if it isn't too cold or rainy. "Let them breathe a little fresh air before they go home," she often says, and I always think it's a splendid idea. It's almost as if Courtney, a twenty-two-year-old girl, understands that none of us gets to live in this world forever.

Hunter is standing by himself, as usual. His clip-on mittens hang like puppy ears at the ends of his jacket sleeves as he stares into space, or maybe at the top of the jungle gym.

"Hunter!" his sister hollers, and he turns at the sound of her voice. His expression brightens as he runs toward us. "Mama! Thithy!" he calls excitedly. "Brayton Clark climbed the jungle gym today and peed on Madison's head!" He is flushed with excitement, recounting the day's centerpiece event. I hear my own sharp intake of breath.

A whole descriptive sentence, the prepositions and articles and everything! His classmate peed *on* Madison's head, on *the* jungle gym. I feel giddy with happiness.

"Eww! Gross, Hunter," Charlotte says. Then I see that she and Courtney are frowning at me as I clap my hands enthusiastically.

"Hunter, this is wonderful!" I cry, scooping him into my arms and twirling him around. Courtney frowns harder, and I explain to her that it's not the naughty boy's behavior we're celebrating, but the way that Hunter has described it.

"He's been talking like that all day," the beautiful preschool teacher assures us. "And on far more socially acceptable topics."

"Fabulous!" I cry, spinning Hunter around again. He laughs and laughs, then asks me to put him down in a complete sentence.

"You know that peeing on Madison's head wasn't very nice," I say to him, more for Courtney's sake than his.

"It was bith-gusting!" he exclaims triumphantly, and even his teacher smiles.

"I notice no ketchup bottle today," she whispers to me. "This trip was really good for him."

Yeah, right, I think, watching Hunter wrap himself around Charlotte's knee.

"I see he brought in an ice pack, though," Courtney says. "And his front teeth are out. Did I miss something?"

"My brother's ridiculous," Charlotte offers, pulling the collar of her jacket higher. "End of explanation."

Since there's no food in the house yet, we eat food on plastic plates at Formica tables at Kentucky Fried Chicken. We're all in the mood for junk food, so it's not a problem. Not much eating goes on, in the case of Hunter. He's busy plopping his mashed potatoes into his soft drink, while Charlotte attempts to subtly interrogate me about the future fortunes of the Cavanaugh family.

"So you're not going to be at the high school anymore," she says.

"Probably not," I tell her.

"But are we, like, home for good?" she asks, picking the crust off a drumstick.

"Yes, we are," I confirm.

"Whereth the toy?" Hunter interrupts, lifting a biscuit and searching beneath it. "I want my toy!"

"Hunter, this isn't McDonald's," I explain, thrilled anew at how well he is speaking.

"Why not?" he asks petulantly.

"Because it's KFC, you turd," his sister snaps impatiently.

"I'm not a turd!" Hunter retorts, throwing his ice pack into the middle of her plate. It lands with a splat in the coleslaw. Charlotte coolly removes it. No one under thirty eats coleslaw. Her mind is on her future.

"So you're sure you have some job back?"

"I don't know yet," I tell her. "I'll find out soon, though, and I'm sure it will be all right."

Charlotte spins her straw in her cola. "Did Dad leave us money in case, you know, we ever needed it?"

I pat her small shoulder. "Of course he did," I tell her. "Don't worry."

"Toy! Now!" Hunter says. We look at him, then turn back to each other.

"We ought to go visit him," Charlotte says softly.

I place my plastic spork carefully down on my plate.

"We ought to, you know, like, go visit his grave. Say hi. Maybe he misses us."

She turns her face from me, unwilling to show me what she is feeling.

"We can go anytime you like," I tell her.

She looks up from her soda. "Can we go now?"

I stare out the window of the KFC as people pass by with turned-up collars and briefcases and take-out dinners in plastic bags. The setting sun has turned the world charcoal-gray.

"The cemetery might be closed," I say.

"I want to go see," she tells me adamantly.

"Me too!" my son whines. "I wanna go thee, too!"

THIRTY-NINE

Family Reunion

I am not the talk-to-your-husband-at-the-grave type of widow, never have been. I seldom think of or even remember this large gracious cemetery in our town's midst. This is probably why Kyle's ghost has had to come to our garage to find me. I do not lay wreathes at his small headstone, but it is not because I didn't love him. I just don't think of this cemetery as his home.

It is almost dusk but the gates are not locked. We turn the car into the sprawling entrance of the Appleton Cemetery, past the stone pillars and a small Tudor-style chapel, then up the sloping hills, looking for Kyle's gravestone for the first time since his funeral. Charlotte sits beside me, quiet as a ghost. We drive around the perimeters of this place every day. We follow Volvos and mini-vans and Saabs, all of us with trunks full of Whole Foods groceries, heads full of our own thoughts, our children's chatter, the rush-hour news. Now here is the Cavanaugh family, inside.

We drive past rows of handsome gravestones, then reflecting ponds, then tall ponderous mausoleums, deep in the land of the dead. On the edge of the horizon, behind the cemetery fence, we can see the red and yellow sign of the Dragon Garden Restaurant, and remember the world we left where people still need to eat. My children are quiet, bundled into their winter coats, scarves wrapped tightly around their throats. It's as if they are fighting off an incipient chill. In truth, it is a warm evening, after an almost perfect Indian summer day. Our smattering of snow was an aberration;

the sun has shone generously since. Behind me, Hunter clutches his ice pack and stares, expressionless, out his window. Charlotte's face is turned away as she gazes out her own window. Her hands are clasped in her lap like a model child.

"This is it," I say, gliding the car to a halt at the side of Beech Lane. "At least I think it is."

I shift into park and turn off the engine. Nobody makes a move to leave the vehicle. We just sit there, seat belts still securing us, shadows falling on us, thinking our own thoughts, feeling our own feelings.

"Which one is it?" Charlotte asks in a soft voice, her face finally turning to look at me. She is like her mother, I see. We are looking for a grave, which is an *it*, rather than looking for her father, who is a *he*. A *he* who is not here, I tell myself again, and have no trouble believing it.

And yet. We are all of us nervous, uncertain, sad, and curious. Why are we here tonight? Why has Charlotte brought us? What's the task that must be done?

"Okay, then," I say with false steadiness. "Let's take a walk to Daddy's grave." I pat Charlotte's knee before getting out of the van. Then I slide open the back door to help Hunter.

"How come Daddy got a grave and I don't got one?" he asks, expertly unbuckling himself with one hand.

"You idiot," Charlotte says. "You're not dead, okay?"

"Okay," Hunter agrees, not taking her on. He jumps to the ground with his ice pack, then waits.

"Come on, sweetie," I say, taking his hand. "It's this way."

Charlotte walks beside me as the Cavanaughs make their way up a grassy incline. The landscape around us is beautiful. The carpet of lawn we tread upon is green enough, even in the waning light, to earn the Marge Seal of Approval. Charlotte strikes out a little ahead of us, our scout.

"There it is!" she whispers loudly, as if we are in a church or at a funeral. And she is right. She has found her father's grave. She is standing on the grass beneath which her father's bones lie. Her daddy. Her champion. Her soccer coach. We stare at his name on the small granite stone. We stare at the dates, as if these are proof that we're not mistaken. No. He was born, he was with us, and then he died; it's all right there on the stone.

And then Charlotte does the most amazing thing. In the waning light, she collapses onto the grass beside her father's gravestone, throwing a great seated shadow across the sod, crossing her legs Indian style and hugging herself. And then she begins to speak to him.

"Hello, Daddy," we hear her say, in the sweet, unperturbed voice that once was hers, once when Kyle was alive and she was his little cowgirl. "How are you?" she asks, brushing one knee of her jeans lightly. "We're all fine here," she tells the stone. "I'm having a great season in soccer and Hunter is getting really big."

Hunter nods, sucking on the unnecessary scarf still wrapped around his throat. His eyes are trained on his sister. He is listening.

"I've got an awesome boyfriend, so that's sweet," she says. "I think you'd like him, though his father is, like, a sleaze, they say."

"Sleath," Hunter whispers, and then he turns to me and asks, "Where are him?," his baby talk returned once more.

Charlotte laughs lightly, tears now brightening her eyes. "Hunter wants to know where you are, Daddy. Did you know Mom has a boyfriend, too?" She looks up at me with a sweet accepting smile. "He's all right," she tells her father, "but it might take Hunter a little time to get used to him."

"I wanna thee Daddy!" Hunter cries, and Charlotte and I look at him.

"He's not here, honey," I tell him, squatting down beside him and taking his hands.

"He's dead," Charlotte says. "But that's all right. He really loved us, buddy." Now the tears are streaming down her pale face. "He really did."

Hunter pulls his hands free and runs to his sister beside his father's gravestone. He climbs into her lap, dropping his ice pack and hugging her around the neck. "Ith okay, Thithy," he says. And I look at the two of them, gathered in their dead father's lap, and feel so much love for them that I sit down on the grass myself.

We walk back to the car in silence, all of us holding hands, like uneven cutout dolls. Then Hunter pulls loose, turns, and runs back up the embankment toward Kyle's grave. "Juth a minute," he calls behind him, but we are in pursuit of him, the yellow-haired child running wild through the near-darkness, all of us only stopping when Kyle's stone is in front of us again. Hunter is panting a little as he walks to his father's stone and bends his small back. We watch him place his offering. He rests the ice pack against the stone, as if it will bring down some inflammation none of us can see. "There," he says, his empty hands resting at his sides. "So you won't get lonely."

FORTY

Gravity

Kyle is visiting with me in the garage again, listening patiently as I fill him in on life as a middle school counselor. I want him to know how contented I've been these past two weeks, so I tell him.

"It's all about bullying and blow jobs and conflict resolution," I explain, hanging the garden hose again on the side wall. I would never describe my job this way to anyone but Kyle. I would describe to others in far more appropriate language how much I love the twelve- and thirteen-year-olds. I'd explain how wide the girls' eyes grow when they view the DVD about childbirth. How frightened they are when they get their first periods in English class. How they don't know what to do with their burgeoning breasts or blighted complexions. It is true that some of the girls are already sexually active. Some don't consider oral sex to be sex at all, just a nice gesture when they're getting to know a boy. This shocks Kyle. *Not our Charlotte!* he says. *No,* I tell him. *Not our Charlotte. She's busy playing indoor soccer now, and also writing for the* Shepard's Staff. *Don't worry,* I tell her father. *It's a girls' sports column, nothing about little trees dying.*

I don't know if I need to return to my old job next fall. I miss Tom Johnson, and miss my friend Jack. But Jack and I meet up weekly for coffee at Appleton's newest Peet's, to exchange gossip and to keep up with his love life. He says he might be in love with a forty-year-old woman he met at a bowling alley. I'm happy for him. I'm as unconcerned as he is about the difference in their ages. I'm no expert on other people's love lives. Marge has helped me to see this.

Jack says I look more relaxed now. He says when he sees Charlotte in the halls she's surrounded by friends. "It's nice you've stopped projecting your own crap on her," he tells me. Quit acting like a shrink, I scold him. And then he tells me a joke.

"This guy walks into the psychiatrist's office stark-naked, everything hanging out. 'I'm sad, I'm angry, I'm scared all the time!' he tells the shrink. 'Doctor, Doctor, what's wrong with me?' The doctor looks at him and says, 'I can clearly see your nuts.'"

I love Jack.

"Is it true I was projecting my own crap onto Charlotte and Hunter?" I ask Kyle now, stashing a wet wash bucket and brushes on a high shelf. This time he doesn't answer. Truth is, he isn't quite a ghost anymore. He's faded more into a warm presence, residing mostly in my heart, but sometimes by the paint cans, too. He doesn't seem to mind that Marge has rearranged all of his stuff in his garage.

I discuss my new job with living people, too. I talked about it with Foster last night, for instance. I told him about the seventh-grader who hasn't hit his growth spurt and came by my office quite upset. "The girls all look like they're the boys' mothers!" the poor kid had confessed, wringing his hands. Foster laughed out loud at the story. He always lifts his chin when he laughs. I like the way his throat looks. He said he remembered exactly being that boy, but I don't really believe him. Foster was born with confidence. It's what saw him through law school and his messy divorce. It guides his parenting and comforts him greatly during our up-and-down relationship. He'd like to see me more; he's already told me this. But I am happy just the way we are.

It's fun being with Foster, but I'm not in love. I'm in deep *like* with a good man who could end up a mere transitional object in my life, like my son's ketchup bottle. For all I know, Foster could one day be relegated to the Huggies carton of life, once enjoyed but no longer needed. Or maybe one day I will look in his gorgeous brown eyes and see that I want to spend forever with him. On this sunny afternoon, while my children walk a huge dog named Cookie $ with a nice boy named Ren, dating seems fine enough for Kate Cavanaugh. Hunter and Charlotte are plenty to come home to.

This may be the last freak day we enjoy of our mercifully prolonged Indian summer. It's the second week of November and the garage door is wide open, admitting mild breezes that run through my hair like fingers. I've been washing the car in the driveway without even wearing a jacket. The ice caps might be melting at the South Pole, but here in Appleton it's hard to criticize the glorious sunshine we've been granted today. Such is life, I think. You can feel bad for the drowning polar bears and happy for yourself, simultaneously. I tell Kyle this and I think he laughs. I don't actually hear his laughter anymore. I can't remember the sound of it as I once did. It's possible that imagining Kyle is all I have left of him. This, and a locked place in my heart where a shrine exists for a man I loved.

The minivan sparkles like a giant blue inflatable in the driveway, all clean and shining and ready to transport the Cavanaughs wherever they need to go next. Regardless of Charlotte's disdain for its looks, our unhip vehicle carried us safely down the highway as we ran away from home, then moved us swiftly into the passing lane as we made our way to the hospital. It carried us through space, no less than Alan B. Shepard's antique capsule did, until the Cavanaugh family, all of us broken, all of us waiting to be made whole, finally found gravity again.

I shut the garage and gaze across my lawn at Marge's house. Perhaps this is the day she'll get her call, the most important phone call Marge ever receives in her life, the one that informs her she's finally a mother.

"This could be the day," I tell Kyle aloud. I close my eyes and imagine Marge's perfect home with crushed Cheerios on her hardwood floors, the smell of pee emanating from a diaper pail. Why not? I think, locking the garage door. Why shouldn't someone we love be visited by a miracle?

"This could be the day," I tell Kyle again.

"Maybe," he says.